FINALLY HOME

JENNIFER CROSSWHITE

Praise for Jennifer Crosswhite

What Readers Are Saying…

"Definitely on my to-buy list now. I can't wait for more!" Hawaiibooklover, Amazon reviewer

"I look forward to reading more of [her] books." Amazon reviewer

"If you enjoy a good, clean love story then give this novella a try. You will not be disappointed." Danielle, Amazon reviewer

Other books by Jennifer Crosswhite

The Route Home series
  Be Mine, prequel novella
  Coming Home, book 1
  The Road Home, book 2
  Finally Home, book 3

Contemporary romance
  The Inn at Cherry Blossom Lane

Hometown Heroes series, writing as JL Crosswhite
  Promise Me, prequel novella
  Protective Custody, book 1
  Flash Point, book 2
  Special Assignment, book 3

In the Shadow series, writing as JL Crosswhite
  Off the Map, book 1
  Out of Range, book 2
  Over Her Head, book 3

Eat the Elephant: How to Write (and Finish!) Your Book One Bite at a Time, writing as Jen Crosswhite

Devotional
  Worthy to Write: Blank pages tying your stomach in knots? 30 prayers to tackle that fear!

To Jane Mathews, my first partner in creative endeavors! Thanks for being my encourager. Miss you, but I'll see you soon.

But now, thus says the Lord, your Creator, O Jacob, And He who formed you, O Israel, "Do not fear, for I have redeemed you; I have called you by name; you are Mine!

— ISAIAH 43:1

Chapter One

~1882, PORTLAND, OREGON

Amelia Martin clapped her gloved hands together before glancing at her father and noticing his scowl. She shoved them behind her back. Still, she couldn't help but rock forward on the pointed toes of her kidskin boots. As they stood in front of the Oregon Express office in Portland, the shiny red stagecoach pulled in front of them. And Josh Benson was driving. She'd know him anywhere from his description in the letters Mrs. Kincaid—wait, she was Mrs. Adams now— had sent them. That dark curly hair. She couldn't see his dimples, as he wasn't smiling. But she'd bet a cutting of her mother's prized blush damask rose that they were there.

He would be marrying the town's schoolteacher, Miss Emily Stanton. So romantic! She hoped she and Father would be invited to the wedding. She just loved weddings. And since schoolteachers couldn't be married, Amelia planned to take the position Miss Stanton currently held. The town had offered it to her. Father hadn't given his blessing yet, but he would.

She slid her arm through Father's. "Aren't you excited for this adventure?"

He patted her hand, a slight smile flitting across his face, barely visible under his neatly trimmed mustache and beard, but not reaching his eyes. It never did anymore. "I'll be happy when we're settled in our new place. There's much that needs to be done before then."

True. And it had been a lengthy journey from upstate New York to Chicago by train, and then another train through some of the most diverse and spectacular scenery of prairies, deserts, and mountains. In Sacramento, California, they switched to the Oregon and California train for the final leg of their journey to Portland. And somehow her cuttings had survived the entire journey. As tired as she was, excitement coursed through her. The end was so near. And she would get to ride a stagecoach! Just like in her favorite dime novels.

An older man and a younger one loaded their valises and trunks into the boot. And most importantly, her cuttings, wrapped in burlap and nestled in damp sawdust that she refreshed each night. They were her mother's legacy, and they meant more to her than anything else she owned.

Their household goods would be coming by freighter at some point. And because of the dime novels she read, she knew all the correct terms for life in the West and what they meant. Her latest novel was safely tucked in the emerald-green velvet reticule that swung from her wrist. Oh, she was living out a proper adventure, just like in one of her books! The only thing that would make this perfect would be if Mother were with them. She swallowed down the thought. No tears, or even the hint of them, would mar this adventure. She brushed her hands over her deep-green wool coat that matched her traveling suit, picking at a speck of dust.

Josh Benson nodded in their direction as footsteps came up behind them. Amelia tore her gaze away from the stagecoach. A man had joined them. He was sharply dressed in a dark suit and crisp white shirt. Taller than her father and possibly a little older than herself, he was lean with shoulders that filled out his suit coat. He smiled and tipped his hat at her, his golden-brown eyes —such an unusual color—twinkling. "Miss." He turned to include her father. "Are you folks traveling all the way to Reedsville?"

Father nodded. "We are. How about you, Mr.—?"

"Hank Paulson." He stuck out his hand and shook Father's. "I've been living there for a while now. It's a friendly town, good people. You'll like it there, I believe."

"Dr. Luke Martin and my daughter, Amelia. I've taken the position of town physician. We're relocating from New York."

"The town is surely in need of a doctor."

This man would be on the stage with them. All the questions she could ask him about the town raced through her brain. "Mrs. Adams has been writing to us about Reedsville and the people. We'll be staying in her boardinghouse until our house is built. I can't wait to get there."

He smiled. "You won't have to wait long. Josh is ready for us. Shall we?" He swept his hand toward the open stagecoach door.

Amelia stepped on the small box, and with Mr. Benson's assistance, entered the stagecoach.

He flashed her a smile, and those dimples appeared.

She grinned in triumph as she took her seat. Father sat next to her and Mr. Paulson across from them. The rest of the stagecoach filled with passengers, making for a tight fit. She kept her skirts firmly tucked under to keep them from brushing against Mr. Paulson.

Soon they were off. The jostling made it necessary for her to grip the seat, but the scenery that passed the window was breathtaking. So many variations of green! Back in New York, everything was still under layers of snow, the trees only bare sticks. Here it looked like it was nearly spring, even though it was only the end of January. Even the cool air had a hint of warmth to it.

Between the scenery, the jostling, and the noise, Amelia didn't ask any questions of Mr. Paulson. She'd discover it all as she experienced it.

A sharp report split the air. The coach jerked, and shouts came from outside. She caught Mr. Paulson's gaze. His brow furrowed, and he leaned to peer out. He reached inside his jacket and pulled out an envelope. He nodded at Father. "Any valuables, best try to hide them. We're being held up."

Robbed? Oh this was just like one of her books. Except she wouldn't swoon like the heroines often did. That was silly, frankly. She whispered a quick prayer for safety.

Mr. Paulson shoved the envelope in the seat cushion behind him then pointed to her reticule. "Anything in there you want me to try to hide?"

"Oh no. Merely a handkerchief and a book." But her hand went to her neck. Her mother's cameo, one of the few things she was allowed to keep for their journey West. It had a gold setting and chain, so it was worth some money, but of far greater value was its sentimental one. She tucked it into her dress, her high collar hiding the chain.

Father's arm came around her shoulders, pulling her close.

The stagecoach slowed to a stop, and horsemen replaced the woods as the scenery out the window.

Mr. Paulson cut his voice low. "Just do as they say. They likely want the strongbox and any valuables. But generally no one gets hurt, and they'll let us on our way once they get what they want."

A man on horseback with a bandana over his face bent to scout out the inside of the stagecoach. "No funny stuff, ya hear? Get on out here, and bring your valuables with you."

The stagecoach door flew open, another masked man holding it. "Don't none of you men try to be brave, or you'll get shot for your trouble."

Amelia trembled. While this was like something out of one of her dime novels, it might be a bit more adventure than she'd like.

What had they gotten into?

HANK FOLLOWED Amelia Martin out of the stagecoach. He couldn't help but notice her comely form, the green coat that highlighted her eyes, or the sun glinting off her reddish-brown hair. He'd been hoping this stagecoach ride would be enjoyable. It was not to be.

He kept to the side and in front of her, her father flanking the other side. What a way to be introduced to their new town. He scanned the robbers for any sign that might help Sheriff Riley identify them or their horses. One horse, a paint, resembled Tim Donnally's that had been stolen last week. So horse thieves too. The men were dirty and scruffy enough that he wasn't sure he could even identify his own brother if he were one of them. Not that Philip would ever be dirty or scruffy.

The final passengers exited the coach. He studied the men. He didn't know any of them, and he hoped no one would try to be a hero. They were evenly matched numbers-wise with the robbers, but the robbers all had their hands firmly on their firearms. Josh had been forced to surrender his shotgun.

The man who had opened the stagecoach door went around to the passengers collecting their valuables, patting the men's pockets to make sure no one was hiding anything. Another two were rummaging in the boot.

And the ringleader had his shotgun pointed at Josh. "Go ahead and toss down that strongbox I know you have up in that so-called secret driver's compartment."

Josh moved slowly, deliberately, but he complied.

The robber stealing from the passengers reached Hank and the Martins. "Easy now. Give me your wallet." His gun shifted to Miss Martin. Hank stiffened and shifted his weight closer to her. "And you, missy, hand over any jewelry and that fancy bag of yours."

Miss Martin paled. A faint sprinkling of freckles stood out

across her nose and cheeks. He'd be enchanted in any other circumstance.

"I'm wearing no jewelry. And there's nothing of value in my reticule. See?" She opened the drawstring pouch and held it toward him.

The man raked his gaze up and down her form. Hank wanted to punch him. Based on the slight movement Dr. Martin made and Miss Martin's restraining squeeze on his arm, Hank suspected he wasn't alone in that sentiment.

The robber grabbed the bag and dumped it into his hand. A scrap of lacy linen and a dime novel fell out. She hadn't been lying about her lack of valuables, thank goodness.

The man scowled. "A book? I ain't got no use for reading." He tossed the bag and its contents to the ground then chuckled. "But I might come back for a different kind of payment."

Over my dead body.

A scuffle at the boot caught Hank's attention. Items flew out the back, including some burlap sacks that broke open and scattered sawdust and plant material over the ground. What on earth was that?

Miss Martin whimpered.

He turned to see her gaze on the sacks, her gloved hand at her lips. They must be her items. But what they were, he had no idea. Her face crumpled, and she blinked rapidly. The encounter with the robber must have upset her more than she let on.

One of the passengers lunged for the robber. Looked like Bill Benchly, a saloon owner. Two others joined in.

Hank snatched Miss Martin about the waist and rolled her under the stagecoach.

The other robbers leaped in and a melee ensued. In the midst of the wrestling match, a gun went off. The shouts and several other gunshots faded from his awareness as the blackness pressed in. *Lord, please. Not now.* Reciting the Twenty-Third Psalm in his head, he deliberately steadied his breath and opened his eyes, which he hadn't realized he'd closed. He could see daylight. The space wasn't that tight. Slowly the blackness receded.

He became aware of Miss Martin's form pressed beneath him. Small and soft. He forced his mind away from those thoughts. She would likely be upset that he had dirtied her dress.

She struggled under him, trying to push him off. The scent of lilacs filled his nose.

"Shh, it's not safe."

She whispered something he couldn't hear over the commotion.

Horses whinnied. Men shouted. Hoofbeats started then receded.

He peeked out from under the stagecoach. Dr. Martin bent over a man. A woman knelt next to him, sobbing.

An elbow to Hank's ribs elicited a grunt, and he rolled over.

Miss Martin shimmied out from the stagecoach and ran—not to her father—but to the burlap sacks.

Hank slid out from under the stagecoach, fast on her heels.

She reached the first sack, scraping the sawdust and plants back into the bag.

Plants?

She glanced back at him. "Help me." Then she began coughing.

Dr. Martin jerked his head in her direction, frowned, and returned attending to his patient.

"What are these?" Hank studied what appeared to be a stick in his hand. Some others had a bit of greenery on them. Odd.

"My cuttings. The only thing I have left from my mother. They can't dry out. Pack the damp sawdust back around their roots and put them back in the burlap."

He did as she asked, taking in the scene around him as he worked. One man had been shot, the one Doc was working on. The rest seemed no worse for wear, picking up their hats, dusting themselves off, and repacking bags the robbers had strewn over the ground.

Josh gave directions and tended to the horses.

Hank packed the last burlap bag and handed it into the boot.

Miss Martin continued coughing.

"Are you all right?" Perhaps Josh had a canteen if she needed a drink.

"I'm coughing because you pushed my face into the dust and wouldn't let me breathe."

Oh. He'd tried to be a hero and had, once again, failed miserably. At least she'd only inhaled a bit of dust.

She rummaged through her father's doctor bag and came up with a small vial, which she opened and placed under her nose.

They loaded the injured man onto the stagecoach. It was Benchly. Some of the men rode up top to make room for him to lie down inside. Miss Martin followed her father onto the coach, carrying his medical bag.

But she didn't glance his way once.

Her reticule lay in the dirt where the robber had tossed it. Hank picked it up and dusted it off. She'd likely want it back. He snatched up her handkerchief and her book as well. *Her Love or Her Life.* The cover promised adventure and romance. Maybe today's adventure was a bit more than Miss Martin had encountered in the pages of this book. Maybe she'd learned that a hero only existed there and not in real life. Thank God He had kept them safe.

He tucked it all into his coat pocket and scrambled up next to Josh once all the other passengers were settled. He told himself Josh could use another set of eyes for the remainder of the trip home.

But the truth was, he didn't want to be near Miss Martin. He'd never felt less like a hero.

Chapter Two

A melia clutched Father's medical bag as he directed the disembarking of the injured man from the stagecoach. She whispered a prayer for his healing and Father's wisdom. They had driven through town and pulled up in front of a white farmhouse with well-mulched flower beds.

A red-headed woman—she'd know Mrs. Kincaid, now Mrs. Adams, anywhere—bustled down the stairs and issued directives. "Bring him inside. Do you need the dining room table?" Before Father even answered, she directed a thin girl on the cusp of womanhood to clear it and fill a pan with hot water. A tall, pale-blonde woman followed the girl inside. Was that Emily Stanton, the schoolteacher? Mrs. Adams had written that Emily and Josh would take over the stagecoach and boardinghouse after they married.

Father and the men carried the wan, unconscious, injured man inside.

Amelia followed him up the stairs. She had his bag. He would need her help. At least to hand him supplies.

"You must be Amelia." Mrs. Adams smiled at her, her apple cheeks and the lines around her eyes falling into their natural places. "I apologize for the terrible introduction you've had to our town. Once we get your father what he needs, I'll get you settled."

"I'm sure Father will need my help." She lifted his bag then climbed the stairs and followed Mrs. Adams into the house.

Father had the man on the table and was washing up.

"I have your bag. How can I assist?"

He nodded to a dining room chair. "Put it there, please. Just stay with Mrs. Adams. I have all the help I need." He gave her a tight smile. "You can pray."

She spotted the two men on either side of the table. She placed the medical bag on the chair. Father dried his hands and began removing the man's coat and shirt, the other men assisting him. Surely they didn't have more experience assisting in medical situations. He glanced up. "Amelia, please leave."

She nodded. She could do more than just pray. She could offer practical nursing help. But he never seemed to let her.

Warmth touched her shoulder. Mrs. Adams. "How about some tea?" She gestured to the hall. "We can take it in the parlor. Emily and I will prepare a cold supper and bring it out shortly."

"Thank you." Amelia turned to move to the parlor and nearly ran into Mr. Paulson. "Oh! I didn't see you there. I apologize."

His hand steadied her elbow. "No need. I didn't mean to sneak up on you. I was helping Josh unload the stagecoach and I wondered—well, since the cuttings were so important to you— what you'd like done with them. Josh has left them in the barn and said it was fine with him to leave them there."

A funny weakness shot through her, and she twisted her hands together, suddenly unsure of what to do with them. A brief flash of him holding her to him, the feel of his warmth and solidity against her... Well, clearly she was a bit—not over- wrought but perhaps worn out from the day's events.

"Thank you. That was very kind of you. Would you mind showing me where they are? That way I can tend to them."

"Not at all. Follow me." His gaze searched her face a moment and then seemed almost relieved.

He led the way to the barn in the fading daylight. The close mountains hid the sun sooner than back home. Inside, a workbench to the left held her burlap bags neatly lined up. She untied the twine on each sack and examined the contents. They didn't seem too much worse for wear. Other than needing to be dampened again. She turned to search for a water source.

"I'll get you some water. I know where the pump is." He gave her a quick nod before disappearing out the door.

It was almost as if he'd read her mind. Or paid attention to her words in the midst of the chaos of the robbery.

He returned with a pail of water before she knew it. He helped her dampen the existing sawdust. "I could use more sawdust soon. Perhaps I can find some tomorrow. But for now, this should be fine. It's kind of Mr. Benson to let me store them in the barn."

"You'll find most folks around here to be neighborly and helpful. I'm sorry that's not what you saw earlier."

"Evil is everywhere." She sighed and dusted off her hands. "Thank you for your help."

"You're welcome. How soon do you have to plant them before they die?"

"The sooner the better. My father and I are having a house built in town that will be his office as well. I'd like to plant them there in memory of my mother. But I'm afraid that will be awhile. I'm hoping I can get some temporary pots that will serve until I can transplant them." The light in the barn grew dim and the air chilly. But she wasn't in a hurry to return to the house. It had been a long time since anyone had asked about her plants. Father had never had the time nor interest. She suspected they reminded him too much of Mother, who spent many hours in their garden back home.

"If you don't mind my asking—"

A gangly, dark-haired young man came to the barn door. "Sheriff's here. He'd like to talk to you folks in the parlor."

"Thanks, James, we'll be right there." Mr. Paulson glanced at the workbench again. "Is everything set for the night, then?"

She looked around. As far as her plants were concerned, yes. They had survived the journey intact. That was one of the most important things.

But had her vision of the future? This was not how she'd ever imagined her first day in Reedsville would look. She'd always pictured adventure as romantic and heart pounding. She'd never pictured blood and gunshot wounds.

What would tomorrow hold? Because today had been nothing like what she'd expected.

HANK AND MISS MARTIN found Sheriff Riley in the parlor. He stood. "I'm Sheriff Michael Riley. I hear you and your father are new to this town. I apologize for the way you were greeted."

Miss Martin extended her hand. "Amelia Martin. And please don't apologize."

The sheriff nodded and took her hand. "Hank, would you mind waiting in the kitchen until I've finished with Miss Martin? I won't be long."

"Sure." Hank turned into the kitchen and sank into a wooden chair.

Maggie followed close behind. "What can I get you? Coffee? Tea? A sandwich?"

"That's kind of you. Coffee and a sandwich would hit the spot. Thank you."

Maggie nodded and bustled about the kitchen. She was a constant in this town, someone who always knew the right word or gesture to make a body feel better. Emily already stood at the counter assembling sandwiches.

If only he knew how to sort out his own thoughts. He'd been

far too aware of Miss Martin's presence. Why had he bothered to help her with her plants? Josh easily could have told her where they were.

After the stagecoach robbery—rather, after experiencing one of his episodes, which he'd thought he was rid of—his pride had made him want to avoid her. He was grateful it hadn't been worse, that the techniques he used—prayer and calm breaths—had kept his episode under control. He knew avoiding her wasn't practical in this small town, but he hoped to at least put some distance between them until she'd forgotten that he'd cowered under a stagecoach fighting the darkness that threatened to engulf him.

Why he'd had another episode was a mystery to him. It wasn't a terribly tight place under the stagecoach. He could see daylight. But it had come on so suddenly it had shaken him. He'd been through a stagecoach robbery before. And this one hadn't even cost him any money. His envelope hadn't been discovered.

But when he'd seen how Miss Martin's face had fallen when her father had turned down her offer of help, he felt compelled to do something to make this terrible day better for her. And she'd not treated him any differently than she had earlier.

Women were puzzling things.

Maggie brought over a mug of coffee and a sandwich of thick, dark bread with slabs of meat and cheese tucked inside.

"Thank you, Maggie. As usual, you're a true gem."

"I'm just glad you've decided to join our town. Helping Seth out with the logging company while Owen Taylor is with his mother has been an answer to prayer. Seth has been known to work too hard a time or two." She smiled.

"It's been my pleasure. He's been teaching me everything I need to know about the logging business. It's been the best education I could ask for."

"I'll let you eat. I'm sure the sheriff will call for you soon. He's been wanting to talk to everyone separately."

Hank took a big bite of the sandwich. He couldn't remember when anything had tasted so good. Then again, breakfast had been a long twelve hours ago.

Emily wiped her hands on her apron. "Maggie, why don't you and Pastor Roy head home? We've got it under control here."

Maggie and the preacher, Roy Adams, had married at a Christmas church service and now lived in the teacher's cottage that served as a parsonage. The town had donated supplies for a true parsonage to be built, one that could house Maggie's children as well. But for now, it was sweet that the two folks who meant the most to the town had some privacy for their new-found happiness.

"I'll help you wash the dishes, and then we'll be on our way. Roy's making his rounds with the passengers after the sheriff is finished with them, offering to pray or hear their concerns. Hank here is the last one."

He'd bunk with Josh tonight, so he'd get Maggie's cooking again for breakfast. Of course, with Josh getting married soon, Hank wouldn't have a place to bunk much longer when he was in town and couldn't make it back up to the logging camp. Since Seth himself was a married man and returned to his own home in Reedsville each night, he relied on Hank to be a presence in the camp.

Which meant he needed to push any thoughts of Miss Martin out of his head. Learning the logging business so he could set up his own outfit or become Seth's partner was his primary focus right now. It was the only way he could get out from his family's thumb and prove that he could accomplish something without their resources and influence. And he only had seven more months to do it.

As if his thoughts had conjured her, Miss Martin came into the kitchen. "The sheriff is ready to speak with you."

No distractions. He nodded as he passed her. Easier said than done as her lilac scent enveloped him.

Chapter Three

Hank tapped the cover of the dime novel sitting on the table next to where he'd bunked in Josh's cabin. He'd discovered it in his coat pocket last night when he got undressed for bed. He'd completely forgotten to return it to Miss Martin last night.

No suit today. He was in his regular work clothes—denims and a broadcloth shirt, both comfortably worn—and that was just fine with him. The suit had been necessary for his visit back home to San Francisco, but here, his work clothes represented his true self.

Josh had already left the cabin at first light and was likely doing chores at the barn. Josh's father, Charlie, also shared the loft. He was up and out too.

Hank would need to hurry to get breakfast and return to the logging camp. He hoped Miss Martin would be at breakfast, as he'd like to return her book to her in person. But given her eventful day yesterday, he didn't expect to see her.

But when he entered Maggie's kitchen door and slipped into the dining room, Miss Martin was already seated with her father and several other passengers. Pastor Roy and Charlie were also at the table nursing their coffees.

She broke off a sharp whisper toward her father and gave Hank a polite smile as he joined the table, choosing the chair next to hers. But she returned to her meal, keeping her eyes on her plate. It was as if they hadn't shared a stagecoach ride or robbery yesterday.

He didn't quite know what to make of that. Perhaps she wasn't much of a conversationalist in the morning. He dug into his food, thinking. Finally, he set the novel on the table and slid it toward her. "I believe this is yours."

Her gaze jerked up to his, her brow furrowed in confusion. Then the lines eased as recognition lit her face. "Oh, Mr. Paulson. I'm so sorry. I didn't recognize you." She took in his clothes and swallowed, and a look crossed her face that he couldn't interpret. But it was tinged with disappointment, though she recovered quickly.

"That's all right." He nudged the book again. "This got dropped in all the, uh, commotion yesterday, and I thought you'd like it back."

She smiled then grew pink, yanking the book off the table into her lap. "Thank you kindly. I appreciate that."

Dr. Martin glanced over and frowned. Hank got the idea the doctor didn't approve of his daughter's reading material. "Mr. Paulson. Good to see you again. Thank you for your assistance yesterday."

"It was nothing." He lowered his voice. "How did Benchly fare?"

Doc leaned closer. "I removed the bullet and stitched him back up. Barring infection, he should be fine."

"That's good to hear. I'm glad we had a doctor with us since something that unfortunate had to happen."

"Mrs. Adams told me he was the owner of the Golden Tree saloon."

Maggie bustled in with a coffeepot, pouring refills. "Please, call me Maggie. We're not formal around here."

Doc smiled and nodded. "Thank you." He wiped his mouth,

set his napkin on the table, and turned to Amelia. "I'm hoping to meet Danny Tillman about the construction of our home and office and find a temporary office space. Though I'm not convinced staying is the right choice after yesterday. I'll make my decision dependent on what I discover. I trust you'll be able to keep yourself occupied today?"

Hank frowned at the mention of Tillman. He hadn't met the man, but his reputation preceded him. And not in a good way. He'd like to take a look at what exactly Tillman had planned for Doc's office. Part of the reason the parsonage hadn't been built yet was that there was a lack of good men available to do the building. And not staying? What was that about? Not that it was any of his business.

Amelia set her fork down. "Yes, I thought I'd take a look around the town and try to meet Mr. Parsons at the hotel about the schoolteacher position."

Dr. Martin frowned.

Emily had been in the hallway, pinning her hat on, but stepped into the dining room. "I'm heading to the schoolhouse now. If you can meet me there before school starts, I'll show you around and answer any questions."

"Thank you so much. I'll hurry."

Emily nodded and disappeared into the kitchen.

Doc turned to Amelia. "I'm not sure you should get your heart set on that schoolteacher position. Do not promise Mr. Parsons anything until we speak about it. Ask Mrs. Adams where it is safe for you to go. I don't like the idea of you running around town unescorted."

"I can take her where she needs to go." Hank was surprised to hear the words coming out his mouth. He needed to get back to the logging camp, not hang around in town all day. But something about Amelia—Miss Martin—did strange things to his senses.

Doc nodded at him. "Thank you, Mr. Paulson. I'd appreciate

it." He rose and kissed the top of his daughter's head. "I'll see you at noon. Then we'll continue our discussion."

Miss Martin watched her father leave the room then turned to Hank with a bright smile that seemed a bit forced. "Just let me run this book to my room and get my hat and coat. Then we can be on our way. I'm sure you have better things to do than squire me around town." She pushed her chair back, stood, and disappeared from the dining room.

Hank belatedly jumped to his feet, then scanned the table. Most were engrossed in their own meals or other conversations. He headed into the kitchen, thanked Maggie for the wonderful meal, and then grabbed his hat and coat off the hook by the back door. He met Miss Martin in the hallway.

"Let's go out the kitchen door. There's something I want to show you." He pushed open the back door and led her down the stairs. "Last night it was too dark to see, but it's a pretty sight." He stepped back and let her take it in.

Beyond Maggie's wash line and vegetable garden, past the barn and corral, the land appeared untouched, turning into a forest that climbed mountains still capped with snow. A meandering stream flowed behind the garden, the riverbank just beginning to bud with what would surely be spring wildflowers. The morning light cast a bright glow over everything.

"Oh, it's beautiful. I noticed how green everything was as we got further west and then into Oregon. I can't believe it's the first of February and no snow."

Warmth spread throughout his chest. After yesterday, it was good to see her happy. "I thought with your love of plants and all, you'd enjoy it."

She turned to him, eyes bright. "Thank you for showing me. I can't wait to explore where that stream goes. It is safe, isn't it?"

"For the most part. Let someone know where you're going and use common sense. There are still wild animals around, though they tend to want to avoid people. And then there are the unsavory folk that drift through from time to time." He'd heard a few stories about past incidences. And what about yesterday's robbery? Was it connected to anything in the past? He pushed the thought aside.

She shuddered. He regretted bringing up the subject. And yet, he didn't want her to unwittingly put herself in danger. Those dime novels weren't exactly true to life.

He held out his elbow. "Ready to see the rest of the town, Miss Martin?"

"Yes." She took his arm. "And please, call me Amelia."

He nodded. "As long as you call me Hank."

"Done." She smiled.

They walked around the front of the boarding house and headed toward town. There were still a few shanties held together with tarpaper, but most were genuine establishments. Some had false second stories propped up from behind with poles. Main Street boasted a livery stable, a blacksmith, a tailor, the office of the Oregon Express and the telegraph, Frontier Bank, and Fulton's Mercantile. The town was just beginning to come to life this morning, with shops opening and proprietors sweeping the boardwalk and wiping down windows.

Her eyes took it all in. If she was this impressed with a small town at the end of the Oregon Trail, what would she think about San Francisco? His mind wandered a bit as he imagined showing her his favorite places.

"Here's Parsons Hotel. As I think you must know our mayor, Mr. Parsons, runs it. You mentioned wanting to speak with him. We should head to the schoolhouse first. It's at the far end of town, but there should be time before school starts."

"Yes, let's do that."

They walked a few more steps, their boots ringing hollow on the boardwalk that ran in front of most of Main Street's businesses.

Amelia looked up at him. "You've been so kind to me. I feel like I owe you an apology."

He frowned. "For what?"

"After the robbery, I was rude to you. You simply were trying to protect me, and I complained about the dirt."

"It's not necessary. It was a difficult time."

She shook her head. "No, you deserve an explanation. My mother had weak lungs. It was the cause of her death." Her voice caught. "My father has always been very protective of me in that way, afraid that I had inherited her weakness. I don't believe I have, but every time I cough, I see the worry cross his face. I can hardly bear it. I shouldn't have taken it out on you."

"Apology accepted, if it makes you feel better, but it is not necessary." However, it made a few things clearer to him. "That's why saving the plants is so important to you. It's a link to your mother."

"Yes." Her voice was so soft he almost missed it.

The schoolhouse rose before them, a thin stream of smoke trailing from the chimney. The schoolyard was empty.

"Tell me something about yourself. What is it you do? Yesterday you were dressed in such a fine suit I assumed you must be a banker. Today you are dressed like most of the men in town, in work clothes. And yet you are escorting me around town this morning. It is a puzzle." She gave a tinkling laugh.

He responded, yet feared his laugh sounded much more strained. He wished he thought through his answer before now. Only one person in town knew his true identity. "I, uh, was returning from visiting my family in San Francisco. But right now, I serve as a foreman for Seth Blake's logging outfit."

She stopped and stared at him. "Oh. I see. I never would have thought that." A shutter came over her face, putting an abrupt end to the amiable companionship.

"Hello there!" Emily exited the schoolhouse and waved. "Hi, Hank."

"Morning, Emily." Hank cleared his throat. "Since you two ladies have a lot to discuss, I'll leave you to it." He tipped his hat. "Have a good day."

Amelia touched his arm. "Thank you, Hank, for everything.

I appreciate your time."

He nodded and left. The way Amelia's face had closed off made Maggie's breakfast set hard in his stomach. There was no escaping it, it seemed. Everyone wanted him to be someone he wasn't and was disappointed in who he really was.

Amelia wasn't any different.

AMELIA GLANCED over her shoulder at Hank's retreating form and repressed a sigh. Their lovely morning had ended on an off note. For someone she had just met, she found that disconcerting. She needed all the friends in this new town that she could get.

Emily was talking, so Amelia turned her attention to her.

"I'm excited that you're staying at the boardinghouse. Since I'm living there until Josh and I get married, you and I can get well acquainted." Emily pushed open the door. "Let's take a quick tour through the schoolhouse before the children arrive. This also serves as our church on Sundays. The cottage next door has become the parsonage, for now." Emily laughed. "It was supposed to be the schoolteacher's cottage, but I never got to use it. Once Maggie and Pastor Roy announced their engagement, he moved in here, over Mr. Parsons's objections. But his wife brought him around. When Maggie and Pastor Roy married at Christmas, she joined him. I know she misses living with her children, Sally and James, but I think it's sweet they get some time alone together. Once the town is finally able to build them a parsonage, then they'll all be under one roof. But a number of people come and go from there throughout the day, folks that need spiritual advisement. I pretend not to notice unless the folks specifically greet me. I figure some of them would like their privacy."

Amelia nodded. "That seems wise."

A section walled off in the back had hooks for coats and

lunch pails. Wooden benches with attached desktops stretched in two rows the length of the room. A blackboard, teacher's desk, and woodstove stood at the front. For a moment, Amelia pictured herself at the front teaching a room full of children. It was a bit frightening and exciting at the same time. Think of all the things she could share with them. The greatest adventure of all, the adventure of learning. She clasped her hands together. Oh, she hoped Father would let her teach.

"Are there any other candidates for the position?"

Emily laughed. "This is not a desirable job, despite what Mr. Parsons would like people to believe from his advertisements. Last fall, he tried to replace me. The woman who came out was greatly disappointed by how she'd been misled and returned on the next stage. Since then, he's altered his advertisement to be a bit more realistic, but there have been no serious takers. Since we planned our wedding to be next month once we heard you were coming, if you're literate, he'll hire you."

Why would anyone try to replace Emily? Maybe Mrs. Adams would have some insight. She hadn't known Emily long enough to feel comfortable asking, and the children's voices grew louder.

Emily glanced at the watch pinned to her blouse. "It's almost time for school to start. Once you've talked to Mr. Parsons, come see me in the afternoon. I'll show you the lesson plans for the rest of the year, and you can come sit in the schoolroom to get to know the children and eventually take over." She squeezed Amelia's arm. "You'll do wonderfully. And I'll still be around to provide you help. Maggie has running the boardinghouse down to a fine art and has taught me everything she knows, so I'll have plenty of time to help you. Silly rule about married women not being allowed to teach."

Emily walked with Amelia outside to the bell.

"Thank you so much for your time. I'm sure I'll have many more questions."

"Happy to help." Emily smiled and pulled on the bell.

Amelia made her way down the stairs, weaving among the children, and headed back toward Parsons Hotel. This time by herself. Disappointment threaded through her. At some level, she had assumed Hank was a professional man, possibly a banker or some sort of businessman. His dress, his speech, his manners all led her to that conclusion. And her heart had leaned that way, too, if she was honest.

It must have been the excitement of the robbery and arriving in the new town and his gentlemanly ways that made her draw parallels between him and the heroes in her beloved novels. Yes, they were fictional, but the Hank of yesterday could have been the inspiration for one. She couldn't help but let her imagination run away with itself. It was a flaw of hers, as Father often pointed out.

But when she had seen him this morning dressed in work clothes, she didn't even recognize him. As they talked and walked, it made sense that he would wear work clothes in a town like this. Likely only Father would wear a suit. It just wasn't practical. Maybe even Father would begin dressing like the other men.

She stepped onto the boardwalk and spotted the hotel up ahead. She'd made it this far by herself in her new town. Luckily, everything she needed was on Main Street.

But when Hank revealed he was a laborer, her heart plummeted. Here she had felt she had found a friend, possibly someone who could even be a potential suitor. But Father would never allow her to be courted by a logger. Even one who was a foreman. She didn't realize how far her dreams had run away with her until the depth of the disappointment surprised her.

And, even worse, she knew it had shown on her face. Hank's coolness toward her proved that she hadn't hidden her feelings well. And hurt someone who had been nothing but kind to her in a trying situation. Father was right. Her imagination had gotten her in trouble. Worse, there was no way to repair the damage that had been done.

Chapter Four

⚜

Hank's strides ate up the town streets, his bootheels raising dust. He was in a hurry and needed to get back up to the logging camp, but first he had to find the homesite where Danny Tillman was supposed to be working on Doc's house. At least that's what he told himself. Not that his pride stung.

He was a logger. That's how he thought of himself. He was learning the business from Seth, and the men respected him. He'd spent his lifetime trying to break away from his family's control, responsibility, and expectations. He was certainly not going to stop now just to impress a woman. Even if she had fascinating freckles and fit perfectly to him.

Just past the mercantile, he turned down Center Street and then onto Second Street. The shopkeepers and store owners that didn't live above their stores lived down this street. It was close to the center of town, so it would be a suitable location for a doctor.

There it was. A vacant lot with a small pile of lumber. And notably silent. Hank strode the boundaries of the lot. It was a good size. It could hold a house and office plus have enough room for a small barn and Amelia's garden.

Amelia. For someone he'd only known for a day, she sure was

taking up a lot of space in his head. Why did he even care what she thought of him?

He examined the lumber pile. Warped boards with knots. He lifted a few. Most of this was worthless. And it had been sitting here awhile based on the yellowed grass beneath it. Uncovered in the rain. He tossed the board down. Where was Tillman anyway?

This looked nothing like the jobsites that he worked on with Jonathan Baker, the man who had taught him everything he knew about creating something with his hands, something that would last. The man who first called him Hank instead of Henry. The man who had first told him he was a good worker.

He crossed the street and knocked on the door. After a moment, a woman answered, wiping her hands on her apron. "Good morning."

"Morning, ma'am. I'm Hank Paulson. I work with Seth Blake up at the logging camp."

"Oh, then you must know my Andrew. I'm Beth Paige." Her face sagged. "He's not hurt, is he?"

"Oh, no, ma'am. I'm sorry to have alarmed you. Yes, I know Andrew, but I'm not here about that."

Relief flooded her features. "Oh, thank you, Lord. I know logging's a dangerous business, but Seth Blake runs a good outfit, and I've never worried too much. I know he treats his men right."

"Yes, ma'am, he does. I'm proud to be working with him." Hank gestured over his shoulder. "I'm actually wondering about that property over there. Do you know if that's supposed to be the new doctor's house?"

"Yes, that's what I'd heard. But there hasn't been much activity over there. When is the doctor supposed to arrive in town?"

"He's already here. That's why I'm checking on things. He said he'd hired Danny Tillman to build for him."

She scowled and shook her head. "That boy is nearly as bad

as his brother. Maybe just as bad but hasn't been caught yet. That lumber was delivered, but I haven't seen hide nor hair of Danny in near a month. Certainly not doing any work."

Hank's shoulders dropped. "About what I expected. If you see Danny, will you send word to me through Andrew?"

"Sure thing."

"Thanks, ma'am." Hank stepped off the porch. He hoped the doc hadn't paid Tillman too much of the money. He'd ask around a bit more before alarming the doc, but he didn't hold out much hope. He walked back to the boardinghouse. There was one more thing he needed to do before heading to the camp.

AMELIA PULLED open the hotel door, crossed the well-appointed lobby, and headed for the registration desk. No one was around, so she tapped the small bell that sat on the oak counter. After a moment, a short, balding man with a thin mustache came around the corner. "May I help you?"

"Mr. Parsons?"

His brow furrowed. "Yes?"

She held out her gloved hand. "I'm Amelia Martin. I've come to speak with you about the schoolteacher position that Miss Stanton will be vacating upon her marriage to Mr. Benson. Is now a good time?" In his correspondence with Mr. Parsons, Father had indicated that his daughter *might* be interested in the schoolteacher position if certain conditions were met. He never said what they were, but Amelia could only imagine. She hoped to present the contract to him as *fait accompli*. Then there would be no discussion of them leaving this town either. Now if Mr. Parsons would cooperate.

He gestured to a grouping of chairs in the lobby. "Let's sit over here, shall we? Would you like some coffee? I believe my wife and cook have whipped up some spice muffins as well."

Amelia took a seat on the velvet settee, folding her hands in her lap. "Oh, thank you, but no. I just finished breakfast at Mrs. Adams's." *Maggie's*, she corrected herself, but it felt foreign.

"Very well." He took the seat opposite her. "As you mentioned, Miss Stanton is getting married and will not be permitted to teach. Before that, my daughter was the schoolteacher. Unfortunately, no one has been able to match the standard she set for our town."

"Oh, Father, don't be ridiculous." A small, pale woman with aquamarine eyes crossed the lobby toward them. She bore a striking resemblance to a delicate china doll. "I'm Cassandra O'Malley."

"Amelia Martin. So nice to meet you."

"I've been looking forward to meeting you ever since Father mentioned you and your father's move to town. When did you get in?" She sat next to Amelia on the settee.

"Just yesterday."

"She and her father got caught up in the stagecoach robbery where Benchly was shot. I don't care for the man, but I don't want to see him shot. Good thing the doc was there to patch him back up."

Cassandra leaned conspiratorially toward Amelia. "Mr. Benchly ran against Father for mayor last year."

"Cassandra, we were discussing the schoolteacher position, not town politics."

An older woman, a slightly taller, darker version of Cassandra, entered the parlor. "Bill, I need your assistance with a matter."

"At this very moment?"

"Please."

He stifled a sigh. "I'll be back in a moment, and we can continue."

"Don't worry, Father. I can tell Amelia everything she needs to know. Just bring back a contract with you when you return." She turned to Amelia. "I was afraid I'd miss you. I'm just home visiting over a school break. My husband, Sy, and I attend Willamette University in Salem."

Amelia's eyes widened. "You attend the university? I've always wondered what that would be like."

"It's difficult and wonderful all at the same time." She told Amelia all about her and her husband's studies and his particular interest in inventions to make farmers' lives easier.

"I'm quite fond of gardening. I brought cuttings with me from back home, but I know very little about what will grow out here. I'm amazed things are so green so early."

"I'm sure Sy will have some books and journals he can share with you. Would you like to come out to his family's farm to see all of his inventions and horticultural ideas? He could explain it all better than I can. Plus, all of my books are out there. I have the largest collection of books in town, and you are welcome to borrow them anytime."

"Oh, that would be wonderful! Truly this has been the most welcoming town."

Cassandra arched her eyebrows. "Other than the stagecoach robbery?"

"Well, yes. That was unfortunate."

"Did the sheriff say who he thought was behind it?"

Amelia shook her head. "Not to me. He interviewed us all separately last night. No one said anything this morning at breakfast." But her thoughts drifted to Hank and how kind he'd been to her. Shame threatened to heat her cheeks again.

When Mr. Parsons didn't return, Cassandra promised to bring the contract over to Maggie's. "I'll bring you some books and a time when Sy can show you around the farm. We leave this Friday on the stage to Salem, so it'll have to be tomorrow."

Amelia left the hotel feeling a bit like she'd been in a whirlwind that morning. She'd met two women who she felt would soon become fast friends. But she couldn't help the disappointment that Hank would likely not be part of her life.

And that was all her fault.

Hᴀɴᴋ ᴏᴘᴇɴᴇᴅ the door to the cabin that served as the camp office, an apology for his lateness ready on his lips.

Seth glanced up from the paperwork on his desk. "Glad you're all right. Josh said you were on the stagecoach too."

Hank eased into his chair. It squeaked anyway. He'd need to oil it again. "Yeah. It would have been straightforward if Benchly hadn't decided to make a fuss. Too used to breaking up barroom brawls. I guess he had money in the strongbox."

"He wasn't the only one. Our payroll was in there." Seth tossed his pencil down and leaned back in his chair. "The money was insured, so it'll be replaced. The problem is that it'll take time. I don't have enough here to cover it. These men have bills and expenses. It's not their fault the stage was robbed." He rubbed his hand over his face. "And I owe Josh still for the mortgage he took out on the Oregon Express to save the logging camp last year. I'm trying to think of solutions. Maybe talk to Fulton at the mercantile and the bank. See if we can work something out for the men to buy on credit and get an extension on any payments if I'm good for it." He leveled his gaze at Hank. "What would you do?"

Hank took a breath and blew it out. It was a double-edged question. One, Seth was teaching him, letting him make decisions that a logging outfit owner would need to make. But, two, Seth was the only person who knew Hank's true identity. And it was his past experience that Seth was drawing on now.

"It should be possible to arrange a line of credit to cover payroll. I know you had some troubles last year, but those are easily explained away, and things have righted themselves." Last year a man had wanted the land under Seth's logging claim because he thought there was gold beneath it. When Seth wouldn't sell, the man tried to drive him out of business and then almost burned the town down. The fire had burned through a good portion of the logging camp last summer. Seth had men repair things, and they'd begun logging again. But in the interim his foreman, Owen Taylor, went to visit his mother to convince her to move to Reedsville, creating an opportunity for Hank. "A telegram and a trip to the bank should arrange it."

Seth frowned. "You're not making any special exemption for me, are you? A line of credit is a standard business practice?"

"It's very standard. I'm surprised you don't have one for situations like these."

"Haven't needed it before. We grew slowly, just bringing on men as we could afford them, paying as we went. In fact, this was the first time I'd had payroll delivered via the stage."

Hank leaned his elbow on his desk. "Which makes you wonder if that was a coincidence or not. Who knew about the payroll?"

"Not many people. The banker here in town and the one in Portland. And whoever there might know of it."

"Could be any number of clerks who saw or carried out the order. Did you mention it to the sheriff?"

"Haven't talked to him yet. I'm guessing we need to make a stop there while we're in town." Seth got to his feet and placed his Stetson on his head.

"I think that's a good idea." Hank followed suit, his mind whirling. How could he use his knowledge from his previous life to help the people he cared about in his current life without the two colliding and blowing up in his face?

Chapter Five

Amelia rounded the boardinghouse to enter through the kitchen stairs. Maybe she could help Maggie with the noon meal.

"Miss Amelia?" Charlie Benson, Josh's dad, came out from the barn. She'd met him earlier at breakfast. "I have something for you."

"For me?"

He beckoned her toward the barn. "Best come see. It's a mite hard to explain."

She followed him into the barn, blinking as her eyes adjusted to the dim light.

He walked over to the bench where her cuttings sat and tapped a bin. "Hank said you could use this. I'm working on a new project, so there will be plenty more if you need it."

That's right. Charlie had mentioned that he did woodworking. Josh helped when he wasn't running the stagecoach line. Curious, she stepped closer. The bin was full of sawdust. Unexpectedly, her eyes filled. She blinked back the tears. No tears. "How thoughtful."

Charlie chuckled. "Never thought I'd see anyone grateful for sawdust."

She laid her hand on one of the burlap sacks. "I use it to keep the roots around these cuttings damp. During the stage-coach robbery, much of it got scattered. So this is very helpful. Thank you so much."

"There's plenty more where that came from. Here, I'll show you. Then you can help yourself whenever you'd like." He led her farther into the barn. A small shop had been added on to the back with a long bench, and a variety of tools that she had never seen hung from the walls. A project of some sort sat on a low bench. Sawdust and shavings covered the ground. "Every night I sweep it all up into a big pile over here." He pointed to the corner. "Sally comes and gets it for the chicken coop. And when it gets to be too much, we burn it. So you're welcome to it."

She took a step toward the project. "This is quite fascinating. I've never seen anything like it. What are you making?"

He laid a work-worn hand on the in-process wood. "This'll be a bookcase. Working on the carcass right now. Done right, it'll easily last a hundred years."

"How wonderful to create something of such beauty and lasting value. My father should speak with you about creating bookshelves and cabinets for his new office."

"Be happy to talk with him."

"I'd better go see if Maggie needs any help. Thank you for showing me your shop."

"You need anything, you know where to find me. Here, at Josh's cabin until he gets married, or at Maggie's table." He chuckled.

Amelia smiled and left the barn, picking her way across the yard. Maybe she was wrong about Hank. Or not about him exactly, but about her idea of a hero. While no hero in her dime novels had ever brought a woman sawdust, Hank had listened to her and given her something she needed. Even if it wasn't heroic, it certainly was sweet. If she hadn't completely offended him, perhaps they could be friends.

HANK FOLLOWED Seth into Sheriff Riley's office. They'd gotten the line of credit set up without too many questions. Just as long as the banker in Portland didn't mention anything to Hank's father, things should go smoothly.

The sheriff stood as they came in. "Howdy, Seth, Hank. What brings you by?" He sat and pointed to the two chairs in front of his desk.

Seth preceded to tell him that the missing payroll was his, which the sheriff knew because Josh had told him. "But here's the thing I realized as Hank and I were talking about it. I've never had payroll delivered that way before. How did they know it was coming? Or were they just lucky?"

Sheriff Riley tapped his chin. "Interesting point. Who all knew about the payroll?"

Seth and Hank named everyone they thought might know. They hadn't come up with any new names on the ride down from the camp.

"I'll check into it. I'll talk to the marshal's office in Portland, see what they know. Hank, you want to search through these wanted posters to see if any look like those robbers?"

Hank thumbed through them. "The men were unshaven and unkempt with bandanas, so I'd be surprised if I find anything. But it can't hurt to look." As the sketched faces passed by him, he couldn't help but think he probably had better, more relevant contacts in Portland. He'd never planned that starting a new life could be so difficult.

"Have you seen Danny Tillman lately?" Hank put the stack of posters down.

Seth crossed his arms, and his face darkened.

The sheriff frowned. "No, come to think of it, I haven't. The saloons have been pretty quiet lately. Why do you ask?"

"Dr. Martin contracted with him to build his new house and office. I went by the site this morning and there was a pile of old, barely useable lumber and that was it. Mrs. Paige who lives across the street said she hadn't seen him there in nearly a month."

"Did the doc pay him any money?"

Hank shrugged. "I didn't ask, but I'd assume so."

"He's no better than his brother. If he's skipped town, so much the better. Though unfortunate for the doc if he paid Tillman any money." Seth scowled and shifted in his chair.

Danny Tillman had come up to the camp looking for work over the winter. Usually Seth gave a man the benefit of the doubt, so when he unceremoniously dismissed Tillman, it confused Hank. Until he heard that Tillman's brother had been involved in an attack on Seth's wife last year.

"Well it's fraud to take a man's money and then not do the work." The sheriff leaned his arms on his desk. "I'll ask around, but the doc better find someone else to build his house. Tillman was a bad choice anyway. Did Parsons recommend him?"

"Don't know, but I'll ask him when I see him." Seth stood. "The boardinghouse is our next stop."

"Let me know. Parsons has been involved with some shady characters in the past. If he and Tillman are running some kind of scam, I want to know about it."

"Will do, Sheriff."

Hank and Seth headed down Main Street to the boarding-house. If they were lucky, they'd get a meal out of their visit. Actually, this was Maggie. They would for sure get a meal out of their visit.

As they came in through the kitchen, Maggie was at the stove and glanced up. "Come on in. You're just in time to eat."

Hank grinned and removed his hat. "I hoped you'd say that."

"Go on in and sit with the others. Sally's got the biscuits, and I'll be out with the stew shortly."

Seth hung his hat on the peg by the kitchen door. "Thanks, Maggie. Is the doc in there?"

"Just sat down. Can he at least eat before someone needs him?"

"No one needs him. We just have some questions for him about his home site."

"Well you can talk while you eat." She shooed them both into the dining room.

Hank didn't have to be told twice. He spotted Amelia and her father sitting where they had this morning. He couldn't decide if he was disappointed or relieved that Charlie, Josh's father, sat next to her. He took a seat across the table next to Seth and next to the pastor, who asked the blessing on the food before they all began.

Amelia smiled at him and actually seemed glad to see him. He smiled back. Women were confusing things. But there was no time to talk as Seth had just asked Dr. Martin if he'd paid Danny Tillman to build his house.

"I wired him a deposit to purchase supplies he said he needed to get started. I tried to find him today, but no one has seen him." He dragged his spoon across his bowl. "I saw the homesite. Nothing has been started. He'd written me that he'd gotten the foundation laid and the walls were going up. That he would need more money soon. I put him off about the money, wanting to see what work had actually been done. I asked Mr. Parsons to look at the site for me, as he was the one who had recommended Mr. Tillman." He looked around the table. "He also recommended Mrs. Adams's boardinghouse."

"He didn't suggest his own hotel?" Hank asked before biting into a flaky biscuit dripping with butter. Maggie's were the best.

"He did, but the expense was more than I wanted to pay for how long we would need the rooms—two rooms—and the costs of establishing a practice. So then he mentioned this place."

Seth let out a breath. "I don't think Tillman is going to return. And neither does the sheriff. He'd like you to come file a complaint."

Dr. Martin paled a bit but then nodded. "Do either of you

gentlemen have a recommendation on who I can hire to build my house and office?"

Hank put down his spoon. "I do, actually." He glanced over at Charlie. "You might be interested in this conversation too." He caught Amelia's gaze. Her wide smile did something funny to his stomach.

AMELIA HELPED Maggie clean up after noon dinner while the men discussed something about building their home and office. Fortunately, Father hadn't brought up the issue of their leaving again. He must have gotten reassurance about the safety of the town. It had been a pleasant surprise to see Hank again, and he'd smiled back at her, so maybe he didn't hold a grudge. She hoped she could make amends. But the men had turned to their conversation, shutting her out.

Cassandra came in the back door.

"Cassandra! What a lovely surprise." Maggie wrapped her into a hug. "I was hoping you'd stop by when I heard you and Sy were in town for a visit. How are you two doing?"

"Oh, we're fine. I came to bring a few things to Amelia and thought I'd visit with you as well."

"Need another cooking lesson?" Maggie smiled. "How about some coffee?"

Cassandra took a seat at the kitchen table. "I'll take the coffee." She set a basket on the table and motioned for Amelia to join her. "I've brought you a few things."

Surprised, Amelia joined her at the table.

Cassandra pushed the basket in her direction. "First, here's your teaching contract signed by my father." She produced a piece of paper.

With shaking fingers, Amelia took it. There was her name across the top. It was only for the remainder of the semester, until June, with an option to renew for the fall semester. But it was enough. She clutched it to her bodice. When she looked up, Cassandra was beaming at her.

"There are a few books for you in there too."

Amelia reached into the basket and pulled out books by Mr. Twain, Miss Austen, and— She jerked her gaze up.

Cassandra's eyes twinkled. "They may not be your taste. I know they aren't great literature, but they are great fun."

Two dime novels rested in the bottom of the basket. Amelia grinned and then covered her mouth.

Cassandra giggled with her. "Now, before I forget, is tomorrow a convenient day for you to come visit the farm? Sy is excited to find someone else interested in plants. You may end up with more than you bargained for. We can fetch you after breakfast. We have supper with my parents that night, so we'll be back in town anyway."

"Tomorrow would be fine." Amelia tapped the certificate. "The only thing I have to occupy my time is reading. And peppering Emily with questions about teaching."

Maggie joined them at the table. "You'll do fine. We've been blessed with good teachers in this town. You'll carry on the tradition." She patted Amelia's hand.

Amelia's stomach fluttered. She wanted to believe Maggie's words. But was she qualified? As the women talked around her, Amelia couldn't help but wonder if she'd made a terrible mistake. After all, even her father didn't want her help. He didn't think she was capable. She stared at the contract. It still required her signature. Father would expect her to discuss it with him prior to her signing it.

Cassandra stood. "I need to get back before my mother sends out a posse. When we come home for a visit, she complains about every second I don't spend by her side." She hugged Maggie and then Amelia. "I put my address on a piece of paper in that book. Please write and tell me how things are going."

"I will."

After Cassandra left, some of the light faded from the room.

"Her parents have always been overprotective." Maggie picked up the coffee cups. "Marrying Sy and moving to Salem has been the best thing for her. She's fairly blossomed."

"It's too bad she lives so far away. I think she could be a good friend."

Maggie squeezed her hand. "You'll find your place in town. You've met Emily. She'll be a newlywed soon, but that doesn't mean she won't need friends. Her more than most, I suspect. She's had a time of it. I'm sure she'll tell you her story at some point."

"She mentioned that Mr. Parsons tried to have her replaced last fall."

Maggie shook her head. "Mr. Parsons—let's just say he gets his feathers ruffled easily. And as the mayor and head of the school board, he has plenty of opportunity to be ruffled. Last fall there was a robbery that ended up involving the town, and inadvertently, Emily. He used that as evidence somehow of Emily's poor character and tried to replace her. The replacement teacher refused to stay, and the town insisted that Emily stay on."

Amelia's hand went to her throat. Would Mr. Parsons find some fault with her?

"So I think you'll find a kindred spirit in Emily. And you haven't met Seth's wife, Becca, yet. She's been a bit under the weather." A smile played around Maggie's lips. "But she's like a daughter to me."

Amelia tapped the contract again. Two people in one day had expressed confidence in her. She wasn't quite sure what to make of it. What would Mother do? She would grasp the opportunity with both hands.

But would Father agree?

AFTER SUPPER, Amelia shut herself in her room and sat on her bed, contract spread on her lap. All she had to do was sign it. She stared at it.

No, she couldn't do that. Not without talking to Father first.

Could she really do this? Her experience teaching had been limited to helping farm children with their reading while the teacher in upstate New York did the actual teaching. But Miss Schneider had told her that she did a fine job and should be a teacher herself. In fact, Miss Schneider's disappointment over the Martins' leaving made Amelia think Miss Schneider had a beau and was hoping that Amelia might be able to take over her position. She'd even sat for the teacher's examination.

But she had to admit that the stagecoach robbery had shaken her a bit. She thought her dime novels had prepared her for life in the West. Yes, she knew they were exaggerations, but still…

Father had just finished eating when someone had called for him to check on an ill family member. Emily sat with Amelia by the fire in the parlor and told her about the children. It was clear by the tenderness in her eyes and her smile that Emily loved her students. If Amelia didn't take the position, who would? Could she in good conscience let these children go without a teacher? An education would make a lifelong difference to them.

And yet, if she didn't do a good job, wouldn't she do more harm than good? Not to mention failing spectacularly in front of the whole town.

What was holding her back?

Fear.

Fear that she wasn't good enough. Fear that she would fail. Fear that she'd freeze when she was most needed. Just like she had with Father. After Mother died, he was running himself ragged, and she tried to help the way Mother had. One day when the waiting room was full, he had asked Amelia to wash and bandage a minor cut on one of the boys. She had fainted, broken the basin, hit her head, and cut herself. She had made more work for him. She tried one more time with something simple, giving medicine or handing him supplies. But she got so nervous that she was going to make a mistake, she dropped things, spilling and contaminating them. After that, he never used her unless there was no one else. He would pat her head and tell her to pray.

She fingered the small scar that crossed the back of her thumb, reminding her of her failures. Would teaching be one more on the list?

Lord, I know fear is not of You. But I don't want anyone to suffer because of my incompetence. And if You had seen fit to leave Mother on this earth, then I wouldn't even be in this situation.

That wasn't fair, but it was how she felt. Of course, they would still be in their small town in New York and she never would have met Emily, Maggie, Cassandra, and Hank.

God, I know you have a plan, but I surely miss Mother. I could use her advice. What should I do?

HANK FLOPPED on the bed in the foreman's cabin. He tapped the letter he held on his thigh. He had to open it, but he knew what it would say. More of the same. Couldn't his family even give him a minute to return to Reedsville? He'd just been visiting them.

He tore open the letter. It was from Mother this time. A change in tactics. She hoped that his return to San Francisco had caused him to come to his senses and give up his silly pursuit. That he would return home immediately—or at least to his former banking position in Portland—and take up his rightful position in the family banking empire.

He nearly tossed the letter in the stove before finishing it, but Mother's last paragraph was different from before. Father was ailing. He didn't want anyone to know—of course not—not even Philip. That wasn't a surprise. Philip couldn't be trusted with escorting an old lady across a busy San Francisco street. But

Mother's panic came through the lines. She was afraid Father wouldn't be able to run the company and that it would be left to Philip. Who would bring it to ruin.

Henry was her only hope. No one in his family called him Hank, no matter how many times he'd asked them to.

He ran his hands through his hair. Nothing he'd said to them in person or by mail convinced them that he had left banking for good, that he wanted to be his own man and work with his hands.

Was Father truly ailing? He had seemed fine to Hank, but he allowed that Father was adept at hiding his true emotions. On the other hand, Mother could be prone to exaggeration to get her way.

Didn't Mother know about the agreement Hank and Father had? Hank had agreed to work in banking in Portland, which he had done, in exchange for the freedom to prove he could make his own way within a year. Seven months were left, and he was well on his way to making his point.

What to do? Did he have an obligation to his family? Why couldn't one of Father's managers run the company? He had hired several excellent ones. Why did it have to be Hank?

His mind drifted to his earlier conversation at Maggie's dining room table. He'd suggested that Charlie Benson take young John McAlistar under his wing and teach him the construction trade. Hank himself had even agreed to help out. Not only did they need to build the doc's quarters quickly, Pastor Roy and Maggie needed a parsonage too. Seth offered to provide a few men for a workday.

And with the railroad knocking on the edge of town, it was only a matter of time before the town would need more buildings. Anyone who could learn to craft a solid building would be in great demand. It wouldn't be Hank, but he'd be happy to help another man get started.

He'd made a good life for himself here. He was a contributing member of this town, and it felt good. He'd nearly proved that he could be his own man, not reliant on his family's status and income.

And then there was Amelia. The doc hadn't flat out stated that they were staying, but he'd contributed to the conversation about building his office and home. Though he allowed that any doctor the town hired would be grateful for the accommodations.

As they'd sketched out the plans, he'd thought of Amelia's plants and her desire for a garden. He had just the space reserved for it on the lot, but he'd value her opinion of it. Maybe he'd ask her tomorrow, show her the site, and get her thoughts on the spot he'd picked out. See if she agreed.

He stood and readied for bed. As for his family, he'd have to do some more praying on it.

Chapter Six

A melia waited until the breakfast dishes had been done, the boardinghouse dining room table had cleared out, and Father was settled in the parlor wing chair flanking the fire with a cup of coffee and one of his journals. He always spent the first half hour after breakfast reading on the latest developments in medicine. If he didn't have any emergencies.

She hadn't been able to bring up the subject last night. He and the men had spent the afternoon laying out plans and discussing things she was clearly not to be a part of. While she assumed that meant he had decided they were staying, she could admit to herself that she was afraid he hadn't.

Emily had given her a broad smile and quick wink before she left for school that morning, and Amelia tried to take courage from that. Cassandra and Sy would be here soon, so she had to do this now. She wiped her hands on her apron and moved into the parlor, pulling the teaching contract from her pocket. She sat in the chair opposite him and waited for him to look up.

"Do you have something with which to occupy yourself today, Amelia?"

"I'm visiting Cassandra and Sy O'Malley at their farm. Sy is quite a horticulturist and is willing to give me pointers about growing things out here. They're fetching me shortly." She handed him the paper. "I wanted to discuss this with you." She studied his face as he scanned it, but it was impassive. Her fingers crept up to Mother's cameo around her neck. She was incredibly grateful it hadn't been taken from her in the robbery.

He met her gaze. "Do you have any idea what life is like out here on the edge of the frontier? That stagecoach robbery was just one of many things that could happen to us. I've been talking to various townspeople. There's been fires, ruffians, shootings, logging accidents, and claim jumping." His face softened. "I know we both wanted a fresh start, but perhaps a place more settled, like Portland, would be a better choice."

She squeezed her hands together. "Perhaps. But there are plenty of teachers—and doctors—in Portland. This town needs both of us." What she didn't say was that Mother would have wanted them to stay. She had a tender heart toward those who were in need. Even with her weak lungs, she would call on Father's patients and bring them food and comfort. She had a touch that Amelia hadn't seemed to inherit.

His gaze bore into her, and she resisted the urge to squirm or defend herself. She clamped her mouth shut and waited. Did he think she was capable of the job?

After a long moment, he handed the paper back to her. "You are of age, and it asks for your signature, not mine. If you think it's the right choice, then I'll support you."

A grin broke free, and she couldn't help but wiggle in her seat. "Does that mean you've decided for us to stay?"

He gave a slow nod. "For the time being. You are correct, Amelia, that this town needs us." His gaze grew troubled, and he blinked. "But I can't risk putting you in danger and losing you. If anything happens—" His voice broke, and he cleared his throat. "If I think the danger is too much, we'll be packed and headed to Portland no matter if it's the middle of the school term or I have patients in labor."

She was certain he meant it about the school term but wasn't so sure about the laboring mothers. He would never put his patients at risk. She hopped up and threw her arms around his neck.

He jerked his coffee cup to the side to avoid spilling it.

"Thank you, Father."

Maggie appeared in the parlor doorway. "Cassandra and Sy are here. Bundle up. It's chilly and foggy out there."

"Have a good time, Amelia." Father turned back to his journal.

"I will." She and Cassandra had plenty to talk about. She headed over to the desk, dipped a pen in ink, and signed her name across the contract with a flourish before dashing upstairs.

HANK PAUSED on the back steps of the boardinghouse to shake off the damp that clung to his duster and hat from the heavy fog before entering the kitchen. The same heavy fog that had limited logging operations that day. Some outfits would work no matter the weather, but Seth didn't like to endanger his men, and low visibility would do that. If they had a lumber mill in town, it would have been a good day to start working on the doc's house. Seth could have spared the men. But as it was, lumber had to be ordered and shipped in by a freighter.

"Hank!" Maggie wiped her hands on her apron. "What brings you out this way?"

"I was hoping to talk to Amelia. Is she here?"

"No. She's out at the O'Malleys'. Sy was going to talk to her about growing plants out here."

A heaviness dropped into his stomach. "Oh." It hadn't occurred to him that she might not be here. Which was silly. She wasn't sitting around waiting for him.

"How about you taste one of these muffins I just pulled from the oven? And have a cup of coffee to warm you up."

Hank gave her a grateful smile and pulled out a kitchen chair. "I promise I didn't come by just to get fed by you."

She pulled a cup off the shelf. "It would certainly be fine if you did."

Maggie mothered most of the town, and her warmth was a contrast to the society woman that was his mother. She was kind, but never could quite see Hank and what he needed.

A moment later, he was biting into a warm muffin and washing it down with a cup of hot coffee, both of which chased the chill away. "Maggie, what would we do without you?"

"Pshaw, you'd be just fine." She pulled out a chair and joined him. "I'm actually looking forward to letting Emily and Josh run things so Roy and I can spend some time together. He's still visiting the surrounding towns once a month, and based on his stories about those people, I'd like to go with him and help out."

Hank grinned. "So, no resting on your laurels, Maggie?"

She waved a hand. "Not as long as the good Lord has given me work to do and the strength to do it."

"Tell me, have you and Pastor Roy talked about what you'd like the parsonage to look like? For example, do you want a kitchen like this? How many bedrooms would you need? Has anyone asked you about any of that?" And why did he go and open his big mouth? Doc's house was one thing, but this was something different. Why was he involving himself with things that had nothing to do with his real job, running the logging camp? But this was Maggie. She'd done so much for the town, she deserved to have something that she wanted.

"Oh, goodness. I hadn't even thought. Seth and the others put up the money for the lumber, but Seth put off ordering it until we had a workday scheduled. I figured between the weather and how busy the logging camp was trying to make up for lost time, it would be some time before anything happened." She smiled. "Roy and I are quite comfortable at the teacher's cottage."

Of course she was. Maggie would never complain. He pulled out of his pocket the small notebook and pencil that he carried everywhere with him. "So just pretend for a moment. If you could have everything you wanted in a house, what would it be?"

It took some prodding and a lot of questions, but by the time Hank had finished another cup of coffee and a muffin, he had a fairly good idea of the plans he could draw up for the parsonage. He'd talk with Charlie on his way out and see if they couldn't come up with a way to get Doc's house and the parsonage both built.

As he left, Maggie wrapped him in a hug and sent him off with a flour sack of muffins.

After he had spoken with Charlie, he turned his horse back toward the logging camp. Why had he just taken on another project? He had to admit he enjoyed drawing up buildings and seeing what he'd put on paper come to life. But his career was as a logger, not a builder. He'd best remember that. After all, if he owned his own outfit and was successful, Father might finally respect him as an equal who'd built his own company. And he would have won his independence. But a common laborer would never win his Father's respect.

He remembered all too clearly Father's lecture to him on being a common laborer. Hank had been helping Mr. Baker after school each day to avoid Philip and his so-called friends. He'd felt useful and strong. Every day there was a little bit more progress on the building. Until the day he was carrying a load of lumber and tripped over a bucket of nails he'd left out. Trying to catch himself, he'd got his arm twisted under the lumber and broken it.

When Mr. Baker had helped him get home, after giving him a lecture on keeping a clean jobsite, Hank had to spill the whole story to his parents as to where he'd been spending his days.

Father's face had turned purple. He hadn't worked as hard as he had to have a son of his work as a common laborer.

Worse, Father had ordered Philip to carry Hank's books home from school each day. Which just gave Philip and his friends an excuse to torment Hank. But swinging a hammer and carrying lumber had given Hank muscles. When he bloodied Russell's nose, that had put an end to the pushing and shoving, though not the taunting. At least he was able to block that out.

As he rode into the logging camp, he reined in his thoughts. No, he needed to keep with his original plan. Charlie Benson was a capable carpenter, and John McAlistar had the energy and muscles to do the heavy work. They'd make a good team.

And Hank could stay out of it.

THE RIDE to the O'Malley farm had been shrouded in fog, so Amelia hadn't been able to grasp the scope of it. But Sy had led her and Cassandra around their orchards. Sy pointed out the varieties of apples they grew, which would be budding soon. They also grew peaches, pears, and almonds.

Sy examined one of the branches. "My folks back in New York grew apples, so that was what drew us out here. The reports touted this soil and climate as being able to grow nearly anything."

"Yes, I'd read that too. Is it to be believed?"

"For the most part. Certainly more than the harsh winters of upstate New York would allow." Sy smiled at Cassandra and reached for her hand. "Which was why my folks finally agreed to relocate out here after delaying two years. This winter was the last straw, so I hope to see them here this summer. And since Jacob is seriously courting a young lady in town, I think we'll be needing to add a few more cabins to the farm."

Amelia continued to ask questions about the care and harvesting of the trees. Sy willingly expounded on his knowledge, clearly enjoying how his work at the university had allowed him to study his passion. He was unlike anyone she had met. He liked to work with his hands but was clearly intelligent. She'd never considered that someone could enjoy both.

She cast a glance at Cassandra, who simply beamed. She was visibly proud of her husband. As she should be. Amelia suppressed a sigh. What would it be like to admire a man like that? And have him reciprocate with adoration? Cassandra was a smart woman, too, and yet she had no problem with Sy's interest in agriculture.

Hank's face flashed in her mind, his golden-brown eyes twinkling. She did enjoy his company, but there could never be anything but friendship between them. Their lives were too different. Weren't they?

As they neared the barn, Sy pointed out a small building that served as a greenhouse. "When I lived here, this was where I did cross-pollination and grafting experiments. Now I don't think anyone is using it. You're welcome to bring your cuttings here." He showed her where he stored small pots and his specially blended soil with amendments. "Use anything you'd like. No one else is, and it would please me to see it being used by another horticulturalist."

Mother would have adored the greenhouse. She'd always wanted one. Amelia couldn't help the smile that spread across her face. Not since spending time in the garden learning plant names with her mother had she felt so fully welcomed for who she was. The only sadness was that the O'Malleys lived so far away in Salem. At least for another year.

Sy tugged open the barn door. It squeaked. "I see my brothers still haven't fixed that. I don't know how it doesn't grate on their nerves." He led her over to a wooden counter covered with neatly lined-up tools. A stack of papers sat to the side. A shelf above the counter held a few books.

"Show her your ledger." Cassandra's eyes nearly danced.

He tugged down a thick, leather-bound volume. "When I

lived here, I took weather readings every day. I have a weather station in the hayloft. I compared the weather data to crop output, checking for correlations. Not that you can change the weather, but maybe you can change its effects on the crops. It's now a part of my research at Willamette University." He flipped some pages and ran a finger down a column. "See? This is the same day last year. In the fifties. Whereas in January we had a bad ice storm." His face turned ever so slightly pink.

Amelia glanced at Cassandra who giggled. "It forced Sy to stay at the hotel and gave us a chance to get to know each other."

"Ah, so it was fortuitous, then."

"I would say so." Cassandra touched her husband's arm. "Show her the hayloft." She turned to Amelia. "You're not afraid of heights or climbing ladders, are you?"

"Not at all. One of my neighbors had a tree house growing up, and I used to love to go up there and read. So peaceful. And you could see over all the rooftops."

Cassandra led the way to the ladder and motioned to Amelia. She grasped the smooth wood rung with her gloved hand and stepped on a lower rung, repeating the movement until the barn floor looked far below. Her stomach dipped.

"I can't look down." Cassandra's voice came from below her. "My stomach gets all swirly when I do. But I still love it."

The teacher's contract in her pocket rustled with each step that she climbed. Father had left the decision in her hands, and she'd signed the contract. But she hadn't given it to Cassandra yet to give to Mr. Parsons. She hadn't even mentioned that she had it with her. She still had time to change her mind. Father had never let her make this kind of decision before. Was it a test? Did he think she'd fail? Or did he trust her to make the right decision?

The hayloft appeared in her line of vision, and she scrambled up into it. Cassandra appeared a moment later followed by Sy.

"I rigged a platform to slide out the hayloft door via a pulley.

All of my instruments sit on it, but I can pull them in to take readings." He spent the next few minutes showing her how he had set up a rather sophisticated weather station.

Once they had studied Sy's setup and climbed back down, he led them into the house. His brother Stephen had a warm apple pie and a pot of coffee ready for them.

As they were eating, Sy encouraged her once again to bring her cuttings out to the farm.

"I'd be happy to help," Stephen volunteered.

"I'd appreciate that, thank you." She took her final bite of pie. "This is just delicious, Stephen. What a lovely surprise."

"Our mother taught me how to cook, and it's a good thing, too, or we would have starved these past two years." He winked at Sy.

Cassandra stood and began clearing the plates. Amelia made to join her but Cassandra waved her down. "You and Sy talk plant things."

Sy chuckled. "I have a steady group of farmers and scientists that I correspond with. If I can't help you with something, I'm sure they'll know the answer. So please write and let us know how things are faring."

"Any time you want to come out to the farm, just leave a note for me at the mercantile. Sy and Cassandra can tell you about how well that works." Stephen nudged Sy's shoulder.

But before he could reply, three men came in the kitchen and headed for the cookstove.

"Amelia, these are my older brothers. Jacob, the oldest, then Patrick and Nicholas. Boys, this is Miss Amelia Martin. She's going to be the new teacher, and her father is the town doc. They've just moved here from New York, not terribly far from where we grew up."

The sound level in the kitchen rose as they all asked her various questions about her trip and her plans and settled around the table. They joked with Cassandra and treated her like a little sister. Amelia took it all in. It must have been wonderful growing up with so many siblings around. Always someone to talk to or a playmate to share adventures with. A bit of melancholy cast a shadow over the day, much like how the fog had blocked out the sun. Which was ridiculous. She shook it off. It had been a perfectly lovely day. And the O'Malleys, like everyone she'd met so far in town, had been warm and welcoming to her.

Cassandra tapped Sy's shoulder. "We'd best be getting back. Mother's got a farewell supper planned for us. You boys are all coming, right?"

Jacob got to his feet. "I'll come along separately with the buggy."

"I'll ride with you," Nicholas said.

"No, you go along with them." Jacob sprinted upstairs.

Patrick grinned. "He's going to stop by Emmaline's house later."

A short time later, they all, minus Jacob, had piled in the wagon and pulled away from the farm. They had just come over a rise when Cassandra touched Sy's arm. "Sy, stop and let her look."

He reined in the horses. "You couldn't see this on the way in, the fog was too thick, but turn around and take a look. It's one of my favorite views."

A slight mist hung over the hills in the distance, shrouding them in mystery. Trees in neat rows raced up and over the hills with a little pond tucked in between.

"It looks like something from a storybook." Amelia's voice was breathy.

Cassandra squeezed her hand. "That's just what I said when I first saw it."

After a moment, they turned forward again, and Sy clucked to the horses.

Amelia's hand slipped into her pocket. It had been a magical day. These were kind people. And Emily would help her with whatever she needed to learn as a teacher. She pulled out the teaching contract and handed it to Cassandra. "Would you give this to your father?" Not only would she teach, she'd do a good enough job that they'd ask her back next year as well.

That's exactly what Mother would do, and it felt like the right thing for her too.

Chapter Seven

S tanley Wallace returned from taking his noon meal at Hotel Pacific and entered his nicely appointed office at the Bank of the Pacific in Portland. On his desk sat a letter with a familiar script, one that notched his heart rate up. He hung up his hat and coat before taking a seat at his desk and slitting the letter with an opener. What news would this contain? Fear and anticipation warred, and he swallowed as he unfolded the letter.

DEAR MR. WALLACE,

BECAUSE YOU HAVE PERFORMED SO ADMIRABLY on the last task I set before you, I have another assignment for you. Bank of the Pacific has acquired Frontier Banks, a small chain of no significance except that they have a branch in Reedsville. Currently, it is managed by a Mr. Hubert Irving, who replaced Horace Wilkins last year after an unfortunate incident.

It has come to my attention that Mr. Irving is working against my interests by allowing a logging company owned by Mr. Seth Blake to establish a line of credit. I am certain my son is behind this, and I need a manager of this bank that I can trust to represent my interests.

Even though you'd be managing a backwater branch, your salary will remain the same as compensation for your work. I need not remind you of the adverse information I possess that would ruin your career in banking if it were ever to be discovered.

Report to the Reedsville branch as soon as possible, no later than two weeks hence. You may take lodging at the Parsons Hotel, the only suitable establishment in town.

Yours,
    Vernon Paulson

STANLEY DROPPED the paper to his desk. He had no desire to move to a dirty little town at the end of the Oregon Trail, even if it meant managing his own branch. He rather liked living in Portland. However, if he wanted to keep Harley's criminal activities a secret, then he had no choice but to do Mr. Paulson's bidding. Before Stanley had been promoted to manager, Mr. Paulson had sent him a letter stating that he'd had him investigated by Pinkerton, like he did all of his managers. And Pinkerton had uncovered his brother Harley's unsavory past.

However, Mr. Paulson promised to keep the matter quiet if Stanley would do his bidding. Since then he'd served as Mr. Paulson's lackey, reporting gossip among the clerks and handling sensitive transactions.

Getting out of Portland wouldn't be the worst idea, though, after what happened two weeks ago. Stanley had been walking home from work when Harley had appeared out of nowhere and stopped Stanley with a hand to his chest.

"Hey, brother. I need a favor."

Stanley tried to push past him.

"Aw, come on. You're my brother; you have to help me."

"I don't. Your 'activities' almost cost me my job."

Harley grinned. "But they didn't." The grin dropped away. "But I could still make that happen. Walk into your fancy bank and tell everyone who I am."

Stanley's stomach dropped. "Don't do that. What do you want?"

"Just information. Nothing much. I just need to know when payroll or large shipments of money head out of here on stage-coach runs. They're insured, and nobody gets hurt. It doesn't hurt anyone except the insurance companies, and they can afford it."

"Is Red Dawson behind this?"

Harley shoved him up against the brick building, the sharp edges cutting into Stanley's back through his suit coat. "Don't mention his name. Forget you ever heard it."

"Okay, okay."

"And if the marshal comes sniffing around, I'll be sure to tell him who my brother is." He shoved a wadded-up scrap of paper in Stanley's pocket. "Leave me the info here." Then he disappeared down the street.

Stanley took a breath. Harley's threat was a real one. And while Mr. Paulson knew, if others knew, Stanley's career in banking would be over. He'd be lucky to get a job as a lamplighter.

But that wasn't the worst of it. If Red Dawson thought he'd ratted them out, then there was nothing that could save him. And Stanley didn't think even Mr. Paulson could manage Red Dawson.

HANK SHIVERED UNDER HIS DUSTER. The morning was cold, and frost glistened on every surface. Logging would be on hold until the day warmed up. If it did.

But the early morning was the only way he could ensure he'd catch Amelia. And before he finalized the project and ordered the lumber, he needed her input. He'd discussed the plans last night with Seth, including the ones for the parsonage that he'd drawn up based on Maggie's input.

Seth had given his blessing but had brought up an idea that Hank wasn't sure what to think of.

"You know, if we had a sawmill in town, we could cut our own lumber." Seth nursed his coffee as they sat in front of the fireplace at his home. Becca brought them each cookies, and he thanked her with a smile. "It's silly to ship our logs out to have them milled and pay to have them shipped back to us. A sawmill would eliminate the middle man. With all the building that's bound to come our way with the railroad, it would be a good business for someone."

Hank met his gaze. "Are you trying to talk me out of logging? This is the second time you've suggested that I might want to do something else."

"Not at all. You're a natural leader, the men respect you, and you've learned the business quicker than anyone I've ever seen." Seth shifted in his seat. "But a sawmill would be good for this town. The Oregon Express's days are likely numbered, and I'm thinking of options. I'd hate for Josh and Emily to have to move on. He's like a brother to me and saved the logging company last summer at the risk of his own livelihood." He took a bite of cookie before continuing. "And you're the only one who has the ability to make that kind of investment." Seth held out his hand. "I'm not suggesting you do anything you don't want to. I'm just tossing out ideas as I see them."

Hank swallowed the rest of his coffee. "What you're saying makes sense. I'll think on it some."

And as Hank put up his horse in the barn behind the boardinghouse, he couldn't help but look in on the woodworking shop attached to the back. Several projects in various stages sat on the workbench. Charlie was keeping busy. But a lack of sheet goods would always slow things down.

Could he figure out how to help the town without revealing who he was? He shook his head and headed inside. Something else to pray about.

Maggie barely moved her attention from the stove when he came in. "Morning, Hank. You're just in time."

Emily carried a plate of biscuits out of the kitchen into the dining room. "Come grab a seat."

He removed his hat and damp duster, the warmth of the kitchen immediately thawing him. Would it be the same once Maggie and Pastor Roy weren't here? What about once the train came through town?

He shook the thoughts off and entered the dining room, tugging out the chair next to Amelia.

She looked up in surprise. "Hank!" A smile lit her face.

"Let's pray." Pastor Roy's booming voice left no room for discussion.

Hank gave Amelia a quick smile before bowing his head. After the blessing, Emily was filling his coffee cup before he even asked.

He passed the plate of biscuits to Amelia. "How was your trip to the O'Malleys? I hear Sy has quite the setup."

"He truly does." She gave him a summary of her trip, including the offer to use his greenhouse, as platters of food passed around the table.

"I'd be happy to help get your plants out there, if you'd like." The words were out of his mouth before he realized it. He shoved in another bite of hash.

She touched his arm. "Thank you. That's very kind. I'd like to get them settled before I start teaching."

"So you signed the paperwork then."

She nodded.

"When do you begin?"

She glanced in Emily's direction. "We'll talk about it tonight, but likely in a week or two."

He nodded. "I thought, if you had the time, I'd like you to look at the plans I've drawn up for your place." He glanced to the other side of Amelia. "And you, too, Doc. But I was particularly concerned that you approve of the area I set aside for a garden."

Doc wiped his mouth. "I have several patients to see this morning, but you can leave the plans, and I'll go over them with Charlie." He stood, dropped a kiss on Amelia's head, and left the dining room.

"Guess the town is happy to have a doctor. He's been busy since you've been in town."

Amelia nodded and gave a tight smile. "Just like back home."

Hank looked down the table as folks were finishing up. "Charlie, are you able to go with us? I'd like your opinion on the site and plans."

"Sure thing. I'll head over to young John McAlistar's. He should be in on it from the very beginning if he wants to learn the trade."

A few minutes later, they were bundled up in hats and coats and walking down Main Street, their breath making small clouds in front of their faces.

Charlie waved toward a building. "I'll go roust John. He and Annie have a small room above the mercantile. He helps out Mr. Fulton with deliveries and does small jobs around town, but I know he wants to learn a trade. He's a hard worker."

Hank nodded. "You're the one working with him. You do what you think is best."

Charlie winked and moved across the street.

Amelia turned to Hank. "Does your logging experience relate to your building experience somehow?"

He thought for a moment about how much to say. "There

was a man, Mr. Baker, who would let me help out on his construction site after school." He paused. "My brother and his friends tried to make my life difficult on the way home from school, so having a place to go was a way to avoid them. But Mr. Baker was a good teacher, and he taught me a lot. There's something rewarding about seeing a building go up by your own hand when there hadn't been anything there before."

She gave him a soft smile. "That sounds a bit like gardening."

He laughed. "I guess it does at that."

They arrived at the site. Hank pulled out the plans and began explaining them to Amelia. John and Charlie showed up shortly after. They all listened politely and asked intelligent questions. But when it came time to talk about the layout of the garden, Amelia began shaking her head.

"Oh, no. That won't work. It won't work at all."

AMELIA WATCHED as Hank's face fell. He'd been so proud of the plans he was showing them. She hated to spoil his hard work. But she had no choice. The area he'd chosen for her garden backed up to the woods. "It is picturesque, but there is too much shade for most of my plants." She turned in a circle, examining the area. "The best spot would actually be here."

"That's the front yard." Hank took a few steps. "The house starts here. That doesn't seem like it'd give you enough room."

She shook her head. "No, it wouldn't. I don't suppose we could move the house back farther?"

Hank squinted. "A little. Not much. We still need to have room for the barn and the privy. You don't want either of those too close to the house." He touched her arm. "Could you put some in the front and some in the back? Maybe closer to the house where there isn't as much shade?"

Her heart sank. It wasn't Hank's fault. He was trying. But

she'd brought Mother's plants all the way out here. To think that there was no place she could put them... She couldn't even imagine. She gave him a small smile. "Thank you for your hard work. I appreciate your kindness in thinking of my mother's plants. I'll—" Her voice faltered, and she swallowed down the lump in her throat. "I'll think on it some and see if there's a solution to be found. Continue with your plans, I need to return to the boardinghouse to help Maggie. There's a stagecoach today."

She spun and hurried away, ignoring Hank's pleas to stop. She hoped he wouldn't follow her, as she turned down Center Street and then Main Street as fast as propriety would allow. *Please, Lord, don't let anyone want to talk to me.*

But Mrs. Fulton was sweeping in front of the mercantile. "Good morning, Miss Martin. My goodness, what could have you in this part of town so early? Helping out your father?"

She squeezed her eyes shut then opened them, pasting on a smile but barely slowing her steps. "No, just looking at our future homesite and reviewing the plans. Father is already so busy, he can't wait for his office to be built. Now I must hurry back to help Maggie. Have a lovely day, Mrs. Fulton."

Speeding up to unladylike strides, Amelia tossed a wave and kept going.

HANK WATCHED Amelia disappear around the corner. He wanted more than anything to go after her and make things better. But what could he do? Those plants meant the world to her, and he couldn't help her find a place for them. Seemed like he should be able to do something that simple.

He turned to see Charlie studying him. "She'll come around. She knows it's not your fault. There's got to be some way we can figure out where to put those plants of hers. Why don't you write Sy O'Malley and get his thoughts on the matter?"

The heaviness in his chest lifted. "That's a great idea. Thanks!"

"Well, you may not thank me when you see what I have in mind. Come here, John."

The three men bent over the plans and made additions and changes. When Hank and Charlie had come up with a mutually agreeable plan, he brought up the other thing that was on his mind. "I talked to Maggie about the parsonage. I figured if we were building one house, we might as well build two. Save on freight charges for the lumber."

"Good thinking. I suppose you drew up some plans." Charlie held out his hand.

"Actually, let's walk over there. I have some ideas I'd like to run by you."

The three of them walked down Center Street and then turned the corner at Main. Hank couldn't help but glance in the opposite direction down Main to see if he could catch a glimpse of Amelia. But given how fast she was moving, she was surely back at the boardinghouse by now.

Charlie pointed toward the schoolhouse steeple in the distance. "Use to be this was the far reaches of town. But folks are building beyond it. Won't be long until it could be the center of town. I think that's something to keep in mind while we're building the parsonage and where we want to put it. Plus, in the summer we have church picnics on the grounds. Need to make sure there's space for that too."

As they drew near, Charlie and Hank pointed out different areas, discussing the advantages and disadvantages of various locations for the parsonage. John stood politely by taking it all in, occasionally adding a comment or two.

The seed of an idea sprouted in Hank's mind. He didn't want to say anything to anyone yet, but he needed to get a letter to Sy, to see if his idea was remotely possible.

And he hoped he could put a smile back on Amelia's face sometime soon.

As he and Charlie marked up the parsonage plans, he couldn't help but think that for someone who had thought he was done with building, he was sure involved in two projects. He had to make sure they didn't interfere with his true plan. But surely he could manage it all. He pushed down the niggle of doubt and gave his attention back to Charlie.

Chapter Eight

Later that week, Amelia helped Maggie and Emily get the stagecoach passengers breakfast and returned to the soon-departing stage in what seemed like record time to Amelia. Not that she had much experience with these things.

Emily breezed through the kitchen. "I think I've just now gotten used to the stagecoach schedule meaning Saturdays are workdays. But right now, they're easier than Tuesdays and Wednesdays when I'm juggling the stage and school."

But watching Maggie and Emily work in concert like they'd done this together for a long time was a wonder to behold. It didn't seem like much of a struggle.

When Amelia went to toss dirty water out the back steps, she caught Emily giving Josh a kiss as he was leaving. It was more sweet than the passionate clenches of her dime novels. What must it be like to know that a man had chosen you to spend the rest of his life with?

Unbidden, Hank's face appeared, and she pushed it away. That was ridiculous. He was kind, and could be a good friend. But they were far too different. Though so were Emily and Josh, if she was to think on it. And Sy and Cassandra had proved that her notions weren't always correct. Oh bother! She did not want to think of Hank right now.

A small, honey-blonde woman entered the back door with a smile, gave a quick grimace, and smiled again. Not as brightly this time. She reached out. "You must be Amelia! I've been wanting to meet you. I'm Becca Blake, Seth's wife."

"It's nice to meet you."

"We're so thrilled you and your father have joined us. We need a doctor and another teacher in this town." She gave Maggie and Emily hugs in turn.

Maggie said, "Let's move into the parlor and discuss wedding plans."

Emily's cheeks pinked, but she pulled down a mug and filled it with coffee. "Now that Amelia's ready to begin teaching, we can do that." She lifted the pot in question toward Becca who made a face.

"No, I'll just have some tea."

Amelia grabbed the teapot left over from breakfast and poured a cup for Becca and herself. "Oh, I'm not sure I'm completely ready. What did you have in mind?" She handed one of the cups to Becca.

Maggie tilted her head. "Let's discuss it in the parlor." She picked up mending from her basket next to the settee as she sat. "What dates were you thinking of, Emily?"

Emily clasped her hands. "Well, now that Amelia's here, I suppose it could be any time in March. What would be good for you and Pastor Roy?"

"He's making rounds in two weeks to the neighboring towns and some of the mining camps. If you can hold things down here, I've a mind to go with him. So sometime after that would be fine."

Becca sipped her tea. "What kinds of things would you like for your wedding? I know you and Maggie have been working on your dress."

The three women chatted about plans and people that

Amelia didn't have much reference for. What she was most concerned about, as selfish as it seemed, was how to take over Emily's teaching duties. Perhaps she and Emily needed to have a private time to talk about it.

"What do you think, Amelia?" Becca asked. "You are the one with the love of flowers, I hear. We can have someone bring them in from Ankeny's Market in Portland."

"You can get fresh flowers this time of year? I mean, of course you can, but usually hothouse flowers cost a small fortune." She clapped her hand over her mouth. That was rude, mentioning money. And it was none of her business. "I'm sorry. I shouldn't have said that."

The women laughed. Emily patted her knee. "It's perfectly fine. There are many greenhouses out here, and our winters aren't as harsh as they are back East, so they aren't terribly expensive. But they are a special treat."

"In that case, I think white roses would be lovely. Or even pale pink peonies if you make sure to get all the ants off them. But did you set a date? I didn't think you had decided on that."

"No, we need to do that." Emily flipped through the calendar she had swiped from Maggie's kitchen. "What if the wedding was March eleventh? That's a little over a month from now. Amelia can take over the classroom in two weeks, and that gives us plenty of time to get Josh's cabin ready for me to move in. I suspect it'll need a thorough cleaning."

"Where's Charlie going to stay?" Becca asked. "Here in the boardinghouse?"

"Yes, he says that's what he wants, so he can be close to the workshop. At some point, we'll build a dedicated workshop with a living space overhead."

Maggie pulled thread through a patch. "And frankly, I'd feel better with Charlie staying in the boardinghouse with Sally and James and whatever boarders come through. Until the parsonage is built, and they can be under my roof again. I know they're both grown, but a mother worries."

Amelia twisted her hands together and look at Emily. "When precisely would you like me to take over the classroom?"

Emily laughed. "Monday?"

Amelia's stomach dipped even though she knew Emily was joking. "I thought you liked teaching."

"I do, but I suppose the wedding plans are a little more attractive than lesson plans right now."

"About that. Perhaps we could go over your lesson plans and discuss what you'd planned for the rest of the year? I've never done that part before."

"You'll do just fine. I have no reservations about that at all."

Maggie and Becca both turned smiles on Amelia. "You will," Maggie said.

While she appreciated their reassurance, and she certainly didn't want to distract from a bride enjoying her wedding preparations, she still felt no closer to understanding what was expected of her. Well, Emily lived at the boardinghouse, and there wouldn't be another stage until Tuesday. She'd find another chance, she was sure of it.

Becca rose and gathered her shawl. "I need to see to things at home. Seth is up at the logging camp today, so it's a good time to get the floors mopped without him underfoot." She hugged Maggie and Emily.

As she embraced Amelia, she whispered, "Could you give this to your father, please, when you see him?"

Amelia looked down as Becca slipped a note into her hand.

"Certainly." She met Becca's gaze. Was Becca ill? She seemed fine. Perhaps she wanted to extend a supper invitation to welcome them to town. Or perhaps... Amelia had been around Father's patients long enough to recognize the signs.

A faint pink stained Becca's cheeks.

"I'll see he gets this as soon as he gets in." She squeezed Becca's hand.

"Thank you." Becca gave her a smile and then left.

The busyness of the boardinghouse was nothing like her

quiet days back in New York. Her life had changed drastically in a few short weeks. And no doubt it would change further when she began teaching. Her hands shook at the thought, but she pushed it away. The best cure was a dose of reading one of those new novels that Cassandra had dropped off. She lifted her skirts and hurried upstairs.

HANK PULLED open the door to Fulton's Mercantile, the tinkling bell announcing his presence. While Seth was up at the camp catching up on paperwork, Hank saw it as a good opportunity to come into town on a sunny Saturday since they didn't work six-day weeks in winter. He stood at the wooden counter, waiting for Mrs. Fulton to finish up with a customer. He glanced around. Perhaps Amelia would be here, as unreasonable of a hope as that was. But since he didn't have a good excuse to stop by the boardinghouse—and he honestly didn't know what he'd say to Amelia—he was left with wishing he'd run into her.

Mr. Fulton came around the back curtain, wiping his hands on his apron. "What can I help you with, Hank?"

"I thought I'd pick up the mail for the camp once Mrs. Fulton was free. And do you have any machinery catalogues?"

He pulled out several thick, pulp-paper tomes from under the counter. "Let's see if any of these will do. What are you looking for?"

How could he handle this without the whole town knowing? "We're looking for some saws related to logging. Possibly a steam-powered one." He kept his voice low, but hopefully not suspiciously so. No one seemed to be paying him any mind.

Mr. Fulton's eyebrows raised. "Never seen anything like that, but you're welcome to look through them. You might also write to Sy O'Malley. He knows more about fancy machinery than anyone else here abouts with his scientific magazines and all."

He gestured to his wife who had finished with her customer. "Jane, any mail for the logging camp?"

"Well, hello, Hank. How are things in the logging business?"

"Just fine, ma'am."

"Good. I'll just get your mail."

"Take your time. I'm in no hurry." He had to find what he wanted quickly, before she came back. Because if she knew what he was looking for, it'd be all over town. She delivered gossip with the mail quite often. He flipped through the first catalogue but didn't see anything. In the second one, he hit pay dirt. Several steam-powered sawmills dotted the page. But which one would be the right one?

"Finding what you need, Hank?" Mrs. Fulton came over with his stack of mail.

He laid his arm across the page in what he hoped was a casual manner. "Possibly. There sure are a lot of things in these catalogues." Which might have been one of the dumbest things he'd ever said.

She placed the mail next to him on the counter and peered over. "Is the logging camp thinking of building a sawmill as well?"

He shrugged. "Seth and I have discussed the need for lumber in town. I told him I'd look into the logistics." He leaned farther over the counter. "I'd hate to get anyone's hopes up, so if you could keep that between us, I'd be obliged." There. He hadn't said anything that wasn't true, and hopefully he'd appealed to her discretion.

She smiled. "Why, Hank, you should know I'm a veritable vault when it comes to folks' private business. The things I see but don't discuss…" She clucked her tongue.

He scooped up the mail and closed the catalogue. "Thank you, ma'am. I was certain I could rely on you." He left the building, not certain at all that he'd be able to keep this sawmill a secret.

And he hadn't even seen Amelia.

Chapter Nine

✦❧✦

A melia filed into the church pew behind Josh and Emily. Father was behind her, with Maggie taking up the end spot. As she glanced around, she realized in the short time they'd been in town, many of the faces were already familiar.

Across the aisle, the O'Malley brothers took up a whole pew. She thought with a pang about Cassandra. Amelia would write her this afternoon.

Her gaze must have lingered too long because Stephen O'Malley winked at her.

She jerked her gaze back to the front, her face hot. Eager to prove to Stephen O'Malley that she wasn't looking at him, simply looking around, she turned her gaze the other direction. Becca and Seth sat in the pew behind them with Hank. Becca gave her a small wave.

Amelia had passed Becca's note on to Father, and as usual, he said nothing to her. He never discussed cases with her unless he needed her help. Which was a last resort for him. As it was, the town had taken immediately to having a doctor, and she rarely saw him. She was thankful she lived in the boardinghouse with Emily and got to see Maggie daily. When she and Father moved to their own house, she'd miss the women's company for sure.

As her gaze passed Hank, he gave her a grin. She couldn't help but return it.

The steeple bell rang, and someone shut the main doors. Pastor Roy moved to the front, motioning to a woman who joined him.

Emily leaned over and whispered, "That's Beth Paige. She sings at every church service and wedding. She's also a town gossip, along with Mrs. Fulton." She pressed her lips tight to suppress a smile, but her eyes sparkled.

Amelia's eyes widened as she bit her lip to stifle a laugh.

Pastor Roy's deep voice drowned out their almost giggles. "Let's begin with 'Amazing Grace,' shall we? Will you stand, please?"

Unlike their church back home, there was no accompaniment from a piano or organ. Just the voices of common people, many not even on key, lifted in praise and gratitude to their Savior. As Amelia sang, she thought of what the daily lives might be like of each of these people. A number of children filled the pews. She would be their teacher. She would help shape their futures. She swallowed the lump in her throat and focused on the words.

After they had returned to their seats from the singing, Pastor Roy began to speak. He wasn't a polished orator like some of the pastors she had previously heard, but he spoke from the heart with plain language about God's love for us, even when we couldn't see it because our circumstances clouded our vision.

It was a cool, drizzly day out, but by the time the church service had ended, the number of bodies had raised the temperature inside the church, and several of the ladies were fanning themselves. When the back doors opened, the fresh air was welcome.

There was no picnic on the church grounds today because of the weather, but as they walked home, Emily informed Amelia that Maggie usually had a full table on Sundays. "She and Pastor

Roy enjoy having folks come by to share a meal and talk over things."

Which explained the amount of baking Maggie had done Saturday after Becca had left.

When they arrived at the boardinghouse, Amelia took her Bible, hat, and coat upstairs, then returned to don an apron and help Maggie and Emily. Becca and Seth were there, though Maggie had shooed Becca out of the kitchen. Father had pulled Becca aside for a moment after church, she noticed.

And several of the O'Malley boys had showed up. Stephen had brought two of his delicious apple pies. Patrick and Nicholas also showed up. Jacob must have gone home with the family of the girl he was courting. It must be hard to not have their parents with them. And Maggie seemed more than willing to mother anyone who needed it. Something Amelia knew firsthand.

"Let's eat!" Pastor Roy's booming voice brought everyone around the table.

Amelia moved to a chair only to have a hand reach out and grasp the back of it. "Allow me."

She looked up into the golden brown eyes of Hank Paulson. She hadn't seen him come in.

He tugged the chair out for her with a grin.

"Thank you." She took her seat and noticed that Stephen O'Malley had slid into the other seat next to her. She glanced around the room, caught Father's gaze as he redirected his steps from his usual seat next to Amelia and took a seat by the Blakes.

Suddenly, she didn't know what to do with her hands or where to look.

Pastor Roy saved her by saying the blessing, and afterwards, dishes and platters were quickly passed so she didn't have time to think of what to do or say. Once her plate was full, she was able to concentrate on eating and listening to the conversation flow around the table and not have to contribute.

"So, Amelia, how do you like Reedsville now that you've been here a spell?" Stephen asked then took a sip of water.

Out of the corner of her eye, she noticed Hank lean forward.

"The people here are exceedingly kind, much more so than I would have imagined. I feel like I've known many of them for a much longer time than I actually have. And Father has been so busy. The town has really taken to his doctoring. And other than the incident on the stagecoach when we first arrived, I've felt quite safe."

"My offer still stands to help you bring your plants to the greenhouse. I can get the wagon, and we can get them all situated. Just tell me when." Stephen picked up his fork and began to eat.

"Thank you. I'll begin teaching soon, so I do need to get them settled before then."

Hank leaned over. "How did they survive the journey? Have you been able to keep them packed in sawdust?"

She turned her gaze to him and leaned back a bit so she could include both men in the conversation. She never expected anyone, let alone two men, to be interested in her plants. "They seem to be surviving. I won't truly know until I go to replant them."

"Then we should do that as soon as possible." Stephen pushed his plate away. "How about I come down tomorrow and help you?"

"I can help too." Hank glanced at her. "Since I've helped you before and know how you want them handled and all."

Amelia didn't know what to make of the two men who seemed to be vying to help her. "Um, thank you. Tomorrow will be fine." She pushed back her chair and stood, gathering her plate and the plates of the men on either side of her. "I'd better help Maggie with the dishes." She retreated to the kitchen where she could have a moment to let her thoughts settle themselves.

ONCE THE SUNDAY dinner guests had moved on, some back home, some to the woodshop to look at Charlie's latest creation, Amelia and Emily moved to the parlor settee. Amelia saw her chance to talk to Emily before Josh returned from the barn.

Amelia clasped her hands in her lap. "We haven't had a chance to talk much about my taking over at the schoolroom. I feel like I still have so much to learn, and I want to make sure I'm as prepared as possible for the children's sake."

Emily touched Amelia's arm. "You'll do fine. I have every confidence in you. Why don't you come with me to school starting tomorrow? You can get to know the children and their lessons."

"Oh. Stephen O'Malley is coming over tomorrow to help me move Mother's plants out to the O'Malley greenhouse. I can send word for him to come another day."

"Oh, no. Don't do that. You already have plans. Tuesday will work just as well. I have a feeling you'll pick up things quickly. And if you have questions, we can discuss them over dinner or in the evenings."

"That won't interfere with your wedding planning?"

Emily laughed. "Maggie will be in her element, so I wouldn't want to interfere with that. And there's not too much to plan. Mainly it will be working on my dress and all the baking and cooking that will take place just before the wedding. But everyone in town will help out."

Emily lowered her voice. "So Stephen O'Malley didn't seem to be the only one interested in assisting with your plants. Hank Paulson seemed quite attentive to you at dinner." She raised her eyebrows. "Anything I should know?"

Amelia's face heated. "I don't know. I think they were both just being kind. I'm new in town, and they both know how much Mother's plants mean to me. I think they are simply good, welcoming folks, like everyone in town has been."

"But not everyone has offered to take time away from their

work to help you move your plants." Emily gave a knowing smile.

Amelia's stomach flipped. Was there more going on with Stephen and Hank than just kindness? She didn't know what to think. If Emily was right, tomorrow portended to be nerve-making indeed.

HANK SAT down at the small table in his cabin at the logging camp and pulled out paper and a pen. He wished he'd have thought to ask Mr. Fulton if he could bring the catalogue home. Then he would have the exact specifications to ask Sy about. Then again, perhaps there was a better place to acquire a sawmill from that Sy might be aware of.

This letter would go out on Tuesday's stage, so it'd be at least a week before Hank would hear back. He spent some time crafting the letter, explaining his discussion with Seth. And leaving out that Hank would be purchasing it. When he was satisfied that he'd asked all the questions about the sawmill, he thought about Amelia's plants.

She had been so disappointed about not being able to plant them at her home. And while he was formulating some options in his mind, none of them would come to fruition right away. In the meantime, what could he do to make her happy? He loved the way her face lit up when she smiled. Her eyes brightened, and her dusting of freckles might be the most charming thing he'd seen.

He continued his letter to Sy, explaining the situation about the doc's house and the shade. He drew a bit of a map with the location of the trees and the house so Sy would know exactly what he was talking about. Then he asked what kinds of plants would work best in that location and where could he obtain them. He'd like to surprise Amelia with something special. They wouldn't be her mother's plants, but maybe they would be something that she'd enjoy looking at from her windows and tending to.

He hoped so, anyway.

He sealed the letter and set it on the table. He'd take it to town tomorrow when he went to help Amelia and Stephen move her plants to the greenhouse. The idea of Stephen being alone with Amelia turned his gut. Which was ridiculous, since he had no claim on her and she didn't seem to like him half the time. Still, if she objected to Hank's being a logger, he hardly saw how Stephen's being a grower was anything different.

Now he'd just have to explain to Seth why he needed to be in town yet again.

Chapter Ten

A melia clutched her shawl closer as she headed to the barn. The sun peeking over the treetops warmed her face, but the air was chilly. The barn cast a long shadow over the yard, and she hurried inside it. She waited for her eyes to adjust to the darkness as she moved toward the bench that held her burlap sacks. The sounds of animals shifting and snuffling in the barn made for a homey, comforting place.

The smell of damp sawdust wafted up to her as she peered in the sacks. Everything seemed as it had been, but in this dim light, it was hard to tell. When they got to the greenhouse and repotted the cuttings, she'd know for sure if they'd survived the trip. She wished Sy were here to advise her, but she'd write a letter to him and Cassandra. She had planned to write yesterday but decided to wait until she knew the status of her plants.

Refastening the sacks, there was nothing left for her to do until Stephen and Hank showed up. She paced the barn a bit. Maggie had the breakfast dishes under control, Emily, Sally, and James were off to school.

She could go read, but she had a feeling that the words on the page couldn't contain her interest. She stepped outside the barn and wandered through the yard, heading a bit toward the stream that flowed across the back of the property. Dew soaked the hem of her skirt, but moving seemed to be the antidote to the restlessness that had overtaken her limbs.

Who would arrive first? Hank or Stephen? And were they really just being kind as she had told Emily? Or was their interest something more? It was that thought that made her restless. She'd never had a beau back home, though she'd had a schoolmate, Matthew, that she'd had fond feelings for. But she wasn't sure she wanted a beau now. When she'd originally thought Hank was some sort of dashing hero straight out of a novel, she'd not entertained more than heart flutters.

But now, she was unsure. Everything she thought she knew of the West based on her novel reading had been… true and not true. Leaving her a bit adrift.

She studied the stream in both directions. Upstream was a small footbridge. That led to Josh and Charlie's cabin. Downstream she could just see a flat rock that jutted out over the water. That would make a wonderful place to sit on a warm summer day and dangle her feet in the cool stream. She could just imagine it. The dense foliage along the banks indicated an abundance of flora come spring. She couldn't wait to see it.

The jingle of harnesses and the crunch of wagon wheels caused her to turn. Stephen O'Malley pulled into the yard, spotted her, and touched his hat with a grin.

Regardless of what the day held, she knew she'd smile a lot with Stephen around.

But her heart sank a bit at the fact that Hank hadn't shown up as he said he would. He was busy, she knew that. But still, she'd hoped.

Gathering her skirts and smiling, she headed toward the wagon.

HANK TAMPED down his disappointment at Seth's words, though he knew they were true.

"Sorry, I just can't spare you. We need to get that ridge cut since today is shaping up to be a mild one. The *Farmer's Almanac* is calling for rain all this week. I'd like to get ahead of schedule if we can." Seth rose from the cook hall table and began calling out assignments to the men there.

Hank joined him, not really paying attention. If there was only some way to get word to Amelia. But there wasn't a man to be spared today since they were on reduced manpower in the winter. Many operations shut down completely, but Seth was trying to make up for lost time from last summer. He understood that. But the thought of Stephen O'Malley smiling at her and helping her made the coffee in his gut turn bitter. He wished he could let her know he wanted to come but couldn't. He wanted to help her, to show her that he was the kind of man she could depend on.

He stifled a yawn. After writing Sy, he couldn't fall asleep, images of Amelia and Stephen, the doc's house and the parsonage all chasing each other through his brain. He finally got up, lit a lamp, and did some work on the plans. But today his eyelids felt coated with sandpaper.

Maybe if they got a lot of work done today, he could go to town later. Or send word with Seth when he returned home.

Seth turned to him, eyebrows raised. "Hank?"

He'd missed whatever Seth had asked him. "Uh, sure." Fine way to impress the boss, not paying attention when he was talking.

"Thanks for agreeing to lead the north team." Seth clapped him on the shoulder as the men dispersed to their assignments and the equipment shed.

The farthest out they'd be working today. So much for getting done early and getting to town. He thought of the letter on the table in his cabin. He'd send it home with Seth.

With a last swig of tepid coffee, hoping it'd give him the jolt he needed, he headed out to the equipment shed to get what they'd need for today's work.

OUT AT THE NORTH RIDGE, Hank handed out assignments and the men got to work. He took a swig from his canteen. His throat was scratchy from his lack of sleep. He hoped today went quickly so they could get back to camp.

Normally, being out among the trees was exactly what he enjoyed about this job. The sun was peeking out, making the dew on the trees sparkle like they were sprinkled with diamonds. Nothing manmade could ever compete with God's glorious creation. The scent of pine and the crunch of bark and needles under his boots beat being inside any day. He knew that was one thing Seth hated about being the boss—more time inside, less time in the woods. It was something to consider if Hank wanted to run his own outfit too. Being the boss meant more paperwork and headaches.

Raised voices came from two of the men working a whipsaw. Hank headed over to settle it. "What's the problem?"

Curtis and Ollie eyed each other. "Nuthin'."

Ollie spit a stream of tobacco.

Hank barely avoided wrinkling his nose. How could anyone stand that disgusting habit? Hank stared at both men. "Back to work then." Sometimes the men out here reminded him of the boys from his school days with their stupid pranks and arguments. Maybe Seth did have the better deal today.

Then again, if using steam engines and locomotives for logging became the standard, as it was already for some outfits, it might not matter much longer.

"Hank!" A voice came down from the treetops.

He searched for the source and spotted it across the clearing.

Willie was topping a tree. "We've got conk rot here. Check the others."

Marvin, up in another tree, yelled his acknowledgment.

Hank trudged across the clearing to mark the tree when a crash sounded upslope from him.

"Log!"

The ground thundered as the runaway log gained on him. Halfway in the clearing, he stood like a frozen rabbit, not sure which way to run.

"Hank!"

A voice yanked him out of his state, and he sprinted forward, catching his boots in downed limbs, but righting himself.

A strong arm yanked him behind a tree.

A piney gust whisked past them as the tree continued on until it crashed into other trees at the bottom.

He leaned against the rough bark and caught his breath. "Thanks."

"Thought you were a goner there for a moment, boss." Reuben scanned him up and down. "You okay?"

"Yeah, I'm fine." He coughed at the stirred up dust and underbrush.

But he wasn't fine. He was stupid. And he almost got himself killed.

AMELIA ENJOYED the pleasant conversation on the ride out to the O'Malley farm. And this time, Stephen stopped the wagon at the top of the rise before the farm, letting its beauty spill out over the gently rolling hills. While the fog had made it seem mysterious, the sunshine made it glimmer like a fairyland.

"I see why people feel like Oregon is the Promised Land."

Stephen clucked to the horses. "Especially with views like that."

As they pulled into the yard, Stephen hopped out of the wagon and then reached up to help Amelia down.

"Thank you."

"Would you like to come in for some coffee first and warm up?"

The ride hadn't been too chilly. Stephen had brought a lap robe and a hot brick for her feet. Her hands were a bit cold, but she was eager to see her plants in the sunlight and get them transplanted.

"Would you mind if we got the plants potted first? I'm not terribly cold."

"Not at all. And with the sun out, the greenhouse will warm up quicker than you can imagine." He lowered the tailgate and grabbed several burlap sacks. "Follow me."

Amelia grabbed a few as well, and they headed into the greenhouse. The smell of earth and plant matter was comforting and familiar. "How wonderful to have space to work with plants all year round."

"Sy did a lot of his experiments here. Grafting and cross-pollinating. Some groundbreaking work."

"I'm just honored that he is letting me use it."

"You get situated, and I'll bring in the rest of the plants. Then you tell me what to do. I don't have Sy's green thumb, but I take direction pretty well." He grinned at her then left the greenhouse.

She turned, taking in the space again. If this were hers, she'd likely never leave it. She couldn't think of a more perfect place to spend time. She spotted the pots Sy had pointed out to her and gathered them near where Stephen had placed the burlap sacks. She began filling them with Sy's special potting soil part way.

After she had several pots prepared, she undid the tie on the first sack and pulled out the plant, brushing the sawdust from it.

Stephen entered and dropped the last of the sacks. He peered over her shoulder. "How's it look?"

"This one looks dormant, which is good."

"It looks like a stick with roots on it."

"Yes, but watch." With a scratch of her thumbnail, green

showed under the bark. "See? That green means it's still alive." A bit of tension left her chest as she nestled it in the soil and patted more on top of it then set the pot to the side.

They found a rhythm working together. She removed the plants, and he took the burlap and sawdust away, leaving her a clear space to work. They had gone through about half of the sacks when she pulled out a plant that had no roots. She looked at the burlap sack. A hole had been gnawed through it.

"Oh no." She stuck her finger through the hole. "Something ate at this one. Are there any others like that?" She hoped against hope that there wasn't.

Stephen turned over all the other bags. "This one looks like something started to eat at it. The burlap is frayed. But the hole doesn't go all the way through."

She let out a breath. One plant gone. She had expected to lose some. That wasn't so bad. But as she opened bag after bag, she found only one more had survived the journey. Only one revealed green under the bark. Her shoulders sank. A little more than half had survived.

"I'm sorry, Amelia. I know you were hoping you could save most of them."

She blinked back moisture that threatened. "How about some of that coffee you mentioned earlier?"

He stared at her for a moment. "Certainly."

On the back porch, they washed up then entered the kitchen, the warmth of it surrounding them.

He patted the back of the chair. "Sit right down, and I'll have coffee for you in a jiffy. And I don't imagine you'd be opposed to some apple spice muffins? Sy might be good with plants, but he can't bake worth a lick."

She laughed. "That sounds wonderful, thank you." She forced her mind away from her plants and thoughts of her mother.

Stephen set a plate of muffins, a dish of butter, and a mug of coffee in front of her. Then he slid over a piece of paper and a pencil.

"What's that for?"

"Make a list of every plant that didn't make it. I'll send it to Sy and see what he can do. If we can't find the exact plant, he might know of what would make a good substitute. He's good at stuff like that."

Amelia ground her fingernails into the palm of her hand to give her something to focus on other than the tears that really wanted to spring from her eyes. "That's so kind of you. Thank you."

But she concentrated on eating muffins, drinking coffee, and making conversation with Stephen and his brothers that wandered in before picking up the pencil.

HANK REACHED a tired hand toward the door of the camp office and pushed it open. He swiped his hat off his head and plunked into his office chair before he met Seth's gaze. All he really wanted was his bed, but that would have to wait.

Seth studied him. "Want to tell me what happened on the north ridge today?"

Hank figured the word would have gotten back to camp before he did. Though he didn't fancy reliving it. He summarized the events. "But I managed to dodge behind a big tree with Reuben's help." In the moment where he didn't think he'd get out of the way, all he could think about was how stupid he'd been in not being alert. His tired mind had wandered over to what Amelia and Stephen were up to instead of remembering he was working in a place that could kill him. His brain hadn't made the switch fast enough and he'd frozen. But that wasn't anything he'd tell Seth.

Seth tapped his pencil on the stack of papers in front of him. "Hank, you've been a big help to me with Owen gone. You have a good sense of the business, and you're a quick learner. But you've got your mind back in town. A man who does that in the forest is likely to get himself killed." He swallowed. "I lost one friend that way. I don't intend to lose another."

Hank squirmed, and the chair squeaked, giving him away. He felt like he had been called into the headmaster's office.

"What you're doing for the doc and Pastor and Maggie, that's important, and it's a good thing to do. But it conflicts with logging. When I need you here on the sunny days, you'll need to be down supervising the work in town. You can't do both; you'll make yourself sick or get yourself killed. I need you to think seriously about where you want to put your attention and energy. I'll back whatever decision you make, but you need to be all in on one or the other."

Hank nodded. "What you're saying is true, and it isn't anything I haven't already told myself." He drummed his fingers on the desk, thinking—hoping—a solution would present itself that hadn't as yet. "Let me talk with Charlie and John. See how they feel about the projects and go over a few final things with them. After that, they should be capable of handling things themselves. And I'll still be in town on Saturdays and Sundays so they can talk to me then."

Seth nodded. "If you think that will work, that's fine with me."

Hank rose. "Thanks, boss. If you don't mind, I think I'll finish up and then turn in early."

"Go ahead. We don't need you getting sick on top of it." Seth turned back to the papers on his desk.

Hank slipped out of the office and headed to the cookhouse. He'd grab something to eat and then find his bed. What Seth said was right, and Hank would feel terrible if his actions got a man hurt or killed.

And yet, he couldn't let the building go. Charlie was capable but getting on in years. But maybe for just the two houses, it would be fine. He'd ask around town, see if there was someone else with building experience. Of course, if there were such a person, surely they'd have stepped forward before now.

He pulled open the cookhouse door, refusing to think of how Amelia's day had gone. Hopefully better than his.

AFTER SUPPER, Amelia sat at the parlor desk with pen and ink to compose a letter to Sy and Cassandra while the other boardinghouse residents enjoyed the warmth of the fire. It was a simple thing, really, but her thoughts were jumbled and didn't want to untangle themselves on the page.

The remainder of her day with Stephen had been pleasant. He did his best to cheer her up with a trip to the barn to examine Sy's journals to see if any would be helpful. And she left her list of plants with him on his insistence.

But her mind kept wandering to Hank. Why hadn't he shown up? Of course he was likely busy and couldn't make the time. Still, there was a twinge in her heart that she couldn't account for.

Finally, she was able to begin her letter by relating to Cassandra her plans for teaching, Emily's wedding, and then ended with a list of questions for Sy.

Just as she was sealing the letter, Father came into the parlor.

Emily stood, putting her book down. "We kept a plate hot for you. Let me get it."

"Thanks." He came over to Amelia and kissed her head. There were fine lines around his mouth and shadows under his eyes. She hardly saw him lately. "How was your day, Amelia?"

She stood and slipped her arm through his, guiding him into the dining room. "I repotted Mother's cuttings at the O'Malley greenhouse. Many survived. Some did not." She hurried on as he took a seat, and she slid in next to him. "The greenhouse is a sight to behold. Mother would have been ecstatic. How was your day?"

"Tiring but good. It'll be a relief to have our own place and office. Trying to make house calls and anticipate what I need and what will fit in my bag has been challenging. Our trunks should arrive next week with the rest of my supplies. I've found a vacant building in town that will work for a temporary office space until ours is built. Once I have my supplies, I can work out of there."

Emily set a plate in front of Father along with a mug. "Not coffee, but some chamomile tea. It should help you sleep but not make you groggy. It's what Maggie always serves at night."

He gave her a tired smile. "Thank you, Emily. I don't know what we'd do without you and Maggie."

Back home they'd had a housekeeper and cook. Amelia wasn't sure what they'd do once they had their own house. With her schoolteaching, she could do the cooking, but not all the cleaning and washing. Surely there were women in town who would want to do that work for them. Well, that was something to think about in the future, not to bother Father with right now. Their house wasn't even built yet. Perhaps tomorrow on the way home from school she'd take a small detour and walk by to see the progress.

"The town really has missed having a doctor, hasn't it?" She studied Father as he shoveled food in his mouth, politely, but clearly it had been some time since he'd eaten.

He nodded.

She began telling him about the greenhouse and the plants, about Stephen's cooking, but it was clear his mind was else-where. "Is there anything I can help you with?" As soon as she said the words, she almost took them back. She'd be in the schoolroom starting tomorrow. But he looked so tired, she couldn't help but want to relieve his burden.

He patted her hand as he scooted his chair back. "Sweet of you to offer, but I've got it under control. As soon as we get the office established, I'll place an advertisement for a nurse." He kissed her head again. "I'm off to bed. See you tomorrow."

"Good night." Amelia sat at the table, a bit stunned. She wasn't quite sure what to make of Father's words. It made sense that he would look for a nurse to assist him. She would be teaching. Yet, she'd always pictured herself helping him in some capacity. She absently rubbed the scar on her thumb.

If he hired a nurse, he wouldn't need her at all. The thought tumbled through her brain all night.

Chapter Eleven

Stanley Wallace lifted the oilcloth covering the windows of the stagecoach that ostensibly protected the passengers from the rain outside. They had pulled up in front of what looked like a white farmhouse. A redheaded, buxom woman descended the stairs— shawl pulled over her head to protect from the rain—and greeted the passengers. So this was the backwater town of Reedsville. He was not impressed. Not that he expected to be.

He exited the stage and glanced around, snugging his hat down over his ears and pulling his overcoat closer.

"Welcome to Reedsville." The woman gave him an unexpectedly kind smile. "Will you be staying in our boardinghouse or elsewhere?"

"Parsons Hotel. Can you direct me?"

"Surely. Just head down Main Street here. It'll be several blocks down on your left."

"Thank you." He took his carpetbag from the driver. "And would you also know the location of the bank?"

"Same side of the street, just two blocks sooner."

He touched his hat. "Thank you, ma'am." He hurried across the muddy street until he could reach the protection of the boardwalk. The bank first, then the hotel. Mr. Irving was to have been wired about Stanley's arrival, so it shouldn't be a surprise to him. He'd get the lay of the land and formulate a plan of action. That was always the best way to go about things.

He pulled open the bank doors. It was a small but well-appointed space, more so than he expected. He shook off his hat.

The one clerk looked up as Stanley entered. "May I help you?"

"I'm here to see Mr. Irving. He should be expecting me."

"Whom may I say is here to see him?"

"Stanley Wallace."

The clerk walked along the counter to an office door and opened it. There was a low murmuring and then the clerk reappeared, followed by Irving. His eyes widened as he spotted Stanley, but he hurried over to the barred door at the end of the counter and opened it. "Come in, Mr. Wallace."

Stanley followed the man into his office, scanning the area. This was all his now. And he would run it to the best of his abilities, awaiting Mr. Paulson's next orders. Whatever they would be. Tomorrow he'd send a telegram regarding his arrival and a follow up with a letter on how he found things.

He'd also pay a call on the sheriff, see what he had found out about the payroll robbery and the Red Dawson Gang. As a concerned banker and new citizen of the town, of course.

And if luck was with him, he'd find out where Henry Paulson was and what he was up to. Information Stanley was sure Mr. Paulson would be grateful for.

AMELIA CARRIED a stack of dirty dishes to the dry sink where Emily scraped them into the slop bucket in the kitchen after supper. Emily swiped the back of her hand across her forehead, brushing back a stray hair. "I appreciate your help, Amelia. I don't know what I'd do without you. Here or in the schoolroom."

"I didn't do much. Mostly just sat next to your desk and paid attention."

"You helped the new readers with their work, freeing me up to work with the older students. Perhaps after you take over, I can come in a few days a week when there isn't a stagecoach and help you."

"That would be a turn of events, wouldn't it?" Amelia smiled. "I'll take whatever help I can get from you."

"You'll do just fine. The children really warmed to you. Especially the younger ones."

"It's the older ones, the boys, that I'm more concerned about."

"Just keep a firm hand with them." Emily handed a plate to Maggie, who had finished shaving soap into the steaming water.

Charlie came into the kitchen. "Sorry to bother you ladies, but, Maggie, do you have any of that willow bark tea?"

Maggie dropped the dishrag into the soapy water.

Emily stepped into her place. "We'll finish up here."

"Is your leg paining you again?" Maggie pulled down her box of tea leaves.

"Some. It's this rain, and I'm not as spry as I used to be. Young John is doing most of the heavy lifting, but I have to guide and direct. He's a fast learner."

Amelia turned from where she had taken over scraping the plates. "Emily and I walked by our homesite after school today since the rain had let up. The foundation looks nearly done."

"It is. And it'll last a lifetime. But those rocks sure are heavy. And we'll need some help digging the cellar. Until we get the lumber in, there's not much more we can do. Which is good. I've got a wedding present or two to work on." Charlie winked in Emily's direction.

Her cheeks pinked up and not from the hot dish water.

"The doc would like to know more about the progress and the plans, so I sent James to fetch Young John and Hank."

Maggie clattered around the stove. "I'll bring this to you in the parlor when it's done steeping. And I think there are some cinnamon cookies left for your discussion. I'll fix you up a hot poultice before I head home tonight. Don't forget to take it with you. It'll help the pain so you can sleep."

"Thank you, Maggie. You're a dear."

"Oh, pshaw."

Charlie grinned and left the kitchen.

They had just finished straightening up the kitchen when Amelia stepped out the back door to toss the dishwater. She hefted the basin and then stopped as a figure rounded the porch steps. Hank.

Her heart did a little flip. "You almost got an unintended bath."

Hank grinned as he mounted the steps. "I could probably use one. Sorry to arrive so muddy, but I came directly from camp."

She tossed the dishwater to the side then opened the kitchen door. "Come on in. We can find you something to eat if you haven't had supper yet."

"I did, but thanks." His fingertip brushed hers as he reached for the door, holding it for her.

Warmth shot up her arm. This was Hank, a friend. One who had plans quite different from hers. She hung up the dishpan on its nail and turned to find Hank close behind her, the smell of pine and bark pleasantly clinging to him.

"I'm sorry I didn't make it yesterday to help with your plants. Seth couldn't spare me. Did you get them situated?"

"I did." She lifted her gaze to meet his. "Not as many survived as I would have hoped."

He touched her hand. "I'm sorry, Amelia. I know how much they meant to you."

"Thank you." She flashed him what she hoped was a bright

smile. "At least a few of them survived. That is something. And I'm grateful for that." She stepped to the kitchen table and picked up the plate of cookies. "They are all in the parlor. We should join them. Would you like coffee or tea?"

"No, but thanks."

They entered the parlor. Maggie and Pastor Adam had returned to the cottage. Emily and Josh shared the settee, his arm laid across her shoulders. Father and Charlie sat in the chairs flanking the fire. Young John sat at the writing desk. Amelia handed the plate of cookies to Josh who took two and passed the plate on. Then she took a chair next to Hank's, careful to keep her skirts from brushing his legs.

Charlie sipped on his tea. "I thought I should get you all in the same room for a moment so we could discuss the next step on the doc's quarters. Young John and I have gotten the foundation laid, but there's not much we can do until the lumber arrives. We've started on the cellar, but with the ground so wet, it's heavy and slow going. We could use a few more strong backs."

Hank sat forward. "The lumber should be here early next week. It's also bringing the lumber for the parsonage to save on freight costs. Would you be up to working on the parsonage foundation until then?"

Charlie absently rubbed his leg while he glanced at Young John, who nodded. "I suppose we could. Now that Young John has sense of how the foundation gets laid, I expect he can do more of the work while I supervise."

His leg must be bothering him more than he let on. She slid her gaze over to Hank who was exchanging glances with Josh.

Hank cleared his throat. "I think we can let Young John plan out the foundation with Charlie's supervision. Then I don't see why we can't get some of the townsmen to help gather stones and put them in place. It's for the parsonage, and everyone in town respects Pastor Roy and Maggie and would be happy to pitch in. I imagine a few would also be willing to help with the doc's cellar." He looked at Charlie. "I'll see when I can get away from the camp to finalize the plans with you both."

Charlie nodded.

Josh spoke up. "We can make that happen. I'll let Ben and Mrs. Fulton know, and they'll make sure everyone else knows."

"In the meantime—" Father glanced between Hank and Charlie— "When can we expect our quarters to be finished once the lumber arrives?"

"Do you want the office finished first or the living quarters?"

"Living quarters," said Amelia without thinking.

"Office," said Father at the same time. He frowned in her direction.

"Of course you're right, Father. We can stay at the boarding-house for as long as we'd like. It certainly makes more sense for your office to be finished first." But she couldn't help but be eager to dig her hands into soil and begin making things grow out here. Working in the greenhouse and seeing what Sy had accomplished had whetted her appetite for more.

Charlie looked to Hank. "Should only be about a month or so. Depends on how many good weather days we get. At least to be useable, if not fully finished."

Hank nodded. "Sounds about right. Might be sooner if we can get some help. Doc, you could consider asking your patients for work in exchange for treatment." He smiled.

"That's not a bad idea, Hank. There are a few poorer folk who can't afford a doctor, so they don't call one. If I let it be made known that I'd take work in exchange, perhaps their pride would be assuaged and they would seek treatment." He took a sip of his tea and looked at Josh. "I am running low on supplies since there was a limit as to what I could carry with me and what the mercantile stocks. I'll need to make a trip into Portland to pick up some supplies and order more. When would be a good time to make that trip?"

Amelia's heart perked up. She would love a trip to Portland. They had so little time to view the city, just one night's stay between leaving the train and boarding the stage. There would be so much to explore in one of the most modern cities in the West.

"Tuesday's stage goes to Portland. Comes back Friday."

Her heart sank. She was helping Emily with the schoolroom. She couldn't possibly be gone that long. She wouldn't be able to go to Portland until the next school break. And who knew if Father would be able to make a trip then?

Father grimaced. "That long between stages? I hate to be away from my patients that long."

"Until the railroad comes through." The edges of Josh's mouth turned down. "You could pick up horses in Oregon City and ride home."

Father's nostrils flared. He wasn't a horseman. He preferred a buggy or his own two feet.

"You could probably catch a ride back with the freighter," Hank said. "Either the one delivering your trunks or the one delivering the lumber."

Father's face relaxed a small amount. "I'll think on it and possibly send some telegrams tomorrow. I'm also planning on hiring a nurse to start as soon as the office quarters are ready." He turned to Emily. "Would there be any problem with a woman residing here for an extended period of time?"

Emily turned to Josh. "I don't imagine there would be. Josh, can you think of any concerns?"

"Nope. I just don't imagine she'll stay unmarried long. Doc, do you have a problem with married women serving as nurses? If so, you'd best be prepared to hire a string of them. Unmarried women are still a rare commodity out here. And they don't stay that way long." He squeezed Emily's shoulder.

"I hadn't thought of that."

The meeting broke up a short while later, the important topics having been discussed. Amelia decided that she wouldn't miss Father too much while he was in Portland since she didn't see him much here anyway.

Hank stood and she joined him, the closeness of their chairs causing her to take a step back. "You must have a cold ride back to camp. Or will you bunk down here?"

"It's a cold ride whether I make it at night or in the morning. But at first light, it's a little easier to see the trail, so I'll bunk with Josh tonight." He glanced over at Josh who nodded. "Hopefully I'll beat the rain back to camp. Otherwise, it's a wet and muddy ride."

"Come to the boardinghouse early to get a hot breakfast before you leave." Why had she offered that? It really wasn't her place. Her cheeks grew warm, and she hoped Emily didn't think she'd overstepped.

Hank gave her a soft smile. "I'll do that. See you tomorrow, Amelia." Then he disappeared into the kitchen.

Amelia said a vague goodnight to the room and headed upstairs, confused as to why she found herself wanting to spend more time with Hank.

Chapter Twelve

H ank awoke to the sound of rain pounding on the roof. He washed up and dressed, and headed down the loft stairs, leaving Charlie snoring softly. The man had slept restlessly last night. His leg must be paining him. Maybe it was too much to ask him to take on the construction of both buildings. John McAlistar was eager but didn't have enough experience to manage it without direct supervision. Unfortunately, the days Hank could take off from the logging camp were days like today. Rainy. Which meant no building, whenever the lumber got here.

Lord, help me think of a solution here that works for everyone. I owe Seth a hard day's work for what he's done for me. And yet I want to help the people of this town with the skills and knowledge I possess. I don't want to see Charlie continuing to hurt because he's taken on a job that I could do. I just don't know what the answer is. Please show me.

Not to mention the clock was ticking on his own deadline to prove himself to his father.

Josh was pulling on his boots. "Heading over to the boardinghouse?"

"I thought I might. A hot breakfast sounds a lot better than a cold, wet ride."

"I agree with you there." He glanced at the loft. "Pa still sleeping?"

"Yeah. Didn't seem to sleep too well last night."

Josh grunted. "It's that leg of his. If Doc can find a way to ease the pain, I'd be grateful. Pa's been too proud to ask, but I think I ought to ask Doc to check on him if he has time. I certainly don't want Pa turning to that nasty patent medicine again."

"Couldn't agree more. I've heard some terrible stories about that snake oil."

Donning hats and slickers, they headed out the door and over the footbridge. The water was well below the steps that carried them up and over the small stream. Soon they were shaking the damp off themselves on the back porch. The moment they entered the kitchen, Maggie hustled them to the dining room with mugs of coffee, where they joined Pastor Roy. The warmth felt good seeping through his hands.

The sound of footsteps on the stairs had him looking up. Amelia entered the dining room and came to an abrupt stop. "Where's Charlie?"

Josh wrapped his hand around his mug. "He'll be along shortly. He moves slower in the damp. I'm sure he can't wait for spring to arrive."

"Father would be happy to look at his leg. Considering all the work Charlie's doing for us on the house, it's the least we can do."

Josh nodded. "I was hoping to ask. Pa doesn't like folks to know much about it, but it's obvious he's in pain. It would be a good thing if he could get some relief." A shadow fell across Josh's eyes, and he sipped his coffee.

"Morning, Pastor. Hank. I suppose you aren't looking forward to the ride back to camp." Her cheeks were a delicate pink that made the dusting of golden freckles stand out.

He grinned. "Morning, Amelia. No, I'm not. I'm hoping to postpone it long enough for the rain to stop at least."

She nodded. "I'd best help Maggie."

Another set of footsteps on the stairs, and Emily appeared. "Morning, boys. Pastor." She touched Josh's shoulder, and he covered her hand with his, giving it a squeeze.

Hank admired their easy way with each other.

Amelia returned with a basket of biscuits, a ball of butter, and a pot of preserves. She set them on the table. "Maggie will have eggs and sausage out shortly. But you can get started with these."

"Let's ask the blessing." Pastor Roy blessed the food with his booming voice, and they dug into the flakey biscuits. Nobody made them better. Hank's mouth watered every time he thought of them.

The rest of the food joined the biscuits on the table and the women took their places. Sally and James came in from their chores. Conversation was family-like and comfortable around the table, something Hank enjoyed now but never had growing up. Children were to be seen and not heard in his family. But Maggie's children were equal participants.

Amelia spoke as she spread strawberry preserves on her biscuit. "I've still not gotten used to having rain this time of year. Normally we're buried in snow, which brings its own set of problems. But it does take longer to soak you to the skin."

Emily patted Josh's arm. "Luckily Josh will drive us in the buggy today so we don't have to walk in the rain. And the covered boardwalks help too."

The heat of jealousy shot through Hank. He was surprised how much he wanted to have that time alone with Amelia in a buggy. But of course there was no way he could offer to drive Josh's buggy. And there wouldn't be any good reason for him to ride along.

"Speaking of which, we'd best be going." Josh tossed his napkin down and pushed his chair back, then held Emily's chair for her.

Amelia gave Hank a warm smile before following after Josh and Emily.

Maggie's biscuits didn't taste quite so delicious after they had left.

Charlie hadn't made an appearance by the time Hank was ready to leave. He didn't want to be responsible for making an old man's condition worse. He hoped the doc had some relief for Charlie. Otherwise, Hank would have a hard decision to make: The well-being of the town or proving himself to his father.

THOUGH IT WAS ONLY her second day in the schoolroom, Amelia was glad that at noontime, there was a break in the rain so the children could eat their dinners outside and burn off their excess energy.

Emily handed Amelia a thick sandwich that Maggie had made them, and they discussed the day's lessons as they ate.

Emily finished her sandwich and reach for the jar of canned peaches. "There's really not much else to show you. You've seen how the day is structured, and the plans are written for the rest of the year. You just have to follow along. I think you should go to Portland with your father next week. Once you start teaching, you won't have the opportunity until summer, and who knows if your father would be able to get away then. It's a wonderful town to explore for a few days."

Amelia forked a canned peach slice into her mouth. So sweet. Such a wonderful taste of summer sunshine. Which was much needed on a gray day like today. Chewing gave her a moment to gather her thoughts. "It doesn't seem right to go gallivanting off and leave you here to teach."

"It's my job. For now." Emily smiled. "I don't mind at all. In fact, I insist."

"Will the townspeople think I'm flighty? I don't want them to think I'm unreliable." Getting asked to come back next fall was important to her, and she wanted to make sure she made a good impression with those who would make the decision.

Emily packed up their dinner. "Mr. Parsons will find a reason to criticize everything you do. I'm not sure why he's like that. Cassandra was the only perfect teacher in his mind, I suppose."

Amelia brushed the crumbs off her skirt. "I just want him to hire me again for the fall. I want him to think I'm a good teacher." She met Emily's gaze. "I want to be a good teacher.

"You'll do fine." Emily squeezed Amelia's hand. "No matter what Mr. Parsons says. Which you cannot control, as you well know."

Amelia nodded and moved to peer out the window to see what the children were doing. The ground was wet, so it was likely at least some of the boys would return covered in mud. There were so many things to manage with being a teacher.

Emily patted Amelia's shoulder as she passed her. "Don't fret. Enjoy your time in Portland with your father." She moved to the back of the room to ring the bell to bring the children in.

Amelia returned to Emily's desk. Yes, spending time with Father would be good. They'd had a lot of time together on the trip out here, but since then, she hadn't seen him much at all.

Hank's grin from this morning at the breakfast table flashed in her mind. Of course, it would take time away from Hank. Which would be a good thing, wouldn't it? She'd be able to sort out a bit her feelings for him. Did she even have any feelings for him beyond friendship? She enjoyed his company and looked forward to seeing him. But she had to admit she was reluctant to get attached to someone and then have them taken away, like what happened with her mother. She wasn't sure she could endure another heartbreak if Hank didn't return her feelings. If she had them.

The noise level rose greatly as the children poured back inside and into their seats. Amelia smiled at them as they came in and tried to remember their names. This was what she needed to turn her mind to.

Emily followed the last child up the aisle and nodded at Amelia, who called the class to order and began their afternoon session.

Chapter Thirteen

H ank sat in the cookhouse sipping on coffee and working
on the house plans he had spread out over the table,
which was much bigger than the one in his cabin. The rain
pelting the roof gave him a particular sense of privacy. Seth
hadn't come up today, having gotten caught up on the books
and paperwork earlier this week. The rain was good for that.

He downed the last of the coffee and glanced over both sets
of plans one last time. He'd made a few adjustments and needed
to talk to Charlie and John before the lumber came in next
week. Also, it wouldn't hurt to see if there was a letter from Sy
on the stage that came in today. Seemed like a trip to town was
in order. He folded up the plans and inserted them in an oilskin
pouch.

Donning his hat and slicker, he saddled up his horse, Prince
—a beautiful bay gelding that had been a gift from his father.
He looked out of place in the camp livery. Hank and Prince
made their wet way down the mountain into town. His first stop
was the mercantile, where there was indeed a letter from Sy. He
took all the mail for the camp from Mrs. Fulton, giving polite
responses to her inquiries. Since Mrs. Fulton knew most of the

comings and goings of folks in town, it was a good bet she'd have the information he needed.

"Do you know where John McAlistar is working today?"

"I believe he's at the livery."

"Thank you. Good day." He left the mercantile. Leaning up against the outside wall protected by the covered boardwalk, he ripped open Sy's letter.

He scanned it quickly, then reread it more carefully. Sy did have a sawmill recommendation and a place to purchase it. Hank's blood rushed through his veins. Yes! This was what the town needed. It wouldn't help with Doc's house or the parsonage, but once the railroad came through, they'd need a lot more buildings, faster than the freighters could deliver the lumber. It would ultimately pay for itself.

Who could run the sawmill? Perhaps Seth would know if one of his men had experience with that sort of thing. He'd head over there just as soon as he checked out the doc's site.

Sy had also included a list of shade plants that would work on the doc's site. Amelia would be pleased to see those. And he hoped she'd be pleased with him.

He tucked all the letters within his slicker to keep them dry then untied Prince and mounted. A short ride and he was in front of the doc's homesite. He dismounted, keeping the reins in his hand. The foundation looked good. The rocks nestled closely into each other, snug in their mortar, evenly touching the string line. It was ready to be built on and the cellar dug. All they needed was the lumber, which would hopefully arrive next week, along with good weather, if the *Almanac* was to be believed. And it usually was.

He remounted and headed for the livery, where he spotted John. "Hey, can you spare a few minutes to meet us at Maggie's to go over the plans for the doc's house and the parsonage?"

John spoke to Max the owner then came back out. "I'll be right over."

Hank nodded then headed on to the boardinghouse, pulling

around back to the barn. Too bad it was too early for school to be out. He'd miss seeing Amelia. He poked his head into Charlie's workshop.

"Hey, Charlie."

Charlie turned from what looked like a box he was working on. "Oh, it's just you. I've ordered Emily to stay out of here." He gestured to the project. "This is her wedding present. Going to be a trunk." He pointed to a nearly completed bookcase. "And that's from Josh for her. He's been in here working on it at night."

"I'm sure she'll love them. You both are talented craftsmen. I'm going to take care of my horse first, but do you have a few minutes to go over the changes I made to the plans?"

"Surely. Sounds like a good time for a coffee break and whatever goodies Maggie has for us to sample."

Hank grinned. "I'll see you inside, then."

After taking care of Prince, Hank was happy to see the rain had stopped as he exited the barn and headed up the back porch steps. Once inside, the warmth of the kitchen enveloped him as he removed his slicker and hat, then took the plans out of their oilskin pouch.

"Coffee, Hank?" Maggie had a cup poured before he'd barely nodded. "You boys can use the dining room table. I'll bring in some cookies leftover from yesterday."

"Thanks, Maggie." He took his cup from her and headed to the dining room where Charlie and John were already seated with their own mugs.

Hank spread out the plans and explained the changes he had made as well as a general plan of where they should begin once the lumber was delivered, based on what the doc had said.

Hank tapped the plans for the parsonage. "Guess the workday is postponed at least a week. Even if it doesn't rain tomorrow, the ground is too wet and muddy to work."

"Might be even better." Charlie finished the last of his coffee. "Pastor and Maggie are planning to go out visiting to the neighboring areas that don't have a pastor. It'll be nice for the town to work on their place without them around."

"And the lumber should already be delivered by then. We might get more than the foundation done if we have enough help and the weather holds."

After they were agreed on the work and Hank was folding up the plans, Charlie spoke up. "Hank, you've got a real knack for this. More so than most anyone I've worked with. Maybe you should be the town's carpenter. We're going to need one, and it'll be more work than me and Young John can handle."

John nodded, perhaps a bit too eagerly.

Hank warmed at the compliment followed immediately by a cold lump in his stomach. He couldn't be a carpenter. "Thanks for the kind words, Charlie. But this is just something I know how to do. I'm working on owning my own logging outfit."

Charlie nodded and met his gaze. "Seems to me they'd both be about running your own outfit. We've got a lot of loggers around here. Not so many carpenters. But you do what you think is best. A man needs to chart his own destiny, not based on someone else's opinion." He winked at Hank.

There was something more to what Charlie was saying, but Hank didn't have time to think about it now. He had to get to Seth's and tell him about the sawmill.

HANK PULLED up to Seth and Becca's house, a snug two-story in the middle of a meadow, surrounded by forest.

Seth pulled the door open as Hank dismounted. "Trouble at the camp?"

"Nope. Heard back from Sy and thought I'd discuss it with you." He flipped the reins over the porch railing and followed Seth inside. A cheery fire warmed the room, and he slipped off his coat, hanging it next to the door.

Becca stood. "Hi, Hank. Can I get you some coffee?"

"Thank you, but no. I just came from Maggie's."

She smiled. "So I imagine you're full too."

"Yes, ma'am." He grinned. Becca left the room, and Hank followed Seth to the chairs flanking the fireplace and handed him Sy's letter.

Seth nodded as he read and then handed the letter back to Hank. "Sy came through for us." He met Hank's gaze. "There's a couple of ways we can go about it. I have no problem with the logging camp buying the sawmill if it gets it here sooner. We can pay for it out of our line of credit. That will work, won't it?"

"Yes, that should be no problem. It's exactly the kind of thing a business uses a line of credit for."

"But my preference would be that someone from town would own it and run it as their business. Frankly, I don't need the hassle of running it. I'd prefer if someone from the town would buy it from me and make it their own." Seth pointed. "Someone like you."

"Me?" Hank leaned back in his chair, his stomach clenching. "Am I not doing a good enough job for you at the logging camp? I told you I was committed to working there."

"You're doing a fine job. But you have carpentry skills, and the town needs that. A sawmill would be a natural extension of that business."

Hank gazed into the fire. "What you're saying makes sense." But his father would never respect him as a common laborer. Still, the good of the town must count for something as well. And if Charlie's leg didn't get better... "I need some time to think on it."

Seth nodded. "I'm not sure I understand why the logging is so important to you. I thought you wanted to prove to your family that you could make it on your own. How is being a carpenter any different than being a logger?"

Hank let out a breath and rubbed the back of his neck. "I don't know if this will make any sense to you, but if I owned my own logging outfit or if I were your partner, my father would respect me as a business owner. But being a carpenter, well that's common labor. And he'd never respect that." His throat tightened. How could he prove to his father that he had succeeded as a carpenter, using his brawn instead of his brain? No, Father would not consider it a success, and Hank would be forced back into banking per their agreement.

Seth was silent for a moment. "Earning his father's respect is a powerful thing for a man." He paused. "But perhaps it's not the only thing that matters in the big scheme of things. Only you can decide that for yourself. Tell you what. Why don't you spend as much time as you need on the sawmill? The logging company will purchase it, but you see if you can't find someone to run it. It's more valuable to the town right now to solve that problem than to have you working in the logging camp. Sound fair?"

Hank stuck out his hand to shake Seth's. "It does. We should swing by the bank to get the sawmill purchase authorized by the line of credit and then we can get it ordered."

The men got to their feet. Seth disappeared into the kitchen where Becca had gone and returned as Hank was donning his coat and hat. How nice to have someone care about where you were going and when you'd be back. Amelia's sweet, freckled face came to mind. But he couldn't imagine her ever wanting to welcome home a logger every night. Let alone a carpenter. Not when her father was a doctor.

The rain held off while he and Seth rode to town. They pulled up in front of the bank, dismounted, and headed inside.

The clerk looked up. "Mr. Blake. Mr. Paulson. How can I help you?"

"Is Mr. Irving in?" Seth asked. "I need to speak to him about the logging camp's line of credit."

Hank studied the bank. He'd been in a few times, but given his background, he couldn't help but examine it through a professional eye.

The clerk's face paled. "Um, Mr. Irving is no longer with us.

That is, he's still alive, I assume. But he's no longer at the bank. Mr. Wallace has taken his place as bank manager."

Hank frowned. Odd. Seems like they would have heard of that happening. It was still a small town. And why did the clerk look so nervous?

"Thanks." Seth rocked on his heels. "May we speak with him?"

"I'll see if he's available." The clerk scurried to the office door and knocked, then whispered when it cracked open.

The door opened wider and a thin man strode out wearing a finely made suit. He unlocked the barred door and opened it. "Mr. Blake and Mr. Paulson, I'm Stanley Wallace, the new bank manager. Please come this way." But his eyes remained on Hank, studying him.

Odder still. But Hank followed Seth into Mr. Wallace's office and took a seat. It hadn't changed much, except that it was completely devoid of any personal touches. Mr. Irving had kept a photograph of his parents on his desk and a few souvenirs from his travels to various Western cities. Perhaps Mr. Wallace just hadn't gotten settled.

"When did you take over as manager? I hadn't heard about it?"

Mr. Wallace shot Hank a tight smile. "It was rather sudden. Now, how can I help you gentlemen?"

Seth explained about the need to access the line of credit to purchase a sawmill.

Mr. Wallace shook his head. "I'm afraid that's not possible. Your line of credit has been closed."

"What? For what reason?" Hank nearly came out of his chair. If this city dude thought that he could buffalo some dumb loggers, he was in for a surprise.

"It's an unsound exposure. The bank can't afford the risk. I don't know why my predecessor thought it was a good business decision to allow it. It's one of the reasons he's no longer here."

He rose from his seat. "Now, if there's nothing else, I have much to attend to."

Hank pointed his hat at the man. "The bank has never lost a penny on the logging company. In fact, it's made quite a bit on it. If you want to talk exposure, I'm sure Mr. Blake's standing in the community could cause quite a few people to pull their deposits if they were to hear how he has been treated. This town sticks by their own."

Mr. Wallace leaned over the desk. "Is that a threat, Mr. Paulson? Because there are established procedures that protect banks. Every town needs a bank. It would be a shame if this one should close."

"I'm sure the shareholders would have something to say about that. And might be interested in how you are managing their investment."

Mr. Wallace smiled, but his eyes narrowed. "I'm sure they would be. You might know something about that, wouldn't you Mr. Paulson?" He shot a glance at Seth.

What did he mean by that? There was something going on. Wallace had no idea who he was dealing with.

Seth grabbed Hank's arm. "Come on. We're not going to make any headway here."

They strode out the bank.

"I'm sorry, Seth. I don't know what's happening, but I'm going to get to the bottom of this. Even if it means going to Portland." Which is exactly what it would mean. Which would mean several days away from the logging camp.

Seth mounted his horse and nodded. "I meant what I said. Take some time to figure all this out. I don't care about the line of credit so much, but the town needs a sawmill. If you can make that happen, we'd be indebted to you. Say hi to Amelia and Emily for me." He grinned, wheeled his horse and rode off.

What? He glanced up the street. Children were streaming down it. School was out. He could see Amelia before he headed back to camp.

Oh.

Seth had seen right through him when it came to Amelia. Had anyone else?

And only Seth knew that Hank could make the sawmill happen with his own funds.

What was the situation at the bank and with that Mr. Wallace? He'd get to the bottom of it, but it'd mean taking the stage to Portland on Tuesday. He touched the letters in his slicker. At least this day could end on a good note. The rest he'd figure out later.

AMELIA CHATTED WITH EMILY, their bootheels making a dull thud on the damp boardwalk. She glanced ahead and noticed a familiar figure down the street watching them. Hank. Her pulse pounded a bit, and she pulled her books closer to her chest. What was he doing in town? He seemed to be waiting for her.

He tipped his hat and started toward them. When he drew near, he reached for Amelia's and Emily's books and lunch pail. "Ladies, may I carry your books?"

"Thank you, Hank." Emily brushed down the front of her dark-blue wool coat. "What brings you out this way?"

Hank smiled at Amelia, and warmth spread through her.

"I had business in town since it was too wet to work at the logging camp. I saw you coming down the street and hoped I could be of service."

Amelia laughed. "Such fine words. Have you been practicing?"

His face fell, and she immediately regretted her teasing. "I only meant that it's a lovely contrast to how most of the men in town speak."

"You mean grunt?" Emily giggled. "Thank you, Hank. It's very kind of you."

Amelia touched his arm. "Yes, it truly is."

Hank's smile returned. "I have an update about the lumber and the sawmill. I spoke to Charlie and John earlier. I hoped to see if I could catch your father as well."

"Your chances are as good as mine. I hardly see him since we've come to town." They had discussed the Portland trip. He did agree that it was the only place he could get the supplies he needed. And while he didn't relish the idea of being gone three days, he was pleased that Amelia would go with him.

"Well, I bring good news. The sooner we can get your house built, the sooner your father will have his own office, and you'll be able to spend more time with him."

"That is good news."

They entered the boardinghouse through the kitchen, which was empty for once.

"Make yourself at home, Hank. There's coffee on the stove." Emily hung up her coat. "Amelia and I will put our things away and then be downstairs. Maybe Maggie's in the parlor and knows where the doc is."

Amelia followed Emily upstairs, ignoring her knowing smile as she put her hat and books away. But she did check her reflection in the mirror over her washstand, patting a few loose strands back into place and pressing out the wrinkles in her cinnamon-colored dress before heading back downstairs.

In the parlor, Hank sat next to the fire, alone in the room.

"Where's Maggie?"

"I think she's in the kitchen."

"You didn't find my father?"

"No, and Maggie hadn't seen him either." He motioned to the chair next to him. "But I do have something to show you." He reached into his coat pocket and pulled out a piece of paper.

She eased into the chair next to him, the fire welcome after their chilly walk home. What could Hank have for her?

"First, about your house. The foundation looks good, and as you know, the lumber will be here next week. But, Seth and I have been looking into getting a sawmill for the town. Sy sent us his recommendations, and I'll be heading to Portland next week to make arrangements to purchase it. It likely won't be too much help for your house, but if we get it up and running in time, it could help if we run out of lumber."

Amelia's heart jumped at the mention of Portland. He didn't know she was going. Had he assumed her father would go and naturally take her? Or did he assume she wouldn't go because she was helping Emily in the schoolroom? Of course, Father hadn't thought a thing about her missing the schoolroom. His dismissiveness of something that was important to her cut her heart. Perhaps on their trip she'd have time to explain to him how important teaching was to her.

"So you'll be leaving on Tuesday's stage with my father and me."

Hank's face lit up, doing something funny to her insides. "That's wonderful. So your father decided to go?"

"Yes, he's reluctant, but it's the only way he can get the supplies he needs. We plan on seeing a bit of the city while we are there. Perhaps you could join us?" Her last words came out in a rush, and she almost wished she could take them back. How forward must he think her? And yet the idea of spending time with him was an enjoyable one. Maybe it wasn't the distance but his company that would help her sort out her feelings.

His eyes crinkled at the corners. "That sounds like the best thing I've heard in a long time. I know the city well and can show you a few of my favorite places." He tapped the paper he held. "And I have some good news for you. This is a list of plants I got from Sy that will do well in the shade of your homesite." He handed her the paper.

It was a drawing of their lot with the house and barn placed, the trees indicated. Then another script had neatly drawn groupings with printed plants in their common and Latin names. A list of all the plants ran down the side of the page.

Tears pricked her eyes, and she blinked. "I don't know what to say. This is so wonderful." She swallowed the lump in her throat. No one had ever done anything so kind for her. "To notice what I needed and to find a solution…" She met his gaze. "Thank you."

"You're welcome, Amelia." His voice was husky. He laid his warm hand over hers. "I just wanted to see you happy."

"Hank, are you staying for supper?" Emily appeared in the doorway, and Hank snatched his hand away.

Amelia's cheeks grew warm at Emily's saucy grin.

Hank glanced at Amelia. "I'd be happy to, if it's no bother."

"It's no bother." Emily flounced into the kitchen.

Amelia concentrated on the paper in order to avoid thinking about her burning cheeks. "I know some of these names, but some are not familiar at all. I do have a book on gardening that was my mother's. I'll get it." She fled up the stairs, giving herself a chance to take a deep breath. What on earth was going on with her?

STANLEY TOOK out paper and dipped his pen in the ink well. Mr. Paulson would be pleased to learn about Henry's visit to the bank today. And his plans to acquire a sawmill. Stanley was certain Henry didn't know that he knew who Henry really was. While Henry might threaten to have people pull their money out of the bank, Stanley could threaten to reveal Henry's true identity. If it came to that.

It was his ace in the hole, so he'd carefully consider how best to play it.

He was certain Mr. Paulson would be appreciative of his efforts and information, especially the closing of the line of credit.

These backwater rubes didn't know how the world really ran. And Stanley would use that to his advantage. When Mr. Blake's logging camp went out of business, Stanley would make sure Blake knew that it was Henry's fault. And then Henry would have no choice but to return to his father and the family business, having disgraced himself in this town.

Yes, Mr. Paulson would be most appreciative. Stanley could picture the big-windowed office and mahogany desk that would soon be his as a reward. He wouldn't be in this dusty town for long.

Chapter Fourteen

A melia and Emily were going over lesson plans in the parlor when a knock came at the front door.

Frowning, Emily stood to answer it. "Why, Stephen, you could come around the back." She opened the door wider and motioned for him to step in.

Amelia rose and stood behind Emily.

Stephen twirled his hat in his hands. "Hi, Amelia. I came to see if you'd like to come check on your plants in the greenhouse. Since it's not a school day." He motioned to the front of the boardinghouse. "I brought the buggy."

"That's very kind of you." She turned to Emily. "Can we finish up our planning when I get back?"

"Certainly. We're nearly done, and I have baking to help Maggie with. Nice seeing you, Stephen." Emily turned and left the room, winking over her shoulder at Amelia.

Amelia gave Emily a hard stare. "Just let me get my coat and hat." She hurried upstairs and collected her things, including the list of plants Hank had brought over from Sy. Perhaps they could look through some of his journals and books to find out about the ones that weren't in her garden book.

She glanced in the mirror over the washstand. Her cheeks

were pink. Likely from her rushing around. It had nothing to do with the fact that two men seemed to be quite helpful to her lately. Nor that Emily seemed to find the whole situation amusing. This was not anything she had expected. In her dime novels, when two men were interested in the heroine, one was a dashing, charming rogue and the other was a steady, reliable man. Both Stephen and Hank were more the steady type.

Not knowing what to make of her own thoughts, she headed back downstairs.

AMELIA POKED at the soil around the plants in the greenhouse. It was just the right amount of dampness.

"I check on them every day when I do my chores and add water just when the soil is barely dry to the touch." Stephen grinned at her, hands behind his back, leaning over her shoulder.

If she stepped back, she'd bump into him. Flustered, she dusted her hands off. "Thank you. That's very kind." She gave a stiff smile. "They are doing quite well. Some are even producing buds. I wonder when I can transplant them. I suppose I'd best write Sy about that. Poor man, he's going to be sick of my letters."

Stephen took her elbow as they left the greenhouse. "Somehow I doubt that. He loves talking about plants, and I'm sure he's thrilled to have someone to discuss them with in detail. In fact, I have something to show you."

Amelia was careful to keep her elbow still and her body pulled away slightly so as not to rub against Stephen. Once they were in the kitchen, he plied her with coffee and his apple spice muffins before heading upstairs. "I'll be right back. I think you're going to like this."

His boots clattered up the stairs and over her head before coming back down. She hardly had time to know what to think.

Was Stephen just being helpful, or was he interested in her in a romantic way? No, surely he was just being a good neighbor.

He returned with a piece of paper that he slipped in front of her before taking his seat. A list of plant names filled the pages in two columns but in different handwriting. The first column she recognized as her plants. The second column looked to be Sy's handwriting.

"What is this?"

Stephen grinned. "I sent Sy a list of all of your plants that hadn't survived the trip and asked him to list ones that would be similar that we could replace them with."

"How very sweet." The similar list that Hank had given her, the one that she currently felt crinkling in her pocket, came to mind. How kind for both men to be interested in something so important to her. Her father had never shown such interest in gardening. He was pleased that it made Mother happy and kept her occupied. Even when she had her breathing spells, she would lay in bed and look at seed catalogues or her gardening books. But Father never helped her with any of it. It was something Amelia and Mother had shared.

She reached into her pocket and pulled out the list Hank had given her. "I have this list from Sy as well. It's the plants that can grow in the shade on our homesite."

Stephen's grin faltered but settled into a soft smile. "So did you draw out this plan for him? It's quite good."

"No, Hank did that. He wrote to Sy on my behalf after I was so disappointed about the homesite's lack of sunlight."

Stephen's smile disappeared completely. "Well, that was neighborly of him."

"It was, wasn't it?" Amelia spread both papers side by side. "I brought it hoping there might be some journals or books here that we could use to look up these plants. Some of them I know, but some of them weren't in my gardening book."

Stephen nodded. "We can do that. Let me go check and see

what Sy left here. Would you like a refill?" He nodded to her mug.

"Yes, please." She sipped on her coffee while Stephen brought down a stack of journals and books.

They spent the rest of the day searching through books and journals, identifying plants on both lists. All in all, it was a pleasant way to spend a drizzly afternoon. But when Stephen brought her home and took extra care to place a hot brick at her feet and tuck in the lap robes around her, she couldn't help but wonder if he was being more than neighborly.

They pulled up to the boardinghouse. To the front again. "You can pull around back and let me out by the kitchen."

Stephen turned to her, appearing not to hear her. "I've surely enjoyed our time together, Amelia. I'm hoping we can do more of that." Was it her imagination or did his face turn a bit ruddier?

"Thank you, Stephen. I enjoyed it too." She made to move the lap robe off her, but he touched her hand.

"Amelia, I know I should speak to your father, and I will when I can find him, but the reason I pulled to the front and not the back is because that's what a gentleman caller does when he's courting a lady." He swallowed. "Would you be receptive to my courting you? Once I got your father's permission, of course."

Heat rushed to Amelia's face. She had not been expecting this and didn't know what to say. Or what she even felt. Did she want to court Stephen? He was kind, but… "Oh, that's so sweet. Um, my father and I are going to Portland on the stage Tuesday. May I have some time to discuss it with him then?"

He grinned, but it lacked some of his earlier confidence. "Take all the time you need. I'm not going anywhere." He held her gaze until she looked away.

She licked her lips. "Thank you for a lovely day and for looking after my plants. I'll see you tomorrow at church." She scrambled out of the lap robes, but Stephen hopped out and made it around to her side of the buggy to help her down before she could gather her skirts.

He held on to her waist a touch longer than necessary. "Yes, you will."

With a quick smile, Amelia gathered her skirts and headed up the stairs to the boardinghouse front door. She fled up to her room without looking back. Now what was she to do? For the first time in her life, church threatened to be an uncomfortable occasion.

Chapter Fifteen

From inside the church, Amelia spotted both Hank and Stephen as they took their seats, but she had surrounded herself with Emily and Becca. However, that didn't keep her mind from wandering during Pastor Roy's sermon. Surely her luck wouldn't hold out after church, and she'd have to speak to one or both of them. Right now, she favored running into Hank since he hadn't asked to court her.

She wasn't sure how she felt about that, either. Or Stephen. They were both kind men, people she was happy to call her friends. They had been helpful and made her feel at home in a new town. But what did her heart want?

Stephen had caught her eye and tossed her his confident grin.

She smiled back but averted her gaze. She enjoyed spending time with him, but she wasn't sure she was ready to court him. If she had more time to get to know him, maybe she'd be able to form a more informed opinion. But wasn't that what courting was for, to get to know a person? She should have asked Emily last night. But she was so confused and in such turmoil over Stephen's words, she hadn't wanted to talk to anyone. She didn't want to be swayed by someone else's opinion.

Well, she'd have time away in Portland to think things over. Time she'd be spending with Hank. She slid her gaze in his direction.

Hank was wearing his suit to church like he usually did. It reminded her of the first time she saw him, dashing in his manner, protecting her during the hold up. Her heart had immediately inclined toward him. But then when she realized he was a logger, she'd felt a bit letdown. Her image of him didn't line up with reality. But now that she'd gotten to know him, spend time with him, she'd seen how much more depth of character he had than any dime novel hero.

How was she to choose between these two men? Then again, Hank had never indicated he wanted to be anything more than her friend. So perhaps there was no choice to be made. She fingered the delicate gold chain on which the cameo hung. She supposed the trip to Portland would be revealing. She'd get to spend time with Hank and decide if he had any romantic interest in her or if she had any in him. And maybe she could sort out her feelings about Stephen.

Emily nudged her as they stood to sing the final hymn. She hadn't heard a single word of the sermon. She hoped Pastor Roy didn't ask her opinion at Sunday dinner.

HANK STOOD in the churchyard watching to get a chance to speak to Amelia. It wasn't raining at the moment. In fact, the sun was trying to poke through a gap in the clouds. As usual, he was invited to Sunday supper at the boardinghouse, along with Seth and Becca. He could talk to Amelia then, but he couldn't seem to take his eyes off her now. The idea of spending time with her in Portland with no distractions had chased through his mind last night, making it hard to sleep. He couldn't wait to show her all his favorite places. And her father, too, of course.

Stephen stepped up to where she was talking with some of the town's women.

Hank clenched his fists and then relaxed them when he realized what he had done. He liked Stephen. He didn't know him too well, but he was a good sort. All the O'Malley boys were.

Stephen handed her a note with a grin. She took it, and Stephen's touch lingered. She gave him a soft smile, and then turned away, slipping the note into her pocket.

Heat rushed through Hank's face. What was that all about? Something from Sy perhaps? But Sy would have sent it to the post office at the mercantile. It didn't make sense to send it to Stephen to give to Amelia. That would be an extra step that made no sense. And Sy was nothing if not logical. Which meant the note was from Stephen himself.

Hank shook his head slightly. It wasn't his business, and he shouldn't be gawking. He tried to turn away.

But Amelia turned and spotted him. He gave her a half wave and tried to smile. It likely wasn't convincing. He turned and walked off to his horse. He wasn't sure where he was going, but he just needed to get out of here to where he could sort his feelings out in private.

Because it certainly looked to him like Stephen had more than friendliness on his mind when it came to Amelia Martin.

But before he could reach his horse, the new bank manager hailed him. Stanley Wallace. Quite possibly the last person he wanted to see.

"Hello, Mr. Paulson."

"Mr. Wallace. What did you think of Pastor Adams's sermon?"

Wallace gave a smile that reminded Hank of a snake. "Not a polished orator, of course. But certainly powerful. Appropriate for a place like this."

Hank held Wallace's gaze. And his own tongue. What was it about this man that turned his gut? "Where do you hail from?"

"Most recently Portland."

Portland? If he was in banking, then they likely knew some of the same people. Of course, Wallace didn't know who Hank really was. He'd do some checking while he was up there. See what information he could dig up on him.

Hank nodded congenially. "Nice place."

"Mr. Wallace." Mr. Parsons came up, saving Hank from having to make another polite comment. "There are some folks I'd like you to meet."

"Of course, Mr. Parsons." Wallace touched the brim of his hat, a smile on his lips but hardness in his eyes. "I'm sure I'll see you around, Paulson." He turned and walked off with Mr. Parsons.

Hank watched for a moment before swinging up on Prince. There was definitely more to Stanley Wallace than met the eye. He'd find out what it was. In the meantime, he hoped Sunday dinner redeemed what had turned out to be an unexpectedly strange day.

How soon could he politely leave? Hank's nerves were stretched to the breaking point. Too many people in the boardinghouse, the rain keeping everyone inside. He wouldn't even mind a wet ride out to the logging camp at this point. The press of people didn't disturb him the way tight places did, but they did make him uncomfortable and antsy to find some breathing room.

And since he hadn't been able to get close enough to Amelia to have a conversation with her, what was the point in staying?

He made his way to the kitchen, stopping to thank Maggie for the wonderful-as-always dinner. Grabbing his hat and coat off the overcrowded hooks, he slipped them on as he stepped out to the back porch.

Amelia stood there in her coat, arms wrapped around her

middle, looking off over the meadow. She turned. "Hank. Leaving so soon?"

He peered out. There was a break in the rain. God must be showing His favor to Hank. "I thought I might. What brings you out here?"

She glanced back inside. "Too many people. It felt close and hot. I wanted some fresh air and was considering a walk since the rain had stopped." She brought out a piece of paper from her pocket. "With this map you drew, I could see if I could envision the plants where Sy had indicated on our homesite." She gave a sheepish smile. "Plants are comforting to me."

He swept out his arm. "Let's go." He paused. "Unless you'd rather be alone?"

"Oh no, I'd be glad of the company. Plus, there are a few things on the map that you could explain to me."

They walked the few blocks to the homesite. Hank was happy to see that the foundation had cured and was holding up. They hadn't made much of a dent for the cellar though. Not surprising with all the rain.

She pulled out the map and studied it in relation to the site. Hank slipped behind her so he could see the map and the land. Ostensibly. In truth, he enjoyed being close to her. He pointed out where a few features on the land corresponded to the drawing, and she picked up the cues quickly. He loved watching her face light up as she saw the correlation between the plants Sy had indicated on the map and visualizing where they'd be on the actual land. He followed her around as she examined each potential bed, her excitement growing.

"Hank, this is even better than I imagined. Sy picked the most perfect plants for each spot. I can see it all coming to life. Thank you so much!" She threw her arms around his neck.

Stunned at her soft body pressed against him, he waited a beat before wrapping his arms around her and gently pulling her closer, the smell of lilacs mixing with the damp of the earth.

She looked up at him, her eyes like deep pools in the forest.

He bent his head.

A door slammed.

Amelia jerked out of his arms, and he took a step back and turned. Beth Paige was standing on her front porch staring at them.

He gave her a small wave. What had she seen? Better yet, what would she tell the whole town? Had he just ruined Amelia's reputation as their schoolteacher before she'd even begun?

Chapter Sixteen

When Amelia and Emily came home from school, a large freighter was pulled around in front of the barn at the boardinghouse.

"Our things must have arrived!"

"Let me take your books so you can go see."

Amelia handed her things to Emily and hurried to the barn.

Father stood and supervised the unloading. "Just stack it over there. Leave that one on top, please." He spotted Amelia and smiled. "How was school?"

"Good. So our things have arrived?"

"Yes, but until our house is built there is no place to put anything. I've asked them to leave my medical supplies and your trunk accessible."

"Good. I'm tired of wearing the same two dresses. Though I'm sure those in the trunk will need a good airing and pressing."

"You and Maggie can work out the details. Make sure you're ready to leave first thing."

She smiled and swatted his arm. "I know when the stage leaves, Father."

The man unloading the boxes and trunks came over to Father. "Once I off-load the buggy, that's it. Does it look like anything's missing? I'll be back in a few days with a load of lumber, and I can bring it then."

"That's all of it. And the lumber is ours too. Though it'll be going to our homesite." He shook the man's hand. "I'll be glad to see you returning."

They watched the man leave. Amelia turned to Father, clapping her hands. "So many exciting things happening this week. Our things are delivered. You have a buggy now. We're going to Portland. The lumber is coming. It's going to be a good week."

"Yes, it is, my dear. I'm going to go through my medical supplies, decide which ones I need to move to my rented office space. Perhaps you and Emily can sort through your things later when I'm out of your way. I'm heading to the livery in a bit to buy a horse. Josh will allow me to house it in the barn." He kissed the top of her head then turned to his crates.

It felt like the first time she'd talked to him in ages, and he could only think about his medical supplies. Well, she'd have time with him in Portland.

Shoulders slumping, she turned and headed back to the boardinghouse. Maggie could use her help, she was sure. Plus, she needed to sort through her things, pack for tomorrow.

Up in her room, she saw Stephen's note on her dresser, the printed pastel candies spilling out. The note simply wished her a good trip and hoped that she thought about him while she was gone, with a sweet treat to remember him by. The candies said BE TRUE on them.

She sighed. Her romantic heart didn't sing at the note as it should.

Maybe it was because Hank had almost kissed her yesterday. Her heart had dropped a bit when he pulled away, and it took her a moment to register why. Beth Paige, the town gossip, was watching them. What had she seen? Would she report Amelia to Mr. Parsons for inappropriate behavior? Would Amelia lose the teaching job before it was even hers?

But Mrs. Paige had simply waved to them and asked when

the building would begin. So perhaps she hadn't seen anything. Only time would tell. That was the conclusion Amelia came to in the wee hours last night after exhausting all the questions in her mind.

She had to give Stephen an answer. Surely her heart wouldn't have anticipated Hank's kiss if she wanted to be courted by Stephen. She wished she could speak to him, but that likely wouldn't happen before she left for Portland. She didn't want him to be hurt by gossip. She could only hope nothing reached him before her return.

And then there was Hank. After their almost kiss, they headed back to the boardinghouse, conversation stilted, the topic of the almost kiss neatly avoided. Would their trip to Portland be awkward?

The elation she felt just a short while ago in the barn collapsed like a soap bubble. Maybe she'd be better off staying and helping Emily and Maggie. It would certainly be less complicated.

Two days after he'd last seen Amelia, Hank settled Prince in the barn at the boardinghouse, with Sally's promise to look after him. He helped Josh with a few things on the stage, and then they were ready to go. He realized he was stalling, avoiding Amelia. After replaying their near kiss all night last night, he couldn't rightly say if she had welcomed his attentions or was just excited over her plants. Had she thought him overstepping? If Beth Paige hadn't interrupted them, he would have kissed her. And then what? Would that have ruined their friendship?

He ran his hand through his hair. He could ask to ride up top with Josh, but James was going along, still learning the ropes from Josh. And that would seem strange since he and Amelia were friends and had talked about this trip. No, he would return to their friendship footing and see what their time in Portland revealed.

He strode into Maggie's kitchen. Maggie plied him with a cup of hot coffee and some biscuits before Josh said, "Let's head out."

He didn't see Amelia until she descended the staircase, valise in hand.

"Let me get that for you." He took her bag, brushing his fingers against hers.

She smiled. "Thank you, Hank."

They walked out to the coach, and he handed her bag to James, who was stowing baggage in the boot. Then he helped her into the stage, waited for her father to board, and climbed up behind them, taking a seat across from them. The rest of the passengers boarded, and soon Josh had them racing out of town.

"It looks to be a nice day. The sun is out." Amelia clasped her hands in her lap as they jostled along.

"I believe it will be. And not such a hot and dusty day as to make the trip intolerable." Hank smiled at her. Had they come to this, exchanging banalities about the weather?

Doc settled his hat over his eyes and leaned his head back against the seat.

Amelia grinned. "He can sleep anywhere. It's a gift for a doctor who is often up during the night."

"I would imagine so." Hank wondered how they could get the conversation to an easier rhythm. Her father might not actually be asleep and could be monitoring their conversation. Not that Hank would say anything inappropriate, though their near kiss dominated his mind.

"How are your plants doing in the greenhouse? Have you been out to check on them?" She had said Sunday that plants were comforting to her, so perhaps that was the safest subject.

Amelia's face brightened. Ah, he'd picked a good subject. "I was out there Saturday. They are doing quite well. Some are even budding. I'll have to write Sy and ask about when I can trans-

plant them safely." She reached forward and touched his arm.
"Thank you again for creating such a detailed plan for the homesite. I don't know if I thanked you Sunday, I was so thrilled with
being able to actually envision it all. Some plants I knew, some I
found in my gardening book, and some Stephen showed me in
Sy's books out at the farm. I'm hoping I can find some seeds in
Portland."

Elation at her touch followed by a stiffening at the mention
of Stephen's name. "Blake's Mercantile—owned by Seth's pa—
should have a good selection." He paused. "Stephen showed you
those when you were out there on Saturday?"

"Yes. He's been taking care of my plants, making sure they're
watered properly. I'm grateful." She looked out the window. Not
overly comfortable talking about Stephen. Why was that? He
would think she would be glowing if she were in love with the
man. On the other hand, since Hank had fairly made his feelings known by nearly kissing her, perhaps she didn't want him to
be uncomfortable. He shifted in his seat.

Her gaze returned to him. "So tell me about Portland. You've
spent some time there. What did you do there? Is that where
you're from?"

His mind jerked away from the kiss and onto the change in
subject. Why hadn't he thought this through better? He'd told
her he would show her the sights of Portland, but he had been
so consumed by her possible courtship with Stephen and then
their near kiss that he hadn't thought through what part of his
story to share. He didn't want to lie to her. If there was any
possibility of a future together, that would be a bad way to
begin.

However, he didn't want all the ears in the stagecoach to hear
his business. As noisy as it was, it wasn't likely anyone could
overhear their conversation. But her father could. And he
wanted to explain things to him as well, man to man.

"No, I'm actually from San Francisco. That's where my
family still lives. That's where I was returning from when we first

met on our last stagecoach ride." He smiled at her, and then realized something. "You're not fearful of another robbery, are you?"

"Oh no. Given the odds, I would imagine that was my one and only stagecoach robbery. Don't you think?"

"I would say that's intelligent thinking. And we are going away from Reedsville, not towards it. Not too much money flows from Reedsville to Portland."

She nodded. "So you are from San Francisco. How did you end up in Portland?"

How indeed. "I took a job there. In banking. But I found I didn't enjoy it much. I did it to please my father. What I did enjoy was building things. Back when I was in school, I met a man who taught me everything I needed to know about building." Hank settled in. This was a story he was happy to share with her.

HENRY DRAGGED his feet in the dirt as he walked home from school. If he waited long enough, maybe Russell and Clovis would already be gone and wouldn't torment him. He didn't know why Phillip's friends were so mean to him. And why Phillip didn't stop them. He was Henry's brother. Shouldn't he be sticking up for him instead of conspiring with his friends to tease him?

The repeated banging rhythm caught his attention. He perused the area and saw a couple of sticks of lumber sticking up in the air that hadn't been there when he walked to school. Curious, he darted down a side street.

As he rounded the corner of a brick building, he spotted the source of the noise. In what had been a vacant lot, a new building of some sort was sprouting up.

A man bent over a saw and cut a longer piece of wood into two smaller pieces. Then he took one of the pieces, laid it next to another, and hammered it into place. A few more times, and the man lifted the skeleton of a wall into place. With some knowledge and skill, a body could create a building where one wasn't before. He'd never thought about how buildings got there, but now he knew. It wasn't quite magic, but almost.

Henry hopped onto a wooden crate, dropping his books.

The man jerked his head up.

Henry's heart pounded. Maybe he wasn't supposed to be here. Would the man be mad?

The builder nodded. "How ya doing?" He talked around the nails that poked out of his mouth.

"Uh, good." Henry swallowed. "Don't mean to bother you. Just never saw a building go up before."

"With a strong back and good tools, a man can pert near build anything."

Henry nodded, but he'd never seen his father do anything but go into an office and read the newspaper at home.

The man waved him over. "Wanna give me a hand?"

Henry jumped off the crate. "Really?"

"Sure."

He took two steps before reaching back to snatch up his books. Then he dashed over.

The man held out his hand. "Name's Baker. Jonathan Baker."

Henry shook the rough, calloused hand. So different than his father's soft one. "I'm Henry Paulson."

"Nice to meet you. Anyone ever call you Hank?"

"Nope, but I like it." He grinned.

"Well, Hank, if you hold this board right here, I'm going to nail this brace to hold the wall in place until we get the others built."

Henry did as he was told, and the rest of the afternoon flew by as Mr. Baker explained everything he did. They were building a house to replace one that had burned down in a fire. Mr. Baker usually had a helper, but he'd decided to work on a ship heading to China.

As the day darkened toward twilight, Henry heard his name being called. Philip! Oh, Mother would be upset he hadn't headed home from school.

"Mr. Baker, I've gotta go. Thanks for letting me help."

"Sure thing, Hank. Stop by anytime. You're a good worker."

Pride bubbled up in his chest. He didn't often hear words like that. He was actually good at something. Huh. "I'll be back!" He scooped up his books and ran toward Philip, who was just rounding the corner.

"Where've you been, Squirt? Mother's worried."

"Sorry. Just helping out a friend." He dodged past Phillip and ran all the way home. Somehow, he'd figure out a way to help out Mr. Baker as much as he could.

Chapter Seventeen

The stagecoach arrived at Mrs. Vandermeer's way station for the noon meal. It wasn't as good as Maggie's cooking, but it was tasty and filling. Amelia studied the way station with fresh eyes. It was clean but small. It appeared she didn't take boarders, just provided the meal and horses for the Oregon Express. Maggie, Josh, and soon to include Emily, had truly created something special. Something that may not last much longer if the rumors of the railroad were to be true.

Hank, Josh, and James ate quickly then left to help Mrs. Vandermeer's husband switch out the horses. Once everyone had eaten and seen to their personal needs, they reboarded the stage.

Amelia settled back into her seat, grateful that this trip was a short one compared to their trip across the country. The jostling and cramped quarters, however short, were not particularly enjoyable. Her father settled back into his seat.

Hank's gaze met hers. She smiled at him. "So you learned carpentry from Mr. Baker? How long did you work with him?"

A shadow fell over his eyes. "Not as long as I'd have liked. I broke my arm, and my parents forbade me from working with him." But then his eyes twinkled. "However, I managed to still learn from him without actually working."

She laughed. "So why did you go into logging instead of carpentry?"

The shadow reappeared and then disappeared with his easy chuckle. "Seth keeps asking me that too." He shrugged. "I wanted to own my own business, doing something that involved working outside instead of behind a desk, like my father wanted. He doesn't hold with common laborers." He leaned forward, forearms on thighs. "He really wanted me to be a banker. That's what I did in Portland to appease him. And then it was my turn to do what I wanted. I have to prove to him that I can be successful at that." And only about six months at that.

"I suppose being a man is much different than being a woman. No one has any particular plans for us other than we marry well and have children. I'm fortunate that Father approves of my being a schoolteacher." She glanced at him, but he didn't so much as twitch. He must be well and truly asleep. "Or maybe not approve, but he tolerates it." She giggled. "Do you see your family much?"

"Before my most recent visit, I hadn't been home in nearly a year. San Francisco is still a fair journey. Of course it's easier with the train instead of the steam wheelers. The Pacific Ocean can get quite violent, despite its name."

"I've never seen the ocean. I would love to."

Hank's gaze grew intense. "Then I'll take you someday. It's more vast than you can even imagine." His gaze lightened. "And I know you can imagine quite a bit."

She laughed. "You know me too well. I would enjoy that."

The rest of the trip Hank regaled her with stories about Portland, places he wanted to take her such as Ankeny's New Market, the Park Blocks, and a ride on the Pacific Railway's streetcar.

She was grateful for the high-necked collar that she hoped hid the pulse ticking in her throat in excitement. Was it just the excitement of seeing the city? Or was it the man himself? She couldn't wait to spend time with Hank tomorrow. She only hoped Father approved and didn't drag her along on his errands.

As they approached Oregon City, she spotted railroad workers carving up the land, preparing the way for the railroad that would soon reach their town. What would that mean for Josh and Emily? She didn't know but worried for her friends.

There was nothing she could do however, and she was determined to enjoy her time in Portland. With Hank. And maybe sort out her feelings for him.

HANK RETRIEVED Amelia's valise as James handed it out the boot at the Oregon Express office in Portland.

"Don't wait for us." Josh handed down another bag. "You can get checked into the hotel, and James and I'll meet you at Josiah's when we're done here."

Hank offered Amelia his arm as they headed down the boardwalk eight blocks toward the hotel. Her father gave him a sharp look but said nothing, trailing behind them. A sense of rightness washed over him. He could imagine a future like this. But could she?

"Father and I stayed at Hotel Pacific when we were in Portland the first time. Are you staying there as well?"

"I thought I might." Anything to stay close to her. To prove to her father that he was worthy of her attentions.

Mr. Hanson checked them into the hotel. When he discovered they were from Reedsville, he sent his well wishes to the Blakes, Adamses, and Bensons. They deposited their bags then walked across the street to Blake's Dry Goods. The bell above the door tinkled, but that was all it had in common with Fulton's Mercantile in Reedsville. The store was about three times the size. He'd been in it before, but it had a new meaning since the proprietor was his boss's father.

Josiah came around the counter. "Hank, good to see you. How's the logging business?"

"Slow this time of year."

"To be expected."

"This is Doctor Luke Martin and his daughter, Amelia."

Josiah extended his hand. "Pleased to make your acquaintance, Doc. Amelia."

"Josh and James will be along shortly," Hank said.

"Mr. Blake, a pleasure," Doc said. "I need to restock my medical supplies, and I wonder if you might help me with that?"

Josiah nodded. "Right this way. I have several catalogues that might have what you need. Some of it I stock. I do carry some things for the local physicians in town." He guided Doc toward the store counter.

Hank turned to Amelia. "Would you like to explore the store while we're waiting?"

She nodded. "It's so big." She smiled. "I see my father and Mr. Blake have hit it off."

"Josiah has a way with everyone." Hank turned down one of the aisles, enjoying watching Amelia take it all in in wonderment. He couldn't wait to show her Ankeny's New Market tomorrow. He paid attention to the things she particularly lingered over, filing that information away. He wanted her to have something to remember this trip by. Hoping against hope that it would always bring fond memories to her recollection.

And maybe something more.

After they had toured the store and found a large number of plant seeds on her list, he guided her to the counter. "I believe Josiah has other catalogues that could help you as well."

Josiah winked and brought out a catalogue for her perusal.

While she was engrossed with the catalogue, Hank slid down to the candy counter. Today was Valentine's Day, and the store had some of the printed pastel candies that had become popular. They were called conversation hearts.

Josiah filled a paper bag and handed them to Hank with a

wink. Which made Hank think maybe he'd made a mistake. But he wanted to acknowledge the romantic day with some small gift for Amelia. And candy seemed like a small but genuine gesture.

Deciding not to think overly much about it—what was done was done—he stuck the bag in his pocket and moved back down the counter to watch Amelia make her selections in the catalogue.

He hadn't been standing there long when Josh and James entered the store.

"I insist on treating everyone to supper at the Hotel Pacific." Doc turned and addressed their small group. "Josiah, you too." He placed his hand on Amelia's shoulder. "You all have been so welcoming to my daughter and me during a difficult time of transition. I'm so grateful. It's a small token."

There were a few murmurs of protest, but Doc raised his hands. "I insist. I won't take no for an answer."

After grumbled assent, Josiah flipped the sign to closed, removed his apron, and their party made their way to the hotel restaurant. Hank was able to help Amelia into her chair, and for a moment it felt like they were courting.

Conversation was flowing easily around the table when Hank spotted Albert Ackerman from his old bank. The man didn't see him, and Hank didn't make any attempt to say hello. He didn't want to stir up any questions. But it brought to mind that he would need to speak to him tomorrow. And somehow do some poking around into who Stanley Wallace was and who he was working for. Hopefully without alerting his father.

But that would mean leaving Amelia alone. Somehow he had to figure out how to achieve both tasks. They would be here two days. Perhaps he could wait until Thursday. She knew he was here to purchase the sawmill. She wouldn't want to accompany him for that, would she? How much should he tell her?

He put all those questions aside for the evening. When they left the dining room and headed upstairs to their rooms, Hank noticed that Doc had walked ahead of them, giving him a bit of privacy with Amelia.

He handed her the small paper bag of candies. "This is for you. Happy Valentine's Day."

The gold flecks in her eyes twinkled in the gaslights of the hallway, and a smile lit her face. "Hank! How sweet of you. I don't think anyone else even noticed it was Valentine's Day."

He shrugged. "Probably not. But I wanted you to have something sweet."

"That's very thoughtful." She placed her hand on his forearm. "I'm looking forward to tomorrow."

"Me too." He held her gaze a moment. "Good night, Amelia. Sweet dreams." He winked at her before heading down the hall to his room, her soft, "You too" following him.

Chapter Eighteen

The next morning, Amelia fingered the paper bag and once again shook out the pastel candies across the dresser. All pale colors of the rainbow scattered with printed messages that said: TRUE LOVE, BE GOOD, BE TRUE, KISS ME, and BE MINE. Her mind flitted back to the note Stephen had given her Sunday with the BE TRUE candy inside. Two men, both with similar ideas. That Hank had remembered it was Valentine's Day was a pleasant surprise. She didn't expect men—unless they were courting—to remember such a day. So did that mean Hank wanted to court her? Perhaps today she would have an answer.

Stephen was sweet, and she enjoyed spending time with him. But she now knew what it was like to have a man set her heart to fluttering. She wasn't looking forward to telling Stephen that she didn't want to court him and hoped it didn't make working on her plants awkward.

Well, it was something to worry about back in Reedsville, not here. Today, she was going to enjoy seeing the sights with Hank. She picked up a candy—BE MINE—and popped it in her mouth.

She was happy her trunk had arrived in Reedsville before they left, and she had pulled out her favorite sage-green dress with golden buttons down the front. It was a long-waisted curiass bodice that fit tightly through her thighs then gathered in back and fell in ruffles to the floor. The two-tiered underskirt was cream with golden sprigs. Her flowerpot hat matched the dress and had trim to match the underskirt. It was her finest dress copied from *Godey's Lady's Book*. She had pored over it the previous winter.

She pulled on gloves and snatched up her matching reticule, dropping the room key inside. She took a quick peek in the mirror and noticed her cheeks were faintly pink.

Hank leaned against the wall outside her door. He was wearing his suit again, making him look like a dashing hero. "Good morning. I'm here to escort you to breakfast."

"Oh, that's lovely. Have you seen my father?"

"He went down just a minute ago. He said we were to join him." He didn't take his eyes off her. The look of admiration in his eyes was not one she'd seen before, and she willed her cheeks not to heat.

He offered his arm. "Your dress is quite lovely. It makes your eyes sparkle."

Now her cheeks did heat, and she studied the front of her dress. "Thank you kindly."

They joined Father in the dining room. Matthew Hanson, the son of the proprietor, waited on them and insisted that they have his mother's cinnamon rolls. As Amelia forked a bit of the hot, yeasty cinnamon-filled sweetness into her mouth, she knew Matthew hadn't steered them wrong.

Father wiped his mouth, giving careful attention to his neatly trimmed mustache and beard. "What is on your agenda for today, Hank?"

Hank shot a glance at Amelia before meeting Father's gaze. "I do have some business on behalf of the logging company, purchasing a sawmill and such. But I thought I'd show Amelia some of the sights, if you've no objections."

Father narrowed his eyes at Hank, leaning forward. It was a

look she'd seen him give particularly recalcitrant patients, meant to brook no nonsense.

To Hank's credit, he held Father's gaze.

Father gave a short nod. "Does that suit you, Amelia?"

"It does, Father. I'm looking forward to seeing the sights."

His gaze softened on her, and he nodded. "Very well. I'll see you both at supper." He placed his napkin on the table, rose from his seat, and left.

Amelia's nerves suddenly felt exposed, and she didn't know what to do with her hands. Something had passed, an understanding of sorts, between Father and Hank. Did it mean— Was Father giving Hank permission— She could hardly bring herself to finish the thought. Fearing her cheeks were pinking, she turned to Hank. "I've never tasted anything more delicious. Have you?"

He leaned toward her. "No, Mrs. Hanson's cinnamon rolls are famous." He placed his napkin on the table. "Where would you like to start today's activities?"

"Oh, I have no idea. Don't you have some business you need to do first?"

"I can attend to it later if you'd like to explore the city beforehand." His gaze on her was more intense than usual.

"Well, if you don't mind—"

"I don't mind." He grinned.

He stood and helped her from her chair. "Shall we catch the Portland Street Railway Company's streetcar? There's a stop not far from here. I thought we could ride it to Ankeny's New Market. If you thought Josiah's store was big, wait until you see this."

"Sounds lovely."

They walked down the sidewalk, the fine wool of his suit firm under her gloved fingers. Her head only came up to his shoulder, and on these unfamiliar streets—as adventurous as she purported herself to be—she was glad for his presence. They only had a few moments to wait before the streetcar arrived. He helped her board and seated himself next to her on the wooden bench. In a moment, they were off.

She gripped the edge of the seat next to her. "It does almost feel like flying. I'm glad the car is enclosed. My hat would likely blow right off at these speeds."

Hank chuckled. "I'd retrieve it for you. But it is a much smoother ride than the stagecoach. I've ridden the cable cars in San Francisco. They are open, and people hop on and off them at will as they travel up and down the hills. It's quite something."

He pointed out the window. "This is Chinatown." The tree-lined streets were crowded with buggies, wagons, and people.

She took in the oriental architecture of rounded windows, awnings, and covered sidewalks. Even the iron work had an oriental flair. She'd never seen anything like it.

Chinese men with straw hats like large, flattened cones hurried up and down the street carrying laundry, produce, and wood in tall, cylindrical baskets suspended from ropes attached to a wooden pole that they balanced across their shoulders. As passengers got on and off the streetcar at stops, the lilting, sing-song sound of their language and the smell of unusual foods cooking would waft in.

A few blocks after they left Chinatown, they disembarked the streetcar and walked to Ankeny's New Market and Theater. If she'd thought the architecture of Chinatown was amazing, the market looked like an engraving she had seen of a Renaissance palace. It had a centralized arcade lined with marbleized columns and arches supporting a high ceiling. Vendors manned stalls that ran down both sides of the arcade for as far as the eye could see. Each stall had its own counter with marble tops and carved wood fronts and was lit by a small gas chandelier. Next to the arcade, a theater marquee announced the next performance.

An exotic blend of aromas filled the air including fresh fruit, coffee, fresh bread, spices, and fish, while music played some-where in the background. Grocers displayed their wares in elegant displays: shiny piles of apples and oranges and plums, warm brown bins of nuts, baskets of fresh herbs.

She turned to Hank. "You were right. This place is simply amazing."

As they made their way around the market, Hank purchased bread, cheese, fruit, cookies, and two bottles of lemonade at various stalls, placing everything in a sack he pulled out of his pocket. "You may not be hungry now, but I do have a spot in mind you might enjoy for lunch."

"You are a man with a plan."

"I try to be."

But the most astounding section of all was the flower market. Metal buckets with flowers spilling out of them in every shade and color filled booths. Some varieties she'd never seen before, in vibrant, exotic hues. She could hardly take it all in. If she lived here, she would come every day just to witness this beauty in all its floral shapes and forms. Hank followed behind with an amused smile on his face, letting her flit from flower to flower like an ecstatic bee.

After marveling at the market and wondering what it would be like to have regular access to this market, they returned to the streetcar and rode through town. The various neighborhoods and the variety of architecture was a feast for her eyes. Her hometown in New York was a small, farming town, not terribly different from Reedsville in many ways. And while she'd seen the cheek-and-jowl houses from the train as they'd passed through Chicago, she'd never spent an entire day in such a diverse city.

They turned up Salmon Street, leaving the business district behind and heading into the residential section. The farther they went from town, the more ornate the houses became. Most were Victorian with a lot of wooden gingerbread decoration and painted with elaborate color schemes. But a few Italianate homes sat among them.

They got off at the last stop and walked a few blocks. Then

they came to a section where the grass covered the whole block, one block wide, and stretched almost as far as she could see.

"These are the Park Blocks," Hank said. "I thought we'd have our picnic here."

Amelia turned in each direction. "It's so lovely. Can you imagine having a park in the center of town? One that everyone could enjoy?"

Hank nodded. "It's something I think would be a real asset to any town. You could have festivals and concerts there. Bring the whole town together." His eyes narrowed in concentration as he scanned the area. "How about on that bench?"

As they ate their picnic, Amelia couldn't remember the last time she'd been so content. Hank had given her a perfect, thoughtful day. Warmth flowed through her, and it wasn't just from the sun which had condescended to join them today.

Hank put the remains of their picnic in the bag and stowed it behind him. He turned toward her, taking one of her hands in his, rubbing his thumb along the back. "Have you had a good day?" His gaze on her was soft and dark.

Her mouth went dry. She dropped her gaze then met his again. "I have. Thank you."

He looked at their hands. "Amelia, I wonder if I might ask you something."

"Yes?" Her heart pounded in her chest. Her corset stays might be the only thing holding it in. His golden-brown eyes were warm and liquid, and the sun brought out matching streaks in his hair. He was every inch the hero she had always imagined.

"Is there an understanding between you and Stephen O'Malley? Do you feel anything beyond friendship for him?" Hank's eyes clouded over.

Amelia hadn't thought of Stephen since this morning. "While it's true Stephen did ask to court me, I put him off, saying I needed to speak to Father about it." She squeezed Hank's hand. "I don't have any feelings but friendship for Stephen."

A weight appeared to lift from his shoulders. He gave a shaky laugh. "That's good news. While I haven't spoken to your father, I believe he understands my intentions, man to man." He raised his hand and traced a finger along her jawline. "You might be the most fascinating, curious, adventurous, and beautiful woman I have ever met." His voice turned husky. "I know I may not be the hero you've read about in your novels, but would you consider my courtship of you?"

She could scarcely believe her ears. How could she have ever dismissed him as unworthy of her attentions? She smiled. "I believe that would be acceptable." She giggled. "Oh, Hank, yes of course."

He gave a hearty laugh. "Amelia, getting to know you will be one of my great joys." His gaze darkened and dropped to her lips. A moment later, his lips were on hers, warm and sweet. His hand came around the back of her neck, pulling her closer.

Her hands crept up his suit jacket as the promise of a future swirled around them.

Chapter Nineteen

Hank joined Amelia and her father for breakfast again the next day at the hotel. But considering the narrowed glances Doc had been shooting at him, they had some talking to do. Last night, they had all had supper at Josiah's, and it was a congenial time of visiting and conversation. He and Amelia had sat on the settee, not touching. But he hadn't missed Doc's appraising gaze of them. Still, it had been one of the best nights Hank had had in a long time. He was part of this community, accepted for who he was and what he could do to help them.

"Amelia, what are your plans today?" Doc wiped his mouth and set his napkin on the table.

She glanced at Hank and then back at her father. "Hank has some business to take care of, so I thought I'd spend the morning at Josiah's perusing his catalogues for plants. And for furniture for the house, if that meets with your approval."

He nodded. "Purchase what we need and have Josiah give me the bill. Why don't you head over there now? Hank and I have business to discuss."

Her cheeks pinked as she pushed her chair back from the table. "I'll see you both later."

Hank followed her with his eyes as she left the dining room.

When he returned his gaze to the table, he found Doc staring at him.

"Am I to assume you and my daughter have an understanding?"

"I asked to court her yesterday, and she gave me her permission. We're enjoying spending time together and getting to know each other. But unless something unforeseen happens, I do plan on asking for her hand in marriage."

The doc held his gaze for a long moment then gave a small nod. "Hank, I don't know anything about your family or where you've come from."

Hank's mind reeled. What would Doc think if he knew who Hank really was? And would he feel deceived? He had made up his mind to tell Amelia everything today. He supposed her father deserved the same courtesy.

"And I don't really care. In the West, all that seems to matter is a man's character and his ability to work hard. You're respected in the community. You're a hard worker. Don't think I haven't noticed how much you have helped us with our living quarters. We couldn't have done it without you. I'm grateful."

He took a sip of his coffee and continued. "I never quite knew how to handle Amelia. She's a sweet girl with a big imagination. A bit flighty at times. She adored her mother. We both did. Since her mother died, I haven't known what to do other than work. I'm a good doctor. That's what I know to do."

He met Hank's gaze with a bit of moisture in his eyes. "If you can make her happy and provide for her, that's all I care about." He stuck out his hand. "You have my blessing."

Hank grasped the man's hand firmly. "Thank you, sir. I appreciate the faith you have in me. More than you know."

Doc nodded. "Someday I'd like to hear more about your background."

"You shall. I promise you that."

Doc pushed back from the table. "I have colleagues to visit while I'm in town and an ad to place for a nurse. I trust you'll take care of my daughter this afternoon after you've taken care of your business."

"I will, sir."

"Then I'll see you at supper." The doc turned and left the dining room.

Hank sat a moment longer, Doc's words washing over him. A man whose opinion mattered greatly to him didn't care that he was a logger, was grateful that he was a carpenter. He saw Hank's heart, and that was good enough for him. Hank wasn't sure what to make of it, but he'd treasure those words.

But for now, he needed to buy a sawmill and do a bit of research.

After finishing his coffee, Hank left the hotel and headed out to Bank of the Pacific. His old place of employment and a branch of his father's bank. This would take a bit of finessing to get what he wanted without having his father find out about it. His feet naturally found the way, allowing his mind to wander, and shortly he pulled open the carved oak doors. He entered the marble-and-mahogany lobby, searching for his friend, Albert Ackerman.

One of the tellers caught his gaze. "May I help you, sir?" Clearly someone who had been hired after Hank had left. So far his luck was holding.

"Yes, I'm looking for Mr. Ackerman."

"Right through that door, sir."

"Thank you." Though he knew the way. He walked down a short hallway and stopped in front of Albert's desk. "How are things since I've been gone?"

Albert glanced up, surprise crossing his face. "Henry! Good to see you." He stood and stuck out his hand, and they shook. Hank hid his grimace at the use of his given name. He much preferred Hank.

"What have you been up to? Rumors are that you left us for a backwoods town."

Hank glanced over the room at the other desks. A few heads

raised. He turned his back to the room. "It's a long story. I need you to set me up with a line of credit for my business."

"Certainly." He grabbed some forms from his desk. "Follow me."

They moved into the more private client-consultation area. Hank filled out the forms while trying to dodge Albert's questions. "I'm running a logging outfit in the mountains not too far from here. We need to make a capital purchase."

Albert shook his head. "Can't imagine leaving banking to go into logging."

Hank smiled. "Beats being cooped up at a desk all day. Hey, do you know a Stanley Wallace from one of the banks around here?"

"I'm surprised you don't. He works directly for your father. Heard he got sent to run a new chain of banks Bank of the Pacific just bought up. He's in the backwater just like you." Albert grinned.

"What bank?"

"Frontier."

Hank's stomach plummeted to his polished boots. That was the bank in Reedsville. And it was certainly no coincidence. Not that his father had purchased it, and not that Seth's line of credit had been closed.

"Thanks for your help, Albert. And if you don't mind, could you not mention to anyone that you saw me?"

Worry flitted through Albert's eyes, but he nodded.

Something was going on here, and his father was behind it. He just had to figure out what. Because he had no doubt that his father would do whatever it took—including ruining Hank's friends—to bring him back home.

HANK HAD TURNED over Albert's words in his mind all morning as he left the bank and ordered the sawmill. He knew his father was trying to force him to take over the family banking business. Every letter from home stated that. And he knew that Philip, while the older brother, would never be able to run it anywhere but into the ground. At least Father had sense enough to know that.

But why couldn't he let Hank make a living the way he wanted? And why should it cost his friends?

Was Stanley Wallace sent to spy on him or just make his life difficult? Maybe a little of both. Regardless, a letter to his father was in order. And he'd write it tonight. It'd get there faster from Portland than from Reedsville.

He pushed open the door to Blake's Dry Goods, the bell tinkling overhead. He glanced around. Amelia wasn't here. He nodded to Josiah, who was helping a customer.

"She's down the street at the millinery shop looking at hats," Josiah said. "I expect she'll be back soon."

"Thanks." Hank wandered the aisles. He wanted to give her something to remember this trip by. He finally settled on a porcelain dresser set with a garden scene painted on it. It was delicate and beautiful, just like she was, and he had seen her lightly run her fingers over it yesterday when they were browsing the store.

Josiah wrapped it up for him just as Amelia blew in the door, her cheeks pink and a package under her arm.

"So you found something you liked?" Hank moved to take the package from her.

She smiled. "I did. A new hat. And this morning I picked out plants and furniture. It's been a fruitful day. How did your morning go?"

"I'll tell you all about it. Shall we have something to eat at the hotel?"

"That sounds lovely." Amelia turned toward the door, and Hank stepped back as Josiah handed him his package with a wink and without Amelia seeing it.

"You two enjoy yourselves." Josiah waved.

"We will."

Once they were across the street and settled in the dining room, Hank slid the package beneath his chair. "Before I tell you about my day, I need to tell about the conversation I had with your father this morning. He asked what my intentions were, and I told him that I had asked to court you, but that my intentions were to lead to marriage." He paused, taking in Amelia's shining eyes. "He has given us his blessing."

She reached over and squeezed his hand quickly.

The waiter came to take their order, and then they continued their conversation.

"I had no doubt Father would give his blessing. He appreciates and respects you."

"It was good to hear." And to hear it again from Amelia. He just hoped what he was about to say didn't destroy that respect.

"You should know a bit about my family. Only Seth knows all of it." He wiped his hands on his pant legs, suddenly not sure what to do with them until their food came. "My father owns Bank of the Pacific. He always expected me to take over the family business, even though I'm not the oldest son. My brother, Philip, is, but he's never really applied himself to anything. Luckily, my father sees that." Though he didn't see much of anything else that Philip did.

"I worked at the bank branch here in town for a while. Our agreement was that I would work for him for one year then work at what I wanted for a year. If I was successful at what I was doing, I could continue on. But if I failed, I'd return and run the banking empire so he could retire. His health hasn't been the best and has apparently worsened."

He paused while the waiter delivered their food. He said a quick blessing then continued while Amelia began eating. "I started working with Seth when his foreman, Owen Taylor, left at the end of last summer to go take care of his mother and hopefully move her to Reedsville. I wanted to be outdoors and work with my hands. Logging seemed like a good fit. Right now, in the six months I have left to make good to my father, I could easily become Seth's partner or start my own logging outfit. I'd have a positive profit and loss statement to prove my words."

Amelia put down her fork. "So what will happen to your family's banking business if you don't return to it in six months?"

"Father has several high-level banking officers who are exceptionally capable. He could make any number of arrangements with them from buying him out to simply running the day-to-day business while he remains the main shareholder. But he is obsessed with keeping it in the family. Personally, I think it's because while Father is head of the bank, Philip has a job title and a paycheck. Even though he does little work. If Father leaves, no one in their right mind would keep Philip on. And Philip would have to learn how to work." He began eating his meal, letting his words sink in for Amelia.

"I take it you and Philip aren't close?"

He shook his head. "He's four years older, but he took a lot of delight in tormenting me. Mostly my parents turned a blind eye. That's why I enjoyed working with Mr. Baker so much. I could actually create something with my own hands."

She lightly touched his arm before picking up her fork again. "Whatever you choose, Hank, I'll support you. I don't care what you do as long as you find it satisfying."

An unfamiliar sense of peace flooded him as they finished their meal. Before they left the table, however, he pulled out the package from under his seat and set it in front of her.

"What's this?" Her eyebrows raised and a smile played on her lips.

"Just a little something to remember our trip by."

She undid the wrapping and her face lit up as the porcelain dresser set came into view. "Oh, Hank. It's beautiful." She ran a delicate finger over the painted flowers. "It reminds me of my garden back home."

"I hoped it would. I'm glad you like it."

"I love it." Her eyes shone, and she nearly wiggled in her chair. "Thank you."

"You're welcome." He loved seeing her excited and made a mental note to make it happen as often as he could.

There would be time enough to tell her what he suspected about Mr. Wallace and his father.

And that his real name was Henry.

Chapter Twenty

It was foggy when they climbed aboard the stagecoach in Portland. Father allowed Hank to sit next to Amelia. She had had a wonderful time but was ready to head home. What would life be like now that she and Hank were courting? And she would have to tell Stephen before he heard from someone like Mrs. Fulton. She was not looking forward to that. She hoped Mrs. Paige hadn't spread any news about her and Hank at the homesite.

Due to the fog, the trip was much slower. Even though she was sure the horses knew the road well, Josh had to be alert for any obstacles in the path. She was grateful that she knew him and his conscientiousness. It was reassuring.

"Are you looking forward to teaching solo starting Monday?" Hank asked.

"I am, but I must confess I'm a bit nervous. I'm glad I came to Portland, but I wish the timing would have allowed for me to teach a few days with Emily by my side."

"There's nothing to be nervous about," Father said. "You're simply teaching the basics to children who only need to learn how to read and figure sums."

Her shoulders slumped along with her heart. Once again,

Father didn't see her as competent to do anything special or important.

Hank gave her a reassuring smile. "You'll do fine. Emily said you were a natural. And you'll be making a real difference in the lives of these kids. Knowing how to read and figure sums will make a world of difference to their future options. Some may even go on to university. Plus, knowing you, you'll add some wonderful bit of knowledge that will make them excited to come to school each day."

She smiled gratefully. She was so fortunate to have a man such as Hank interested in her and be so supportive of her.

While she had been surprised at Hank's revelation about his family, it hadn't changed her perception of him at all. In fact, it heightened her respect for him. How many people would leave a life of wealth and family expectations to do what their hearts called them to do? And look how the town had benefited.

Hank had asked her not to reveal the information to anyone. He didn't want anyone treating him differently because his family had money. He had told Father the same story at supper that night when it was just the three of them. She thought Father's impression was similar to hers—increased respect for a man who chose to make his own way instead of depending on his family's money.

When they finally pulled into Reedsville, she was happy to see Emily greeting them and ushering them inside to a hot meal.

Once they were seated and eating, Amelia asked, "How was your last day teaching?"

"A little bittersweet. I'm going to miss the children, but I know that I'll see them in church and around town. And I can tutor any that need extra attention. They made me a beautiful card that they all signed and drew pictures on. It was very sweet. It's nice to know that I touched their lives in a positive way." She smiled at Amelia. "It helps that I know I'm leaving them in good hands."

"Did Maggie and Pastor Roy leave for their visiting rounds like they planned?" Josh buttered another biscuit.

Emily nodded. "They did. Left this morning even in the fog. I don't think I've ever seen Maggie ride a horse."

Josh chuckled. "It's been a long time."

Charlie pushed his plate back "Looks like the town is still planning on working on the parsonage tomorrow. Young John and I got the foundation laid, so we should be able to start putting up walls first thing. "

Hank wiped his mouth. "That's great news. So the lumber got delivered?"

"Yep. There and at Doc's house. Covered it all up with tarpaulins. We'll have to build a good bonfire tomorrow to keep warm. *Farmer's Almanac* calls for it to be chilly. I can feel it in my bones." Charlie turned to Emily. "Know where Maggie keeps that willow bark tea?"

Emily stood, gathering plates. "I'll get you some."

Amelia joined her, bringing more dishes.

Hank stood and leaned toward her, his words for her ears only. "I'll wait for you so I can say goodnight."

She smiled and hurried into the kitchen before anyone saw her pink cheeks.

Emily prepared the willow bark tea while Amelia ladled water from the reservoir into the washtub. "So I take it you and Hank got better acquainted on your trip to Portland?" Emily grinned at her.

"We did." Her face was definitely hot now. "Don't tell anyone yet, but we're courting. Father gave his blessing."

"I knew it was just a matter of time. But why the secret?"

"Stephen O'Malley had already asked me to court him before we left. I told him I needed the trip to talk it over with Father. It was because my heart wasn't in it. So I need to give him my answer before he finds out from someone else."

Emily headed toward the dining room with the tea. "Sounds like tomorrow will be a perfect day to have that conversation."

Amelia hesitated. No, she definitely wasn't looking forward to tomorrow.

THE NEXT MORNING, Amelia could see her breath as they loaded up the wagon with food and supplies. The men had already gone on to the parsonage after a hearty, warm breakfast. Seth had gone with them after dropping Becca off. She, Amelia, Emily, and Sally spent the morning cooking and baking so the food would be hot. A few times, Becca ducked out of the kitchen. Amelia smiled and wondered when they would make an announcement.

She climbed up to the wagon seat next to Sally, while Becca and Emily sat in the second seat. It would be a short trip with Sally driving, but she wished they had grabbed a blanket for their laps.

As they pulled up to the schoolhouse, Amelia was amazed at the flurry of activity. The foundation had been laid, men were digging the cellar, and skeleton walls rose in the air. The new parsonage was perpendicular and set back from the schoolhouse, nestled up against the forest, leaving a wide-open space for picnics and festivals.

Amelia's gaze found Hank. He held a hammer with ease in one hand and the plans in the other, talking to a few of the men. She watched him work, her cheeks heating at the memory of his good-night kiss on the back porch last night. As if he could sense her gaze on him, he turned and waved. She smiled and waved back.

He returned to work, and she scanned the rest of the jobsite. Stephen was also there, digging the cellar. So she could deliver her news to him if she could find the time and privacy. Luckily, he didn't spot her.

Even Father was hard at work. She had rarely seen him do physical labor, but he held a board while another man hammered. She supposed every pair of hands was welcome, and it pleased her that Father had considered himself part of the community enough to pitch in. Of course, the sooner the parsonage was done, the sooner their house could be done as well.

Sally reined in the team, and they joined the other women who had arrived and were laying boards to create makeshift tables, which got filled with food as soon as they were set up. A roaring bonfire in the middle gave a place to warm up, but many of the men had shed their jackets and rolled up their shirt sleeves.

Amelia hefted a pot of stew wrapped in a cloth to keep warm. "I'm amazed at how well everyone is working together. It's like you've done this before."

Becca grabbed several baskets of warm rolls. "We've done a few barn and house raisings. But we also had the fall festival."

"And last Valentine's Day, Cassandra organized a box supper to raise money for the school," Emily added.

They continued talking while unloading the wagon. "Those sound like wonderful ideas. The Valentine's box supper sounds romantic. Too bad that day has passed." The memory of the sweet candies Hank had given her flitted through her mind. "Perhaps I should plan something as well. Maybe an end-of-the year picnic? The children could show off their accomplishments for the year."

Emily laughed. "I think that's a great idea, but you have plenty of time to worry about that."

"You'll help me? After your wedding, of course."

"Certainly. And I can guarantee it'll end up better than the fall festival I planned."

Amelia frowned. "What do you mean?"

Emily shot Becca a glance and sighed as she closed the tailgate on the wagon. "I was kidnapped by Dillon Rogers at the end of the fall festival. He ran with the Red Dawson gang. It's a long story, but they stole some money in a payroll heist and stashed it in my bag on the ferry when I came into Portland from Seattle so they wouldn't get caught. I didn't know about it. When I found the money, I mistakenly assumed someone I knew had put it there. Once I learned the truth, I turned it in to the sheriff.

"The Rogers boys were trying to get the money back from me, and Dillon Rogers kidnapped me so I would tell him where the money was. Once he discovered I didn't have it, he was willing to turn me over to Red Dawson." Emily shuddered. "Luckily, his twin brother McKay wasn't in on the heist and was able to help me escape. But none of them was caught."

"Do you think they were behind the stage holdup that I was on?" Amelia walked with Becca and Emily toward the food tables.

"It's possible. Apparently Red Dawson lets others do his dirty work."

Beth Paige set her food on the tables, giving Amelia a smile. Was there any meaning behind it, or was she just being friendly? Mrs. Paige put her hands on her hips. "I think that Danny Tillman is running with Red Dawson. His disappearance was mighty coincidental. And then Bill Benchly was saying that it sure looked like Tim Donnally's paint at the holdup, and it could have been Danny riding it."

"How is Bill?" Emily asked.

Mrs. Paige nodded toward the building. "He's out there swinging a hammer. Looks like Doc did a great job sewing up his leg. He's still using a cane."

"That's to be expected after an injury like that," Amelia added. "There's a lot of damage to the muscle."

"Well, Danny Tillman best hope never to show his face in this town." Mrs. Paige rearranged the food on the table. "Are we about ready to call the menfolk over?"

"Looks like it." Emily caught Josh's eye and waved him over.

Josh cupped his hands around his mouth and hollered at the jobsite. "Time to eat, boys."

Hammers and saws dropped as men swarmed toward the tables like locust. Josh picked up a ladle and pot lid and banged. "Hey! Before you dig in, I know Pastor Roy isn't here, but let's ask the blessing on the food these wonderful ladies have provided." He dropped the ladle and removed his hat.

Silence descended over the crowd, and the men whipped off their hats.

"Dear Lord, we ask Your blessing on this food that has been provided for us. Bless the hands that made it. Keep us safe from harm today. And we ask a special blessing on Pastor Roy and Maggie. They've been a blessing to everyone here. Keep them safe as they minister to those in neighboring towns. In your Son's name we ask all this, Amen." Josh replaced his hat. "Let's eat!"

The men continued moving through the line. The women stepped back, other than to help replenish a dish. Mr. Parsons approached Amelia. She hardly recognized him in work clothes. "Miss Martin, may I have a word with you?" He grasped her arm and moved her a few steps back.

"Certainly." She tugged her arm free as discreetly as she could. This was not starting out well.

"I hear you spent last week in Portland instead of sitting in the classroom with Miss Stanton. I hope you take your duties seriously. This isn't some lark for you to take up whenever you please."

Blood rushed through her body as she sorted through the thoughts and words crashing through her mind. She let a breath pass. "Mr. Parsons, yes, I accompanied my father to Portland, as was his desire, and with Miss Stanton's blessing. We have worked hard on the lesson plans, which I take very seriously. I am prepared to take over the classroom Monday. You need not concern yourself on that point." Her words contained more bravado than she felt, but Mr. Parson's implications rubbed her the wrong way.

"I do hope so, Miss Martin. I do hope so." He gave her a

hard stare and then strode off to the food table. How someone as sweet as Cassandra could have a father so overbearing, she'd never know.

She moved toward the bonfire to warm her hands until the men had gone through the food line. Her father was off looking at someone's hand and hadn't made it through yet. She spotted Stephen, and he made his way toward her as he left the food line. She gave him a soft smile, her heart not in what she had to say to him. Instinctively, she sought out Hank, who was still in the food line behind Charlie Benson. He smiled and winked at her.

Stephen approached. "How was your trip to Portland?"

"It was wonderful." She gestured to his plate. "Please eat. I know you men have to get back to work."

"Thanks." He dipped a biscuit into gravy and bit into it.

"It's such an amazing city. So many sights and such diversity. I saw men from China with their cone hats balancing buckets strung on poles across their shoulders. I rode the streetcar and visited Ankeny's New Market. It truly was wonderful."

"So your father took you all those places?"

She glanced down at her apron and then up. "Stephen, I need to speak with you about…"

He swallowed. Then gave her a slow nod. "Yep. Okay. I'd better let you get some food." He moved off.

She hated disappointing people, hated that she'd made him feel bad. But it couldn't be helped. She glanced toward his bowed shoulders and then headed toward the food line.

Hank intercepted her. He nodded at Stephen. "Did you talk to him?"

"A little. He guessed. I didn't get the chance to tell him that you and I were courting. I simply said I needed to talk to him. I guess not many good conversations start out that way."

"No, I suppose they don't. Why don't you get some food before it's all gone?" He leaned in. "Beth Paige may be a gossip, but she makes a mean peach cobbler."

She smiled.

"I'll grab us seats along the foundation."

Amelia filled her plate, along with the other women and children. Even with the men's appetites, there was still plenty of food left. Because the ground was so damp, no one was spreading out blankets to sit. Many leaned against wagons and buggies, against trees, or sat along the foundation wall. She found Hank and joined him, realizing the moment she did, she was as good as announcing their courtship to the town. Well, it would happen eventually.

She searched for her father, who was talking to Bill Benchly. When he looked up, she waved him over.

He wearily eased himself down to the low wall, a plate of several desserts in his hand.

Hank leaned over. "For someone without much construction experience, you've been a big help today, Doc."

"Thanks, Hank. I think I'll need some liniment tonight for sure. My hat's off to you boys who do this for a living."

Hank grinned, and Amelia could feel the pride radiating off him at her father's words. Given what Hank had told her about his own father, she didn't expect he heard much praise growing up.

She finished off her food while Hank and Father talked about the construction on the parsonage and how it was similar to what their own house would be. She glanced around, looking for Emily, taking her cue from her as to when she should begin to help clean up.

Instead she caught Stephen's gaze. And the hurt in his eyes about brought her to her knees.

HANK WAS PLEASED that he and Doc could have a conversation about the construction project, that Doc trusted his opinion, and most of all, that Doc trusted Hank with his daughter. At the lull in his conversation with Doc, Hank noticed that Amelia had gone quiet. He followed her gaze and caught the look on Stephen's face, studying the two of them.

His gut twisted. He had no ill feelings toward Stephen and probably should have spoken to him man to man before today. But with only arriving back from Portland yesterday, there hadn't been time.

Amelia took both their plates and moved off, while he and Doc stood and headed back to work. After sitting and eating, they had started to get cold again. Work was just what they needed to get warmed up. He called Charlie and John over to go over the plans and discuss this afternoon's work. Josh, Seth, and a few of the other men gathered around as well. He handed out assignments, and the men headed toward their work.

Charlie limped away. He was trying to hide it, but it wasn't working. Clearly his pain had gotten to be too bad. Blast it. This was not what Hank wanted. He had hoped with John helping, the work wouldn't be too much for Charlie.

Hank found Doc. "Would you come with me a moment? Charlie's limping pretty badly."

Doc frowned and put down the board he was holding. "Is it a new injury?" They both headed toward Charlie.

"I think it's his old one. I didn't see him get hurt today, and no one said anything."

"I checked with Charlie before we left for Portland at Josh's request, but Charlie brushed it off as nothing."

"Yeah, he's like that. Stubborn." Hank and Doc reached Charlie, who was a bit pale and clearly favoring his leg.

Doc lowered his voice. "Hey, Charlie. I'd like to look at that leg. Want to head over to the wagon?"

Charlie hesitated then nodded.

It really must have been bad for him to agree. Hank slipped his arm casually around the man, taking on some of the weight off his bad leg. They got him to the wagon and he and Doc hoisted Charlie up on the tailgate. Doc rolled up Charlie's pant leg. The knee was red and swollen.

"Want me to grab your bag?" Hank asked. At Doc's nod, he grabbed the bag from the front of Seth's buggy they had arrived in. He also signaled Josh to come over.

When they arrived at the back of the wagon, Charlie was trying to brush it off. "I just need another poultice from Maggie. I forgot to get the recipe before she and Pastor Roy left."

"This is more than a poultice can fix." Doc pressed gingerly around Charlie's puffy knee.

Charlie clearly tried not to wince but wasn't entirely successful.

"While that could help with the pain and swelling, you have some damage to this joint that will get worse if you overwork it." Doc reached into his bag. "I'll put some salve on it and wrap it to help with the swelling, but you need to stay off it and keep it elevated until the swelling and redness goes down."

Charlie swung his gaze to Hank, apology written in it.

Hank squeezed his shoulder. "It'll be fine. Listen to the doc. We'll get things handled from here."

Josh said something to Doc and Charlie as Hank left and returned to the building site. It was important to help the town, and Charlie needed to rest his leg. John could help Hank with a lot of the work, and possibly some of Doc's patients. But Hank's presence would still be required.

An impossible choice. Help the town and be forced back into banking in six months. Or continue working with Seth and earn his freedom from family obligations. *Lord? Help me here.*

There was really no choice to be made.

He'd need to talk to Seth, but it looked like he was in the carpentry business. He clenched his fist. Now how was he going to prove to his father that he was a success?

Chapter Twenty-One

Amelia approached the schoolhouse, the key clutched in her gloved hand, her breath making puffs in the air. Her solo walk through the empty town had been thrilling and slightly terrifying. She'd be doing the teaching on her own today.

The parsonage nearly looked like a building after Saturday's effort. It was fully framed and some of the roof and siding had begun to go on. Maggie and Pastor Roy would be so surprised when they returned next Saturday. The thought made her smile.

But the crunch of frosty grass under her feet worried her. They'd had two frosts, and she hadn't been out to the greenhouse in over a week. She knew her plants were probably fine. But still, if she could check on them, she'd feel reassured.

Plus, she hadn't had her conversation with Stephen. He'd clearly avoided her the rest of the day and had headed for home before she could talk to him. She hoped he would still take care of her plants; she didn't think he was mean or vindictive. But would it be awkward for her to go out there to see them? And when would she have time?

She climbed the steps of the schoolhouse and inserted the key in the front door, turning the knob and letting herself in. She stood and took in the room. Today, this was her schoolroom. Pushing thoughts of her plants and Stephen from her mind, she got to work readying the room for her first day of teaching. *Lord, please give me the ability to teach these children well, to know what they need, and provide it for them.*

With a final look around the room, she glanced at the watch pinned to her bodice. She touched the cameo that hung from her neck. Mother would have been proud of her. She blinked back dampness in her eyes, smoothed down her dress, and went to ring the bell.

AFTER HELPING Josh with the morning chores, Hank rode over to Seth's house. It was too cold to log today, so he'd be home. Saturday, Seth had simply said that they'd discuss their plans on Monday.

Sunday, the town had gathered in the schoolhouse that served as their church, even though Pastor Roy wasn't there. It was what they used to do when he was their circuit preacher and only came on occasion. They sang hymns, and Seth read a passage of Scripture. Afterward, several of the men wandered around the parsonage and talked about what parts they could help finish up this week.

Sunday had been a quiet day after the hard work of Saturday. Emily had prepared a simple dinner with Amelia and Becca's help. Afterward, Hank had sat next to Amelia in the parlor and visited with Josh, Emily, Seth, and Becca. He noticed Stephen had left as soon as church ended. Amelia hadn't had a chance to talk to Stephen, and Hank hoped things wouldn't be awkward with her plants in the greenhouse. Well, soon as he got their house built, they could move her plants into the yard. And those that wouldn't survive in the shade, well, he was thinking of a solution for that too.

Pulling up at Seth's house, he tossed his reins over the porch railing. Seth let him in, and Becca provided him with a hot cup of coffee and left the two of them to talk in their usual spot in front of the fireplace.

"With Charlie needing to be off his leg for a while—a couple of weeks at least, Doc says—I don't have much choice other than to be more involved in the building of the parsonage and Doc's quarters."

Seth tapped his thigh. "I got a letter from Owen Taylor. He and his mother are on their way and plan to be here in a week or so. She'll need a small house as well. In the meantime, she can reside at the boardinghouse. The timing is good so you can concentrate on getting those things built. And then the sawmill should arrive, and you can get that up and going."

Hank's stomach dipped, but what Seth was saying made sense. "I'll clear my things out of the foreman's cabin, then, so he'll have his space back. I can bunk at the boardinghouse as well. No point in getting in Emily's way as she's trying to clean the cabin and get it ready to move into."

"God has a funny way of making things happen, doesn't He?"

"What do you mean?" Hank frowned.

"Just that it's like you've been kicking against the goads in regards to this carpentry work. You're clearly suited for it, and the town needs it. But you've been reluctant to take it on. Seems like this might be God's way of directing you."

Hank stared into the fire. "I guess if I had my own choice about the matter, I would choose to be a carpenter. I enjoy the work. But as I've said before, my father doesn't respect laborers." He met Seth's gaze. "My father wants me to take over the family banking business. He's not in good health, and my older brother isn't capable of running it. I made an agreement with him that I would work in banking in Portland for a year, which I did. I then would have a year to prove to him that I could be successful running my own business. Running a logging outfit like what you do or being your partner, that would be something that he would respect, even if he didn't like it."

He took a sip of his coffee before continuing. "But he hasn't had kind words for laborers. He considers them beneath him. When he found out I was working with Jon Baker, he forbade me to go back there. Just about threw the man out of his house when he brought me home with a broken arm. If I began a carpentry business, I'm not sure there's enough time or money for me to live up to my end of the bargain. I'd have to return to Portland or San Francisco and take over the family business."

"When you made this bargain with your father, did he know the specific work you were going into?"

"He didn't care. Scoffed at it when I tried to tell him the details. He was certain I'd come crawling back before the year was up."

Seth stared into the fire. "Anyone in town would consider you a success. That may not be your father's definition, and you have to work out what you think is best in regards to your family, but consider that you might still be judging yourself based on your father's standards. You might ask God what He thinks of you instead."

Hank mulled over Seth's words as he rode to the foreman's cabin and packed up his things. He hoped he'd have some time to talk to Amelia tonight after supper, though he didn't think they'd find much privacy at the boardinghouse. Still, she thought of him as a logger. It was only fair for her to know that plans had changed. Might still change significantly more.

He dropped his bag off at the boardinghouse, told Emily about the change in plans, grabbed his toolbox, then headed to the parsonage. The good thing about this was that he'd be able to walk Amelia to school each day and maybe even have a noon meal with her. Perhaps there was a silver lining in this cloud. His step was certainly lighter than he would have expected given he'd just lost the job that could have won him his freedom from his family's expectations.

A RUMBLE in her stomach caused Amelia to look at the watch pinned to her shirtwaist. Almost noon. No wonder she was hungry. The morning had flown by. "Children, close your books. Grab your lunch pails." The room erupted in the slamming of books, boots on the floor, and the chatter of children. Over it all was the distinctive ringing of a hammer. Someone was working at the parsonage. She hoped it would be even further along by the time Pastor Roy and Maggie returned.

It wasn't raining, so it would be good for the children to run off some energy before the afternoon lessons. "After you eat and put your things away, you can play outside. Do not go near the parsonage, however, or touch anything that has to do with the work site."

The boys inhaled their food while the girls sat talking and giggling in groups, playing with yarn or jacks. Amelia tucked into her own lunch pail at her desk, opening one of the books Cassandra had loaned her, *Sense and Sensibility* by Jane Austen.

When she had finished eating, she peeked out the window to make sure the boys weren't bothering the work site. She angled to see who was working on it. Though his back was turned to her, she'd recognize his form anywhere. Hank. Her heart ticked up. She glanced at the watch; there was still plenty of lunchtime left. She slipped on her coat and headed outside.

Hank spotted her descending the stairs and grinned. "Howdy, teacher," he said as she got close enough. "How's the first day?"

"It's going well." She scanned the area. The boys were playing tag and staying away from the parsonage. "I told the boys not to bother the site."

"They've stayed away. John will be joining me soon." He glanced around. "I'll be here every day the weather permits until it's done. Then I'll move on to your quarters."

"Because of Charlie?"

"That and Owen Taylor will be back soon to help Seth." A shadow passed over his face, and then he grinned. "I'm now staying at the boardinghouse with you all. I can walk you to school and carry your books."

She smiled back. "That's most kind of you. I have to get back inside, but perhaps we could give the children a tour of the parsonage at some point, and you could explain some of the science behind the building. The same things that attracted you as a boy."

"I'd like that. Let's talk more about it tonight."

With a soft smile and a wave, she turned and headed inside. Comfort settled over her shoulders like a warm blanket knowing he was outside. But if he was no longer working as a logger, what did that mean for his future? And hers?

WHEN AMELIA TOLD the children to put their books away for the end of the school day, she barely suppressed a sigh of relief. It had gone well, and the children had listened to her. Emily's lesson plans had been a godsend since she knew what to do for each hour of the day. At some point, she'd be ready to add her own touches and activities, once she felt comfortable. It was only the first day, she reminded herself. She didn't need to get too far ahead.

She told Sally and James they could head home without her. They had chores to do. She had straightened up the room and slipped on her coat, when the schoolhouse door opened, and Hank slipped in.

She smiled.

"Came to walk the teacher home." He reached for her books and lunch pail.

"Are you done working for the day?"

"John has it covered, and a few men were planning on joining him. I have a few things to attend to." He waited while she locked up, then took her arm as they descended the stairs and headed down Main Street.

"I wanted to stop by Father's new temporary office on the way home." Walking and talking with Hank felt like the most natural thing in the world. And now that he was staying at the boardinghouse, they'd have more time to get to know each other.

"That was one of the things I wanted to attend to. See if he needed help with those crates."

They found his new office on Center Street, just around the corner from their homesite. The door stood open. It was one bare room, stacked with partially opened crates. His desk and chair had been unpacked, and books were piled in a row along the wall. Father was bending over another crate.

"Looks like you've been busy." Amelia stepped inside.

Father straightened. "Amelia. Hank. How was the first day of school?"

"It went well. How are things going here?"

"It's not much but it will do for now. A place to hold my books and supplies and for patients to find me. I can't keep using Maggie's parlor as a waiting room." He smiled, but it didn't quite reach his eyes. Perhaps he was more tired than he wanted to let on.

"Anything I can help with, Doc?" Hank stepped forward.

"I could use your strong back." The two of them muscled a crate around the floor, opened it, and began removing the contents.

Amelia watched, pleased that Father seemed to enjoy Hank's company. For the moment, at least, all seemed right in her world. "I should leave you to your heavy labor." She smiled. "I need to hurry to the boardinghouse and tell Emily about my day, plus see if she needs any help with supper."

Both Hank and Father looked at her. Indecision clouded Hank's eyes.

"Hank, you stay here and help. I can find my way back to the boardinghouse." She gave a saucy grin and picked up her books and lunch pail from where Hank had set them.

His gaze said he wanted to say more, but he simply nodded. "We'll be along for supper, then."

She stopped at the mercantile before heading home. She had written a note to Stephen last night. While she'd have preferred to talk to him in person, she didn't know when that would be since she'd tried on Saturday and Sunday. So a letter it would have to be. She had explained as best she could about Hank and her appreciation for all Stephen had done for her plants and that she hoped he would still continue to care for them and allow her to check on them from time to time. It was the best she could do. She left the letter with Mrs. Fulton and headed to the boardinghouse.

When she entered the kitchen, Emily was at the cookstove. "How was your first day? I want to hear all about it."

"And you will. Just let me put my things away, and I'll tell you as I give you a hand with supper." Amelia put her books upstairs and came back to the kitchen and pulled on an apron. She told Emily all about her day, including Hank's appearance. "Thank you for creating such complete lesson plans. It was like you were there holding my hand. How was your day?"

Emily laughed. "Well, I spent it trying to keep Charlie off his feet. I headed to Josh's cabin to give it a good top-to-bottom cleaning, and I found Charlie trying to head out to the workshop. I managed to persuade him to give his leg a couple of days' rest under the guise of needing to know where things go in the cabin. I don't think he was convinced, but it was a fabrication that allowed him to keep his pride intact."

They had a full supper table that night. Amelia sat next to Hank but it wasn't until the supper dishes were done that they had a moment alone in the kitchen while everyone else was in the parlor.

She put a few cookies on a plate for them to share. "Thanks for helping Father with his office. I'm sure he appreciated the help."

"Happy to. We got it all set up and functioning. I think it

was a relief for him to have some sort of office space, even if it was only temporary. Especially since he ordered more supplies in Portland."

"It will be nice having you around the boardinghouse more."

He grinned. "It'll be good to be here."

"So does it mean that you are done with logging?"

"I hope not. Right now the plan is for me to get the parsonage and your house done, get the sawmill up and running, and then see where we're at." His gaze dropped to the table, and he fiddled with his cup handle.

"Will you still be able to prove to your father that you are successful?"

"That is the question." He tapped the table. "Seth and I discussed it a bit today. He gave me some words to chew on. But I know you thought you were courting a logger. Being a carpenter is a different thing. And if I have to go back to being a banker, life could look very different."

Amelia covered his hand with hers. "Hank, I chose *you*. Not what you did for a living. I do love living here in Reedsville. I don't know if I would enjoy big city life as much, even though I find it adventurous and fascinating to visit. Still, that decision is down the road. I can't believe your father wouldn't consider you a success and let you do what you're good at."

He shook his head. "That's because you have had loving parents. You can't understand what it's like living under the obligation of a family name and wealth." He squeezed her hand back then stood. "I think I'm going to turn in." He gave her a soft smile but his eyes were troubled.

And he didn't try to kiss her goodnight before he headed up the stairs.

Chapter Twenty-Two

After a day of rain yesterday, the children seemed particularly restless. She had to raise her voice several times to get the girls to stop talking and the boys to settle down. She needed to come up with some physical options for learning on days like this. Only one more day this week.

They could at least stand while they did their lessons. She lined them up—boys on one side of the room, girls on the other—and had them volley spelling words back and forth, the older ones coaching the younger.

"Ow!" Eleven-year-old Dahlia Drake flinched and rubbed her cheek. She looked around and picked up a tiny wad of paper off the floor. "Someone hit me with this."

The boys giggled. Amelia studied their faces, trying to determine the perpetrator. "That's enough. Flossie, the next word is yours. Bicycle."

Amelia glanced down at the spelling word list for the next word, and two more girls cried out. She shot a look at the boys. Both Jospeh Spitzky and Robert Reinfeld had their hands behind their backs.

She strode over in front of them. "Hand them over."

Joseph shot a look at Robert then reluctantly handed over

his pea-shooter straw. "Go sit down and write a letter of apology to the girls you hit."

"What?" But he shuffled off to his desk, flopping into it with great flair.

"Robert, now yours."

He grinned at her. "I don't know what you're talking about, teacher."

Considering he was bigger than her by almost a head, she couldn't physically take it from him. She couldn't make him do anything.

Robert turned around from his desk, snickering. Other boys did too. If she didn't get control over this situation, she'd lose the respect of all the students.

Hank was working again at the parsonage. Too bad she couldn't ask him to give the boys a talking to. They would respect a male.

However, this was her classroom. "Everyone, take your seats. Since Robert and Joseph have ruined the fun for everyone, they can stand up by the blackboard and write out their lessons." She turned to both of them. "And for homework, letters of apology to all the girls you hit, signed by your parents so I know they've seen them."

She returned to her desk and sat, stifling a long exhale. Robert and Joseph ambled up to the blackboard, but based on the giggles coming from the class, they surely weren't doing their lessons up there. But she chose to ignore it and focus on the students who wanted to learn. She glanced at her watch. Only two hours to go.

As she called the third-grade readers to stand, Robert tossed down his chalk and walked to his desk.

"You haven't finished your work."

"Don't care." He grabbed something from his desk, headed to the back, and grabbed his coat.

"Robert! School's not out yet." She couldn't physically stop him, and the sense of powerlessness was overwhelming.

"It is for me." The door slammed shut behind him.

Tittering swept through the room.

"You all still have work to do." She glanced at the blackboard. A cartoon drawing of what she imagined was supposed to be her festooned one corner of the board. Joseph had partially answered one question. She suppressed a sigh and began composing a note to their parents.

She was sure word would get to Mr. Parsons about how she hadn't been able to keep one of her students from walking out. She couldn't maintain control of her classroom. Would other students follow suit?

Why had she even thought she would be good at this?

HANK WAS BACK at the parsonage with John after the rain delay. John was a quiet worker, which left Hank alone with his thoughts most of the time. They worked in a rhythm: lifting a board, measuring, cutting, nailing, repeat.

He hadn't been able to get Seth's words out of his head. Yes, he had an agreement with his father, but why would his father's definition of success be the only one that mattered? If Hank was happy and able to provide for himself, and potentially a family, shouldn't that count?

It should, but he couldn't seem to quite wrap his mind around it. What if his father got so upset he forbade Hank to set foot in their house? Could he stand not seeing his family again? What would it do to his mother?

Hank was convinced that Stanley Wallace was sent by his father to spy on him. Why else would he buy up Frontier Banks? Hank wasn't surprised. Father had always used questionable tactics to get the upper hand on his competition. So that must make Hank the competition. But closing Seth's line of credit was a pretty low thing. He hadn't heard back from his letter to his father. Not entirely surprising, but he was curious, even a bit

anxious, as to what his father would say to Hank's finding out
about Stanley. Which reminded him that he hadn't even told
Amelia yet about Stanley. There'd be time enough to tell her
when he heard back from his father.

A lot of questions and not a lot of answers. He stretched his
back. He and John should be able to get the parsonage watertight today with the rest of the siding up. Then they could work
inside even when it did rain. There was certainly something
satisfying about seeing the proof of a hard day's work right in
front of you. The progress seemed slower at this point, since it
wasn't as dramatic as walls going up. And the finish work would
take even longer. But perhaps by that time Charlie would be able
to help, since his finish carpentry skills were the best in town.

He glanced toward the schoolhouse. What was Amelia doing
right now? How was her day going? He loved her ability to see
the adventure in every situation. She wasn't afraid to strike out
on something new, a trait they both shared, and one that was
helpful in a small frontier town. The way her eyes danced and
those cute freckles dusted across her nose—

"Hank?"

He jerked his head up.

John gave him a questioning look.

"Did you say something?"

"Yeah, I wanted to know if you were ready to cut the next
group of boards."

Hank dropped the end of the board he was holding. "Yeah. I
want to get this house watertight today." He glanced over at the
schoolhouse again. It didn't matter what his father said. He and
Amelia were going to build a life together; a life they wanted.

As the last student left the schoolroom, Amelia let out the
breath she felt she'd been holding all afternoon. She sank into
her chair as the doubts she'd fought to keep at bay assailed her.

She'd lost control of her classroom, a student had walked out, and it was only the first week of teaching.

As soon as Mr. Parsons heard, he'd surely fire her. And she'd be a disappointment to her father yet again. She wasn't able to step up and do what needed to be done. She was weak and a failure. Just like when Mother died.

Tears welled up and she blinked them back. No crying. Ever. They were shameful and accomplished nothing. Mrs. Mason's words rolled through her mind from the day Mother died. They only kept one from thinking clearly. She looked toward the ceiling, but the tears persisted and overflowed, running down her cheeks. Great wracking sobs shook her, and she could barely catch her breath. She had to get herself under control, but she couldn't. She was at the mercy of the tears that had been bottled up since the day Mother died.

She put her head on her desk and let the tears flow.

SPENT FROM HER TEARS, the sleeves of her dress soggy, she raised her head and searched for her handkerchief in her reticule. She wiped her face and nose. She must look a sight. She attempted to repair her appearance in case Hank came looking for her. From the steady sounds of construction coming from the parsonage, she was guessing that he was too busy to walk her home today. And for once, she was grateful. She needed the time to gather her thoughts and compose herself before arriving at the boardinghouse.

The door opened, and her heart sank. She hoped she had repaired her appearance enough.

Hank walked down the aisle, his boots echoing through the empty room. He grinned. "Working late?" Then his smile disappeared, and his brow furrowed. "What's wrong? Bad day?"

She shook her head and forced a smile. Her feelings were too raw and tender to be exposed right now. She couldn't break down in front of him. She waved her hand. "I'm fine. There's no problem."

She made to stand, but he pulled over the other chair and sat next to her. "You're not fine. Tell me what happened."

Her lip trembled. "Oh, it's ridiculous. I don't know why it's bothering me so much." But she poured out the story of Robert and Joseph's antics and Robert's early departure from the schoolroom. "I sent home a note to Robert's parents with his younger sister Clara explaining what happened today and asking for them to talk to their son about what was expected from him in the schoolroom."

Hank nodded. "Perhaps that will help. Often a boy thinks he's getting away with something, and will continue until he faces consequences." A quick shadow flitted across his face and then was gone. "Hopefully, his parents will set him straight." He touched her arm. "But is that all that is bothering you?" His voice lowered, becoming something like a caress. "I've seen you survive a stagecoach robbery without as much emotion. Is there something else?"

She swallowed. She'd never told a soul about the day Mother died.

AMELIA LEANED against the maple tree, the bark ridges rough through her cotton dress, listening to Mother's voice. She loved this tree because it gave them maple sap that Mother boiled down into syrup, the first sign that the long New England winter would soon come to a close. It also produced the prettiest leaves in the fall. But most of all, it was where she and Mother would read books on summer afternoons like today, when the house was too stifling.

They were reading through *Little Women*. Right now it was her favorite book because she could imagine that she had sisters like the March girls did. And their father was often gone helping others, just like hers was.

Mother coughed, and Amelia looked up. Was it a regular cough or a bad cough?

Mother swallowed and then reached over to squeeze Amelia's hand. It must be a regular cough. She began reading again but didn't get far before Mother cleared her throat. After a few more coughs, she closed the book. They hadn't even finished the chapter.

"Let's go inside." Mother's voice was strained. She pushed to her feet, seeming to glide up.

Amelia hopped up next to her and took her arm. Mother's grip seemed tighter than usual.

The coughing started again, forcing them to pause on the way back to the house. Mother let go of Amelia's arm and rested it on her shoulder. Should she run inside and get the water boiling or wait here with Mother? What was the right thing to do? And she didn't want to make Mother talk by asking her.

Mother was able to catch her breath between coughs, and they moved to the house. She collapsed into a kitchen chair, dropping *Little Women* on the floor.

Amelia hurried to pull the teakettle over the burner. It was too light. She opened the lid. Empty.

Mother glanced up at the grating of metal over metal. Her face was pinched. It got that way when she had a bad lung attack.

Amelia's stomach fluttered. She wished Father were here. He was a doctor and knew how to help people. He was always helping people. She grabbed water from the reservoir on the stove, slopping it across the stovetop in her haste. Once the kettle had enough water, it only needed to heat up.

She dashed into the front parlor and through Father's office door, opening up the cabinet that held the peppermint and eucalyptus oils. She grabbed them, knocking something else in the process. The bottle shattered. She froze. Father would be upset. Should she clean it up? But Mother needed the oils.

She ran back through the house clutching the oils.

Mother was leaning over the table, a wheezing sound coming from her, lips tinged blue. This was a bad one. Where was Father? She'd never been alone for one of Mother's bad episodes before. She thrust a bottle at her, but Mother just shook her head.

Amelia twisted off the top of one bottle and held it under Mother's nose.

Mother jerked back but nodded.

The teakettle whistled.

She left the bottle open on the table and went over to the shelf where the big basin sat. She couldn't reach it, so she dragged over a chair and climbed on it. Her fingers grabbed the cool edge and pulled it toward her until she could wrap her hand around it. Gripping the basin, she climbed down and set the basin on the dry sink. Grabbing a cloth, she lifted the teakettle up and poured the steaming water into the basin. When it was nearly full, she carried it to the table, sloshing hot water on her sleeves and down the front of her dress. It burned, and she sucked in her breath. But she didn't cry out. Mother needed her.

She slid the basin in front of Mother and dumped in the oils. She didn't know how much to add. She draped the dish-cloth over Mother's head like she'd seen Father do, trapping the steam that came off the basin.

But Mother didn't seem to be getting better. Tears welled in Amelia's eyes. What should she do? Where was Father? Who could help them?

"Hello?" A voice called from the front parlor.

Amelia ran in there. Mrs. Mason stood looking around. Amelia grabbed her hand and pulled her to the kitchen. "Help. Mother can't breathe, and Father's gone!"

"Julia?" Mrs. Mason came into the kitchen and clucked her tongue. "Amelia, did you make this mess? Clean it up so your mother doesn't have to." Mrs. Mason sat next to Mother and talked to her, helping her.

Amelia grabbed the rag, but tears filled her eyes, and she couldn't make her feet move.

Mrs. Mason looked up. "Stop your tears. They're shameful and accomplish nothing. Do you want to help your mother? Run next door and send one of my boys after your father. Do you know where he is?"

Amelia shook her head and ran for next door, sobs wracking her chest, making it hard to breathe. She could hardly get the words out when Matthew opened the door. She ran back to her house, but this time to the backyard, under the maple tree.

Which was where Father found her that night. To tell her that Mother had died.

HANK PULLED Amelia close to him, wrapping his arms around her shoulders and letting her cry against his chest. He'd like to have a few words with Mrs. Mason. Who said such a thing to a child? He could tell Mrs. Mason's words carried far more weight than they should have. And that Amelia blamed herself in some way for her mother's death.

At some point, he'd like to talk to her father about what really happened. Perhaps he had information that would ease Amelia's burden of guilt. An adult perspective. Even from Amelia's story, he could tell that her mother had a chronic illness, and there was nothing Amelia could have done, even if she'd been older.

As her sobs quieted, he handed her his handkerchief. She dried her face, and he eased her away from him. He went to the bucket of water in the corner, getting a dipperful for her.

She gave a watery smile and dipped the handkerchief in it, wiping her face, before taking a swallow. Her eyes were swollen and her face blotchy, but he thought she'd never looked more beautiful. He wanted her to share her memories so he could show her that she was safe with him.

He kissed her forehead. "Thanks for telling me. I know it wasn't easy."

She nodded. "I just wish I could have done more. And even now, I sometimes see a look in Father's eyes, like he's disappointed in me. And then today, another failure." Her voice cracked at the end, but she swallowed.

"Hey, I don't think that's true. I've talked to your father about you, remember? He loves you and thinks you're adventurous. He's not disappointed in you. In fact, he's very protective of you." He lifted her chin with his finger. "I promise, I'm telling you the truth."

She nodded, but still looked unconvinced. He'd talk to Doc and straighten it out. She'd need to hear it from her father himself.

She glanced at her watch. "Oh my, I'd better get back and help Emily. She'll be wondering where I've gotten to." She pushed to her feet.

Hank gathered her books and lunch pail then offered his arm. "I bet Emily will have some words of wisdom for you. She knows these students, and she wants to help you."

Their walk home was fairly quiet. While Hank hated to see Amelia distressed, he was pleased he could share it with her. She'd spent too much of her life alone.

"I can't help but think what my mother would have done." Amelia looked up at him.

"She taught school?"

"No, she was never well enough, though I think she would have liked to. But she had a way of charming all the neighborhood children. Even the rascally ones. How would she have handled Robert?"

"Robert is responsible for his own behavior. He chose to act badly. That's not your fault, and there's likely nothing you could do about it."

They rounded the boardinghouse, and Hank held the kitchen door for her.

Emily was at the stove. "How was your day?"

Amelia didn't stop. "I'll tell you when I get back downstairs."

Emily turned to Hank with raised eyebrows.

He shook his head. "Not a good day. She'll tell you the details, but Joseph Spitzky and Robert Reinfeld acted up in class, and Robert walked out."

Emily shook her head. "I'd hoped they'd give Amelia a bit more time before acting out."

Amelia came downstairs tying on her apron. She told Emily the tale.

Emily shoved a roast into the oven. "I've had my share of trouble with both of them. Robert seems to want attention, and Joseph just follows along. I ignore them both as much as possible. I've spoken to both of their parents. Robert's father doesn't see much value in schooling, but his mother does." She dropped into a kitchen chair, motioning them to do the same. "If Robert doesn't want to learn, you can't make him. In fact, it's better if he stays away so he's not a distraction to the other children."

Amelia's eyes widened. Hank didn't think she'd considered the possibility of asking Robert not to come to school. But he could see the value in it, and he'd back up Amelia if it came to that.

"On a brighter note." Emily smiled. "Mrs. Parsons paid a call today looking for your father."

"She's not sick, is she? Did you send her to his office?"

"No and yes." Emily smiled. "She wanted to let you both know that she and Mrs. Fulton are throwing a reception to welcome you and your father to town. It will be Saturday at the hotel, and the whole town is invited."

"Oh." Amelia's eyes went wide. "With just a few days' notice? And why us?"

Emily laughed. "Oh, we don't need much notice or much of an excuse to get together. Those two ladies would like us to act more like a sophisticated town than we actually are. But it is fun to come together. And I think they want to make sure that you feel properly welcomed to town."

Amelia glanced down at her hands. "They might think twice about having me for a teacher once they hear about today."

Emily clasped her hand over Amelia's. "Nonsense. Keep your chin up. It will be fine."

Hank smiled. "That's what I keep telling her."

"See? We're in agreement. Now, tonight after supper, let's figure out what we're going to wear."

Hank sat back and sipped coffee, watching the women chat. The sadness had slipped off Amelia at Emily's insistence. She was a good friend to Amelia. Though if she were a better friend to him, she'd have let him and Amelia have some alone time tonight instead of planning dresses. Maybe he'd get a chance to talk to the Doc about the day Amelia's mother died.

Chapter Twenty-Three

❧❦❧

The day of the town reception was a rainy one. Emily had insisted Amelia wear the sage-green dress she wore in Portland. And when she saw Hank's eyes and the memory of their day together in Portland surfaced, she knew it was a good choice.

Seth and Becca were picking up Emily and Amelia in the buggy. They'd squeeze Sally in too. But Josh, Hank, Father, and James would brave the weather in the open wagon. Charlie was staying home close to the fire. His leg had gotten better, and he'd been in his woodshop working on his secret projects because he didn't have to move too far and could sit if he needed to.

Seth pulled up to the front of the hotel and hopped down, hurrying around the buggy to help Becca down.

"You don't need to do that," Becca protested.

"I think I do. Don't want you slipping." He made sure she was steady on her feet before hustling her under the covering.

Emily and Amelia got themselves down, but Amelia thought it was sweet how considerate Seth was being of Becca.

The three women entered the hotel while Seth took care of the horses and buggy.

The hotel was lit with more lamps, candles, and chandeliers

than Amelia had ever imagined existed in this town. They turned the lobby and dining room into a warm, glowing atmosphere. The dining room had been cleared of tables, except for several along the wall that held food, a cut-crystal punch bowl, and a silver tea and coffee service. It was hard to imagine this was a small town at the end of the Oregon Trail. And she couldn't help but feel a bit disingenuous that all of this was being done for her benefit. Hers and her father's. Perhaps her father far more than her. Especially after her handling of the schoolroom this week. She needed to get through the evening without anything embarrassing happening.

Mrs. Parsons spotted her and took her elbow. "Welcome, Miss Martin. Is your father with you?"

"He'll be along shortly."

"Good. I think you probably know most people, but let me introduce you around."

Amelia glanced over her shoulder at Becca, who smiled, and Emily who gave a tiny wave. They were going to be no help. She pasted on a smile and listened to Mrs. Parsons as she nodded and introduced Amelia to everyone as they made their way around the room.

"Have you met Mr. Stanley Wallace? He's our new banker."

The thin man with a finely made suit that looked out of place took her gloved hand and bowed over it like a gentleman out of a Jane Austen novel. "I certainly haven't had the pleasure, Miss Martin."

She nodded. "Pleased to make your acquaintance." She gave what she hoped would pass for a genuine smile and discreetly tugged her hand free.

"Oh, may I leave you in Mr. Wallace's capable hands? I've spotted your father." Mrs. Parsons glided off in her watered-silk gown.

Mr. Wallace smiled at her. "I hear you are the schoolmarm. I must say, if I had a schoolmarm that looked like you, I would have paid more attention in school."

"But you must have paid some attention in school since you are now a banker." She gave him a polite smile and tried to scan the room without appearing too obvious. If Father was here, then Hank should be too.

He tilted his head in acknowledgment. "But who knows what greatness I could have achieved with even more attention to my lessons."

She resisted the urge to roll her eyes. "How do you find our town?"

"It has its charms." His lips thinned, and then his gaze narrowed. "Some of which I was previously unaware."

An unpleasant chill raced up her spine. Her mind reeled for a polite way to extricate herself from this increasingly uncomfortable conversation. A touch at her elbow caused her to turn. Hank. Relief loosened the knot in her stomach.

"Amelia, there you are. Looking lovely as usual." Hank's smile and the light in his gaze sent warmth through her.

"Thank you. I see you didn't get too wet on the ride over."

"A good rain slicker and hat are worth their weight in gold. Wouldn't you agree, Wallace?" Hank nodded in Mr. Wallace's direction, but his gaze had definitely chilled.

"Oh, so you two have met." Amelia looked between the two men. "Of course you would have with your business dealings."

Hank opened his mouth, but Mr. Parsons appeared at Hank's elbow.

Mr. Parsons shot Amelia a cold gaze before turning to Hank. "I need your expert opinion on something. There are a few railroad representatives here tonight that I'd like you to meet." He pulled Hank's arm.

Hank gave Amelia a pleading look. "I'll be back as soon as I can."

By Mr. Parsons's glare, it sounded as if he'd heard about what happened in her classroom. Perhaps she could avoid him tonight, especially if he was concerned with the town's involvement with the railroad. But for now, she was stuck with Mr. Wallace. Wasn't there anyone who could rescue her?

Another woman approached them with a warm smile. "Miss Martin, I'm Mrs. Drake, Flossie and Dahlia's mother." She reached out and took both of Amelia's hands in hers. "Thank you so much for taking over the schoolroom. We love Miss Stanton, but we are delighted with your teaching as well. The girls just adore you."

Amelia smiled, feeling a bit of the tension leave her shoulders. "Thank you. Your girls are a delight to teach. They are good students and eager to learn." She indicated Mr. Wallace. "Have you met Mr. Wallace, our town banker?"

Mrs. Drake's smile faltered. "How do you do?"

Mr. Wallace nodded. "A pleasure."

"Well, I just wanted to tell you how much we value your contribution to our little town. Enjoy your evening." Mrs. Drake moved off.

Amelia took a breath. Hank was engrossed in a conversation with Mr. Parsons and several other men. Mr. Wallace still hadn't left her side. She pasted on a smile. "And where did you come from before arriving in our town?"

"Portland. Quite a charming town."

"Yes, I think so too. I was there recently. I enjoyed my visit. My father, Mr. Paulson, and I made the trip last week." Perhaps mentioning Hank's name would chill Mr. Wallace's interest. "We toured Ankeny's New Market and the Park Blocks. The streetcar was a wonderful ride. You must have enjoyed living there."

Something shifted in Mr. Wallace's gaze, but he remained steadfast in his attention on her. "I did. I hope to return again someday."

"Well, it's not a far trip on the stagecoach."

"Infernal contraptions." He grimaced. "I'll be grateful to see the railroad come to town."

Amelia's stomach twisted. While she agreed that railroad travel was more comfortable, she didn't want to see Josh and

Emily lose their business. Luckily, several other townswomen approached her, mothers of her students. They introduced themselves, invited her to supper, and said how much they were pleased with her teaching. "Our children don't have a lot of opportunities. Many of us never learned to read or write much. So we're pleased you're helping our youngsters have a better life." This from Mrs. Parker.

Mr. Wallace had been forced to the side by the women, but he hadn't left. Surely he had more interesting people to visit with? She would make her excuses and find her father. He'd been sorting things at his office all day.

"Excuse me, but—"

"Miss Martin." Mr. Parsons strode up. "I would have a word with you." He glanced at Mr. Wallace. "In private."

Was this her salvation, or was she out of the fire into the frying pan?

HANK GLANCED OVER HIS SHOULDER. Parsons had made his way back over to Amelia. He clinched his fist. He wanted to be by her side and defend her over whatever ridiculous thing Parsons would say to her. But the two railroad men needed his attention. They had plans to use Reedsville as their base while surveying the railroad route through this area and wanted to know how soon he could build them quarters that would also serve as an office. Seth's words about God's ways drifted through his mind. Sure seemed like God was providing plenty of carpentry work.

Wallace was still by Amelia's side, which both grated and reassured Hank. Surely Parsons wouldn't be so rude as to castigate her in front of someone else? At the same time, what was Wallace's continued interest in Amelia? Did he know Hank was courting her? Had he reported it to his father? He needed to find out what Wallace knew.

He turned his attention back to the men. "How long will you be in town? There are a few places I'd like to show you, and I could get some ideas down on paper."

"We leave Tuesday on the stagecoach." The tall one, Jeremiah Crowley, grinned at the apparent irony.

"Let's meet at the hotel Monday morning, then." Hank shook their hands again and made his way over to where Amelia had been. Wallace was still there, though. Parsons must have dragged Amelia off somewhere. He wasn't sure if that was good or bad. He glanced around but couldn't spot them. The room was crowded. Looked like nearly everyone from town was here.

In the meantime, he'd see what Wallace knew. He stepped over to the man. "Did you see where Miss Martin went?"

Wallace gave him a smile that almost passed for a sneer for a split second. "I believe she's talking with Mr. Parsons." He paused. "I heard you had a trip to Portland last week. How did you find the town?"

Hank stared at him. "Informative."

"Hmm? In what way?"

"Hank, could you join us?" Pastor Roy appeared, Maggie by his side. They must have returned from their visiting. "We want to thank you and the others for all the work on the parsonage you've done. It's far more than Maggie or I ever expected.

Maggie's eyes brimmed bright with tears, a smile filling her face. "You took my thoughts and ideas and made them even better than I could have dreamed."

Hank scuffed his boot on the carpet. "Aw, I'm happy you like it. The whole town helped." Stories of the workday floated around. He scanned the crowd, looking for Amelia. He spotted her coming from the back corner of the lobby, her face pale.

"Excuse me." He left the crowd surrounding Maggie and Pastor Roy and headed to Amelia. "What happened?"

"Mr. Parsons heard about my inability to handle the classroom, as he put it, and has placed an advertisement to search for another teacher." She lifted her chin and blinked.

He rubbed her arm. "I think Emily will tell you about how well that turned out last time he tried that."

She nodded. "Let's find my father. I don't want to think about it during what is supposed to be a party."

He took her elbow and guided her through the crowd when there was a tap on his shoulder. He turned. Wallace.

The man shoved his hands in his pockets as he grinned. "Just wanted to say nice chatting with you. Henry."

Hank's stomach dropped. Wallace had just told him all he needed to know.

AMELIA GLANCED BACK AT HANK, who had been waylaid by Mr. Wallace. She didn't want to get stuck in his clutches again, so she slipped away from Hank and headed toward her father. Hank would find her when he was ready.

But Stephen stepped into her line of vision, a small smile on his face, head ducked. "Hey, Amelia."

"Hi, Stephen. I haven't seen you around since the workday at the parsonage." She clasped her hands. "Did you get my note?"

"I did, and I'm sorry I haven't responded before now." He gave a small laugh. "I guess I needed some time to simmer down. Not that I was angry at you. I had just hoped— Well, anyhow, your plants are doing fine. I've been taking good care of them, and you're welcome to come out and look at them anytime you'd like."

"Thank you, Stephen. You've been a good friend to me, and I appreciate that."

He nodded then looked past her shoulder. She turned. Hank was coming, brow furrowed.

"I hope he makes you happy. If he doesn't, he'll answer to me." Stephen's gaze narrowed.

"He does. Thank you."

Hank arrived and took her elbow, nodding at Stephen. "Stephen."

"How are you, Hank? I heard you had a fine trip to Portland."

"We did, thanks."

"Well, I was just telling Amelia that her plants were doing fine, that she had nothing to worry about. She's free—you both are—to come out any time you'd like to check on them." Stephen stuck out his hand and shook Hank's. "I'd best be going or my brothers will leave without me. See you soon, Amelia." He turned and left.

Hank glanced over his shoulder, but it wasn't Stephen he was staring at. It was Mr. Wallace.

"I still haven't talked to my father this evening. I keep getting stopped by people. I know they mean well." She lowered her voice "Except for Mr. Parsons."

Hank threaded her arm through his and squeezed her hand. "Don't worry about him."

They headed toward Father. Easy for him to say. It wasn't his occupation on the line.

Chapter Twenty-Four

After walking Amelia to school, Hank spent a drippy morning showing the railroad men around town. He hadn't seen Wallace at church on Sunday, but Hank had no doubt now that the man knew who he was. Only his family and banking associates called him Henry. So his suspicion that his father was spying on him through Wallace was likely correct. What did his father know? He wasn't sure, but did it really matter? Would his father's knowledge of his life change things? Probably not. He wished for the thousandth time that he'd get a letter back with some answers. Perhaps he needed to write another one.

He pulled his mind back to the railroad men. He had a couple of ideas where they could build. But they'd have to get in line behind Doc. Once Doc's quarters were built, the surveyors could use his temporary office as theirs and continue staying at the hotel. Hank was sure Parsons wouldn't mind the railroad paying for their stay.

They ended up back at the hotel dining room with coffee and some of Mrs. Parsons's muffins to warm up as they went over plans and options. Hank considered the fact that once the surveyors left, their quarters would be available. While he was grateful for the work, he wanted to keep the town's best interests in mind as well. He would design a building that could be easily taken over by another business owner that wanted to live above his shop. Which meant that Main Street or Center Street were the best locations, and the plans he showed them were adaptable for this idea as well.

They seem pleased with it and promised to bring a contract back when they returned.

Mr. Parsons hovered, under the auspices of refilling their coffee cups or providing more muffins. But Hank could see the pleased look on his face at the way the conversation was going. And perhaps Hank could use that to Amelia's advantage. He'd think on it. She probably wouldn't care for his meddling, but it was surely hard to stand by and let the woman he loved be berated over some kid's antics.

The thought made him pause mid sip. He loved her. He did. Now he just had to tell her. Perhaps they could find some time alone tonight. Being in the same boardinghouse had not made their courting as easy as he would have liked. He was walking her to and from school most days, but the weather had not cooperated for further walks or rides. He'd think of something.

He'd been busy with the railroad men and missed stopping in to see Amelia at lunch. He returned to the boardinghouse, his stomach gnawing with hunger. Emily greeted him in the kitchen. "I've kept it warm for you. Go sit down." She shooed him into the dining room with a smile. She was becoming as motherly as Maggie.

A stocky, bald man sat at the table with an older woman. He looked up when Hank entered and stuck out his hand. "Howdy, I'm Owen Taylor, and this is my mother, Judith."

"Hank Paulson. It's a pleasure to meet you both." He eased into his chair. "I cleaned out the foreman's cabin for you."

Taylor nodded. "Thanks for helping out Seth while I was gone. I know you were a godsend to him."

Mixed emotions that Hank didn't want to think about swirled in his gut. "How was your journey?"

"Wet." Mrs. Taylor smiled, and he saw the resemblance to her son in her round face. "It's good to be inside and warm and dry instead of in a wagon. Oilcloth only does so much good."

"That is true." Hank turned to Taylor. "If there's anything you need or that doesn't make sense, just let me know. We didn't make many changes to things while you were gone."

Emily entered and slid a plate and cup of coffee in front of Hank.

He smiled at her. "Thanks. It'll hit the spot for sure." It'd warm him up for the trip out to the parsonage to keep working for the rest of the day. On rainy days, Seth was loaning out the men from the logging camp, but most of them lacked finish carpentry skills and required supervision.

Depending on the progress they made, he might even walk Amelia home from school. Though telling her he loved her on Main Street seemed less than ideal. He'd have to come up with another plan.

AMELIA MISSED Hank walking her home from school, but he'd stopped by to explain about his busy morning with the railroad men and how he was trying to get the parsonage far enough along so he could start on their quarters as soon as there was a day without rain. She hoped it was soon, but back home, the ground would still be frozen solid and covered with several feet of snow. So she was grateful.

She entered the boardinghouse kitchen to find Emily and Maggie at work.

"How was school today?" Emily wiped her hands on her apron and pulled down a mug. "Any more trouble?" She filled it with coffee and handed it to Amelia.

"Thanks." She set her books on the kitchen table, took the cup, and sat. "No. A few sullen glances but that's manageable."

"Good." Emily eased into the table as well. "Owen Taylor and his mother arrived today. We're getting short on rooms. Until the wedding, do you mind if I double up with you so she can have my room?"

"That's perfectly fine. I've never actually shared a room with anyone. Being an only child and all. I know that's unusual. I'll help you move everything around."

"Finish your coffee first." Maggie set a plate of cookies down and joined them.

The warmth of the room and the friendship seeped into Amelia's bones. It had been a long time since she'd felt this sense of belonging. How would things change when Emily married and moved into Josh's cabin and Maggie moved into the parsonage? She treasured this memory and tucked it away.

After their snack, Amelia and Emily headed upstairs and hauled extra bed clothes and ticking from the attic. "There have been times we've had people bunked on the parlor floor. People need a place to stay, and most can't afford Parsons's prices."

As they worked, Amelia told Emily about her conversation with Mr. Parsons at the reception Saturday.

Emily shook her head. "I think that's the only tool he has in his toolbox. Placing an advertisement for another teacher. You don't have to worry. Look how long his ad had been out before you accepted it."

"What will I do if something else happens? He might fire me on the spot." Amelia fluffed a pillow and tossed it on the ticking. "Are you sure you don't mind sleeping on the floor?"

"The ticking's soft. And it's for less than two weeks." She hung her dresses on the empty pegs. "He wouldn't dare fire you. I saw how the townswomen rallied around you. They did it for me, too, and Parsons was forced to back down. He just likes to throw his weight around and remind people he is mayor. There's nothing else to distract him right now. Maybe we need to push him to bother the railroad surveyors." She giggled.

But Amelia sobered. "What will you and Josh do when the railroad comes to town?"

"We've talked about it a bit. We'd like to expand the wood-working shop. Josh and Charlie could be busy every day filling those orders. And if Josh and I have a family" —her cheeks pinked— "then I'll have plenty to keep me busy. Maggie could sell the boardinghouse to someone who wants to run it that way. We've all known this day was coming at some point. We'll be okay. God has gotten all of us through far worse things. We can trust Him in this as well."

Amelia nodded and finished making room for Emily's things, gently moving her porcelain dresser set that Hank had gotten for her. Memories of that day flooded back. That trip had had an outcome she hadn't expected. But it hadn't been a surprise to God. He knew what was going to happen with her teaching. He was in control; Mr. Parsons was not. She let that thought comfort her.

And what were God's plans for her and Hank?

Chapter Twenty-Five

Hank had peeked in the school windows as he walked toward the outhouse. It looked like Amelia had the children up and moving around. A good idea when today was the first sunny day after a few rainy ones. He had come to a good stopping point with his work. John and a few of Doc's patients were working on framing the doc's house during what looked to be a string of dry days and had made good progress, so he thought he'd fix the leak in the outhouse roof. School would be out fairly soon, and he'd be able to walk Amelia home, part of their routine that he'd grown to look forward to. Then he'd head back and work until dark. The days were growing infinitesimally longer, but he'd take what he could get.

He propped the door open with a rock. Better to do this in cool weather than when the smell was nearly unbearable in the heat. He stepped inside and looked up, letting his eyes adjust to the dim light and searching for the light seeping through the roof for signs of where the leak was originating. He traced the water stain back to the point of origin. Right there. He stood on the seat and used the handle of his hammer to test the shingles. Yep, that was the—

The door slammed shut, and the light disappeared. The

darkness pressed in on him. *Just breathe.* A breeze must have knocked it loose from the rock. Which was odd; he thought he'd braced it good. Careful not to misstep, he stepped down and pushed on the door. Stuck.

How could it be stuck? He felt around for the wood slat that spun to latch the door shut from the inside. It was straight up and down. He shoved at the door again, the darkness heavy against him.

Was that snickering he heard outside? Was this some idea of a joke? "Hey! Let me out! Who's out there?"

Laughter floated and then disappeared.

"Hey! Let me out!" He banged on the door with his fist then began kicking it. The door bowed at the edges but held fast. His breath was in short pants now, and the walls were closing in. He couldn't get enough air.

He slid to the floor and wrapped his arms around his knees. Some part of his brain tried to tell him to breathe, to pray, but it was so hard.

Breathe. Pray. Breathe. Pray. In. Out.

Moment by moment, he still had his sanity. But only for this moment.

After an eternity, he heard scuffling outside the door, a scraping against the wood. Was his mind playing tricks on him? "Hello? Anyone out there?"

"Hank?" Amelia's voice came through the wood. Was he delirious from lack of air?

The door swung open. Fresh air rushed in, and he took his first full, deep breath. He blinked, barely able to make out Amelia's silhouette. The light nearly blinded him. Maybe she was an angel.

"Hank, are you okay?" She bent over and pulled him up by his arms.

His knees nearly buckled. As the world flooded back to him, he realized how he must look to her—red-faced, hot, sweaty, and cowering like a child.

She pulled him to her, wrapping her arms around his waist. "Are you hurt? I saw Robert Reinfeld take off through the woods. Did he lock you in here? This barrel was shoved in front of the door."

He pulled her close and drank her in, letting her presence slow his heart rate. Her lilac scent was soothing. "Yeah, that must have been what happened. I went in to fix the leak in the roof and had propped the door open with a rock. Then it slammed shut, and I couldn't budge it."

He pulled back and looked around. The schoolyard was empty. "Is school out?"

She nodded. "When I didn't see you at the worksite, I wondered if you had stayed to work on our house. And then I saw the barrel in front of the outhouse, and Robert darting off in the woods." She let out a breath. "I suppose I'll need to have a conversation with his parents." Concern filled her eyes. "Are you all right?"

He let go of her. He could only imagine what she saw. "Let me wash my face and get something to drink." He headed over to the water pump and worked the handle, splashing his face, then scooping water from his hand to his mouth. Finally, he felt more like himself. But he was terribly embarrassed that Amelia had witnessed him in one of his spells. What should he tell her?

She studied him from a few paces away, arms wrapped around her waist. Could he brush it off, pretend it was nothing? No, he'd been curled in a ball, just as he had been that time in his father's cupboard. The same position he always found himself in after these spells. There was no way to explain that.

Except the truth. And that was the last thing he wanted to tell her.

AMELIA STUDIED Hank as emotions flicked across his face. She waited for him to speak when he was ready. When she had opened the outhouse door, he had looked terrible. His eyes were wide and unfocused, his face red and hair sticking up in all directions as if his hands had raked through it numerous times. At first she thought somehow Robert had hurt him before shoving him in the outhouse.

She didn't quite know how to explain Hank's behavior. Other than the fact that he had been in a small, dark space. And her father had told her about people who had overwhelming fears of such places. Perhaps Hank was one of those.

"Maybe we should go back in the schoolhouse. There will be some residual warmth from the stove."

Hank stared at her for a moment. The silence stretched so much that she feared he wouldn't break it. Finally he said, "Okay."

He walked next to her up the stairs and waited for her to unlock the door, acting very much like someone who had been awoken from a bad dream. They slid into the two chairs at her desk. She wasn't entirely sure what to do. Should she encourage him to talk about it? Pretend that everything was fine? Or do something to get his mind off things? It was so hard to know what the correct thing was to do when all she truly wanted to do was take away the pain she saw in his eyes.

"Perhaps you can give me some advice." She folded her hands in her lap. "I'm not entirely sure how to handle Robert. I sent a note home to his parents last week, and now this today. Your male perspective might be helpful."

Hank's features relaxed, and he leaned toward her as he spoke. "You need to speak to his parents in person. Especially his father. At his age, his father will be the one that he truly listens to. And if his father doesn't care how he behaves in the class-room, you're better off knowing that now so you can dismiss him on your terms."

She blinked. "It never occurred to me to ask a student to leave my classroom. But Emily hinted at the same thing."

"If they are disruptive and don't want to learn, they are

hurting the other students. You can't make someone learn if they don't want to. And frankly, that's the only way he and the other students will respect you. Foolish choices have consequences."

"Very true." She touched his arm. "I'm glad I talked to you about it. And after what he did to you, I think I need to figure out where he lives and talk to his parents today."

Hank nodded. "I know where the Reinfelds live. I'll walk you there." He stood.

She remained seated. "Hank, will you tell me what happened when you're ready?"

He studied her a moment, his eyes growing cloudy and troubled. But finally he nodded. "I will. While we walk."

"ONE, TWO, THREE..." Twelve-year-old Philip had his head buried in his arms, but Henry wasn't sure if he was still peeking. It would be like Philip to do that. He hated to lose.

Henry tore around the corner. He had the perfect spot. He'd beat Philip at hide and seek for sure. He slid down the hallway and into Father's office. He left the door ajar. If it was closed while Father was gone, Philip would surely notice.

Henry slipped inside, his footsteps quiet on the soft carpet. He looked around. Father was gone, but they weren't allowed to play in here. Still it felt like Father would walk in any minute.

Giving his head a little shake, Henry moved around the big desk that sat in the middle of the room. Several weeks ago, he had watched as his father opened a secret cupboard in the big desk. Henry had tucked that bit of information away for the next rainy day when he was forced to be inside and play with Philip. He knelt down in front of the big desk and ran his fingers along the edges, looking for the hidden latch that would spring open the panel.

His heart pounded as he heard Philip call, "Ready or not here I come!"

He could crawl under the desk and pull the chair in front of him. But he had used that trick once before, and he knew Philip would look there. Frantically, he ran his hands around the panels again, finally finding the barely perceptible notch just below the desktop. He pushed, and the panel shifted slightly, just enough for him to get his fingers into the lip and pull it open.

He scrambled inside. Philip's footsteps pounded up and down the hall. It was only a matter of time before he looked in Father's office. But Henry realized he couldn't reach behind him to pull the panel shut. He slid out, turned around, and scooted in backward. It was a tight fit, but he could just reach over his knees to pull the panel toward him.

Then he realized there was no latch on this side. He couldn't pull the panel completely shut. He did the best he could and prayed Philip wouldn't notice.

The door snicked open over the carpet, and Philip's footsteps thudded across the room, heading straight for the desk.

Henry slowed his breathing, which seemed so loud in this small space.

"Ha! I've got you. Why would you reuse an old trick?" Philip's voice was just outside the desk, and the sound of the desk chair wheels squeaking across the carpet sounded right next to his ear.

"Hmm. Not here." The floor creaked. Henry could picture Philip thinking, scanning the room. "Where else could he be? I've checked all the other hiding places."

The chair squeaked again. Philip had to have sat in it. The sound of drawers opening and closing almost made Henry jump as they were right next to his ear. At least they covered the sound of his breathing.

"Ooh, I wondered where this went." The chair squeaked again and then there was the sound of a foot on the carpet. "Wait a minute."

The panel slammed shut, blocking the sliver of light that had come through.

Henry held his breath. Had Philip found him?

Philip's laugh floated to him as footsteps ran out of the office.

Henry pushed on the panel. It was stuck. He felt around the edges for the latch. His breath came harder now. Would he suffocate in here?

Winning the game didn't matter anymore. It didn't matter if Philip gloated for ten years. Henry pounded on the panel. "Philip! Help! Let me out!

He stopped his pounding long enough to listen. He thought he heard footsteps. But then, nothing. Mother was at some ladies' function, so she had given the help the afternoon off. Who knew when someone would find him?

Pounding and yelling until he was hoarse, tears flowed down his face. What if no one found him? The air grew close and stale. Was there less of it? He struggled to draw a breath. *Please, God.*

He tucked his head further on his knees, his pants soaked from tears and snot. He must have fallen asleep because something awoke him. He jerked, banging his head on the desktop above him. "Ow!"

"Henry?" Father's voice penetrated the wood, unleashing a torrent of tears.

"I'm stuck in here! In the cupboard!"

"Henry!"

A rustle across the wood and then a scraping. Then light flooded him, making him blink. Fresh air poured in, and he gulped it. He tried to scoot out but his legs wouldn't work. He couldn't feel them.

Father leaned in the space, and with a grunt, pulled on Henry's legs until they straightened, and he slid him out of the space. "What were you doing in there? How did you get in there?"

Henry was too weak to move, so he leaned against the desk. His tears couldn't be stopped, and he couldn't talk.

Father handed him a handkerchief. "Now, now, stop those tears. That's no way for a big boy to behave."

Mopping his face, he tried to stop the sobs with great gulps of air. "We were— we were playing— hide and seek." Deep breath. They came easier now. "I thought this would be a good hiding place. I had left the panel open a bit, but Philip shut it and locked me in."

Father scowled. "It was foolish of you to be in there to begin with. First of all, you boys are not to be playing in my office. Second, this is my private property. You need to respect that. Someday this will be yours, but for now you are not allowed in here without permission. You got what you deserved, boy. Foolish choices have consequences."

Henry nodded and scrambled to his feet, somehow feeling even worse.

"Go wash up for supper. Your mother is waiting."

Henry stumbled out of the room.

Philip was just outside the door, a grin on his face. "Such a crybaby! That's what you get for trying to cheat!" He shoved Henry's shoulder.

Henry tried to move past him. "I wasn't cheating. I was hiding."

Philip laughed. "Crybaby! Crybaby!"

Henry ran upstairs and flung himself on his bed, hoping Philip didn't follow him. He never wanted to play with Philip again.

"Oh, Hank, that's terrible. Is that why you and your brother don't get along?" Amelia clung to Hank's arm as they walked towards the Reinfelds'.

"That's part of it. He and his friends used to tease me on the way home from school. To avoid them, I started working with Jon Baker. So in a way, I have Philip to thank for my carpentry skills." He gave a shaky laugh. "But I never could understand why my parents let him get away with all of his antics. And now look at him. Father is still coddling him. I don't understand it."

"I suppose being a parent isn't easy, but I certainly see things that make no sense to me either." She looked up at his face that had regained its normal color. "So is that when your spells started? The fear of small spaces?"

He nodded. "Yes, I think so. I can't remember having that feeling before then. Mostly I can avoid spaces I don't like. But don't ask me to go down into the cellar." He gave her a weak grin.

"I'm fine with doing all the retrieving from the cellar." She nudged his arm, then her face heated at what her words implied.

But his soft chuckle set her at ease. "You have a deal."

"That's the Reinfeld place there."

They turned up the lane, and a woman came onto the front porch. "You must be Miss Martin." Her face was unreadable, but her fingers clutched her apron.

"I am. And this is Mr. Hank Paulson. Are you Mrs. Reinfeld? Could we speak to you for a moment?"

She gave a short nod and gestured for them to come inside and sit in the parlor. "May I get you something to drink? Coffee or tea?"

"No, thank you, ma'am." Amelia wanted to get this over as soon as possible. She clasped her hands together to keep from twisting them. She couldn't tell what Mrs. Reinfeld was thinking about her visit.

Clara appeared from around the corner and waved shyly at her.

Amelia smiled and waved back.

Mrs. Reinfeld whispered something to Clara, and she took off, the back door slamming a moment later. Mrs. Reinfeld perched on the edge of the chair. "I've sent Clara for my husband. I think he should hear this as well. I'm assuming this involves Robert."

"It does. You received my previous note?" Amelia knew she had because Clara had told her she had given it to her mother, but it seemed like a way to ease into this conversation.

"I did. And we discussed it. Robert promised to behave himself." She let out a sigh. "I so hoped he would have more schooling than his father and I did."

Bootsteps sounded on the porch, and then a large, broad-shouldered man—an older version of Robert—appeared.

Hank rose to shake his hand. "Hank Paulson and Miss Amelia Martin." He gestured to Amelia before taking his seat.

"Pleased to meet you both. I'm sorry you have troubled yourself to come all the way out here." He sat next to his wife. "What's he done this time?"

Amelia glanced at Hank, who began speaking. "He locked me in the outhouse after school while I was fixing the leaking roof. He pushed a barrel in front of the door so I couldn't get out. I heard snickers and laughter, and Miss Martin spotted him running away."

Mr. Reinfeld looked at his wife. "The boy's too old to be in school. He needs to put his efforts to work around the farm. I told you he could stay in school as long as he behaved himself and learned something. Seems like that's come to an end."

Mrs. Reinfeld looked at her lap. "I had just hoped he'd have more schooling than we did."

"What we had was good enough for us." He shrugged. "It'll have to do for Robert too. Clara might go further in school, though I'm not sure why she'd need to either."

Amelia's heart sank. She hated to see someone not get a full education. Emily and Hank's words about letting a disruptive student go flitted through her mind. They were likely right, but it still seemed like she should make an effort to salvage Robert's education. Even if only she and Mrs. Reinfeld were advocating for it.

"Robert's a good student when he applies himself. He's smart. Perhaps there's a way we could work something out so he could continue his schooling but not be disruptive or harm others." Her mind reeled trying to think of a solution. If only she'd had more experience at this.

Mr. Reinfeld opened his mouth, but Hank sat forward. "If I may, I have a suggestion. I'm in charge of building the parsonage and the doctor's quarters. The railroad will also be needing a place for their surveyors shortly. There's a lot of building to be done, but not enough men available to do it. If you're willing, I could use Robert's help after school—" he turned to Amelia "— and any other boys who were willing to form a sort of apprenticeship for carpenters. As long as they behave in school, they can work afterwards and even earn a small amount of pay."

Why hadn't Hank shared this idea with her earlier? Or perhaps he had only just thought of it. It seemed like a good one. But what would Mr. Parsons think?

She smiled. "I think that's a fine idea if you are willing, Hank, and if you think your son would be interested, Mr. and Mrs. Reinfeld."

Mrs. Reinfeld's eyes widened with hope as she turned to her husband.

He nodded slowly. "He does have an aptitude for numbers that I never could understand. If he could learn a trade and be useful, I'm for that. But if he acts up in school again, he's back to working on the farm."

"Perhaps this is the motivation he'll need." Amelia was eager to leave so she and Hank could talk over the details. She didn't want to say the wrong thing and appear as if she hadn't been behind this idea from the beginning. She rose to her feet, and Hank and the Reinfelds followed. "Thank you for your support. Hank and I will discuss the details and send them home with the boys tomorrow after school."

Mr. Reinfeld shook Hank's hand. "I appreciate you thinking of this. I hope it'll be a good solution for everyone."

"Me too."

They took their leave. Amelia waited until they were on the

road and out of earshot. "That was a wonderful idea, Hank. Had you been thinking about it long, or did it just come to you?"

"I think because we had been talking about my working with Jon Baker. I thought other boys should have a similar chance, and then I realized I could provide that chance. Plus, we'd talked about giving the children a tour of the parsonage and explaining the science and math behind carpentry. So you think it's a good idea?" His eyes warmed as he smiled at her.

"I do. But do you know what you're getting yourself into?"

He gave a mock grimace. "For someone who didn't want to be a carpenter, I seem to have embraced that role rather fully, wouldn't you say?"

She squeezed his arm. "Yes, I would. Now, would you be willing to explain your apprenticeship program to Mr. Parsons so he doesn't fire me? Somehow I think he'd think it a great idea coming from you and a sign that I couldn't control my classroom coming from me."

His gaze darkened, and he dropped a kiss on her forehead. "Anything for you, Amelia."

Chapter Twenty-Six

In the afternoon before school let out, Hank approached the schoolhouse. He and Amelia had discussed it last night after supper and again on the way to school. The apprenticeship program was a real winner. It would help him—maybe not at first, with all the training he'd need to do—but mostly he thought it would help Amelia's standing as a teacher with innovative ideas to keep young minds eager to learn.

He had spoken to Parsons before heading over here. He hated to lose the time at work, but if word got back to Parsons before Hank had talked to him, Parsons could cancel their plans just on the basis that they hadn't gotten his approval first. But all in all, Parsons had been amenable to the idea, especially since Hank sold it as something that set their school apart, made it progressive, and by extension, made him look like a forward-thinking schoolboard president.

All eyes turned to Hank as he entered the schoolroom. A wave of chatter started, but Amelia raised her voice. "Children, this is Mr. Paulson. He is going to give us a tour of the parsonage today and explain how the math we are learning is used in building houses and other things. Say hello."

A chorus of "Hello, Mr. Paulson" made him smile. He made

his way to the front and stood next to Amelia. "How many of you like math?"

A few hands went up.

"Anybody ever built anything?"

"I built a birdhouse with my pa." "I helped my pa repair the wagon." "We fixed the chicken coop." And a few other comments he couldn't make out as the children talked over each other.

"It's pretty fun to make something, isn't it? You start out with some wood and nails. And with a few tools and some elbow grease you can create something completely different. But you know what you used, probably without knowing it?"

"What?" The children chimed back to him. This was fun. He could see why Amelia enjoyed teaching.

"Math. Let me explain." He moved to the blackboard and picked up a piece of chalk, drawing something that sorta looked like a piece of wood. He walked them through the basics of measuring pieces of wood, cutting them down to size, dividing, multiplying, and figuring supplies. "So see how many ways you need math to build something? Math is everywhere. It's good to know."

He glanced over at Joseph and Robert, both of whom seemed to be paying attention. "Let's head over to the parsonage, and I'll show you in person how we used math to create that building."

Amelia raised her voice over the chatter. "Put your coats on and head over to the parsonage but do not go inside." Amelia smiled at him, and it was all he could do not to touch her.

He helped her with her coat and walked next to her on the way over.

"I think they like your math teaching better than mine." She glanced up at him, the afternoon sun glinting red in her hair.

"Nah, they wouldn't have been able to follow what I was saying if you hadn't taught them the basics."

"That credit probably goes to Emily."

He shook his head. "Can't you take a compliment?"

She laughed. "Maybe not."

He lowered his voice. "Guess we'll have to work on that."

They arrived at the parsonage, and he maneuvered his way to the front. "Now, this is a working jobsite, which means you need to watch where you step, don't wander off, and don't touch anything. Mr. McAlistar and Mr. Paige are still working, so don't bother them." He led them through the rooms, explaining their purpose and how he had designed them, along with all the things they considered during the construction.

Amelia stayed behind the group to keep any stragglers from wandering off, but he caught her gaze often. And the admiration that shone in her eyes could about carry him off his feet. He needed to find some time alone with her.

He was pleasantly surprised to see Joseph and Robert near the front of the group, paying attention, as well as a few other boys. At the end of the tour, he turned and faced the group. "How many of you would like to learn how to build something like this?"

Hands shot up around the room, including a few girls. Interesting. He didn't think Parsons was progressive enough to let girls in the apprenticeship program. But perhaps they should think about something for the girls as well. He'd mention it to Amelia.

"Those of you boys who are twelve and older, with your parents' permission, can join me after school each day to learn how to build houses." He raised his hands to calm the chatter. "Now, listen, there are rules for participating. You have to keep up your schoolwork and not get in trouble with Miss Martin or anyone on the jobsite. Miss Martin has more information back in the schoolhouse that you can take home to your parents. Discuss it with them and bring back the signed form."

He and Amelia had stayed up later than normal last night writing out copies of the forms, one for each boy over twelve, but certain they wouldn't all be used. Now he wasn't so sure.

Amelia herded the children back to the schoolhouse where she reminded them of their homework and dismissed them. Hank helped her hand out the flyers and then close up the schoolroom after all the children left.

She took his arm as they walked home. "That went better than I expected. Mr. Parsons agreed to the plan?"

"He did. I might have emphasized how good it would make him look to be the head of such a progressive school. And once he was on board, I made sure he knew how much you had contributed to the idea."

She squeezed his arm. "We make a good team."

He gazed down on her. "I was thinking the same thing."

STANLEY WALLACE SAT at his desk in the bank, penning his weekly update to Mr. Paulson about the latest developments in town and the bank. There wasn't much to report—nothing happened in this town—but he wasn't sure what Mr. Paulson would consider important or not, so he erred on the side of too much information rather than not enough. He'd just blotted the letter when the clerk knocked on his door.

"Come in."

The door opened, and the clerk's head appeared in the gap. "There's someone here to see you."

"Who?"

"Didn't give a name. Said you'd be happy to see him."

A sinking feeling filled Stanley's stomach, and he slid the letter in the desk drawer. "Send him in."

He wasn't surprised when his brother, Harley, appeared. The stockier of the two, they both still had dark curly hair and easily looked like brothers. He hoped no one else in town had made that connection.

"What are you doing here?"

Harley grinned as he eased himself into the chair across the desk from Stanley. "That's a fine way to greet your brother."

Stanley just stared at him. The sooner Harley got out of here and left town, the better.

Harley toyed with his hat. "Red Dawson has found it mighty interesting that you're here in this town. He has a particular grudge against it, you might say."

His heart ticked up at the mention of Dawson, but he tried to look bored. "What has that got to do with me?"

"See, this town took some money that belonged to Red. He was going to take a girl—an Emily Stanton, the schoolteacher—instead of payment. But those dad-blamed Rogers boys let her get away. So you can see why Red might be a wee bit upset."

"Again, what does that have to do with me?"

"Well, Red would look kindly upon it if you helped him get the girl." He gave an evil chuckle. "Or, I hear the new school-teacher is pretty. He'd take her as well. You just let me know where they'll be, and I'll snatch them up. You provide the info, and I do the hard work, just like always."

Acid filled Stanley's mouth. Money was one thing, but harming someone else wasn't anything he wanted to get involved with. How could he appease Harley and make him go away?

Harley scanned the office. "Nice place. Not as nice as your Portland office. What'd you do to get sent here anyway? And why didn't you let your dear old brother know where you'd gone?" He leaned forward. "I'm sure it was an oversight on your part, right? You weren't trying to hide from me, were you? I don't think the town folks here would appreciate knowing what you really do any more than the folks in your fancy Portland office would." He made to push up from his chair. "But we could go find out."

"No, don't do that." Stanley stuck his hand out. "Look, the girls are never left alone. And if one of them disappeared, this town would turn the woods upside down looking for them, including the sheriff, and he'd bring in the marshals. They would immediately suspect Red. I don't think he could get away with it."

"Well now, that's not your concern, is it?" Harley got to his feet. "You give me the information, and I make it happen. That's how this works. But I guess you've forgotten that."

"Wait!" Stanley pushed to his feet. "I've got something better. Another payroll shipment."

Harley cocked his head. "Red might be amenable to that. Give me the details."

"Where are you staying?"

"Close enough. You don't need to know where."

"I don't have the details yet. I need to know how to get them to you." Stanley gave Harley a hard stare. He hoped this worked. Red was greedy. And Stanley was under no illusions that this would buy him off permanently. But it was the only idea he had. With more time, he could come up with something better for the future.

Harley considered this. "You can slip the details to me at Danny Tillman's barn." He turned toward the door and paused. "It better be soon. Or I'll snatch one of those women myself." He slipped out and the door closed behind him.

Stanley sunk into his chair. This had gotten out of hand. It was one thing to let them know about payroll. Insurance would cover the losses. But taking the women? Nothing good would come of that. And he still had a bit of a conscience left.

Perhaps he should visit the sheriff again. Warn him somehow that Red Dawson might be looking to kidnap women. But how would he explain his knowledge? No, best to try to buy some time with the payroll. Maybe by then he'd develop a better plan.

He prayed Mr. Paulson would not find out about his involvement with this.

HANK HAD LET Maggie in on his plan because he needed her assistance. He was a little nervous as they put the finishing touches on the picnic lunch she had packed that morning.

At breakfast, he'd whispered to Amelia not to make any plans after church. She'd blushed, but her eyes had lit up. He hoped his plan would live up to her expectation.

Maggie put a hand on his arm, stopping his pacing in the small kitchen. "It'll be fine. She'll love it just because you thought of doing something special for her."

He nodded. "Thanks, Maggie." He hadn't even been able to pay attention to Pastor Roy's sermon with Amelia sitting next to him. But he'd been praying constantly the last few days, so perhaps that made up for it.

Amelia had been surprised at Maggie's statement that she didn't need help with Sunday dinner just yet but had obviously figured out that it had something to do with Hank's plans.

He ducked into the parlor. She looked up, but thankfully no one else did. She slipped out and joined him.

"Ready to go?"

"I just need to put on my coat."

They headed out the back of the kitchen, Maggie giving them a wink. He helped her on with her coat from the hooks piled with coats, then shrugged into his own. He picked up the basket and the blanket and they headed out.

Amelia looked up at him. "Is our destination a surprise?"

"It is." He grinned.

She gestured to the basket. "I'm assuming Maggie helped."

"Yes. I wanted you to enjoy your food. I'm not sure I could cook anything edible."

She nudged his shoulder. "I think you could do anything you put your mind to."

He warmed at the compliment. Her high opinion of him made him feel stronger and smarter than he ever had. Made him think that even his father's opinion didn't matter.

They walked across the boardinghouse yard to the footbridge

over the stream. This was the way to Seth and Becca's house, but instead of heading there, he turned off deeper into the woods, following a faint path. He wrapped his hand around hers. They walked in comfortable silence, the warm sun making the trip pleasant. At the edge of the woods, a small trail appeared only when they walked right up to it.

Hank stopped. "I have to make you promise me something."

"What's that?"

"You can't tell anyone about this spot. It's Josh and Seth's secret fishing spot. Becca told me about it."

Her eyes twinkled. "I can keep a secret."

"I knew you could."

They stepped into the forest and walked a short ways. The trees separated to reveal a perfect emerald pool surrounded by large boulders and fed by a small waterfall, lush with winter rains. The sound of splashing water surrounded them.

"Oh, Hank. It's so beautiful and peaceful here. I'm glad Becca let you in on the secret."

He led her over to one of the big boulders. It was large enough to stretch out on. He set the basket down and spread out the blanket, then helped Amelia lower herself before joining her.

"This is lovely. Thank you for thinking of it." She gave him a saucy smile, one he particularly liked since he didn't see her share it with anyone else. "So how did the topic of you needing a secret place come up with Becca?"

"I was discussing things with Seth and Owen Friday, catching up on the logging operations, which men could be spared to help with the building, the apprenticeship program, and so on. When Owen left, Becca asked about our trip to Port-land and then said I might like to take you to this place. Seth mentioned that it was his and Josh's secret fishing spot, but that it had become special to him and Becca. And I guess when the big fire came through here last summer, it was where they saved the horses and the stagecoach. So maybe not a big secret." He chuckled.

"I think it's perfect. I can just see sneaking off here in the summer to do some fishing or to cool off."

He unpacked their lunch, and they ate it, staring out over the water and watching the wildlife. It was a perfect and peaceful place just to sit and be with her, not having to do anything.

When they were done, he got to his feet. "There's something else I want to show you. I did some scouting here Friday after I left Seth and Becca's, to make sure I could actually find the place."

He jumped down off the backside of the boulder they had been sitting on, then held her around the waist as he helped her down. His gaze met hers, and the urge to kiss her almost overpowered him. But he would wait. He had something to show her first, and he didn't want to be distracted and forget. He took her hand and helped her clamber over the boulders that were strewn about. They headed generally in the direction of the waterfall, but they reached a meadow before they got there.

He stopped and watched her reaction. He knew the moment she spotted it as her eyes grew wide and her mouth opened. He chuckled.

"Oh my word! I've never seen anything so beautiful." She took a few steps forward and crouched down, surrounded by the early spring wildflowers that dotted the meadow in shades of pink and purple. Several of the shrubs surrounding the meadow had also sprouted blooms. She touched the delicate petals of the different varieties, oohing and ahhing over their early blooms as she gathered a bouquet of them together.

"I'll hold them while you pick." He held out his hand, gathering her flowers together. He'd never thought he'd enjoy holding flowers so much. She stood in the middle of the meadow, her face glowing, surrounded by wildflowers. He studied her, capturing this moment to pull out in the future.

"The willows by the pond I recognize by their fuzzy catkins. But the rest of these are unfamiliar to me. I'll take some and compare them to my books or Sy's. I wonder if they are strictly wild or if they can be cultivated." She spun around and then looked at him, taking slow steps toward him until she stood a breath away. "Thank you. This is the sweetest thing anyone has ever done for me."

He slipped his arms around her waist, flowers and all, and pulled her closer. "I want to make you happy, Amelia. Whether it's finding wildflowers or eating a meal together or exploring a big city, I want to do it all with you." He swallowed and lost himself in her gaze. "I love you, Amelia." For a moment, it was like he'd stepped off something tall, not sure if there was a step below to catch him.

Her eyes widened and her arms went around his neck. "I love you too, Hank."

Elation shot through him, and he felt like he was floating. He lowered his head as she came up on her tiptoes. He bent and kissed her, tenderly then more deeply, hoping to convince her just how much he loved her and wanted a future with her.

Chapter Twenty-Seven

Amelia wiped down the blackboard at the end of the day to the sound of hammers and saws ringing out. The apprenticeship program began today with four boys. More than they could have hoped for. One unintended consequence was that Hank wouldn't be able to walk her home from school anymore. It couldn't be helped, of course, and she was grateful for the times they had had together.

She thought back to yesterday, to their picnic and his declaration of love. She hadn't intended to say the words, but they popped out of her heart. It felt so right. Hank saw who she really was. He paid attention to what was important to her and did his best to make it happen. He valued her, not despite her quirks and eccentricities, but because of them. If that wasn't love, she didn't know what it was. She couldn't imagine a future that didn't include Hank.

But schoolteachers couldn't be married. And she had wanted to teach again next year. It almost seemed irresponsible to start this job and then leave it soon after. On the other hand, it wasn't like Hank had proposed. She was definitely getting the cart before the horse. Besides, Mr. Parsons had been advertising for a teacher. If one showed up, would it be horrible? Still, she'd rather leave on her own terms, not because she'd been replaced. Either way, it wasn't something to decide today. She would be the best schoolteacher she could be, and the rest would be up to God and His timing.

The schoolhouse door opened, interrupting her thoughts. Emily came in, looked around, and smiled.

"How's it feel to be back in your old schoolroom?"

"You've done a great job. I think your handwriting is neater than mine." She nodded to the board that Amelia was in the middle of erasing.

Amelia scoffed. "If that was all it took to be a good teacher."

"The boys seem busy out at the parsonage. I think you and Hank had a fantastic idea."

Amelia set the eraser down and gathered up her things. "It was mostly Hank's idea. But I do think we should think of something for the girls as well."

Emily nodded. "Most do get training in cooking, cleaning, and sewing at home. What else could we offer them?"

"I don't know. What would make them successful in this modern world?"

"It's changing quickly, that's for sure. And I'm not entirely sure this town is ready for modern women."

"Cassandra and Becca make it look easy." Amelia touched the wildflowers that sat in the jar on her desk and plucked out a sampling.

"They do. But they have people who love and support what they do. Not all the girls in town would have that." Emily gestured to the flowers. "Did you find those out by the pond?"

"I did. With Hank." Amelia laughed. "So I guess the pond's not so secret?"

They walked out the schoolroom doors and down to the waiting wagon.

"Well, the boardinghouse folks know about it." Emily clucked to the horses, and they headed off. "Not many people from town do. They'd have to follow the stream past the boardinghouse and Josh's cabin. Most folks would consider that being too intrusive to someone else's land."

Amelia nodded. "Thanks for taking me out to the O'Malleys' today. I'd like to see what these wildflowers are before they wilt. That way I can press them in my book and put their names underneath. Plus, I thought we could talk about your wedding. I can't believe it's this Saturday."

Emily let out a sigh. "Me neither. I was thinking we were quite ahead of schedule. My dress is done. Josh's suit is pressed. The menu is planned. But we're going to have to start the baking soon. There's only so much that can be done in advance."

"I'll help in any way I can. The flowers, at least, you can leave up to me." Amelia smiled.

They arrived at the O'Malley farm, and Stephen was as friendly and good-natured as always. A weight dropped off Amelia's shoulders. She had worried that things might be awkward between them. He gave Emily a tour of the farm, which wasn't quite as thorough as Sy's since they didn't go see the weather station in the hayloft, but it was still impressive and took a bit of time. They ended up at the greenhouse.

"Oh, this is wonderful, Amelia. All of your mother's plants here. And doing so well." Emily bent over to examine one of the pots.

"Yes, I'm grateful for the ones that made it. And for this perfect space to house them. They seem to be thriving. Some are even putting out shoots. I can't wait to get them in the ground."

"You need your house built first."

"Yes." A bubble of happiness rose in her chest knowing her plants were well cared for and Stephen wasn't upset with her. For now, things were moving forward smoothly. She hoped they stayed that way.

Back inside the farmhouse, he served them his apple spice muffins and coffee while Amelia perused one of Sy's plant books. "Oh, here they are! This is a snow queen. *Synthyris reniformis.*" She pointed to one of the flowers with delicate purple bells. She turned a few pages. "And this one is oaks toothwort, also known as spring beauty. Because it is. *Cardamine nuttallii.*" She gently touched the four-petaled purple flowers. "They are some of the first flowers of spring. I continue to be astounded by the flora out here."

Stephen and Emily shared a grin.

"Okay, I know I'm a bit silly about it, but it does bring me happiness."

Stephen picked up their plates. "It did Sy too. He'd be thrilled to see you making good use of his books."

Amelia looked at her watch. "Oh my. It's later than I thought. We're going to be late getting supper started." She and Emily thanked Stephen and headed home.

"Are you nervous about the wedding?" Amelia asked as they rode in the wagon toward the boardinghouse.

"Maybe the wedding. All those people focused on me. So much attention. But not the marriage. Josh is a good man, and I can't wait to begin our lives together. It's been too long of a wait already. He proposed New Year's Eve so we could begin the new year together. Though I guess if you hadn't come to take over teaching, I'd have had to wait until May. So I owe you a debt of gratitude." Emily shot Amelia a warm smile.

"It's the least I can do. You all have made me feel like I belong here." The wagon jerked and lurched, forcing her to grab to the edge of the seat. "What—"

The horses shied and sidled. Emily tugged on the reins. "Whoa, easy there." They came to a lurching stop.

"What happened?"

"Hopefully not what I think." Emily wrapped the reins around the brake and jumped down. She went around the back of the wagon and disappeared as she bent down. When she straightened, she blew her hair out of her face and put her hands on her hips, her mouth turned down. "We have a broken wheel."

Amelia scrambled down and joined Emily. "What does that mean?"

"I suppose it means we walk into town. We're closer to it than to the O'Malleys'." She glanced over her shoulder. "I think. It's only a few miles."

Amelia studied the fractured wheel. "Do they always break this cleanly? It looks like what happens when you nearly cut a branch through and then the rest splinters off."

Emily scowled. "My thoughts precisely. Someone's idea of a prank?"

"Robert Reinfeld did lock Hank in the outhouse. But this seems a lot more destructive than that." Robert didn't know about Hank's fear of small spaces, so to him it would have seemed like a simple prank and not a terrifying ordeal. She wasn't going to share that with Emily and reveal Hank's secret. "Plus, I think he was working at the parsonage with Hank."

"He would have access to a saw then."

"True. But I think Hank would have noticed. And wouldn't the wheel have given out before now? It seems like it might have happened at the O'Malleys'."

Emily sighed. "And that doesn't make any sense either. The O'Malleys wouldn't want to hurt us." She chewed on her lip and scanned the surrounding area, her brow furrowed in thought.

Amelia's stomach twisted as she scanned the lengthening shadows. She didn't want to think about the conclusion Emily was drawing. "We're not going to make it home before dark. We could unhitch the wagon and ride the horses if they'd tolerate being ridden bareback."

Emily shook her head. "Uh, no."

Amelia raised her eyebrows. "It's the fastest way."

"I don't actually like horses that much. They scare me."

Amelia blinked. "I wouldn't have imagined that you were scared of anything."

Emily gave a short laugh. "Oh, yes. Josh— Well, I'll tell you about it on the walk home. We'd best get started. Let's gather our things."

Amelia grabbed her books, lunch pail, and flowers from the wagon while Emily made sure the horses were secure. Amelia patted their noses. "I hate to just leave them here."

"I can't think of what else we could do. They'll be fine. The men will come back for them as soon as we get home."

They headed down the road, Emily telling Amelia stories of when the stagecoach got stuck in the mud and she had to ride bareback with Josh. And then later getting stuck in a thunderstorm and having to ride home with Josh. "Both times I was stuck between two terrible things, one of which involved being on a horse. I wasn't sure which was worse."

Amelia shook her head. "I would never have imagined." She thought of Hank's fear of small spaces. Seemed like having fears didn't make a strong person any less strong. "But you had Josh with you both times."

Emily gave a sweet smile. "Yes, I did. I think that was the only reason I could handle the situations. Because I trusted him, even before I had realized it."

The trees lining the road cast long shadows. Both women scanned the woods as they walked, peering into the darkness. The sun dipped and disappeared behind them, leaving the sky glowing but dimming quickly. Emily's long strides were hard for Amelia to keep up with, yet she was just as eager to get back to town. She'd never been outside of town this far on her own, let alone in the near dark. And with the apparent deliberate damage to the wagon wheel, she didn't like thinking about someone wanting to do them harm. She pulled her coat closer around her. The dark also brought the cold. At least walking fast would keep them warm. *Lord, keep us safe.*

Emily chuckled hollowly. "I wonder if they'll come looking for us when supper is late on the table."

"I guess it's a race then to see if we'll get home first." She thought through the dime novels she'd read to see if any of the heroines had ever been in this situation. She'd think of it as an adventure. Though simply walking didn't seem terribly adventurous. Still, with the darkness closing in and the chilly air, she'd be happy to be safe at home seated next to Hank on the settee in the parlor next to the warm fireplace.

Night sounds from the woods filtered over to them. Crickets, tree peeper frogs, hooting owls, and other rustlings she couldn't make out. A shiver coursed through her. "Do we have to be worried about wild animals?" Or people?

Emily glanced at her. "I don't think so. We're making enough noise." She bit her lip. "But perhaps we should keep talking loudly. Did I ever tell you how I ended up in Reedsville?"

"No, I'd love to hear about it."

Emily told Amelia about her past with a man who posed as her grandfather but really wasn't. She had just gotten to the point where she had been kidnapped last fall when Amelia stopped her.

"Did you hear that?"

Horse hooves sounded on the road. It took a minute to determine the direction. They were coming from the direction of the town. So was help on the way?

Or was it danger?

HANK ARRIVED BACK at the boardinghouse to find the kitchen empty and the stove banked. No delicious aromas greeted him. Odd. He had watched Emily pick up Amelia after school. He knew they were going out to the O'Malleys', but they should have been home by now. Worry wormed its way through his stomach. There were many logical reasons why they weren't home yet. But he couldn't bring any to mind. Emily would never make them wait for supper.

The back door opened, and Charlie wandered into the kitchen. He sniffed. "Where's Emily? Is she sick?"

Hank shrugged. "I don't know. I just got here. She and Amelia were going out to the O'Malleys', but they should have been home by now."

The door banged again, and Josh crowded into the kitchen. He frowned. "Where's Emily? They aren't back yet?"

"I don't think so. You haven't seen them?" Hank turned to Charlie.

"Not since noon."

Hank met Josh's gaze. "Think we should go look for them?"

Josh gave a short nod, his mouth a tight line, and Hank followed him out the back door and to the barn, pushing away all the possible trouble that could have beset them.

He and Josh saddled up their horses. "They probably just got talking and lost track of time. Amelia loves that greenhouse and her plants."

Josh gave a short nod. Yeah, Hank didn't believe it either. Emily wouldn't let them get home so late as to miss fixing supper.

Josh checked his revolver and rifle before mounting his horse.

"Anything in particular we need to be worried about?" Hank mounted Prince and followed Josh out of the boardinghouse yard.

All traces of Josh's normally jovial personality were gone. Instead, a narrowed gaze met Hank's. "Those Rogers boys that kidnapped Emily last year. They've not been seen since. They ran with Red Dawson, and I'm convinced that he was behind the stagecoach robbery. I don't think we've seen the last of him. Not by a long shot. He didn't get what he wanted from Emily, several thousand dollars of bank notes. Now, taking Seth's payroll might have made up for that, but Dawson's not known for being an equitable man. I could see him taking revenge however he could find it." He shook his head. "Emily's generally never in a position where he could grab her again. I should have gone with them."

Once they cleared the far end of town, they broke into a gallop.

Hank hoped that Josh was wrong. And began praying.

EMILY GRABBED Amelia's elbow and moved her to the side of the road. "I'm sure it's someone we know." But the waver in her voice caused Amelia to shrink back deeper into the shadows as the hoofbeats grew louder.

Emily bent and rustled around in the forest floor debris before grabbing a sturdy branch. She slid a glance at Amelia, but they remained silent, waiting.

Dark forms on horseback appeared in the road, two of them. Amelia studied them as they came into focus and distinct shapes formed.

Emily dropped her branch and stepped out into the road.

Confused, Amelia waited a heartbeat, and then the second rider became clear to her. Hank. And Josh. She joined Emily.

The men reined in and dismounted. Hank took long strides to her and wrapped her in his arms. Being enveloped in his warmth and scent was just about her undoing, and tears pricked her eyes. She was safe.

"Are you okay?" His voice was tender in her ear, and she nodded against his chest, not trusting herself to speak. He moved her slightly away from him, his eyes examining her in the dim light. "You're not hurt?"

"No, a wagon wheel broke."

Hank glanced at Josh who was holding Emily close. "How far back?"

"About halfway to the O'Malleys'."

Emily eased out of Josh's grasp. "And I think it was on purpose. Looked like one of the spokes had been cut through part way."

Josh and Hank exchanged a look that Amelia couldn't interpret. There was something going on here. What did they know?

Josh pulled Emily back toward his horse. "Let's take a look. We can at least bring the horses home."

Hank helped Amelia mount then swung up behind her.

A snap and rustling drew her attention to the woods. Safe in his arms, she peered into the darkness. She grabbed Hank's arm. "Look!"

Was it her imagination or had a man just darted deeper into the forest?

Chapter Twenty-Eight

❧❦❧

Hank ran his hand through his hair, trying to keep his mind on his work. The parsonage was nearly done. He didn't want to make a costly mistake. And his apprentices were looking to him to set an example. His gaze kept drifting to the schoolhouse, even though there was nothing to see.

Yesterday's events had left him spooked. After picking up Emily and Amelia, he and Josh had found the wagon. It was hard to see in the dark, but it definitely looked like a clean cut on a few of the spokes. And it would have had to have been done at the O'Malleys'. Which meant someone had followed the women out there or had known they were going out there. He didn't suspect the O'Malley boys at all. There was no reason to. Even if Stephen had wanted to play a hero to Amelia and rescue her, he hadn't shown up.

Which gave credence to Josh's theory. And if it had truly been a man that Amelia had seen darting away in the woods… Or was it just a deer? He only saw branches swaying. But the idea that someone had sabotaged their wagon and had been following them… He got sick at the very thought. He didn't want to worry Amelia, but he also didn't want her putting herself in a dangerous situation if there really was someone out there trying to kidnap either her or Emily.

Hank had paid a visit to the sheriff right after he'd dropped Amelia at school and discussed with John the plan for the day. Sheriff Riley was as concerned as Hank, especially since he'd been involved in the search for Emily last year when she'd been kidnapped and had a vested interest in seeing Red Dawson locked up. He was going to talk to the O'Malley boys and see if they saw anything, then check out the wagon.

Seth and Owen were going out in the drizzle today with a spare wagon wheel to make repairs and bring the wagon back since Josh had a stage run today. He'd get back the day before his wedding.

Until Hank knew who had targeted the women and to what purpose, Amelia wasn't walking home from school alone. Walking through town with James should have been safe enough for her, the logical part of his brain argued. But the part that had kept him up all night argued that he couldn't let her out of his sight. She'd promised to stay at the schoolhouse until he could retrieve her.

He had a suspicion that Stanley Wallace was behind this somehow. No, he wouldn't have gotten his hands dirty, but he could have hired someone to do it. But how and why? That was what Hank couldn't figure out. And what was the connection to Red Dawson's gang, if Josh's suspicions were correct?

School let out with noisy children bursting from the school-house doors. His apprentices shuffled in, gangly and awkward, but eager to work. He got them started and had John supervise them while he headed over to the schoolhouse.

One more thing that niggled at him. Still no letter from his father. Which only contributed to his suspicions.

Sheriff Riley stopped by the parsonage just before Hank was ready to retrieve Amelia from school. He studied the nearly finished building. "Great job you've done here."

Hank set down his hammer. "Thanks. I've had good help." He nodded toward John.

"I'll not keep you, but I wanted to let you know what I found out. Went out to the O'Malleys'. They hadn't heard or seen anything, but the wagon was parked in front of the house, and they were all out in the orchards, so it seems like if someone had followed the women, they could have cut through the spokes then. Perhaps they meant to cut through more and someone returned to the house. Or perhaps he'd always planned to have them break down about halfway between the two places. Regardless, I looked at the wheel. In fact, it's evidence in my office right now. It was clearly cut."

Riley removed his hat and ran his hand through his silver-threaded hair. "I don't like this one bit. I checked out the woods near the O'Malleys' and near where the wagon broke down. Someone was there based on the broken branches and trampled underbrush. The question is, who? Someone in town is feeding Dawson information. Who else knew that Emily and Amelia were going out to the O'Malleys'? We need to answer that because those women will never be safe until we do."

The knot that had lived in Hank's stomach tightened. He'd hoped he'd been wrong, overreacting somehow because of his feelings for Amelia. But the sheriff confirmed every fear of his. "I suppose we should ask Amelia and Emily that. I think they had made arrangements Sunday at church with Stephen to visit. Anyone could have overheard. Even if they weren't the perpetrator but just reported it to someone else." His mind instantly went to Stanley. He could see the man being involved, but to what end? Should he tell the sheriff? It would mean revealing his own identity. Yet if it protected Amelia and Emily, it was a cost he'd gladly pay.

He glanced around. "Can we take a walk outside?"

Sheriff Riley frowned but nodded.

Once out of earshot, Hank crossed his arms and rocked back on his heels. "I'm not who you think I am."

THE SCHOOLROOM WAS ALMOST as chaotic as the day before a holiday. All the children knew tomorrow was their beloved Miss Stanton's wedding, and most were eager to help prepare for it. Amelia had given up even trying to teach lessons. Instead, under her watchful eye, they cut branches and vines and greenery from the schoolyard which they tied with twine and decorated the schoolhouse with. The fresh evergreens smelled amazing. She placed candles strategically throughout that she would light tomorrow and taught the girls how to make fluffy bows for the benches.

Since nothing unusual had happened since the night of the sabotaged wagon wheel, Amelia had been able to breathe a bit easier. But Hank insisted on accompanying her everywhere. She didn't mind at all. But more than anything, she hoped Emily had a beautiful wedding with no distractions.

The boys moved the desks out and moved in the benches, as well as swept the floors and washed the windows until they sparkled with the sunlight shining through.

And they all contributed to the banner at the back of the schoolhouse that Josh and Emily would see once they were married and headed back down the aisle: Congratulations, Mr. and Mrs. Benson.

Emily would be so touched. Amelia was thrilled with how the children had pitched in and made the schoolhouse festive for their teacher's special day.

She let the children go early. There was much she needed to do back at the boardinghouse, and no one was in the mood to concentrate anyway.

Hank appeared in the back of the schoolroom, his eyes

taking in the transformed space. He gave her a gentle smile. She couldn't help but wonder if someday the schoolhouse would be decorated for their wedding. And was he thinking the same thing? She pushed the thought away, afraid it might show on her face.

"The decorations are amazing. You've worked a miracle."

Amelia warmed under his praise. "Well, I had help. The children did a lot. Emily will be so thrilled."

He drew near and took her hand for a moment, holding her gaze. Maybe he did have the same thoughts she did.

He let go of her hand and helped her into her coat. "Let me take your things."

She handed them to him. With a final look around, they left the building and she locked up.

They were halfway down Main Street, when Hank chuckled and covered her hand with his. "You're in a hurry to get home."

"I am. I'm hoping Josh is back with the flowers from Ankeny's that I need to make the bouquets. And then there is the baking and cooking to do."

"I think every woman in town is baking and cooking right now."

"I hope so. The whole town will be at this wedding."

Amelia helped Emily and Maggie prepare supper for the passengers as well as the final preparations for the next day. The three of them went over the list of things for tomorrow, making sure nothing had been forgotten.

Amelia glanced up to see Emily biting her lip.

"What's wrong?"

"The stage is late."

Amelia glanced at the watch pinned to her blouse, visible above her apron. It was. Quite late. They'd been so busy with the preparations, she'd lost track of time.

Emily glanced out the kitchen window. Maggie squeezed her shoulders. "It's not the first time. Let's get everyone else fed."

Hank came in the kitchen door. "Hold supper for us. Seth

and Owen and I are going to ride out to meet the stage. We'll take James, too, if you don't mind, Maggie."

"That's fine. Take care of yourselves. There's a wedding tomorrow."

Hank nodded then met Amelia's gaze. "I'll see you tonight." He winked.

Relief eased some of the worry from Emily's face, but Amelia knew Emily wouldn't feel peace until she saw Josh. And given what had happened to them earlier in the week, she knew Emily had to be thinking the same things she was. What if the stagecoach had been sabotaged or held up?

Maggie dished up the food. "We should eat. Take these into the dining room, and call Charlie and Sally. And Doc and Roy."

The meal was silent other than the scrape of utensils across dishes. Emily mostly pushed her food around.

"Eat," Maggie urged her. "You don't want to faint from hunger on your wedding day."

Emily gave her a small smile but did take a few more bites.

Amelia thought about the flowers from Ankeny's that were supposed to be on the stage. Should she think of alternate plans in case the flowers didn't make it? Then again, if the groom didn't make it, why should she worry about the flowers? No, Josh would make it. And if the flowers were damaged in transit, she'd think of something.

As they were clearing the supper dishes away, the rattle of the stagecoach wheels and hoofbeats came nearer. Everyone jumped up and ran to the front porch.

Hank, Seth, and Owen rode up behind the stagecoach. Hank waved at Amelia but headed for the barn. James dismounted his horse and opened the stagecoach door, helping passengers down. Josh climbed down from the driver's seat, looking haggard and drawn. Something had definitely happened. He glanced up at Emily and gave her a tired smile but moved to the boot to begin unloading baggage.

Amelia went inside, through the kitchen and back out to the

barn, catching up with Hank as he was putting Prince away. "What happened?"

"The stage had been held up. We got there after the robbers had left. And no one was hurt this time. But once again, they got Seth's payroll." Hank glanced at Seth who was taking care of his own horse.

"I had changed the delivery date because I didn't want it on the stage when James was driving next week while Josh is on his honeymoon. So it's mighty suspicious."

Hank's jaw could have been carved from granite. "I'll get to the bottom of this. There are only a few people who knew about it."

The stagecoach rolled up to the barn, and Josh hopped down. "Amelia, those flowers you ordered are in the boot. Where do you want them?" His words dripped with exhaustion and frustration. And on the eve of his wedding as well.

"Hank, could you help me? We can put them on the bench where my cuttings were. I'll make the bouquets tonight after you all have eaten supper."

They unloaded the flowers while the other men took care of the horses and stage. Then the men headed inside for a much-needed hot supper. They were quiet at the meal, answering basic questions. But she didn't miss the looks that passed between Hank, Josh, and Seth. There was plenty going on that they didn't want her and Emily to know.

After supper, she worked on the bouquets for Becca, Sally, her, and Emily. But her mind couldn't stop thinking about what had happened this week. And what might happen next. *Please, Lord, let Emily and Josh have a beautiful wedding with nothing to mar it.*

Chapter Twenty-Nine

✦❈✦

Amelia couldn't help her excitement as the recently repaired wagon driven by Hank carried the women, food, and flowers over to the nearly completed parsonage.

Maggie wandered through the rooms, exclaiming over how wonderful everything was.

Emily laughed. "If it weren't for my wedding, we could have the town move you and Pastor Roy in here today."

"Now hush. This wedding is more important than that." Maggie finished buttoning up Emily's gown. "And it's wonderful that you can dress here instead of having to ride in a wagon in your gown."

As Maggie helped Emily primp, Amelia and Sally carried in the food and the flowers. Being able to store the food inside until it was ready to eat was a true blessing. No one would have to stand next to the food tables shooing away bugs and curious animals.

Becca arrived and toured the parsonage, making many of the same comments Maggie had. "Maggie, it's just wonderful. I'm sure you can't wait to have all of you back under one roof again."

She smiled. "I've been so blessed by my friends and this town. This is more than I could have ever imagined. There's even a study for Roy to meet privately with people or work on his sermons."

Amelia handed out the bouquets. The white roses and pale-pink peonies from Ankeny's New Market had arrived in pristine condition. With a bit of greenery and wrapped in a blush ribbon, they were the perfect touch.

"Oh, Amelia! These are just beautiful." Emily stuck her nose in the blossoms. "I can't even imagine how you found these flowers."

Amelia grinned, thrilled to have pleased her new friend with something special.

Mrs. Parsons and Mrs. Fulton arrived, and after touring the parsonage, they took charge of the food. "I'd best get seated." Maggie kissed Emily's cheek and bustled from the room. Soon after, the wedding party headed over to the schoolhouse serving as the church today. Amelia peeked in the doors. The church was full. Josh and Pastor Roy stood at the front. She turned back to Emily and grinned. "It's time!"

Sally started down the aisle, followed by Amelia, and finally Becca. When it was Emily's turn, Amelia fixed her eyes on Josh instead. The look on his face when he spotted Emily was inde-scribable joy. Josh smiled a lot, but she'd never seen him so happy.

Emily made her way down the aisle and joined Josh, handing Becca her bouquet and taking Josh's hands. Pastor Roy gave a touching ceremony, knowing both of them well. And soon he was pronouncing them husband and wife, and Josh was tenderly kissing his beloved bride.

They exited the church to cheers and clapping. Amelia saw the moment Emily spotted the banner her schoolchildren had made. Her hand went to her mouth, and she glanced back.

The rest of the day was a true celebration. The sun shone, people filled their plates, congratulated the newlyweds, and visited with each other. It was the first all-town event—other than the parsonage raising—since Christmas. And even though the winters here weren't terrible, it was clear people were happy to have an excuse to get out and gather together.

Hank got many compliments on the parsonage, and the plan was to move Maggie and Pastor Roy in next weekend if all went well. Amelia stood by his side, or rather, he wouldn't let her out of his sight. She hoped that was the only result of the week's events, that Emily and Josh were as thoroughly enjoying themselves as they appeared to be.

Amelia was helping load the food into the wagon, what little of it remained, when Sally grabbed her hand.

"Emily's going to toss her bouquet. You have to come."

She allowed Sally to drag her to the bottom of the church steps, standing toward the back of the crowd gathered there. Emily stood at the top with Josh, laughing. "Is everyone ready?" She turned her back to them and tossed her bouquet over her shoulder. It bounced off a few hands before landing squarely in Amelia's.

Everyone looked her way and clapped. She glanced over at Hank who gave her a rakish grin. Her face heated.

Luckily, the crowd dispersed as folks headed for home.

Hank came to take her arm, his gaze warm on her. "So do you believe in those superstitions?"

She dropped her gaze to her good kidskin boots. "They are rather silly."

"Maybe. Maybe not." He covered her hand with his and led her home.

HANK TOOK FAR TOO much pleasure in making Amelia blush. But her pink cheeks dusted with freckles were so becoming, he couldn't help himself. The boardinghouse clan made their way home in a happy parade. And he was content to have Amelia on his arm.

He took great satisfaction in that Maggie and Pastor Roy, as well as the townspeople, were pleased with the parsonage. He'd have more work on his hands than he could handle. And once the sawmill got here, hopefully this week, things would really move forward. He'd have to see if Seth could spare more men to do construction work.

Except that they'd have to resolve the payroll robberies. He'd looked for Stanley Wallace and had spotted him a few times, but Josh and Emily's wedding was not the time to make a scene.

After Hank had told the sheriff about his true identity and Wallace's work for Hank's father, the sheriff had said he'd pay a visit to the man. But like Hank had thought, there wasn't anything connecting him to any of their troubles. Except now perhaps the payroll robbery. He was one of the people who knew about it. But that didn't mean he'd somehow gotten the information to Red Dawson. There was a missing link somewhere.

Still, the man had made himself scarce. He was one of the few people who would have known about the payroll. But what would he gain by having it stolen? And what could be his connection to Red Dawson? He didn't know, and today he just wanted to enjoy celebrating with his friends and the love of his life.

When they reached the boardinghouse, Josh waved them over the bridge. "Come see our wedding gifts in the cabin."

Hank helped unload the wagon with the gifts the townspeople had brought to the wedding, but he had also helped Josh and Charlie wrestle a few bigger pieces over this morning. He thought Amelia would enjoy seeing Emily's reaction to them.

He took her hand as they crossed the footbridge and up to the cozy cabin. Josh had the door propped open, and they arrived just in time to see Emily's reaction to his gift to her. A beautiful carved bookcase stood in the living area, already filled with her books. Her hands went to her cheeks, astonishment on her face.

Next to it sat a painted trunk from Charlie. "I figured you might want it at the foot of your bed for storing linens and such." Charlie opened the lid, revealing a compartmented tray nestled inside. "It's got a cedar lining."

She bent down and touched the top. "Charlie, it's beautiful. Thank you so much."

"Turn around." Josh took her by the shoulders. On the low table in front of the fireplace sat a delicately painted china tea set complete with eight settings of fine cups and saucers. "It's from Maggie, Pastor Roy, Becca, and Seth."

Emily burst into tears and wiped them away. Maggie handed her a lace handkerchief. "I can't thank you all enough. It's all so beautiful and thoughtful. And now I can have all you girls over for tea."

Becca leaned over and whispered something to Emily. Emily's eyes went wide, and her mouth dropped open before she wrapped Becca in a hug.

After hugs all around, everyone left the newlyweds alone. They would leave for Portland in the morning by horseback. Seth, Hank, and Josh had discussed it and figured that moving quickly was their best safety move. None of them thought it likely someone would try to take Emily from Josh, who was more familiar with the backroads than anyone and would be armed.

Hank hoped they were correct. And it was all the more reason he needed to have a talk with Stanley Wallace. Since Hank knew who Stanley was, perhaps he'd get somewhere the sheriff couldn't.

AMELIA AND HANK headed down the porch steps from Josh and Emily's cabin. She headed for the footbridge but he tugged her arm. "Feel like taking a walk? Let's go view the meadow."

She smiled. "I'd love to." After all the excitement of the day, a quiet walk in beautiful surroundings sounded perfect.

Hank's gaze kept darting to their surroundings. She didn't

think anyone would harm them out here so close to the boardinghouse and in a place so few people knew about. But she found his protectiveness sweet and endearing. It had been a long time since she'd felt so cared for.

They reached the meadow, the afternoon sun touching everything with a golden light. She examined the flowers with new eyes, now that she knew their common and Latin names. There were even more than there had been the last time they were here. She gathered up another bunch, which was a bit silly since she now had two bouquets at home, but she couldn't resist. Wildflowers were ephemeral.

She glanced up to see Hank gazing at her with amusement. She laughed. "It probably seems silly."

"No, if it makes you happy, it's not silly." He took the bunch she had gathered from her. "How did you first get interested in plants and flowers? Was it from your mother?"

She nodded. "My earliest memories were of being in the garden with her. I would hold her hand as she held the basket that contained sharp clippers. I was never to touch them. But I got to hold the garden book that told all about the flowers and plants."

She glanced up at him. "I still have it. Even though it isn't as thorough for the plants out here as some of Sy's books, it's dear to me. She showed me how to prune plants, where to cut them so they'd grow back the fullest. When we cut the flowers for our bouquets and vases, she showed me where to do it." She giggled. "I remember her showing me the names of the flowers in the garden book. I thought peony was the funniest word because it didn't look like the way you say it. We would sit on the porch swing and go through that book for hours."

Hank had a thoughtful look on his face. "There's a porch swing at the boardinghouse."

"That there is. A bit chilly right now, but I can see spending some summer nights out there."

"Perhaps you'd let me join you?" He grinned down at her.

"I think that could be arranged."

As they headed back to the boardinghouse, she thought that Mother would have loved Emily's wedding. She would have been amazed at the flowers Amelia was able to get from Ankeny's New Market, and she would have adored all of Amelia's friends in this town. The sharp ache in her heart that occurred whenever she thought about what Mother was missing wasn't quiet as sharp this time. She looked forward to sharing more memories of her mother with Hank. Because she would have liked him too.

Chapter Thirty

Hank was working at the doc's quarters with John, trying to make good progress on this house so Doc and Amelia could have their own space. Charlie's leg was well enough that he could do the finish carpentry on the parsonage, something he enjoyed and was good at. After school, Hank would get the apprentices started over here at the doc's house. Rough carpentry suited their skillset better than finish work.

Sheriff Riley strode up. "Gotta minute, Hank?"

"Sure." Hank dropped his hammer. He glanced across the street at Mrs. Paige's house then motioned the sheriff toward the back of the lot, where they wouldn't be overheard.

"I wired Marshal O'Connor. He was here last fall when some of Red Dawson's stolen money had been traced to Emily's bag."

Hank nodded. "I remember him."

"I told him what had happened around here and asked if he knew anything about Dawson's activities. I'll let you know what I hear back. Hopefully he'll have information that is useful."

"I thought I might talk to Stanley Wallace today. I know you did, but he doesn't know that I know he's working for my father. If I tell him that, then the wind goes out of his sails and he might fess up to what he knows."

"Let me know if you learn anything."

Horse hoofs sounded on the street behind them and they turned. Two men on horseback stopped in the street. They were the surveyors, Jeremiah Crowley and Davis Shoun.

"Welcome back to town." He glanced at the sheriff, and they headed toward the men. "This is our sheriff, Mike Riley."

They dismounted and shook hands. "Nice to meet you, Sheriff." Crowley pulled out several papers from his saddlebags. "We're back and ready to begin our work. Headquarters liked what we discussed enough that I have a contract for you."

"That was fast. You know I can't get to your quarters until this building is finished."

Crowley nodded. "We've got to stay ahead of the construction crew, and they're laying track faster than anticipated. We're staying at Parsons Hotel. We have a contract with him until July. In the meantime, we're authorized to provisionally approve plans for our quarters and forward them on to headquarters for final approval."

"I'll get the contract back to you tonight. The plans will take a bit longer."

"You know where to find us." Crowley touched the brim of his hat, and Shoun nodded. They moved off.

Hank looked at the sheriff. "They got back here quicker than I expected."

The sheriff lifted his hat and reseated it on his head. "Going to bring a lot more changes here sooner than expected." He extended a hand to Hank. "Let me know if Wallace says anything."

WHEN JOHN TOOK a break for lunch, Hank headed over to the bank. The clerk showed him to Wallace's office immediately.

"Henry Paulson. What a pleasure. Won't you have a seat?" Wallace gestured to the chair in front of his desk with a smirk.

Hank grimaced at the use of his given name. "I'll stand. I want to know what you know about Red Dawson and his gang." He folded his arms over his chest and glared down at the man.

Did the man pale and wince? It was so fleeting, so quickly replaced by a glib smile that Hank wasn't sure.

"The infamous stagecoach robber? Everyone knows about him. He's suspected in the last two robberies of the Oregon Express, for example."

"And I find it curious that the only time the Oregon Express has ever been held up was when the payroll for Seth Blake's logging company was on it."

"How unlucky for Mr. Blake."

"It'll be unlucky for whoever leaked the information to Dawson about the payroll. Would you have anything to do with that?"

"A banker wouldn't last very long if he divulged his patrons' information, now would he?" Wallace placed his hands on top of his desk.

"No. He wouldn't. But if he was being supported by and supplying information to the owner of the bank, well now, that would be a different story."

Wallace did pale this time.

Hank allowed a small smile. "I know you're working for my father, reporting to him what goes on here. That's fine. Feel free to tell him anything you like. I'm actually waiting for a letter from him." He leaned forward. "If anything happens to Amelia or Emily or anyone in this town, I will personally hold you responsible. So if you have any information to share, I suggest you make sure that the sheriff learns about it."

Wallace raised his chin, but his swallow ruined his defiant attempt. "Of course. Any good citizen would. Even in this back-water town."

"If you don't like it here, you should go." Hank gave him a hard stare before leaving.

AMELIA HELPED Maggie get supper on the table. Emily's absence was felt, leaving a hole in the ordered routine that she and Maggie had. Amelia tried to be as helpful as possible, but she knew she was a far cry from Emily's practiced hands. Still, she hoped Emily and Josh were enjoying their honeymoon in Portland.

She and Maggie got the food on the table and sat with the others. Becca and Seth had joined them for supper, which was good because Hank had told her the railroad men had come to town and the sawmill was due this week. He was going to be busy. And Seth and James were taking the stage run tomorrow.

Pastor Roy said the blessing, and they all began eating. Saturday, he and Maggie plus Sally and James would move into the parsonage. The boardinghouse would feel quite empty without their steadying presence.

She turned and caught Hank's gaze as he sat next to her. "Deep thoughts? You've hardly eaten."

"Just thinking about how everything changes." She took a bite of the shepherd's pie she had neglected.

Hank gave her a slow smile. "Me too. But some changes are good."

She nodded.

"Becca and I have an announcement to make." Seth scanned the table, making sure he had everyone's attention. Then he broke out in a grin and slipped his arm around his wife's shoulders. "Becca and I are expecting."

The table erupted in cheers. Yes, some changes were definitely good. Amelia glanced at her father who didn't seem surprised. She had suspected it too. And so had Maggie, by her twinkling eyes.

Pink flushed Becca's cheeks. "We'll be blessed late summer. So far, I've felt fine, other than tired and a little stomach upset.

And Emily and Josh already know. I whispered it to her before they left."

Ah, so that's what that had been about. Amelia smiled. She never thought she'd be part of something that felt like a large family. But the sense of fullness and satisfaction that fell over her had little to do with Maggie's delicious cooking and a lot more to do with the company she was sharing it with.

The chatter continued around the table while Amelia began clearing plates and putting away food. She waved off Becca's help. When she and Maggie had put the kitchen to rights, they carried trays of coffee, cups, and cookies out to the parlor.

Hank patted the space next to him on the settee, and Amelia joined him. "I was just telling everyone about the surveyors coming to town today and how we're going to need more builders, especially once the sawmill gets here this week, and we won't have to order lumber in."

Seth took a mug from Maggie. "The lumberjacks are starting to come back now that winter is over and the weather is warm enough to log again. Which means I'll have more men to choose from. Several who have helped you out, Hank, seemed to enjoy it. Men like Andrew Paige and Tim Donnally who have homes and families in town."

Charlie took a cookie off the plate from his place by the fire. "We're going to need a woodworking shop sooner rather than later. We don't have room in our little shop to build cupboards, and more people will want bookcases, dressers, and other fine woodwork."

The men discussed where to put the sawmill, where the train depot might go—Hank would ask the surveyors tomorrow— and the logistics of setting up a construction and fine wood-working shop. Amelia didn't understand all the details, but watching Hank's face light up as he discussed the options with Seth warmed her heart.

Not all change was bad. She was sad at what it meant for Emily and Josh, but according to Charlie, they were already planning to run the boardinghouse as just a boardinghouse, and Josh would join the woodworking shop. Their little town was booming and soon wouldn't be so little much longer.

Her eyes grew heavy at the talk. Hank nudged her, a slow smile around his lips. "It was a warm day today and tonight's not too cold. Want to try out that porch swing?"

She nodded. Her father and Charlie had gone to their rooms apparently. Becca and Seth, as well as Maggie and Pastor Roy, were getting ready to leave. She said her goodbyes and pulled the quilt off the back of the settee. They slipped out the front door and settled on the porch swing, setting it to a gentle motion. She spread the quilt over their laps.

The sounds of the town settling down for the night slipped over her. The faint sounds of crickets and tree peepers floated to them from the woods. How would all of this change? And how would things be different between her and Hank? He would be so busy. Then she and Father would be in their own quarters, and she wouldn't see Hank so often.

"You've been thinking a lot tonight. No wonder you're tired." Hank's gentle teasing tone washed over her.

"I guess I expected the biggest adjustment in my life to be when we moved out here. It never occurred to me that things would still change. Which is silly. Of course they would. But I just never thought about it." She gave a small shrug. "I like things the way they are. I'm a bit afraid of what the future will bring."

Hank covered her hand with his. "Whatever happens, we'll face it together."

She nodded and laid her head on his shoulder, the motion of the swing lulling her into a sense of contentment.

Except for that nagging sense that the change coming wouldn't be anything like they expected.

Chapter Thirty-One

"Hank!"

He looked up from hanging siding with John on the doc's house to see Mr. Fulton hurrying down the road, apron flapping. He put another nail in then dropped his hammer and headed toward him.

"What is it?"

"The freighter is here with the sawmill. It's a beast of a thing, and he wants to know where you want it. Also, you'll need to round up some men to help unload it."

Excitement flashed through his veins. It was here. All the plans they'd talked about began with this first step. "Come on, John. Let's go see this beast."

John dropped his hammer and followed suit.

The freighter had pulled up in front of the mercantile. In the main wagon, a jumble of belts, gears, giant saw blades, and pulleys filled the wagon. In the second wagon, something that looked like the front part of a small train took up the wagon bed. This was going to be fun to put together and get running. He only wished Sy was here to advise him. He'd write him tonight.

"John, you can take Prince—he's at the boardinghouse—and

ride up to the logging camp to let Seth know the sawmill is here. He'll come down with some men."

"Sure thing, Boss."

Hank chuckled. He looked up at the freighter in his high seat. "We're actually going to go back the way you came. Past the schoolhouse."

The freighter motioned him up. "Climb on up, and you can show me." He extended a beefy paw. "Curtis Frank."

Hank scrambled up and shook it. "Hank Paulson." School would be out soon. He bet the children—not to mention his apprentices—would love to look at this. Anything new in town brought excitement. He directed Curtis Frank around the block and back the way they came. After talking to the surveyors and their general plan for where the train depot might go, Hank and Seth had marked out a lot past town across from it. He hoped that the town's growth would keep it at the edge of town for some time. Being near the depot would be convenient for shipping cut and finished goods. And it would help Seth's logging business as well.

They'd still need to build at minimum a large shed to protect the sawmill and workers so they would work in most weather. His mind reeled with the possibilities and what still needed to be done. If only he could be in two places at once. Doc's house still needed to be built. At least the shed would require only rudimentary construction skills. Something the apprentices and John could handle. Tim Donnally and Andrew Paige could help him finish up Doc's place.

He and Frank arrived at the location and discussed the best way to unload the sawmill. While they waited for help, Frank leaned up against the huge wagon wheel and ate.

"I'm going to head over to the schoolhouse and get some of the bigger boys to help as well."

Frank nodded.

Hank strode back toward the schoolhouse. The distance from the sawmill and the trees between should keep the sound from traveling too far. He didn't want learning to be disrupted by the noise. It was another thing they had considered.

He skipped up the schoolhouse steps and cautiously opened the doors, peeking inside. He caught Amelia's eyes immediately. Her eyebrows shot up as her brow furrowed. He grinned to let her know everything was fine.

She handed the book she was reading from to one of the bigger girls and headed down the aisle to him. The children's eyes followed her. "What's going on?"

He grinned. "The sawmill is here. I thought the children might like to see it, if it wouldn't be a disruption to your schedule. And I need the help of some of the bigger boys."

She glanced back over her shoulder. All the children were staring and whispering. She gave him a saucy grin. "I think that can be arranged." She raised her voice. "Children, Mr. Paulson has just informed me that the sawmill for the town has been delivered. Would you like to go see it?"

Pandemonium ensued as the children shouted their agreement.

Amelia raised her voice. "You can go home after you've seen the sawmill, so note your homework assignments and gather your things."

He stood back out of the way as children rushed around them then he followed Amelia to her desk where she gathered her things.

She smiled at him. "You look like a little boy on Christmas Day."

"I feel a bit like one." In fact, there was really only one thing missing from making his happiness complete, and that was having her by his side—his—forever.

HANK COULDN'T REMEMBER the last time he felt this focused and confident. Amelia had headed home to help Maggie, which had given him a twinge of disappointment, but he couldn't expect her to stand around and watch him work. He sent one of the bigger boys to escort her home and then hurry back. Most of the school children had cleared out by the time Seth arrived from the logging camp. The sheriff and a few other men from town were with him too. With all their help, they'd get this unloaded quickly.

They had gotten nearly everything out of the two wagons when a man rode up. Sheriff Riley moved to intercept the man as he dismounted. "Marshal O'Connor. I didn't expect you to make a personal visit." He waved Seth and Hank over. "I believe you know Seth Blake. This is Hank Paulson."

The marshal shook hands with the men. "Blake, it was your payroll stolen, correct?"

"Twice." Seth's lips pressed into a thin line.

"There's been other reports of stagecoach holdups and robberies in the area, but the Oregon Express was the only one hit twice in a short span of time. You suspect an informer?" The marshal lifted his hat and resettled it.

"I think it might be Stanley Wallace, the bank manager." Hank kept his voice low. Even though the man was a snake, he didn't want the townsfolk thinking their money wasn't safe in the bank. "I can't prove anything, but he's one of the few people that would have known about both robberies."

Sheriff Riley tilted his head. "Wallace wasn't here when the first robbery took place."

"No, he was working for my father's bank in Portland. Where the money originated." Hank didn't see the point in hiding what he knew about Wallace. Seth and the sheriff knew about his family's wealth.

Marshal O'Connor coughed into his fist and pulled out his canteen, taking a swig. "I'll check into him. See about his Portland connections. Anything else going on that I should know about?" He glanced at the sawmill. "Quite a contraption you've got there."

Hank shifted his weight. "With the railroad coming through, we expect to need a sawmill sooner rather than later."

The marshal nodded. "Saw how far they'd gotten on my way in. Things sure are changing. Before you know it, I'll be able to take the train here instead of riding." He coughed again. "Does Mrs. Kincaid have room at her boardinghouse? I'd planned to stay a few days."

Seth nodded. "Yes, but it's Mrs. Adams now. She and the pastor married at Christmas."

"Well, I'll be sure to give her my best wishes." He mounted his horse. "I'll see you soon."

They watched him ride off. Seth shook his head. "Josh is not going to be happy to come back from his honeymoon to find the marshal here."

The marshal had been hard on Emily last year, believing her to be part of Dawson's gang. No one was sure if he was ever convinced Emily had been a victim.

The sheriff clapped Seth on the shoulder. "Maybe he'll be gone by then."

Chapter Thirty-Two

A melia joined Maggie on the front porch of the boardinghouse to meet the stage. Seth and James were driving it back, and Josh and Emily would be on it.

"How do you think Josh will feel about riding in his own stage?" She turned to Maggie.

Maggie smiled. "Knowing him, he might have kicked James off the driver's spot and driven it himself with Seth. Just like old times."

"Even with his bride inside?"

"He's been a stagecoach driver longer than he's been a married man. It might take some adjusting for him."

The stage came down Main Street and into view. Sure enough, Josh was at the reins. Amelia laughed. "You know him well."

"Like one of my own."

James hopped out of the stage and set the step down, helping the passengers off. Emily emerged, bright as a freshly blooming rose. She was followed by a man that looked somewhat familiar. Probably because he resembled a hero on the cover of one of her dime novels. Dressed in fine clothes, he stood a bit taller than Emily. And his eyes were a light brown, almost golden color. Just a bit darker than Hank's. He tipped his hat at Maggie and Amelia. Amelia's thoughts raced back to her early perceptions of Hank. This man reminded her of that time.

Amelia and then Maggie hugged Emily. "Welcome back. I can't wait to hear all about your trip."

"Oh you will." She turned to the newcomer. "And may I present Mr. Philip Paulson. Hank's brother."

Now she knew why he looked familiar.

"Welcome, Mr. Paulson." Maggie gave him her warm smile. "Will you be staying with us?"

"If you have room, I'd be pleased to."

"I'm sure we could arrange something."

Amelia did a quick count in her head. With the marshal still with them, Philip would have to share Hank's room. He wouldn't mind, would he? She recalled what he'd said about how Philip had treated him as a boy, but Philip seemed charming enough now. Surely he'd outgrown his behavior. But would Hank be glad to see him? She had to think he would. Philip was family, after all.

"Thank you, Mrs. Benson, for making this trip more enjoyable." Philip climbed the porch stairs after them.

Amelia glanced at Emily. Her cheeks were pink, probably from being called Mrs. Benson. Amelia smiled. The name—and the blush—suited Emily.

"Oh, I'm sure I talked your ear off. Thank you for indulging me."

Amelia pulled Maggie aside. "I'm assuming you mean for him to share with Hank. Should I go let Hank know his brother is here?"

"Hank would not be pleased if I let you wander through town unescorted. He'll be here soon enough. But I won't send Philip to their room just yet, in case Hank feels the need to make other arrangements."

Emily had shown Philip where to freshen up and introduced him to Pastor Roy and Charlie who were seated in the parlor awaiting supper. She then tried to join Maggie and Amelia in the kitchen, but Maggie wouldn't hear of it. "You've been traveling all day, and Amelia and I have been getting along just fine. There's not much left to do. Go entertain our guest until the rest of the menfolk show up. Which should be any minute."

And Maggie was right. The kitchen door swung open regularly admitting Josh and James, followed by Hank. While Josh and James knew better than to linger in Maggie's kitchen while she was getting supper on, Amelia stopped Hank.

He smiled down on her. "It's good to see you. Meet me on the porch swing again tonight?"

"I hope to. We have a passenger on the stagecoach who is staying over with us."

"The marshal hasn't left yet, right? One of them can room with me. That's fine." He started to move away.

She caught his arm. "It's your brother. Philip."

HANK'S FEET KEPT MOVING. He needed to wash up. But then Amelia's words sunk in. Surely he had misheard. "Philip. Are you sure? Why would he come out here?" In fact, out here was the last place he ever thought Philip would venture. It had nothing to entice him and involved an inconvenient journey. Not to mention it was a long way from San Francisco.

"You can ask him that after supper. He's in the parlor."

Hank's mind spun as he washed up outside the dining room. He poked his head in the parlor. Charlie, Pastor Roy, Marshal O'Connor. And Philip. He couldn't believe his eyes.

And there wasn't time to say anything. Maggie called them into supper. The men rose and made their way toward the dining room. Hank stepped out of the hall and into Philip's path.

"Amelia told me you were here, but I couldn't believe it. Yet here you are." He extended his hand.

Philip took it. Hank was surprised at the softness, the lack of callouses. He'd been around working men in Reedsville and had forgotten that most of the men in the banking world he had come from had hands just like Philip's.

"Here I am. I survived the journey and lived to tell the tale." He gave a rakish grin.

"Well let's get into supper. Maggie is an amazing cook, but she doesn't brook tardiness at her table."

"Indeed." Philip made his way into the dining room and seated himself in the open seat next to Amelia, smiling at her.

Hank met Amelia's gaze with a strained smile and took a seat across from her.

Josh and Emily both had strained looks, likely from the marshal's presence.

After the blessing and the food was passed, the conversation consisted of details of Josh and Emily's trip and Philip's trip from San Francisco.

"Marshal, did you discover any more information about the stagecoach robberies?" Hank asked after he had wiped his plate clean.

"Nothing solid. I have my suspicions that Danny Tillman is still hanging around. He might be your informer. There are far too many footprints and hoofprints around his family's old barn. But nothing I can prove. Proof seems in short supply in this town." His glance took in Josh and Emily. A fine sheet of sweat beaded across his forehead, and he seemed pale.

"Will you be staying long then?" It bordered on being a rude question, but everyone wanted to know, so Hank figured he'd risk it. Though the man didn't look well.

"I plan on leaving tomorrow. But perhaps after supper—" he coughed into his napkin "—we could discuss an idea I have."

Doc Martin frowned. "How long have you had that cough?"

"A few days. It's nothing."

"I'd like to take a listen to your chest."

"I wouldn't want to bother you."

"It's no bother, I assure you." Doc paused. "I insist. There are always various sicknesses in big cities. There is less worry out here with all of this fresh air and open space." He pushed his chair back. "Let me grab my bag, and I'll meet you in the parlor."

The marshal nodded and followed him out of the dining room.

Pastor Roy pushed his empty plate away and leaned his arms on the table. "Philip, what brings you all the way from San Francisco?"

Hank had never been more glad that he had told his true identity to Amelia and her father. Most people in town thought he was from Portland. He hadn't counted on the relief a clean conscious could bring.

"I came to pay a long-overdue visit to my brother." He grinned in Hank's direction. "I wanted to surprise him."

"You succeeded." Hank's return smile felt tight. "How long do you plan on staying?"

"Well, that all depends on you."

Hank was nearly certain he didn't want to hear the next words that would come out of Philip's mouth. And he was absolutely certain he didn't want the whole table to hear it. "How about we take a walk, and I'll show you where everything is in town? I'll be at the jobsite tomorrow and won't be available then. Unless you'd like to help build Doc's house?" He pushed back from his chair and mouthed *I'm sorry* to Amelia. He'd much rather sit on a porch swing with her than walk the darkening streets of the town with his brother. But he wanted to know what Philip's play was before he announced it to everyone else.

Philip tossed his napkin on the table. "Every bit as delicious as was promised, Mrs. Adams."

Maggie smiled. "Please, call me Maggie."

Philip nodded and pushed back from the table. "Lead onward, brother."

As they passed the parlor, the marshal spotted them. "Hank, we still need to talk."

"We will. If not tonight, then in the morning."

He continued out the door and down the porch steps, heading down Main Street, assuming Philip would follow. Most of it was dark and shuttered, other than the saloons, but it gave them some privacy for what was sure to be a conversation Hank wouldn't like.

"Wait up." Philip jogged a few steps and coughed.

"You sound like the marshal. You should have Doc listen to you too."

Philip waved it away. "It's just the dust from that stagecoach ride."

"I wrote Father almost a month ago. Did he get my letter?"

"That's why I'm here."

"So you know Father hired Stanley Wallace to spy on me and interfere in my friend's business."

"Hank, you always were too serious." Philip clapped him on the shoulder. "I wouldn't consider it spying. Father was just looking out for your interests."

"I can run my interests just fine." Hank shoved his hands in his front pockets. "Father and I had an agreement. He agreed to let me make it on my own."

Philip shook his head. "I don't know how you can consider any life successful that is lived in this dusty little town." He kicked at a rock and coughed again. "Why here? You have enough money to live anywhere you want."

"It doesn't matter what you or Father think. It's my life, and I'm happy here."

"You have an obligation to your family. It's your birthright. You can't just turn your back on it. You need to come home and run the banking business. Father would even agree to let you do it from Portland instead of San Francisco. And that's all the concession you're going to get from him."

"So Father doesn't intend to hold up his end of the agreement? Of letting me prove that I can make it on my own?"

Philip laughed. "Don't you get it? There was no agreement. Just a chance to let you sow your oats and get this idea of physical labor out of your system. But it has to be cut short. Father's health isn't good. It's his heart. The doctors say he mustn't get himself worked up over things, and that means someone else needs to run the day-to-day banking operations."

Hank stopped and whirled on Philip. "You do it, then."

Philip laughed, and then stopped abruptly. "Oh, you're serious. You can't be. You know me. I'm the family disappointment. Never can hold a job. I represent us in San Francisco's society. I get named in the papers for whom I'm seen with, and I remind people that my father has a lot of money and they should do business with him." He scowled and his gaze narrowed. "That's my job." He nearly spat the words.

A thread of something that nearly felt like sympathy wound its way into Hank's heart. But it was overpowered by what could only be considered his father's treachery. Hot anger coursed through his veins like lightning in a thunderstorm. Why had he been so concerned about keeping up his end of the deal? About proving to his father he could make it as his own man? His father never had any intention of letting that happen. He wished more than anything right now that he could go pound some nails as an outlet for his frustration. His thoughts chased each other in circles so that he couldn't make sense of any of it.

He spun on his heel and headed toward the boardinghouse. "You're rooming with me," he tossed over his shoulder. He didn't care if Philip kept up with him or not. He could find his way back.

As Philip coughed again behind him, Hank hoped that it didn't keep him up all night. One of them had to work in the morning.

Chapter Thirty-Three

＊＊＊

Amelia and Emily got breakfast on the table at the boardinghouse the next morning. Maggie had wanted to come over and help, but they insisted that she and Pastor Roy stay at the cottage and get everything ready to be moved into the parsonage. Becca showed up with a pan of her famous cinnamon rolls based off Mrs. Hanson's recipe. It was still a mystery how Becca got that recipe, but Amelia wasn't going to complain. They were one of the most delicious things she'd ever tasted.

A bowl of scrambled eggs with diced ham joined the cinnamon rolls while Emily finished frying up the bacon.

Hank slipped into the kitchen, wrapped his arm around Amelia, and gave her cheek a quick kiss. "Morning, beautiful."

She gave him a swat of pretend annoyance. "Go sit down. Where's your brother?"

"Still sleeping. I don't think he's used to rising early."

"We'll leave him a plate warming on the stove then." She wanted to ask about his conversation last night with his brother, about why Philip was here, but this wasn't the time. There would be time later, though. She just had to be patient. Not something she was good at. Plus, the tightness around Hank's eyes along with the shadows under them told her he hadn't had an easy night. Perhaps his brother's visit wasn't going to be as enjoyable as she had hoped.

Everyone was soon seated around the table, minus the marshal and Philip. Josh asked the blessing.

"The marshal isn't joining us?" Emily glanced around the table, and her gaze landed on Father. "Is he ill then?"

Father wiped his beard and mustache, nodding. "I believe it's influenza. I'd like him to stay confined to his room so the rest of you don't get it. However, it's possible that it's already too late. Perhaps it'll be a mild case that will pass soon. Becca, it would be best if you didn't visit here until he's well." He returned to his meal, but Amelia saw the tight way he held his mouth. That happened when he delivered bad news. He didn't think it would be a mild case.

"Emily and I can thoroughly clean the boardinghouse. I'd be happy to take care of his meals." Amelia tried for a reassuring smile.

His fork hovered over his plate, indecision etched on his face. She knew what he was thinking. He was trying to protect her, always worried that she had weak lungs like Mother. But he didn't want to seem callous by suggesting Emily do it. He gave a terse nod.

A clatter on the stairs had them all turned expectantly toward the doorway when Philip appeared, dressed in shirt-sleeves and a brocade vest. A necktie hung loose around his collar. Not exactly working attire. But perhaps he didn't own any. Though he was shorter than Hank and not as broad through the shoulders, he could certainly wear some of Hank's clothes. Amelia about opened her mouth to suggest the very thing when she realized that it would be a better conversation to have with Hank in private first. Or maybe not her business at all.

"Food smells wonderful." Philip pulled out a chair and sat, while dishes were passed to him. He gave a light cough, which caused Father's gaze to shoot to him.

She knew that look. Every cough and sniffle would be under suspicion while Father was trying to prevent an illness. But Philip did look pale. Then again, he wasn't a man who worked out of doors, so perhaps that was his normal complexion.

"Did you sleep well?" This from Emily, already taking on the role of mistress of the boardinghouse.

"I did, thank you. I don't think I've ever shared a room with my brother before."

Hank's jaw firmed up. She could imagine how awkward it felt for him—who had hid his wealth and dressed like all the other townsmen—to see his brother flaunting their wealth, even if it was unintentional. Which Amelia was choosing to believe it was. The table fell silent, since no one could relate to Philip's experience.

He didn't seem to notice as he polished off his food with refined manners. The men excused themselves to head over to the parsonage.

"We'll be right behind you." Amelia lifted dishes off the table. "We won't want to miss the ribbon cutting ceremony."

Hank gave her a wink and then pulled Philip aside. She could only imagine what he was saying. Perhaps he was offering the use of his clothes.

One thing she was certain of. The town would be quite interested in Philip.

HANK GUIDED Philip into the parlor. Last night, he'd been too angry to think straight. He'd laid on the pallet on the floor in his bedroom, having given Philip the bed, and turned Philip's words over in his head until sleep finally claimed him in the wee hours.

Philip had continued to cough regularly through the night. Hank would insist the doc look at him today.

"I can understand why you stay here, Henry. The food is delicious."

"I was going to suggest that you stay at Parsons Hotel. You might find it more to your liking than sharing a room with your little brother."

"There's a hotel in this town? Are you sure it's not a fleabag?"

"It's quite respectable. And you wouldn't have to share a room with me. I can take you there on the way to the parsonage." Hank leaned in. "And it's Hank here. That's what people know me by. And they don't know anything about my money. They know me as the man who came and worked with Seth in the logging camp and now runs the carpentry business in town." He gave his brother a hard stare. "That's it. And I want it to stay that way." He didn't need Philip to come in here like a tornado and rip up Hank's life and turn it upside down, leaving Hank to deal with the destruction.

Philip grinned and shook his head. "I don't understand you at all. I can't promise not to slip up, but I'll try. Will that work?"

Hank gave a brief nod. "Thanks. Now I'm going to be gone most of the rest of the morning. Can you occupy yourself here at the boardinghouse? We can talk more when I get back."

"Why would I stay here? I want to help. I'd like to meet the people in this town, to see what has drawn you to stay here beyond all reason."

Breakfast turned into a hard ball in Hank's stomach. He wanted Philip to stay away and hidden until he could put him back on the coach Tuesday. But apparently Philip had other plans. He looked him up and down. "Fine. But you'll need to change into work clothes. You'll get your hands—and clothes—dirty."

Philip ran his hands over his brocade vest. "These are the kinds of clothes I have. I don't have work clothes."

"Then you can borrow some of mine. They might be a little big on you, but they'll fit."

"Why would I do that?"

Hank shifted his weight toward his brother. "Because these

are simple people. You will stand out, and people will ask questions."

"Then you can simply say I'm your eccentric brother." He waved his hand. "Now let's get going."

"I'll see if Amelia and Emily are ready."

"Amelia. She's the doctor's daughter, correct?"

"Yes." Hank ground out. "And I'm courting her, so keep your distance." Red jealousy flashed over him and he pushed it away. The sooner Philip left town the better.

IT LOOKED like most of the town had gathered in front of the parsonage, Hank noted. A wide ribbon swept across the front porch pillars. Pastor Roy and Maggie stood nearby. Good, the ceremony hadn't started yet.

Philip had chatted with Amelia most of the walk into town. She was kind enough to point out various buildings and establishments, as well as a bit about the people in town. She was the perfect hostess, and even Philip with all of his society snobbishness couldn't possibly find fault with her. Though Hank shouldn't care what Philip thought, it warmed his heart.

Pastor Roy spotted them and waved him over. Hank glanced at Amelia.

"Go on. You deserve the credit. I'll be fine here." She smiled at him. "Emily and Becca are just over there. I'll go join them. Perhaps Philip can help Seth and Josh."

He nodded and wove his way through the crowd, gathering his apprentices and John McAlistar as he went until he arrived at the porch steps.

Parsons trundled up to the top porch step. "Your attention please! Thank you all for coming. I want to thank Pastor Roy and Maggie Adams for choosing to make Reedsville their home and ministering to our spiritual needs. An established church is one of the things that makes for a civilized town. In appreciation for all you have done for us, the town would like to present you with this parsonage."

Cheers and clapping went up. Leave it to Parsons to take credit for something he had contributed very little to. Hank shifted his weight.

Pastor Adams raised his hand and the crowd quieted. "I know I speak for Maggie as well when I say it is an honor to serve you, to be your shepherd. We are beyond blessed at your generosity. In particular, I'd like to thank Hank Paulson for drawing up the plans and coordinating the building. Hank, come up here."

Applause started again. Hank's face warmed, but he climbed the porch steps, gesturing to his workers to follow him. They shuffled up until they filled the steps top to bottom. The applause grew until it was uncomfortable. Hank finally had to raise his hands. "All right. Thank you. That's kind of you. But I can't take credit for it alone. I had all these workers helping me out, in addition to the community build we did, which gave us such a good start." He turned to Pastor Roy and Maggie. "It's the least we can do to repay you for all you've done for us." Parsons would be mad at Hank stealing his glory, but he wanted this done with. "Maggie, Pastor, why don't you cut that ribbon and go see your new house?"

Cheers went up as Hank nodded to his men to slip down the steps. Maggie held up a pair of shears and Pastor Roy covered her hands with his as she snipped, and the ribbon fell away. Another cheer went up, and they stepped back as the whole town tried to push up the steps and into the parsonage. Many had seen it last week for Josh and Emily's wedding, but it didn't stop them from wanting to view it again.

Hank stepped over to Philip. "Come on. There's Parsons."

Philip obediently followed. Hank noticed the curious looks from the townsfolk, but most were too interested in the parsonage right now. They'd get to Philip later.

"Mr. Parsons, I'd like to introduce you to my brother, Philip

Paulson. He's visiting our town and would be interested in staying in your hotel. Philip, this is Mr. Parsons."

Parsons eyes went from narrowed to lit up as he spotted Philip and saw how he was dressed. He extended his hand. "A pleasure to meet you. How long will you be staying in our fine town?"

Philip shook his hand. "I'm not certain. But Hen—Hank assures me that your fine establishment will suit my needs."

"I'm certain that we can. As soon as we're finished here, I can see that you're settled in one of our best rooms."

Hank resisted the urge to scoff at Parsons's words, but he was pleased that Philip made an effort to get along, even using Hank's preferred name.

Philip nodded, but before he could say more, several towns-people had made their way over, asking to be introduced. Philip was polite, repeating that he was here to visit his brother and that he didn't know how long he'd be staying.

Hank didn't miss the speculative looks people gave the two of them. While it was clear they were brothers, it was also clear that Philip had means. It wasn't something that was easily explained away. A flash of fear jolted through Hank. It seemed almost inevitable that his true identity would come out. Then his whole status in town would change. People would see only his money and not him.

He needed to get Philip on the stagecoach as soon as possi-ble. Before he ruined Hank's life.

AMELIA NOTICED the strained lines on Hank's face as she moved to stand next to him, taking his arm.

He smiled warmly down on her, a smile that vanished quickly as he glanced over the crowd that had gathered to meet Philip. He frowned. "Where's your father?"

"I think he was going to ask Ben to send a wire for him."

"How's the marshal doing?"

She had taken him some soft scrambled eggs while Hank and Philip had talked at the boardinghouse. "Feverish and coughing. I doubt he'll have eaten much of the breakfast I left him. I need to sanitize the boardinghouse today. Would you mind if we left to do that? It seems like there are plenty of people to help Pastor Roy and Maggie." Except that only a few people were hauling items from the teacher's cottage to the parsonage. Philip was a more interesting attraction.

He nodded and lowered his voice. "The sooner the better. I'll get Philip to come with us so some work will actually get done." He turned to Philip. "We need to return to the boardinghouse. We can fetch your clothes, and you can get situated in the hotel."

Philip's brows raised but he merely nodded. "It was a pleasure to meet you fine people. I look forward to further conversations with you all."

The three of them headed down Main Street, Amelia struggling to keep up with their long strides. Hank noticed and slowed.

Once out of earshot of the townspeople, Philip said, "Now how was my performance, brother? Surely you can find no fault in it. I didn't even call you Henry." He was seized with a coughing fit that took a block to get under control.

Amelia didn't like the sound of that at all. Had Father looked at Philip yet? She would insist on it when they returned to the boardinghouse.

"I appreciate that. But it's important that the townspeople don't know about my wealth. They would treat me differently. I've worked hard to be respected for what I do, not how much money my family has."

Philip shook his head. "I don't know why you feel that way, but I won't let your secret out. At some point, however, we do need to talk."

By the way Hank's arm stiffened under her hand, Amelia

suspected he was not looking forward to whatever it was his brother had to say. The thing that had brought him out here.

At the boardinghouse, Amelia spotted Father in the parlor. "Did you miss the ribbon-cutting ceremony?"

"I caught the end of it. I'm pleased for Pastor Roy and Maggie."

"Have you checked on the marshal? I left him some scrambled eggs earlier."

"I did. I don't think he ate but a few bites, but it's good to keep food in him. Perhaps you or Emily could prepare a broth that we could give to him in small amounts." He leaned forward on the settee. "I don't want anyone to panic, but if it is the influenza, I need you to be very careful around him. I don't want anyone else to get sick. Wash your hands and anything that comes into contact with him. I sent a wire to some of my colleagues."

She nodded. "Have you looked at Philip yet? He had quite a coughing fit as we were coming back."

Father's brow furrowed, and he pushed himself off the settee, weariness already evident. "I'll go right now." His steps retreated upstairs.

She headed to the kitchen where she set a kettle to boil. Emily would help her get a broth ready, but in the meantime, she could start cleaning. With water from the reservoir, soap, and boiling water from the kettle, Amelia soaked a rag in water almost too hot to stand and began wiping down doorknobs.

Father came down the stairs as she swiped the railing. "Philip won't be going to the hotel. He'll need to move into the marshal's room. He has influenza as well, I suspect. Keep an eye on Hank. He isn't showing any symptoms, but it can take a few days. He's had the most contact with Philip."

Amelia dropped her rag in the bucket. "Emily rode with him inside the stagecoach as well."

"Then we need to keep an eye on her too."

Chapter Thirty-Four

A melia wiped down the blackboard as the last of the children left. Hank would be here soon, and she was looking forward to a moment of privacy with him.

Sunday hadn't been terribly restful. She watched as Father sat stiff in church, alert to any cough or sniffle. Philip and the marshal—she learned his name was Logan—now shared a room, and she spent time trying to keep nourishment in them. Logan mostly slept, but Philip wanted to be entertained like a sick child. So Amelia read to him.

The scuffle of boots in the schoolroom alerted her to Hank's presence. She went to him and wrapped her arms around his waist. He pulled her tightly against him, dropping a kiss on her head, before holding her away from him. "What was that for?" He gave her a slow smile. "Not that I'm complaining, but usually you're conscious of being spotted by a student or parent."

She stepped back. "You're right. My nerves are just a bit frayed with the illness. I hope it doesn't get worse. I've seen Father when an illness grips a town. He doesn't eat or sleep. I worry about him."

"He's a good doctor. And he has people around to assist him."

She nodded, knowing that Hank was trying to help, but it didn't ease her worry much. "How is my house coming?" She smiled up at him.

"Good. It'll be watertight today now that we have everyone working on it. Well nearly everyone. The apprentices are building the shed to cover the sawmill. But your house should be done in about a month." He walked her out of the school-house, waited while she locked up, then carried her things as they headed home.

"Have you checked on Philip today?"

He shook his head. "No, I stayed on the jobsite at lunch."

She squeezed his arm under her hand. "We haven't had much time to talk since he got here. Why did he decide to pay you a visit now?"

"My father. I had sent him a letter when we were in Portland and found it strange that I hadn't heard back. Stanley Wallace, our banker, works for my father. And my father owns Frontier Bank in town. He bought it for the purpose of being able to keep an eye on me and apparently to interfere in my life. Philip came to tell me that Father and I never really had a deal. His plan all along was for me to take over the business, and he was just indulging me in my fantasy." His words turned hard and bitter at the end.

Amelia couldn't find any comforting words. She couldn't imagine her father treating her like that, like her own wishes and plans didn't matter. "That must be difficult to hear. What will you do?"

Hank let out a long sigh and was silent for a moment. "He has a bad heart. Apparently the doctors want him to give up control of the company now. Philip was sent to fetch me home. To fulfill my obligations to my family."

Ice shot through her veins, weakening her legs. She clasped Hank's arm tighter. "Are— are you leaving?" He wouldn't leave her, would he? But family was a powerful draw. She blinked back moisture.

He stared down at her for a long moment, his gaze unreadable. "I'm not leaving you, Amelia. Ever."

Her body began to return to a normal temperature, but a core of ice resided in her midsection. Perhaps Hank wouldn't have a choice.

HANK HAD DROPPED Amelia off at the boardinghouse, waiting until she went inside before leaving. He had taken two steps down the street when the doc called his name.

"Hank, a word, if you have a moment." Doc hurried down the porch stairs.

"Sure."

"I'll get right to the point. I got a wire back. There have been influenza outbreaks in both Portland and San Francisco. I believe that's how both of our guests got infected. And they've both come into contact with numerous townspeople. We need to keep an eye out for anyone else who shows the signs of getting sick and keep them from spreading the disease, if possible."

Hank nodded. "I'll keep an eye out on my men."

"I'd be obliged if you'd keep an eye on Amelia." He shifted his weight. "I don't know what she's told you about her mother, but she had weak lungs, and it was the cause of her death." He swallowed and looked away before meeting Hank's gaze again. "I've always worried that Amelia inherited her weakness and so have tried to protect her from illness whenever possible. I have a new nurse coming. She's supposed to be on Friday's stagecoach. But until then, with the close quarters of the boardinghouse and me having no one else to help with the patients, there's not much I can do to keep Amelia from being exposed. But if you could help minimize her exposure and make sure she rests and eats properly, I'd be indebted to you."

"Of course." Hank felt for the man. First he'd lost his wife, and he'd lived in fear of losing his daughter. He understood his desire to protect Amelia. "I'd do anything to protect her."

Doc met his gaze. "I know." He slapped Hank on the shoulder and headed back inside.

AMELIA WAS HELPING EMILY GET breakfast prepared before school. Father had asked Maggie and Pastor Roy to stay away from the boardinghouse. He didn't want anyone here who didn't live here. Luckily, James and Sally had moved into the parsonage as well. It was easy enough putting breakfast on the table for the residents, but what about this evening when Josh would bring in stagecoach passengers? Amelia would be at school all day.

Emily shook her head. "Maggie did this for years without any help. I can manage." She suppressed a small cough.

Amelia glanced up and frowned.

Emily waved her off. "I'm fine."

They put breakfast on the table to a somber group.

Father looked up from his plate. "Josh, I think you need to consider housing any passengers at Parsons Hotel. No one should be in the boardinghouse except us." He scanned the table. "Both Portland and San Francisco have had influenza outbreaks. Let's not have one here."

Josh frowned. "I hear what you're saying, Doc. But Parsons charges double what we do per night. Passengers shouldn't have to pay that without advance notice. And I'm not sure I can cover the difference and still turn a profit." His mouth tightened in a firm line.

"Let me talk to Parsons," Hank said. "He seems to have taken a liking to me. Perhaps I can persuade him to be generous for the good of the town."

"I wish you luck with that. But if you can persuade him, I'd be much obliged."

Hank nodded and glanced at Amelia. She instantly knew

that it didn't matter if Parsons would agree or not. Hank would work something out.

After breakfast, Hank walked her to school carrying her books, lunch pail, and his toolbox. As they passed Parsons Hotel, she glanced at it.

"Are you going to speak to Mr. Parsons before you head to our house site?"

"Yep."

She gazed up at him and squeezed his arm. "You're planning on making up the difference yourself, aren't you?"

He gave a light shrug. "I might not have to. Parsons might care about this town. He is the mayor, after all."

She briefly touched her head to his shoulder, her heart falling a little harder for this kind man. "I won't say a word. But you are my hero. Whether you believe it or not."

Hank hesitated a pace, his gaze on her warm and tender, full of promise. Then they continued on their way, his step a bit jauntier than usual, if she wasn't mistaken.

HANK PLAYED Amelia's words over in his mind all day. He couldn't quite believe that she not only believed what he was doing was right, but she believed in *him*. Not since Jon Baker had anyone shown that kind of confidence in him. With Philip in town, her belief in him stood in stark contrast to his family's desire to manipulate him to their wishes, not caring one whit for his own.

It was hard to hold a grudge against Philip at the moment since he was quite sick. So was the marshal. Luckily, Emily was home all day to attempt to keep nourishment in them. It sounded selfish, but he didn't want Amelia spending too much time with them and catching influenza. And for now, they seemed to be the only two sick people in town. He hoped it stayed that way.

Josh had been right; Parsons didn't feel the need to accommodate the Oregon Express since it was their guests who had brought the sickness to town. At least that was his reasoning. So Hank worked out a bit of a deal with him, on the condition it was kept private. He'd tell Josh that Parsons had come to see reason. Which he had. It just involved money as well.

At supper that night, Emily appeared exhausted. A faint sheen of sweat beaded on her forehead. Doc hadn't returned home yet. He had stopped by the hotel to check out the new passengers, wanting to make sure no newcomers brought illness as they were passing through. But Hank saw the concern on Amelia's face as she studied Emily.

Amelia stood and began clearing the plates. When Emily started to join her, Amelia put her hand out. "No, I have it. You look tired. Go sit in the parlor, and I'll bring you some willow bark tea."

Emily just nodded, which told him that Amelia's assessment was correct. Emily was sick too. But that meant the cooking and caring for the sick would fall on Amelia's shoulders, something he didn't like. And Doc wouldn't either.

Josh helped settle Emily into the parlor, worry etching lines around his mouth.

Hank carried plates into the kitchen.

"You can set them in the dry sink." Amelia tilted her head in its direction. "I need to take some broth up to the men."

"I'll do it. I don't want you exposing yourself to them anymore than necessary." He put the dishes in the sink.

"I don't want you to get sick either."

"I'll be careful. Besides, it's my brother."

Doc came in the back door, worry creating fine lines around his eyes.

"I kept a plate warm for you." Amelia pulled a plate off the warming shelf.

"I'll eat here in the kitchen, if you don't mind." Doc lowered himself into the kitchen chair, setting his bag on the floor.

"I don't mind." Amelia fixed tea and bowls of broth. "I think Emily's sick too. She's in the parlor. I'm making willow bark tea for her and chamomile for you."

"I'll check on her after I eat."

Amelia took a tray into the parlor, and Hank started on the dishes. "Anyone else in town sick?"

"Not yet. My nurse is supposed to arrive on the stagecoach Friday, so we'll have help then. If Emily's sick, then most of the nursing duties will fall to Amelia. And since she's teaching as well, not only does she risk infecting the children, she risks exhaustion from all of the extra work." He rubbed his hand over his face. "Until the nurse gets here, and as long as no one else in town gets sick, I should be able to handle the patient care so Amelia doesn't have to."

Hank began drying dishes to make room. He wasn't sure where they all went, but he could put away the obvious things. "I'll help Amelia with the cooking and chores."

Doc nodded. "I appreciate that. The wires I have been receiving say that it is hitting the big cities hard. I'm hoping we'll have a better time of it here. I pray we do."

Hank prayed that too.

Chapter Thirty-Five

✦❧❦✦

Amelia and Hank were walking home from school when she spotted Father outside the Oregon Express office, which also housed the telegraph. He'd been wiring fellow doctors about the spread and effective cures. He spent each night poring over his books. He had directed Amelia to sanitize the boardinghouse, to keep separate plates and utensils for the sick. Four more townspeople had fallen ill. Each one seemed almost a personal affront to him.

"Any news, Father?" she asked as they drew near.

He removed his bowler, rubbed his head, and replaced the hat. "The nurse I hired can't leave her current job. They've doubled her salary for her to stay on during the outbreak."

He walked with them to the boardinghouse. "I wanted to discuss with you considering shortening the school day, if not cancelling school all together. I'm concerned about you getting sick from exhaustion, if nothing else. You're teaching all day plus preparing the meals for eight people, three of whom are sick. And you're keeping the boardinghouse sanitized. It's too much."

Her stomach plummeted. What would Mr. Parsons say? Somehow she suspected that it would be one more reason for him to find fault with her. Nothing she could do was good enough for that man. If at all possible, she needed to make as small of an impact on the school day. "I don't think Mr. Parsons would care for that much. If you as a medical professional made the call because it was a danger to the community, that would be one thing." Though she thought Mr. Parsons would still somehow blame her. "But if it's because I can't handle the work, Mr. Parsons will renew his desire to find a replacement for me."

"I'll help Amelia," Hank said. "I can take food to Philip and Logan, help with the dishes. I'm not sure I'll be much help with the cooking, but I can do whatever you tell me to." He turned to Amelia.

"Maggie stopped by the schoolhouse at lunch today. She wants to know how she can help."

Father shook his head. "I don't want anyone at the boardinghouse who doesn't have to be there."

"I was thinking she could do cooking and baking at her house. She's used to managing for a crowd. And then she could coordinate meals for anyone else who gets sick."

Father nodded. "That's a good plan. Hank, when you pick up Amelia from school, you could help her carry the food home."

They entered the back door of the boardinghouse. Father headed upstairs to check his patients. Amelia slipped on an apron. "Thank you for your offer to help. I appreciate it. And it means I get to spend more time with you." She smiled.

"It's an unusual way to court, I'll give you that. But I want to help in any way I can. I'll take your books upstairs for you, if you'd like."

"Thanks."

Josh entered the back door. "Is your pa here?"

"He's upstairs checking on Philip and Logan. How's Emily doing?"

He ran his hand through his curly hair, making it stand up. "She feels like she's been through a stampede. She's not getting a lot of sleep because she's coughing so much."

"Take some broth with you when you go back." She moved the pot on the stove, lifting the lid to check the fire. "We'll keep praying you don't get it. Wash your hands often and try to avoid her when she's coughing."

A clatter of footsteps on the stairs brought Hank and then Father into view.

"Hi, Josh." Hank turned to Amelia. "How can I help with supper?"

"Don't you have to get back to the jobsite?"

"They can manage without me. They know what to do."

"Doc, I wanted to talk with you and Hank. You might as well know, too, Amelia." Josh tipped his head toward the dining room. "Can we all sit down?"

"I'll bring the coffee." Amelia grabbed mugs and the pot, following the men into the dining room and getting them all served.

Josh toyed with the cup in his hands. "I don't want to leave Emily alone to go on the stage runs. But the Oregon Express isn't financially stable enough to go without the income, let alone the mail contract that I have. I also don't want to bring any more sick people to our town. So I have a couple of ideas. Could Emily stay here while she's sick? It'd be easier for Amelia or anyone else to look in on her. I don't like the idea of her in the cabin alone."

"Of course." Amelia nodded. "I should have suggested it." She had thought of it but had dismissed the idea because Josh and Emily were newlyweds and likely wouldn't want to be separated. "It makes the most sense."

"Thanks. My other thought, Doc, was to not stop in town at all. Nor at Mrs. Vandermeer's. We'd pack some provisions for a rest stop, and we'd swap horses at her place, but no one would get off the stage at her place or here in town."

"I think that's wise. Most people are just passing through Reedsville anyway, aren't they?" Father looked at Josh over the rim of his coffee cup. He'd emptied it fast.

Amelia refilled it.

"For the most part. Unless they have logging business with Seth."

"If someone needs to get off in Reedsville, keep them separate from everyone else, and they must see me first before they stay. If they are sick at all, I'll put them back on the stage."

"That's fair. I'll try to discern any of those needs before we leave Portland or Salem. I may wire you if I have any questions."

Father turned to her. "Now, Amelia, I've decided to talk to Mr. Parsons. I won't recommend changing anything yet, but I will let him know that I am instructing you to send home any children who are coughing, feverish, or look sick. And that anyone who feels sick should stay home. I'm on my way there now. I'll check on my other patients and be home for supper." He got to his feet just as there was a knock on the front door.

Josh answered the door. It was one of the boys who worked at Parsons Hotel. "We need the doc. The surveyors are sick."

HANK WAS WORKING on the doc's quarters with his team. It was a beautiful day, sunny and just the right amount of warmth. It made it hard to believe sickness was in their midst. But Andrew Paige had fallen ill. So far, none of his other men had.

They had gotten the building watertight and were making good progress now that the weather was cooperating.

"Hank!" The doc called from across the street at the Paiges'.

Hank dropped his tools and came near. But not too near. "How's Andrew doing?"

"He's feeling pretty miserable right now, but I don't see anything that indicates he won't make a full recovery. I'd expect him back at work in a week or so."

"Good to hear."

"I'm headed back to my office. Andrew was my last patient on my morning rounds." He glanced down the street before meeting Hank's gaze again. "Thanks for helping Amelia and looking after her. I don't like that she's having to take care of the sick."

"She's good at it. Must be from years of watching you." Hank smiled.

"Her mother had a touch, that's for sure. A way with people and plants."

"I know you're concerned about Amelia getting sick. It's understandable given that you lost your wife. I think Amelia just wants to please you."

Doc's brow furrowed. "She does. Why would she think she didn't?"

"I think—" Hank shifted his weight, not sure how much he should say. "I think she harbors some guilt over her mother's death. She feels that she should have been able to help her or to have done more."

Doc paled slightly, and his eyebrows rose. "I had no idea. There was nothing she could have done to save her mother. It was always just a matter of time. Her lungs were simply too weak to work well."

Hank nodded. "Perhaps you should tell Amelia that some time. I think it would mean a lot to her."

"Thank you, Hank." The doc was quiet for a moment. "I appreciate your care of my daughter. You are good for her."

"I try to be, sir."

The doc gave a nod and moved off down the street.

AMELIA LOADED A TRAY WITH BROTH, tea, and biscuits to take upstairs after school. More townspeople had fallen ill this week, including both the Drake girls. And some folks were keeping their children out of school for fear of the illness. She had eliminated homework and extra assignments. She didn't have time to do any grading in the evenings and once again praised Emily for her thorough lesson plans.

She knocked on Emily's door then pushed it open. Emily was reading.

"How are you feeling?"

"Slightly better. I think the worst is over, I'm just so weak."

"Well, drink your broth. It'll build up your strength." Amelia set the items on the dresser next to Emily's head.

"I will. Then I think I'll take a nap. I can only read for short periods of time before my head aches."

"That's to be expected. I'll check on you after I see to Logan and Philip." Amelia eased the door shut behind her and headed across the hall to the boys' room, as she'd taken to calling it. Low voices came through the door. She knocked. At the "Come in," she pushed the door open.

Both Logan and Philip were awake and sitting propped up.

"How are you feeling?" She doled out bowls and cups.

"Feel like I've been in a barroom brawl," Logan answered.

"You know that from experience?" Philip asked.

Logan just stared at him.

"Philip?"

"I hurt everywhere. Can't the doctor give me something for the pain?"

Amelia tapped the cup. "Willow bark tea. It'll help." The room was stuffy, and it was a nice day out. She opened the window. A light breeze blew in. "It might feel a bit cool, but the fresh air is good for you." She touched each of their foreheads. Both a bit warm but not worrisomely so.

Philip reached up and grasped her wrist. "What would help would be for you to stay and read to me." He gave her a rakish grin. "I need a distraction from a pretty lady."

He was incorrigible. And he knew it. Amelia sighed and glanced at Logan. He was concentrating on his broth, but the hopeful glance he shot her seemed to indicate he'd like the distraction too.

"All right. But just for a few minutes. I need to check on supper." She darted to her room for the book she had been reading. It was a dime novel. No, she couldn't read that to them. She scrambled to find something else, but her other book was down in the parlor. Well, too bad. They could just listen to her read *All for Love of a Fair Face*.

She sat in the chair in the room and opened the book to where she'd left off. With a quick synopsis to bring them up to speed, she began reading. She heard a few scoffs from Logan and a chuckle from Philip. But she kept on going. After a while, there were no more comments, but she was into a good part of the story so she kept reading, taking them all to a land of adventure.

HANK STOOD in the doorway for a moment, watching Amelia read. Logan's eyes were closed, but Hank didn't think he was asleep. Philip stared at her with the kind of rapt admiration that made Hank want to put his fist in Philip's face, sick or not. He'd told Philip that Amelia was off limits. Then again, Philip did what pleased himself, everyone else be hanged.

What was Amelia doing reading to these men? And a dime novel? Something she usually kept hidden? How had she developed such a rapport with them? An ugly feeling snaked through his stomach. When they were growing up, Philip had tried to ruin everything that brought joy to Hank. Had anything changed?

He rapped on the doorframe, a bit harder than necessary. When Amelia about fell off her chair, he regretted it. He shot Philip a hard look before touching Amelia on the shoulder. "How's everyone doing?"

Amelia smiled up at him, closing her book but keeping a finger marking her place. "I was just reading to them for a bit."

She glanced at her watch on her blouse. "But I need to get supper going." She squeezed his hand as she stood.

"Thanks for reading to us, Amelia." Philip winked at her. "I hope you'll find time to make it a regular thing. Sure makes the time pass faster. Even if it is a romance."

She smiled at him. "I'll see what I can do. Anyone need anything?" She gathered the dishes on her tray.

Logan gave a quick nod. "Thanks. It did make my nap more restful." He grinned.

Hank about couldn't stand the attention they were paying to Amelia. Perhaps he should ask her not to come up here anymore. Which was ridiculous. He was just edgy with the illnesses, worry about Amelia, and Philip being in town.

Amelia headed out the door. Hank turned to follow.

"Hank? We need to talk." Philip's voice was serious.

Hank turned and stared at his brother, weighing his choices. But the sooner he learned all that Philip wanted to tell him, and Philip was well enough, the sooner Philip could leave. If Philip hadn't gotten sick, he could have been on his way back to San Francisco by now.

Hank reluctantly stepped back into the room.

"Close the door." Philip waved his hand.

Hank raised his eyebrows and glanced at Logan.

"I think the marshal can hear what I have to say. He might have some insight. He and I have been talking a bit."

Hank eased into the chair Amelia had used.

Philip reached under his pillow and pulled out a yellow slip of paper. A telegram.

"When did that come?"

"Ben sent a boy around this afternoon. It's from Father. He wants you to get to Portland as soon as possible. The regulators are inspecting the books, and he wants you to represent the family's interests."

Philip's words didn't make any sense, like they were part of a conversation with someone else. "What are you talking about?"

Philip gave a sheepish look, eyes downcast. "It was the other part of the conversation I never got around to telling you about. Not only is Father's health bad, the bank is in trouble. There have been some... discrepancies, and we're being investigated. In danger of losing our charter."

Hank was surprised Philip even knew what those words meant. Maybe he didn't and was just repeating what he'd heard Father say.

Hank ran his hand through his hair. He couldn't leave now. Not only did he need to keep working on Doc's quarters, he had to help Amelia with the boardinghouse. She couldn't do it all on her own. "Father's just going to have to get one of his vice presidents to take care of it. I can't leave here." He stood and started to leave the room.

"It's bigger than that. I don't understand all the details, but Father said something about a double liability that could ruin us."

Hank stopped and sank back in the chair. Double liability. Where the bank was liable not only to the depositors but to make good to the shareholders too. Philip was right. It would ruin the family. He looked up to see Philip studying him.

"Father has made some poor business decisions, as I understand it. But can you imagine what would happen to Mother if she were shunned by society?"

Which is exactly what would happen considering most of the bank's shareholders were fellow society members.

"I don't like this. I don't know anything about Father's decision-making or about the condition of the books. What if there's nothing for me to do?"

Philip adjusted the blanket covering him. "Father thought you could help."

Or he thought he could rope Hank back into the banking business with a crisis. Or alleged crisis.

Logan cleared his throat. "I don't know anything about the banking business other than when they're robbed. But if you do go to Portland, I have a favor to ask of you. I need you to meet with Marshal McKinely and find out about Red Dawson's activities of late. I don't want to send a telegram because I don't know who all is involved. But if you suspect an informer, then as soon as I'm well, I say we set a trap. But I need some information and more men."

Hank stood and tried to pace the small room. He really needed to go pound some nails to work out his frustration. Or go help Amelia with supper.

Perhaps he should pray. He turned toward the doorway. "I'll let you know my decision after supper." He headed toward his room and closed the door behind him.

Chapter Thirty-Six

Hank found Amelia in the kitchen after breakfast. He wanted a moment alone with her before the stagecoach left. He'd told her last night on the porch swing about his conversation with Philip and Logan, and how, after spending time in prayer about it, he felt obligated to at least see about the situation with his family. God had impressed on his heart the need to forgive his family and Philip for the pain they had caused him. Hank came to his decision mentally kicking and screaming. But ultimately, he either trusted that God knew what was best for him or he didn't. He decided to trust and obey.

He didn't expect to be much help to his family on this trip since he had no idea what was going on. In fact, he felt the most profitable part of the trip might be his meeting with Marshal McKinely about Dawson. If he and Logan could spring a trap and catch Dawson, a load would be off his mind and their town would be much safer.

Even this morning, he wasn't completely convinced that a trip to Portland was a good idea. The timing was terrible. He worried about leaving Amelia unprotected and without help. And under Philip's charming influence.

It had shaken him to see her reading to Philip yesterday. As

Philip began to get better, he'd demand more of Amelia's attention. And of the two brothers, Philip resembled the dime-novel hero most, with his fine clothes and charming ways. Hank remembered how Amelia had reacted to him when she'd first seen him in his work clothes. The disappointment that he wasn't the dashing business man he'd appeared to be on the stagecoach.

Yes, they'd gotten past it. But would Philip change that? He'd always had his share of female attention, something he encouraged.

He slid his hand across her shoulder. "Can you step out on the back porch with me?"

She smiled up at him. "Of course."

Outside, the morning sun already held a touch of warmth, promising to be another beautiful day.

"Please be careful while I'm gone."

"I will be."

"I mean it, Amelia. Have James walk you home each day. Don't spend too much time with Philip. You can't believe anything he says."

She gave him a look that she must have practiced on her recalcitrant students. "I thought you two were getting along better."

"I don't trust him. He's spent most of his life trying to take happiness away from me. I don't know what the family situation is, if any of what he's said is true. And his desire to get attention from you could just be a maneuver to get at me."

Her gaze narrowed. "Hank Paulson, what has gotten into you? He's sick. I'm simply caring for a sick man. Logan is in the same room. I'm not giving Philip any attention that I'm not giving to Logan too."

"I don't have a history with Logan." Hank tried to make her understand. Why wasn't she getting it? Usually she was so understanding of his situation. "I have every reason to believe he was sent here by my family to force me back into the family banking business. He's stated that is my father's desire. And it benefits Philip as well. What better way to do that than to make me miserable here so I'll leave?" He tucked a loose strand of hair behind her ear. "And believe me, losing you would make me miserable."

Her face softened. "You're not going to lose me. And Philip hasn't been anything but a charming gentleman since he's been in town. He's even made the effort to call you Hank instead of Henry."

He wished he could believe in Philip's good intentions the way she did. "I know him better than you. He's not what he seems."

Amelia let out a sigh and tilted her head. "But neither are you."

The sound of the stagecoach leaving the barn alerted Hank that his time was up. Frustration and something unsettling carved through his gut. He gave Amelia a quick kiss on the forehead. "Be safe." He slipped down the stairs and around the boardinghouse without looking back.

What would change while he was gone? What would he come back to?

AMELIA FINISHED the supper dishes alone. She missed Hank's help in the kitchen. Not just the extra pair of hands but the companionship he provided. She hated how they'd parted. Her own worries had made her prickly and not open to truly listening to the concern for her behind his words. She wished she could do it over.

She made a mug of chamomile tea and carried it to the parlor to Father. He was asleep on the settee, exhausted from caring for the number of sick that grew daily. Each day she waited for him to order her to close the school. Fewer children came each day, and frankly she'd be glad for the break. But she was still wary enough of Mr. Parsons not to want to suggest it herself.

She eased into one of the chairs flanking the cold fireplace and sipped on the tea. She'd just rest a minute before sending Father to bed, though she suspected he'd been sleeping on the settee anyway in case anyone came to the door. It was better than on a pallet at his office, she supposed.

A knock at the front door had her glancing at Father. He didn't stir. He really must be tired since he usually was a light sleeper. She hoped he wasn't getting sick too. She hurried to the door before whoever it was knocked again. She wanted to let Father sleep as long as possible.

A young man about the age of the O'Malley boys stood at the door. "Is the doc here? My sister, Emmaline Parker, is sick."

Emmaline was the girl Jacob O'Malley was courting. She glanced back at Father sleeping. She hated to wake him. And there wasn't much he could do for her if she had influenza.

"What are her symptoms?"

"Same as everyone else's. Feverish, weak, pale, achy." He glanced past her. "So is he here?"

"Just a minute." She hurried back into the parlor and checked again. "Father?"

He didn't stir.

Mind made up, she popped open his medical bag where it was sitting at the end of the settee. A thermometer and packets of willow bark tea nestled inside among other things. But those were all she'd need. She snatched up the bag and started to return to the front door.

Oh, she should tell someone where she was going. She scurried to the writing desk and scribbled a quick note, dropping it on the dining room table before she hurried out the front door, shutting it behind her.

Emmaline's brother frowned. "Where's the doc?"

"I'm going with you. I have his bag."

The boy shook his head. "Uh, I don't know. They sent me for the doc."

"I'm his daughter. I've worked with him all my life, and I've been taking care of patients. I know what to do. He's exhausted and needs his rest or he won't be any good to anyone."

The boy shrugged. "We'll have to ride double."

She nodded and clung to the boy's waist as they trotted through town. At the Parkers, the surprised looks of the family members gave way when Amelia began her expert ministrations. No one else in the family was sick. But what about the O'Malleys? She'd send Father to check on them tomorrow. Emmaline's temperature was high but not alarmingly so. She left willow bark tea and instructions to keep her well supplied with broth and cool cloths. She also instructed them to wash their hands after coming in contact with Emmaline.

Mr. Parker stepped forward. "What about whiskey? I heard it was medicinal for influenza."

Amelia shook her head. "Father, uh Dr. Martin, doesn't believe it's helpful. Just follow the instructions I gave you, and he'll be out tomorrow to check on her."

The Parker boy brought her home. Once inside, she checked on Father. Still asleep. She dropped his medical bag at the end of the settee and went to wash her hands. Exhaustion settled over her like a blanket. She still had to get up early and teach school tomorrow as well as fix all the meals.

But something else settled deep inside her as well. Satisfaction of a job well done. She had helped Father and Emmaline. She didn't think he would have done anything any differently. Perhaps she was capable of helping him. But would he see it that way?

Now, did she tell him what she had done tonight or wait until tomorrow? And what would he say when he found out?

Chapter Thirty-Seven

Amelia loaded a tray with breakfast items for the boys and Emily, her feet dragging from the shorter night's sleep she'd gotten. It gave her even more empathy for Father, who she had yet to see this morning.

Had Hank made it safely into Portland? Worry for him had nagged at her like an itch she couldn't quite reach since Philip had come to town. Hank was going to be pulled back into his family's business. She was certain of it. He'd be forced to relocate to Portland at the very least. He was an honorable man, and he would feel obligated to take care of his family. Even now, when Reedsville needed him—she needed him—he was answering his family's beck and call.

She stopped at Emily's room first. Emily had already opened the curtains and was sitting up in bed. "You look a little perkier today."

"I don't hurt quite as much. I can't wait until I get back on my feet. I feel terrible that you're having to do all my work on top of yours as well."

Amelia patted her hand. "You just work on getting well. I'm managing fine." She stifled a yawn with the back of her hand.

"How is the rest of the town? Are more people getting sick?"

Amelia nodded. "Some. Emmaline Parker is the latest. I went to see her last night." She scooted closer. "Father doesn't know. He was sleeping on the settee when Emmaline's brother came, so I went instead."

Emily's eyebrows raised. "Are you going to tell him?"

"Yes, at breakfast. He'll need to check on her when he does his rounds." She gave a wry grin. "So if you hear yelling—"

Emily reached for Amelia's hand. "You're doing a masterful job of taking care of everyone. Please take care of yourself as well. Consider closing school for a few days."

Amelia swallowed. That would be like admitting defeat to Mr. Parsons. "I'll check on you when I get home from school."

She moved to the boys' room and knocked, getting permission before entering. They were awake but that was about it. She handed out breakfasts and opened the curtains. "Do either of you need anything before I leave for school?"

Philip dug into his breakfast. "These eggs are better than our cook's."

"Thanks, Amelia," Logan said. "I think my appetite is finally beginning to return a bit."

Philip gave her his most charming smile. "You are a godsend. Such beauty and talent wasted out here. Are you sure you don't want to return to San Francisco with me?" He gave her a rakish grin.

Hank's words about Philip trying to sweep her off her feet filled her mind. "You're too kind, Philip. I'm not sure I'm a big city girl anyway. I like it here in Reedsville. The people here have become like family to me." And as she said the words, she realized they were true.

Philip shook his head. "You don't know what you're missing. But perhaps it is for the best. Hank will be in San Francisco before either of you know it. Of course Mother's already got a sweet socialite daughter of one of her friends already picked out for him. He'll need a wife equal to his station who will know how to perform all of the social functions that will be required of him." All jovialness left his face. "Hank has his duties. If you genuinely care for him, you'll give him the freedom to embrace the role he was born for."

His words drained the life from her legs, and she fought to remain standing. A veil of moisture coated her eyes. "I—I've got to get ready for school." She fled the room and downstairs. She'd get their dishes later.

She dashed into the kitchen and stood in front of the stove, not seeing it. She should have known. She wasn't good enough to keep anyone in her life, not her mother, not Hank. Her father rejected her help so much that she had to sneak behind his back to offer it.

She blindly put dishes of food on the table for Charlie and Father, pouring coffee and going through the motions, her mind —and heart—miles away. Did Hank feel the way his family did? Did he know that he'd have to return and find a suitable wife, one his family would approve of?

Would he give in to his family's pressure? Even if he loved her and wanted her for his wife against his family's wishes, would she be content living in a big city like Portland or San Francisco? No flowers, no gardens. She loved Hank, but would both of their sacrifices just make them miserable? Could love really conquer all? She wasn't sure, no matter what her dime novels said.

She was well on her way to school before she realized she hadn't told her father about Emmaline Parker.

HANK SAT in the vice president's office at the Bank of the Pacific poring over the books. The table was stacked high with ledgers. But his meeting with the regulators was tomorrow, and he had to have a strong enough understanding of what was going on to answer their questions. Hank's eyes were beginning to blur.

Thoughts about Amelia distracted him. He wished they'd

parted on better terms. He should have told her that he loved her and reassured her that he would be back, that nothing about his family would change anything between them.

Instead, he'd let his familiar anger with Philip come to the forefront and control his words. Without even trying, Philip had come between them by Hank's own words and actions. A letter wouldn't get there in time, and a telegram wouldn't come close to saying what he wanted to.

What was Philip telling her about him and their family? He should have more trust and confidence in her. She hadn't cared about his money or his past. But worry still slithered through him. It seemed inevitable that the town would find out who he was. And that he'd have to play some sort of role in his family's affairs. How would that change things between him and Amelia?

It already had.

He needed to pray. He closed the book in front of him and unloaded all of his concerns about his family, Philip, the bank, and Amelia onto his Heavenly Father the way the freighter unloaded lumber.

When he had said everything he needed to and left it before the Lord, he pushed back from the table. He'd head over to the marshals' office and meet with Marshal McKinely. The walk would do him good. And the situation with Red Dawson might actually be a problem he could help solve. It would relieve one worry from his mind if Amelia and Emily were safe in town.

As he walked the streets of Portland, memories of his time here with Amelia threaded through his mind. The grayness of the day had less to do with the clouds and more to do with the fact that she wasn't here with him. The sights and sounds were less interesting and more irritating. He missed the trees and the nature sounds of back home. And while Mrs. Hanson at Hotel Pacific was a wonderful cook, he missed helping Amelia in the kitchen at the boardinghouse. He missed everything about her.

He pushed open the door to the marshals' office and waited

for the clerk to look up. "I'm Hank Paulson, here to see Marshal McKinely. Marshal O'Connor sent me."

The clerk's eyes widened. He nodded and disappeared around the corner. He returned a minute later, followed by a burly man with a bushy salt-and-pepper mustache. "I'm Marshal McKinely." He extended his hand, and Hank shook it. "I hear O'Connor sent you. Come back with me."

Hank followed the man to his office where he closed the door behind them. "Got a wire from Logan yesterday. He told me you were coming and that you had information for me. Didn't say much more than that."

"We think there's an informer in town, so I'm sure he didn't want to say too much to you and give it away. But we're hoping to use that to our advantage to set a trap to catch Red Dawson or at least his gang. Unfortunately, Marshal O'Connor has fallen ill with the influenza that has come into our town."

McKinely nodded. "It's hit my men here too. What did Logan have in mind?"

Hank told McKinely what he and Logan had discussed, and the plan they had devised. McKinely agreed with it, and said he'd do a bit of checking on Dawson's whereabouts, and they could set their plan into motion.

Hank whistled as he left the marshals' office. At least one thing looked like it would be resolved soon. One big thing. Which just reinforced to him one other decision he had made. But it would require a stop at a certain shop and a letter to Sy.

EXHAUSTION PULLED at Amelia like a leaden hem in her skirt as she wiped down the chalkboard, gathered her things, and locked up the schoolhouse, hoping she wasn't forgetting anything. She'd only had five students today, which was fine with her. It meant they were able to end school early.

She headed over to the parsonage. A visit with Maggie, even

though it would have to be a short one, was just what she needed. James had left directly after school to deliver food from Maggie to various families in town. He'd come back and walk Amelia home once he had finished.

And, as she might as well admit to herself, she was delaying heading home and seeing Father. She had had James take a note to him this morning in which she'd written about Emmaline Parker and suggested that he also check in on the O'Malleys.

She had no idea what she would face when she got home, but she didn't think it would be pleasant. Still, she didn't regret what she had done.

Maggie opened the parsonage door even before Amelia had finished climbing the porch steps. "Come in, come in. Let me get you some tea. You look dead on your feet."

"Thank you." She set her books and lunch pail down in the sitting area while Maggie moved into the kitchen. Maggie had put her own homey touches everywhere. She'd only taken a few things from the boardinghouse, and she and Pastor Roy had acquired a few other things since moving in. But anyone visiting here would instantly feel at home.

Maggie returned with a tray set with a tea service and a plate of cookies. She served Amelia and then took a seat next to her. "You look plumb tuckered out."

Amelia gave a short laugh. "That's exactly how I feel."

"How has it been having Philip in town? Is he much like Hank?"

"No, they're about as different as two brothers could be." Philip's words from earlier came back to her. Hank's secret wasn't hers to share, but she sure could use Maggie's wisdom. "Philip told me this morning that their mother already has a suitable woman picked out to be Hank's wife. They are all expecting him to return home to San Francisco."

"Does Hank know this?"

Amelia shook her head. "I don't know. I don't think he knows about the potential wife. Although, I suppose that's not something you'd mention to a woman you're courting. He does know that his family wants him to return home. But he doesn't want to."

Maggie gave a soft smile. "Families are complicated. While it would hurt me something fierce to have my children move away from me, if that's what they felt they needed to do to fulfill the yearning God put in their hearts, then I'd send them on their way. With tears and a smile."

"I don't think Hank's family is like that at all. Philip's goal, I believe, is to convince him to return."

"How does Hank feel about that?"

"He says he doesn't want to go back. But his trip to Portland was mostly for family business. I think he does feel an obligation to help out. I just hope he doesn't get pulled back in out of a sense of duty."

Maggie patted Amelia's knee. "Hank has a good head on his shoulders. Yes, he does like to help people. It's an admirable quality, and the town has certainly benefited from it. But I've also seen how he looks at you. I don't see him as the kind of man to play with your heart if he thought he'd be leaving or if there was another woman in the wings."

Amelia's head and her heart agreed with what Maggie said. Mostly. But that small corner of her heart that told her she was useless to help the people she loved when it really mattered kept speaking up. There was nothing she could do to help Hank. Would his interest in her wane as well?

She leaned over and gave Maggie a hug. "Thank you. I'm glad the parsonage is close to the schoolhouse so I can still see you often."

"Me too, my girl."

The front door swung open, and James entered. Now she had to face Father.

Chapter Thirty-Eight

Stanley set on his desk the scrawled note that the clerk had just handed him. Harley had spent more time getting in trouble rather than going to school, and his writing showed it with its misspellings and poor penmanship. It took Stanley two tries to understand what Harley was saying in the note.

Red Dawson had heard about the illness in town and that both Josh and Hank were gone. Probably from Harley. He was planning on swooping in and snatching up Amelia from the schoolhouse tomorrow. Stanley was supposed to keep the sheriff occupied as long as possible.

This had gone too far. He'd hoped by putting them off with a payroll shipment that he'd be able to make them forget about the women. They'd gotten the money. But Dawson was known for his penchant for revenge. It's what kept people from double crossing him, his unrelenting desire to make them pay.

So now what? Knowing what would happen to that pretty schoolteacher wasn't something Stanley could live with on his conscience. But to tell what he knew would put him in Dawson's crosshairs. And would likely cost him his career if Mr. Paulson found out. Which he most certainly would.

If Hank were still in town, Stanley would consider talking to him. But he wasn't. That left the marshal or the sheriff. Neither of which he was keen to talk to.

Or Philip Paulson. He'd seen the man at the parsonage dedication and around town but hadn't introduced himself before Philip had taken sick. He'd have to consider this carefully. Anything he said to Philip would likely get back to his father.

Stanley didn't have long to decide.

AMELIA AND JAMES entered the kitchen of the boardinghouse. James left the food he'd carried on the kitchen table. Bread, a pot of stew. It would be a simple supper, but she wouldn't have to cook. God bless Maggie.

"Is there anything else you need me to do before I head home?" James asked.

"No, thank you for your help, James. I appreciate it. You really don't need to walk me to school in the morning."

"It's no trouble. And I promised Hank I would."

She smiled. "Well, thank you then. I'll see you in the morning."

James left out the back door, and she lifted the stove lid, checking the heat. Once she got the stove hotter with more wood, she set the stew to warm.

Father entered the kitchen. So much for her attempts to avoid him.

"How was your day? Would you like some coffee or tea?" She reached for a mug.

He pulled out a kitchen chair. "Have a seat. We need to talk."

She sat and slid her gaze over to his. His face was lined with fatigue, but she wasn't terribly surprised to see anger there too.

He let out a breath. "You've been working hard taking care of everyone here in the boardinghouse and teaching school. And I appreciate that. But what would possess you to see a patient?"

Shame washed over her, as familiar as the back of her hand. She dropped her gaze to her lap. "I thought I was helping. You were exhausted, asleep on the settee. You didn't hear the knock at the door or hear me call your name. Her symptoms were consistent with influenza. I simply took her temperature, saw that it wasn't alarmingly high, gave her willow bark tea and instructions for her family to use cool cloths on her. If there had been anything out of the ordinary, I would have come back and woken you. But it seemed to me that the best thing for everyone was to let you get some rest."

Silence strung out taut between them so long that she finally looked up.

His gaze was soft on her. "Your mother would on occasion send patients away if I was sleeping, and she felt their symptoms didn't warrant waking me. She did it so kindly, no one was ever upset. And she was never wrong in her assessment. If my nurse were here, I would have instructed her to do just what you did. As it turns out, you were right. She didn't need anything more than willow bark tea and rest. I also checked on the O'Malleys. They are all well."

The shame drained away, leaving a lightness in its wake.

Father reached across and took her hand in his. "In my zealousness to protect you, I see how I might have given you the impression that you weren't needed or helpful. I didn't want to lose you the way I lost your mother."

Something broke inside her chest and tears gushed out of her eyes unimpeded. She tried to rein them in, but none of her methods made a dent in the flow from her eyes.

Father passed her his handkerchief then scooted his chair closer, putting his arm around her shoulders and pulling her close.

HANK RETURNED to the Hotel Pacific to find a telegram waiting for him at the front desk. He scanned it. It was from Logan. TOMORROW AS PLANNED STOP.

Tomorrow? Tomorrow was too soon. He and McKinely wouldn't have time to get everything set in place. And it wasn't the day the stagecoach normally ran. Wouldn't that tip off Dawson that something was up?

Plus Hank was supposed to meet with the regulators tomorrow. Why had Logan moved it up?

Only one reason. Logan had come into information that made it urgent they act tomorrow. He'd have to trust him.

He'd go by the Oregon Express office and grab Josh before heading back to the marshals' office to talk to McKinely. He only hoped they could get enough men together to get the trap set in time.

What he'd do about his meeting with the regulators, he still had to figure out.

Chapter Thirty-Nine

Hank, Josh, Marshal McKinely, and six of his men rode out of town before the sun's rays cleared the horizon. They had decided not to bring the stagecoach since it wasn't the day it would normally run but go with the rest of the plan for the trap. What would be the bait, Hank didn't know. But he assumed Logan had come across information that made him think Dawson's gang would be in the vicinity today.

"O'Connor thinks Danny Tillman is running with Dawson and that they are using his family's barn as either a stopover or a place to leave messages. We're going to set up a mile down the road from there."

McKinely stroked his mustache. "I've heard the name. Nothing to prove it, but I trust O'Connor's instincts about these things. He's not often wrong."

Josh glared. "But he has been wrong."

McKinely glanced at him. "The evidence pointed to Miss Stanton being involved. He would have been derelict in his duty to take her statements at face value."

"She was a victim." The hard edge of Josh's words could have cut a tree.

"We know that now. But she didn't do herself any favors by not coming forward with the money immediately."

Josh's mouth set in a firm line.

"For what it's worth, O'Connor doesn't believe that she had anything to do with Dawson. And neither do I."

Josh gave a single nod.

Hank hoped the tension between Josh and the marshals didn't create a problem for the trap they were trying to set. He wished they had more time and more information. But they didn't, so they had to work with what they had.

And when Hank had left Reedsville, Logan was still sick. Hopefully he'd either gotten better or had the sheriff get some men together.

Hank had gotten Albert Ackerman to sit in at the meeting for him with the regulators. He'd given Albert the notes he'd taken on the books, which only scratched the surface. But he hoped that with a promise of cooperation and a plea to reschedule at a future date, that Hank would dodge the bullet for now.

And if he hadn't? Well, he would still make the same choice. The people of Reedsville were more important than his family's banking troubles. Today that was clear to him.

Nearing the designated area, they dismounted and slipped into the woods, setting up their positions. "I'll go find O'Connor and the sheriff and see what they know," Hank told McKinely. He and Logan had mapped out this plan in his sickroom. He hoped Logan was sticking to the plan.

Hank cut the long way around the Tillman barn until he came to the spot where Logan had planned to set up. He cut his voice low. "It's Hank. Don't shoot me."

Seth appeared from behind a tree. The sheriff and Logan did as well a moment later.

Logan looked pale and leaned heavily against the tree. "You got the telegram."

"Yeah. I have Josh, McKinely, and six other marshals back on the other side. Why the change in plans?"

"Stanley Wallace came looking for you," Logan said. "It was with great reluctance that he told me Dawson had planned to snatch Amelia from school today. I'm guessing Wallace was our informer. He was okay with payroll robberies, but he didn't want Amelia's blood on his hands. He's sitting in the sheriff's jail cell until all this is over and we can sort it out. We didn't want him tipping off anyone in case it was a trap for us. Might still be."

Hank's blood ran cold then hot. He forced down his emotions to keep his wits about him. The thought of Amelia in danger made a hard knot rise from his stomach and threaten to choke him. He swallowed it down.

They reviewed the plan, though every nerve in Hank's body screamed to go to the schoolhouse and make sure Amelia was safe. But if he did that and blew the trap, Dawson would never get caught and Amelia and Emily and any other women from the town wouldn't be safe.

Hank snuck back through the woods until he returned to Josh, McKinely, and his men. He passed on the information, and they hunkered down to wait.

They didn't have to wait long. Four men approached on the road headed for Tillman's place. McKinely and three of his men stepped out into the road in front of them, rifles pointed at the riders. Three of his other men plus Hank and Josh stepped out to the rear.

"Stop right there. Hands where I can see them." McKinely's authoritative voice carried far. "Drop your weapons and dismount."

The leader slanted his eyes to the side, like he was considering making a run for it or shooting his way out. But Logan, the sheriff, Seth, and other men from town—including the O'Malley boys—emerged from the woods, armed.

The marshals carefully searched the riders and handcuffed them.

Seth nudged Josh. "That's Danny Tillman. Looks like Tim

Donnally's paint that he's riding."

Josh nodded. "Then I was right. I thought that was him in both of the stagecoach robberies. Wonder if we'll get any of your payroll back."

Seth shrugged. "It'd go to the insurance company anyway."

Tillman looked nervous, scanning the road around them. Like he was expecting someone else.

Hank stepped over to Logan. "What's up with Tillman? Think there's another part of the gang on its way?"

McKinely and his men had taken each of the robbers away separately for questioning.

"Could be he's just nervous about getting caught. But let's find out." Logan moved toward Tillman, Hank, Josh, and Seth on his heels.

"You got something you want to share with us, Danny?" Logan nudged his hat back, sweat beading on his forehead. He needed to rest somewhere before he fell over.

It spoke to something in his chest that this man had risked his health to come out and protect Amelia.

Tillman swallowed and looked around at the other men.

Logan stepped in front of him, blocking his view. "What do you know, Danny? You don't want blood on your hands, do you? You'll hang if anything happens just as surely as they will. So it's in your interest to cooperate."

"It's Harley. He's already gone after the schoolmarm."

Ice shot through Hank's veins, and his feet were already sprinting toward his horse as he heard Logan say, "Who's Harley?"

AMELIA HEARD the schoolhouse doors open at the back as she was writing on the chalkboard. Her heart hitched up briefly, thinking, hoping it was Hank. But no, it couldn't be. He was in Portland, and the stage wasn't due until tomorrow.

She turned. A strange man made his way up the aisle. Thin shoulders, clothes that looked like he'd slept in them, and a leering grin.

"May I help you?" She drew herself up tall as fear slithered through her stomach. She glanced at the children who were staring at the newcomer. James had tucked his feet under him as if to stand. She shot him a small shake of her head.

"We're going for a ride, teacher. You and me." He closed the steps between them and grabbed her arm, hauling her up against him.

James shot to his feet and grabbed the man from behind.

The man had three inches and fifty pounds on James. He elbowed James in the stomach, sending him to the floor. He produced a revolver that he pressed to Amelia's chest.

Oh, Lord. Don't let these children see him shoot me.

"It's okay, James." She peered around the man.

James lay sprawled in the aisle. He clinched his fists as he scrambled to his feet and stepped to the side, anger hardening his face.

She turned her attention to the man who had grabbed her. "What do you want with me? Please don't hurt the children. I'll do whatever you want."

He grinned. "We're going for a ride. You'll make a nice present for Red Dawson."

Bile rose and her whole body trembled. *Lord, please, no. Help me.*

But no one knew this man was here. No one would come help her. The best thing she could do was cooperate with the man until her children were safe. She met James's gaze and cut her eyes to the back door. She hoped he understood to get the children out of here.

She forced her feet to move down the aisle, toward the main doors and away from the children. Her brain spun with how to get out of this situation. She had no illusions about what would happen once she was delivered to Red Dawson. She had to get out of this man's clutches before that happened. But she couldn't allow anything to happen to her children.

When they got to the cloakroom, she thought she heard footsteps behind them. If James was getting the children out, she didn't want this man to hear them. "So who are you? How did you become associated with Red Dawson's gang? And why me?"

"That's an awful lot of questions for someone who doesn't need to know anything." He tugged on her arm.

She scanned the cloakroom for anything that could be used as a weapon. Nothing. "What do I call you, then?"

He gave her that awful grin again. "Well, sweetheart, you can call me Harley."

"Are you from around here, Harley? Have we met before?"

He guffawed. "So prim and proper. This ain't no tea party, lady." He yanked open the doors and shoved her through.

A horse ran through the yard in front of the schoolhouse, reins dragging. James must have gotten the children out and untied the man's horse. *Good job, James.*

Harley cursed. He scanned the area around them, but no one was visible.

This was her chance. But it would likely hurt. She let her weight drop at the top of the stairs and allowed momentum to carry her forward down the stairs. She tucked her head and arms in, but the steps cut into her back. She came to an abrupt stop at the bottom and scrambled to her feet. A sharp jolt shot up her leg, stumbling her and halting her breath. She glanced up. Harley was just steps away.

Grabbing her skirts, she ran for the parsonage, trying to push the pain away. She was taking the chance that Red wanted her alive, that Harley wouldn't shoot her.

"Maggie! Pastor Roy!" She didn't want them to get hurt either, but they needed to be alerted. She glanced around the yard. A flash of color caught her eye in the woods but disappeared. Hopefully the children had run far and fast.

The parsonage door flew open. Pastor Roy appeared briefly

then disappeared, reappearing with a shotgun. Five more steps. She felt something whisk by her back, grabbing at her skirt. Was it Harley's hand? She pushed the pain aside, flew up the porch steps. She ducked around Pastor Roy and inside.

Maggie had the cellar door open in the kitchen floor. "Get inside."

Amelia tumbled down the stairs into the blackness.

HANK'S MIND scrambled to make sense of what he was seeing down the road. James and children running out the back of the schoolhouse. James ushered the children into the woods then went for the horse that was tied up to the long hitching post along the side of the schoolhouse. He slapped the horse's rump and it took off, just as Hank galloped his horse into the schoolyard.

James spotted him. "A man has the teacher. He's got a gun." His words were fast, punctuated with gulping breaths. He waved toward the parsonage.

Hank flew by on his horse. "Help's right behind me. Get into the woods."

He rounded the corner of the schoolhouse. A man chased Amelia across the yard, was within steps of reaching her. Harley.

Pastor Roy had his shotgun raised, but he couldn't fire at Harley without risking hitting Amelia.

Hank spurred his horse toward Harley and leaped off, grabbing the man's shoulders, taking Harley with him as he hit the ground. Harley rolled on top of him and came up swinging. Hank ducked and kept Harley rolling. The punch grazed the side of his head.

Harley pinned Hank with his weight. Hank swung but couldn't get momentum, and Harley blocked the punch easily, an evil grin twisted his mouth. "I'll finish you, and then your little lady too. Red will be—"

A blur passed in front of Harley's face, his head snapped back, and he flopped backward off Hank.

Hank scrambled to his feet.

Pastor Roy stood there shaking his fist. "Haven't had to do that in a long time. Help me truss him up."

Hank's chest heaved, catching his breath. He vaguely remembered Pastor Roy having been a fighter before he'd gotten right with God. His burly frame and no-nonsense demeanor made him popular with the lumberjacks in the area. He reached his hand out. "Thanks. Guess God uses our pasts in strange ways."

"That He does."

A thunder of horse hooves rumbled through the ground as Seth, Josh, the sheriff, Logan, and a few others rode into view. Harley was in fine hands. Hank needed to find Amelia. He took a deep breath, ran his hand over his face, and headed up the porch steps and inside the parsonage.

He looked around. No one was in sight. "Amelia? Maggie?" The trap door to the cellar stood open. A muffled voice came up. "In here."

Cold sweat popped out along his forehead. He hated cellars. Never went in them. Ever. It was the worst of all the small spaces with the darkness and smell of damp earth surrounding him. But Amelia was there.

He walked on unsteady legs to the opening. "You can come out now. We've got the situation under control."

Maggie's head appeared in the opening. "You'll have to come down here and get Amelia. She's hurt and can't walk."

"What happened?" Had Harley hurt her? Had she been shot? He ought to go pound the man good.

"It's my leg." Amelia's voice was like a balm for his soul. She was well enough to speak. "I twisted it. It can't bear any weight." She paused. "It's okay, Hank. I can probably scoot up the stairs."

She was the one trying to protect him. Not after everything that had happened. "I'm coming down." He could do this for her. He'd do anything for her. He closed his eyes, pictured the time they were at the pond surrounded by wildflowers, and took a few deep breaths. Then he lowered himself into the opening. The darkness seemed like a physical presence pushing on him.

But he pushed back, focusing on Amelia's face, glowing in the candlelight. She was safe, and that was all that mattered. He finished the last few steps concentrating on her. "Are you okay? Did he hurt you?"

She smiled and reached for him. "I'm fine. Just threw myself down the schoolhouse steps to get away from him. I thought you were in Portland."

He gathered her in his arms, her closeness more powerful than the darkness. He headed upstairs. "I was. Logan wired us that something was going to happen today, so we moved up our plans. I had no idea they were coming after you or I never would have left." The smell of lilacs filled his senses as he emerged into the light of the kitchen. He was nearly weak with relief at being out of the cellar and finding Amelia safe and unharmed. He carried her to the settee and laid her on it.

"I'll get some wet cloths." Maggie's voice came from some-where behind him.

The front door burst open and Doc Martin flew in. "Amelia? Are you okay?"

She smiled. "I'm fine. Thanks to Hank." She squeezed his hand. "You were my hero today. You grabbed Harley before he could grab me."

Her words set to glow something deep in Hank's chest, something that had been lying dormant for years.

Doc flashed him a grateful smile as he moved next to the settee. "Would you give us a minute?"

He met Amelia's soft gaze. "Sure." One more caress of her hand then he stepped out onto the porch to let Doc examine her leg and give them some privacy.

The men were standing in a group, talking. Harley was tied up and on his horse.

Hank shook Logan's hand. "Thanks for protecting Amelia."

"Just doing my job. She took pretty good care of me when I was sick."

"You still look sick."

Logan shrugged. "I've felt better. But I didn't want you to have all the fun. We'd better get on the road." He nodded toward Hank's horse that someone had been kind enough to catch.

"What?" Hank wasn't about to leave Amelia.

Logan squashed that though like a bug under his shoe as he mounted his horse. "We need as many men as possible to escort the prisoners to Portland. I'd hate to get ambushed by Dawson in his attempt to free his men. I don't think it's likely, but I don't want to put anything past him. And then you and I will have to give our statements so these men can stay locked up."

He nodded reluctantly. The last thing he wanted was for these men to go free because there hadn't been enough witnesses to testify against them.

Hank clasped Seth's shoulder before he and the other townsmen headed back to Reedsville. "Check on Amelia for me, okay? Doc's with her now." It wouldn't be proper for him to go in there while Doc was examining her leg. And Logan and the other men were clearly waiting on him.

Seth nodded. "Sure. Anything you want me to tell her?"

So many things, but nothing he wanted Seth to say on his behalf. These words he wanted to tell her himself. "Just that I'll be back as soon as I can."

Hank mounted up and followed McKinely, Logan, and the other marshals with the prisoners back to Portland. But he couldn't help but look back over his shoulder at the parsonage, wishing he'd had one more opportunity to hold her, kiss her, and tell her that he loved her.

Chapter Forty

A melia was in the parlor with her leg wrapped and elevated. She had twisted her ankle and then aggravated it by running on it. It had given out when she flew down the cellar stairs and now was quite swollen. But nothing was broken, and Father assured her that it would heal quickly. Though not quickly enough for her liking. Still, he warned her that being up and around on it would delay its healing. So she reluctantly agreed to stay in the parlor like an invalid.

Emily was recovered enough to help out, even though she was still weak. And Father had allowed Maggie to return to the boardinghouse to cook, now that everyone was on the mend. Philip even went for a short walk today to get some fresh air.

There was a knock on the front door, and Amelia had to restrain herself from answering it. A moment later, Emily appeared in the parlor doorway. "Mr. Parsons is here to see you."

She groaned inwardly. She didn't want to hear that he was going to fire her. She'd done the best she could. If that wasn't good enough for him, well, there was nothing further she could do.

Mr. Parsons entered the parlor and sat across from her, hat in his hands. "I'm sorry for your injury. Your Father assures me you'll recover soon."

"Yes, it shouldn't be too long. But I've already sent word to the families and asked the children to come here. They can read their lessons to me, and I can give them assignments. I assure you, learning will still continue despite my injury."

He nodded. "That's, well, that's above and beyond what I expected. Given everything that's happened in town lately, it wouldn't be uncalled for to close school for a few days."

Was she hearing him correctly? "Oh, I don't think that will be necessary. The children are quite good at adapting to whatever needs to be done. They soldier on like frontier families do."

Mr. Parsons studied his hat for a moment. "Yes, they do that, don't they? I've done some thinking on the subject, and I believe our unique situation here requires a unique type of teacher, something I hadn't quite realized before."

So here it was. Why she wasn't qualified and would be replaced. Her heart sank. But somehow, she would manage. Perhaps she'd help Emily with the boardinghouse. Or Father with his work. She'd proved her usefulness during their time in this town.

"And that's why I realized I haven't given you enough credit. Both you and Mrs. Benson recognized the uniqueness of the students and our town and adapted your methods to ensure the children got the best education. Yesterday was a perfect example. You got the children to safety. I can't imagine a teacher from the city who would maintain her wits about her the way you did. So I came to tell you that the teaching position is yours for as long as you'd like it. I've pulled the advertisement."

Now she was certain she was hearing things. And Father hadn't even given her any laudanum for the pain. "Um, thank you." What on earth had caused such a change in Mr. Parsons's attitude?

He got to his feet. "The community has faith in you. I've heard from a number of families today. Even Mr. Philip Paulson came to sing your praises. If someone from San Francisco recognizes your talent, who am I to say otherwise? I hope you heal quickly."

He was out the door before she could say another word. Why had Philip spoken on her behalf? After his remark that she wasn't wife material for Hank, she'd kept her distance from him, her sensibilities smarting. She didn't know what to make of this.

She was still pondering Mr. Parsons's words and Philip's actions when Emily and Maggie hurried to the front porch. The stagecoach had arrived. Amelia had lost track of time. She'd hoped to look in the mirror and freshen up a bit before Hank arrived. She patted her hair into place and wished for the best. There would be no passengers on Father's orders still, though he'd allowed that things could return to normal next week if no one else got sick. She listened for the clatter of boots.

Eventually they came. She looked up. Josh appeared in the parlor with two baskets. Where was Hank?

"These are for you. Mrs. Hanson's cinnamon rolls." He handed her a cloth-covered basket. "And these." A basket of pale-pink peonies and baby pink roses came next.

She set the cinnamon rolls on her lap and reached for the flowers. A delicate scent tickled her nose. "I don't understand. Where's Hank?"

Josh gestured to the baskets. "He sent these. He's still tied up in Portland with the Dawson case and some banking business. He plans to be back on the Tuesday stage. I think there's a note in the flowers."

"Thanks, Josh."

He nodded and left the parlor, probably eager to get away from the feminine emotions and get to his supper.

She found the note tucked between the blooms.

My Dearest Amelia,

I'm sorry I can't be there to give these to you in person. Please know that I am thinking of you constantly and can't wait to return to your side. I wish I had been able to say a proper goodbye before my return to Portland. But I hope to be back in Reedsville as soon as business here allows. We have much to talk about.

In the meantime, please take the cinnamon rolls (you can share them if you'd like) and the flowers as a small token of my deep affections for you.

Ever yours,
Hank

AMELIA STUDIED THE LETTER. He said they had much to talk about. Was that a good thing? She would have thought so prior to Philip's remark about Hank's future wife not being her. Perhaps this was Hank's way of letting her down gently? And how long would his business in Portland take him? The old fear that he would be back in his family's business sliced through her. She wished she could ask Josh if he knew more, but she didn't want to come across as a sniveling female.

Emily called her in to supper. She took up the cane Father had left her and hobbled into the dining room. But her mind could only think about the fact that Tuesday was a long way away.

HANK AND LOGAN strode away from the courthouse and down the sidewalk. Hank had hoped to be on the stagecoach today, but it had turned out to be impossible. The judge wasn't available until Monday to take their statements. Hank hoped the gifts he had sent to Amelia would please her and reassure her of his feelings for her until he could return and tell her in person.

The only good news was that the banking regulators had met

with Albert yesterday and were willing to allow Hank more time to review the books and develop a plan.

He glanced at Logan, who still looked pale but was steadier on his feet today. "How are you feeling? You looked pretty puny yesterday."

"I was glad to find my bed last night. But I seem to be on the mend. Amelia was a good nurse."

Hank frowned. "I'm not sure I like that you spent so much time with the woman I'm courting."

"She was never improper, if that's what you mean. Neither was I." Logan paused and then continued. "This is none of my business, you understand, but Philip said something that doesn't quite line up. I've gotten to know you. You're an honorable man. So I don't understand why you'd be courting Amelia when there's a woman back home your mother has picked out for you."

Hank stopped on the sidewalk, causing people to veer around him. "What are you talking about?"

Logan nodded. "So you didn't know."

"Know what?"

"Like I said, this is none of my business, but Amelia's a sweet girl and I'd hate to see her heartbroken." He gestured for them to keep moving.

"So would I. What's going on?" Frustration tightened Hank's voice. If Philip had done something…

"Philip told her that she would never make an acceptable wife for you, that your family wouldn't approve, and that your mother already had the daughter of one of her socialite friends picked out for you to marry."

Hot anger shot through Hank, his fists clenched. When he saw Philip, he'd pound him into next week. How dare he. Maybe he could send a telegram to Amelia.

And say what?

"Did you know anything about that?"

"No! Of course not." He thought back to his last trip to San

Francisco, before he'd met Amelia. There was one woman that Mother seemed to continually be inviting over and encouraging Hank to spend time with. He hadn't paid much attention because he wasn't staying and had no intention of returning except to visit. Perhaps that's what Philip meant. "It doesn't matter what my family thinks. I love Amelia, and I'm going to marry her."

Logan gave him a cockeyed grin. "Does she know that?"

Hank stopped again. No, she didn't. He only hoped his letter and gifts would speak to her in his absence. He wished once again that he'd taken the time to tell her he loved her one more time.

Chapter Forty-One

As the stagecoach rounded the bend and made the descent into Reedsville, Hank felt like he'd been gone a lifetime. He couldn't wait to see Amelia. The only good thing about his absence was that it had allowed him to put some final plans into place. He patted his coat pocket.

The stagecoach had a few passengers. They'd be staying at Parsons Hotel until Dr. Martin was sure they weren't bringing in the influenza. Which meant the supper table at the boarding-house would be just the people he'd come to think of as family.

As they pulled up in front of the boardinghouse, an over-whelming sense of coming home flooded him. It had been a long journey, but he'd finally found the route home to where he belonged. Would Amelia be waiting for him? Or was her leg injury too severe? He hadn't even been able to stay long enough to find out.

As the stage swayed to a stop, Hank practically leaped out the door. He held it for the other passengers while scanning the front porch. Emily and Maggie, but no Amelia.

He started to help Josh with the bags, but Josh waved him away. He nodded his thanks, grabbed his valise, and headed up the porch stairs.

Philip exited the front door.

Anger welled up, but Hank pushed it down. There'd be time to confront Philip later. For now, his focus was Amelia.

Philip extended his hand, and Hank took it reflexively. "How did it go with the regulators?"

"Fine for now. I'll tell you about it later. Where's Amelia?"

"In the parlor, I think. She's been keeping off her ankle."

"Is it hurt bad?"

"Just a sprain, I think. I'll let you get to her. We can talk tomorrow."

For someone who had tried to ruin Hank's life, Philip seemed awfully amenable. Hank didn't have time to think about it now. He pushed the front door open and made his way to the parlor. No Amelia. He peeked in the dining room. Not there either. But the flowers he had gotten her sat in a vase on the low table. He headed into the kitchen. There she was, sitting at the kitchen table. But Maggie and Emily were there too. Barely enough room for him.

"Hank, you're back," Maggie said. "Supper's almost ready. How about you put your bag away, wash up, and come join us at the table?"

Amelia's gaze darted to him. A soft smile lit her face. "You made it. I wasn't sure if you'd be on this stage or not."

"I did everything I could to make it happen. I'll tell you about it later." He squeezed her shoulder, frustrated he couldn't do more. By the time he'd washed up, everyone was filing in around the dining room table and seating themselves. He took his seat next to Amelia.

After Pastor Roy asked the blessing and the food began to be passed, Hank leaned over. "How's your ankle?"

"It's just a sprain. Father's been making me stay off it. But it's been nearly a week, and it only hurts a little when I walk." She was far more subdued than he'd expected she'd be. She said her ankle didn't hurt much, but perhaps she wasn't telling him how bad it was. Or had she believed what Philip had said?

He'd get her alone on the porch swing tonight and explain it to her.

But after supper, everyone wanted to hear what had happened to Dawson's men. So they ended up in the parlor with Hank explaining about the testimony he gave at the arraignment. He'd have to go back for the trial as well. But for now, most of Dawson's men were locked up. And a few of them were willing to trade information about Dawson's whereabouts and activities to the marshals. Reports were that Dawson had high-tailed it to California or even Arizona Territory. Regardless, the town of Reedsville could rest easy for now.

By the time Josh and Emily and the parsonage folks had left, Amelia was covering a yawn with her hand. It was too late to get her alone. Besides, he had big plans for tomorrow.

He helped her up the stairs, his hand hovering beneath her elbow in case her ankle gave out. "Has school been cancelled until your ankle is healed?"

"I've been having the students come here for their lessons in the morning then working on assignments in the afternoon."

He smiled down at her. "So resourceful."

"That's what Mr. Parsons said." The first true smile he'd seen since he'd been back lit her face. "He said he came to realize that frontier towns needed a particular kind of teacher. Like me. And that the position was mine for as long as I liked."

"It's about time that man recognized your worth."

She nodded. They stood in front of her door. He wanted nothing more than to kiss her good night, but she opened her door and stepped inside. "Good night." The door snicked shut.

He moved to his room. He had his plan in place for tomorrow. But something had changed between them. He thought back to his conversation with Logan. Amelia had cared for Logan and Philip while they were sick. And Philip had told her that their mother had a wife picked out for Hank. So was that what was bothering her? Or had she fallen for his dashing, dime-novel hero brother?

It was a long time before sleep found him.

AMELIA WAS CONFUSED, her thoughts whirling as she ate breakfast with the rest of the boardinghouse folks. Hank was still as attentive as usual, though he seemed a bit distracted. He had returned from Portland and hadn't left her to run his family's business. Unless he was only back in Reedsville temporarily. But Philip's words about her being unsuitable as a wife for Hank ran through her mind.

Yet Hank had always said he never wanted to run his family's business. And if he stayed in Reedsville, he would certainly have no use for a society wife. She didn't know what to think.

But the still, small voice inside her whispered that she needed to speak to Hank. He was here in town now, so they could talk. She could speculate all she wanted, but only Hank would have the answers she needed.

As the last student left the parlor, Hank appeared. "Let's go for a ride. I have something to show you." He fiddled with the cuff of his sleeve.

"All right. Is it still raining?"

"No, the sun has popped out, but I'll run up and get your coat." He practically sprinted from the room.

She made her way gingerly through the kitchen. Her ankle could hold her weight, but she'd been used to not walking on it.

Hank appeared and helped her into her coat then ushered her out the back door where Josh's buggy awaited. He helped her up, and soon they were headed toward the center of town.

This was when she should ask him about what his mother meant. The silence felt heavy around them, not awkward, but not as easy as it had been before he'd left.

He fingered the reins and glanced at her repeatedly.

"Where are we going?"

He grinned. "You'll see."

Perhaps she should wait until they arrived before broaching the subject. They headed out the far end of town and toward the schoolhouse. He swung the buggy around the large open space, away from the schoolhouse and parsonage, toward the edge of the woods and came to a stop.

He turned toward her. "I've been thinking about a few things. Remember when we visited the Park Blocks in Portland?"

She smiled. That had been a wonderful day. "Yes, and our picnic there."

He nodded. "It got me to thinking about how to do something similar for our town. Can you picture it?" He swept his hand over the open space toward the parsonage and schoolhouse. "This could be the town park and garden. Let me show you." He hopped out of the buggy and came around to help her down, grabbing something from behind the buggy seat. He kept hold of her hand as he led her to an apparently predetermined spot.

"Right here, we could build a gazebo, surrounded by your mother's cuttings, the ones that won't fit on your house site."

Tears sprang to her eyes. She couldn't believe he'd thought of that.

He unrolled the paper he held in his hand. It was a drawing of what the whole park area would look like when complete. Green space, paths, the gazebo surrounded by planting beds. "The gazebo will be big enough to serve as a bandstand so we can have music in the park."

He set the plan down and took hold of both of her hands. "I want a future in this town, with you. I know my brother said some ridiculous things about a society wife my mother had picked out. I don't know anything about it, and I don't care because I'm not going to be living in San Francisco. I'm living right here." His gaze softened and steadily met hers.

Her heart warmed and glowed. Hank wasn't leaving. "I can't believe you thought of this. And the tribute to my mother and her cuttings. I just can't even comprehend it all." She was afraid she was going to start blubbering. After years of not crying, she seemed to be shedding tears at a rapid rate.

He let go of one of her hands and pulled out a seed packet of sweet peas and handed it to her. "This is the start of our future."

She took the seed packet with raised eyebrows. Sweet peas? What did he mean? The packet was heavy and lumpy.

"Open it." His smile was slow, but questions danced in his eyes.

Inside the packet nestled among the tiny seeds was a ring. Her hands shook. "Oh, my."

He took the packet from her and pulled out the ring. He took her hand in his. "I love you, Amelia Martin. I can't imagine any future that doesn't include you. Will you marry me and be my wife?"

Tears and laughter poured from her uncontrollably. "Hank Paulson, I love you. You make dreams I didn't even know I had come true. You're my hero in every way that matters. I'd be honored to be your wife."

Hank slipped the ring on her finger, the coolness instantly warming. She threw her arms around his neck, and he kissed her deeply, tenderly, and with all the promise their future held.

They had both come home to exactly where they belonged.

Chapter Forty-Two

Hank watched as Joseph Spitzky and Robert Reinfeld picked up the last scraps of lumber and swept the last of the sawdust out of the doc's house. The job was done, and Doc and Amelia would soon be moving in. Though Amelia wouldn't be living here long. As soon as he could build a house for them, they were getting married.

He turned at the sound of footsteps. Philip sauntered up the street. "So it's true. You finished it. Great job, little brother." Philip stuck out his hand.

Hank shook it. "How are you liking Parsons Hotel?"

"The room is nicer. The cooking is good, but not quite as good as Maggie's. Don't tell Mrs. Parsons I said that."

"Ready to go over the bank's books?" Hank picked up his toolbox. "Boys, thanks for your hard work. I'll see you at the sawmill Monday." They had the shed built and the mill put together. Monday would be their test run. They'd cut the lumber they'd need to build the gazebo for the park. He wanted Amelia to have the wedding of her dreams.

"I am. I have a few questions." Philip turned, and Hank came alongside him as they walked back to the center of town toward Frontier Bank.

Over the past several weeks, Hank and Philip had had some long discussions. Hank had come to realize that Philip was as much a victim of their father's expectations as he was. Together they'd come up with a plan. Hank bought Frontier Bank from his father. The divesture, along with a few other arrangements, satisfied the regulators. And while Stanley Wallace would not be allowed to work in banking anymore, his testimony about his brother Harley and what he knew of Red Dawson's activities would likely help him escape jail time.

That left Reedsville's bank without a manager. Hank insisted that it be Philip. Hank had no desire to run a bank, and he could teach Philip everything he knew. Philip was reluctant at first. Having been treated as a spoiled child most of his life left him insecure about his own abilities. But Hank was persistent, and they had lessons every day after Hank finished building.

"You always have questions. Which is good. I have answers." Hank smiled. "Any letter back from Father yet?"

"A telegram saying he got the letter and that we should come to San Francisco immediately."

"Which we won't."

"Nope." Philip scanned the dusty street. "I never thought I'd say it, but I like this little town. Thanks for convincing me to stay. Once the railroad gets here, I can easily head into Portland when I need to experience the excitement of a big city."

Hank nodded, unable to speak. Their father might not be satisfied with the arrangement. But Hank found that with Philip on his side, they made quite a team. They'd drawn up a proposal for the most senior vice president to take over the day-to-day operations of the bank with a profit plan to Father and then his heirs. He wouldn't have to worry about a thing.

"I never thought I'd see the day when you'd run a bank, let alone live on the edge of the frontier." Hank clapped his brother on the shoulder and then grinned when he saw the figure waiting outside the bank doors.

"Guess we both finally found what we were looking for."

Hank took Amelia's hand as he drew near her. "Philip, I think I'll meet you back at the boardinghouse. I have an appointment with this lovely woman here and the porch swing."

Epilogue

Amelia grasped Hank's hand as they stepped onto the wooden train platform. Seemed like the whole town was here to see the arrival of the first train to Reedsville. It had taken most of the summer, but here in late September, the day was still warm enough, and the sun was shining.

The depot wasn't too far from the sawmill. And if she looked hard enough, she could see the town square with its baby plants, green grass, and the crowning glory of the gazebo, where her wedding to Hank had taken place three months ago on another perfect June day.

Seth and Becca came up to stand beside them. Becca cradled their new daughter, just three weeks old.

Amelia pulled back the edge of the lace bonnet to admire the sweet baby face of Sophia Margaret Blake. "Are you getting any sleep?" She glanced at Becca and Seth.

Seth slid his arm around his wife's shoulder. "Some." They exchanged a tender look.

Becca tilted her head. "There's Josh and Emily."

Amelia hoped the whole boardinghouse group—even

though only Josh, Emily, and Charlie lived there now—would be near each other when the train came to town. She knew it was a bittersweet day for the Bensons. Josh had made the last stagecoach run yesterday. But the new woodworking shop next to the sawmill was nearly complete, and he and Charlie had more work already than they could handle. The railroad contracts were turning Reedsville into a boomtown.

But Josh and Emily seemed content. They both smiled, and Emily appeared to be glowing. She leaned between Amelia and Becca. "We'll have one of those to occupy us come March."

Amelia squealed and hugged her. Becca did the same, careful not to squish baby Sophia.

The school board had changed the rules to allow a married woman to teach, as long as her husband allowed her and it didn't interfere with her home life, adding to Reedsville's reputation as a progressive town. So her contract had been renewed this fall, and she and Hank had agreed she should teach until they had a little one of their own.

A sense of satisfaction fell over Amelia as she scanned the crowd. She was honored to call these people her friends. The O'Malleys stood closest to the tracks. Stephen had been instrumental in helping plant around the gazebo, under the watchful eye of Sy. Jacob and Emmaline were engaged, and their parents were coming on the train. Finally after years of delays.

Her father and Charlie stood off to the side. Father had a busy practice that now included a nurse.

She leaned into Hank as he slipped his arm around her shoulders and pulled her to him. She couldn't imagine her life without these people. A year ago she didn't even live here. But together they'd been able to handle all the changes thrown at them as they battled their various routes home.

Together they could face whatever came down the road.

What's Next?

Find out by signing up for my latest news and updates at www.JenniferCrosswhite.com and you'll get the prequel novella, *Be Mine*.

My bimonthly updates include upcoming books written by me and other authors you will enjoy, information on all my latest releases, sneak peeks of yet-to-be-released chapters, and exclusive giveaways. Your email address will never be shared, and you can unsubscribe at any time.

If you enjoyed this book, please consider leaving a review. Reviews can be as simple as "I couldn't put it down. I can't wait for the next one" and help raise the author's visibility and lets other readers find her.

Acknowledgments

This book would not be possible without the patience and willingness to read my drafts by Jennifer Lynn Cary, Diana Brandmeyer, and Liz Tolsma. Special thanks to Sara Benner for her expert proofreading.

Much thanks and love to my children, Caitlyn Elizabeth and Joshua Alexander, for supporting my dream for many years and giving me time to write. And to my Lord Jesus Christ for giving me the ability to live out my dreams and directing my paths.

Author's Note

The 1880s was a fascinating time in American history. The country was recovering from its greatest wounding, the Civil War. People were moving West to make new lives for themselves. Progress, in the form of trains, telegraphs, gas, and electricity were making life easier, and new inventions were just around the corner. Out West in particular, women were becoming more independent and taking charge of their own lives, including careers and schooling.

I chose to set this story in Oregon, because I visited there on a trip in high school and fell in love with its beauty. The very kernel of this story started as an AP English project that year. The characters never left me alone and over the years the story grew, morphed, and changed as my writing skills developed. Reedsville is inspired by the real town of Molalla, Oregon, which was the end of the trail and the beginning of a new life for many pioneers of the time.

I enjoyed watching as my characters adapted to the changes of their time, drawing on their strength, love, and community to continue to thrive and make a life for themselves.

I hope you have enjoyed this trip back in time as much as I have.

About the Author

My favorite thing is discovering how much there is to love about America the Beautiful and the great outdoors. I'm an Amazon bestselling author, a mom to two navigating the young adult years while battling my daughter's juvenile arthritis, exploring the delights of my son's autism, and keeping gluten free.

A California native who's spent significant time in the Midwest, I'm thrilled to be back in the Golden State. Follow me on social media to see all my adventures and how I get inspired for my books!

www.JLCrosswhite.com
Twitter: @jenlcross
Facebook: Author Jennifer Crosswhite

Instagram: jencrosswhite
Pinterest: Tandem Services

facebook.com/authorjennifercrosswhite

twitter.com/jenlcross

instagram.com/jencrosswhite

pinterest.com/tandemservices

Preview of *The Inn at Cherry Blossom Lane*, a contemporary Christian romance novella

At the sight of the cherry-tree-lined lane, Claire Thornton took her first deep breath since leaving Grand Rapids. *Home.*

Ironic, since she'd just left her home of eleven years, with a sold sign in the yard.

She turned the moving truck onto the gravel lane and reached over to squeeze the knee of her ten-year-old daughter, Lizzie. "This is going to be a great adventure. Gigi Ma is going to be so excited to see you! You've grown at least two inches since she saw you at Christmas."

Christmases that had been forever altered by the one three years ago when her husband, Ben, had announced that their marriage was over and he was moving out. So Claire and Lizzie braved driving through Michigan winters each Christmas to head north to Claire's grandma's house. As usual, Grandma's was a safe haven in Claire's stormy life.

She drove past the main house and around back to the carriage house, glancing in the rearview mirror to see that her friends, Mark and Suzanne, had followed her. They had volunteered to drive up her car and help her unload. She hadn't seen the carriage house since her trip here on spring break when Lizzie was with her dad. She hoped Alex had carried out her plans to make the carriage house a new home she and Lizzie would share with Grandma.

Alex had grown up here and had been her best friend every summer she spent here with Grandma. Back then, he always went along with her plans and seemed able to read her mind. Now, though they communicated by friendly-but-business-like emails, she had confidence in him. She hadn't actually seen him in fifteen years. Her heart trembled at the idea, a thought she pushed down whenever it poked up.

Parking the moving truck next to the carriage house, she shut off the engine. "We're here! Wanna check out your new room?"

Lizzie grinned and hopped out of the truck. Claire followed.

Suzanne and Mark came around the truck, stretching from the long car ride.

"This is so cute! I want a tour after we unload and before we leave." Suzanne turned, looking around.

Claire tried to imagine what it looked like through Suzanne's eyes. How her future bed-and-breakfast guests would see the property that had been her home every summer growing up. Grandma's idea to convert her home and property to a B-and-B to provide income for her and Claire just had to work out. They were running out of options.

Mark lifted the roll-up door of the moving truck. "Where do you want things?"

"Let me go find my grandma—"

"Right here!" Grandma stepped off the back porch.

Claire flew into her arms, the scent of Shalimar enveloping her. She blinked back tears as Grandma squeezed her then reached for Lizzie too, who had flung her arms around Grandma's waist.

"Gigi Ma!" The nickname sounded just as cute coming from ten-year-old Lizzie as it had from the two-year-old who couldn't say great grandma. So Gigi Ma had stuck.

The next few hours were a whirlwind of activity as they unloaded the truck and set things in the new home. Claire was pleased to see the walls painted with the exact colors that she had picked out in March. Alex had done a good job, and the carriage house had transformed into a cute little home. His touches were everywhere, and she was half surprised he hadn't shown up. She had figured Grandma would have asked him to come over. But it was a Saturday; surely he had other things to do.

After the truck was unloaded, Grandma had cookies and lemonade for them on the wraparound porch of the main house. It was a warm day for late spring. Claire gave Mark and Suzanne a quick tour of the whole property. The main house included a living room, a library stocked with books on the area's history and legends, a dining room, and the newly-installed commercial kitchen. Upstairs were six bedrooms with private baths waiting for Claire's designer touch.

The wraparound porch still needed seating. But the biggest challenge was the barn. It would be a wedding venue with a honeymoon suite upstairs. And the Inn at Cherry Blossom Lane —what they had named the B-and-B—had their first wedding booked in four weeks during the Traverse City Cherry Festival. Which Claire hoped would launch the bed-and-breakfast.

"Anything else you need before we go?" Mark opened the door to his car.

"You guys have done enough. Thanks so much. I don't know what I would have done without you. You have to come back in the fall as my guests when I can give you the full experience." Claire hugged Mark and then Suzanne.

Grandma came around the car and handed Suzanne a sack of cookies. "In case you get hungry on the drive home."

Claire waved as their car disappeared down the driveway. The excitement and logistics that had kept her focused on the move bled away as the weight of her undertaking settled in for good on her shoulders. Her attention would shift to the Inn. She had Lizzie and Grandma to support now.

Alex Wilder pointed his truck toward Cherry Blossom Lane with Lucy, his black Lab perched on the seat next to him. He wanted to be there to help Claire unload the moving truck. His hands shook a bit at the thought. It'd been fifteen years. He had still been doing seasonal work in California last March when she had been up here making arrangements about the Inn with her grandma. At first, he'd been disappointed to have missed her. Later, he realized it had probably been a good thing.

His phone chirped. He glanced at it, and hit the speaker-phone button. "Hi, Mom."

She got right to the point. The summer camp his parents ran had a cabin with a roof leak. They had a new crop of campers coming in tomorrow, and they needed it fixed today. Since he had carpentry skills, he was their de facto handyman. At least it gave him an excuse to see them. It seemed like his doing repairs was the only time that happened.

He sighed as he turned onto Cherry Blossom Lane and stopped. There she was, directing people as they unloaded a moving truck. Fifteen years hadn't seemed to hurt her much. Light-brown hair swept her shoulders, shoulders that seemed slightly weighed down when she thought no one was looking. He wondered if freckles still dusted her nose.

Putting the truck in reverse, he backed out onto the main road. A twinge of guilt shot through him at not helping. He patted Lucy's head. "At least it seems like she has plenty of help, huh, old girl?"

He'd see her soon enough. They had a plan to meet Monday and go over the project. He hoped she liked the work he had done. He'd been careful, taken his time, and had done what he thought she would like. His eagerness was equal parts desire to see an old friend and a desire to please a client with a job well done. That was it.

It had been fifteen years since she'd broken his heart. He wasn't fooling himself; he wasn't over it completely.

Buy it now! Click here.

Books by Jennifer Crosswhite

Contemporary Romance

The Inn at Cherry Blossom Lane

Can the summer magic of Lake Michigan bring first loves back together? Or will the secret they discover threaten everything they love?

Historical Romance

The Route Home Series

Be Mine

A woman searching for independence. A man searching for education. Can a simple thank you note turn into something more?

Coming Home

He was why she left. Now she's falling for him. Can a woman who turned her back on her hometown come home to find justice for her brother without falling in love with his best friend?

The Road Home

He is a stagecoach driver just trying to do his job. She is returning to her suitor only to find he has died. When a stack of stolen money shows up in her bag, she thinks the past she has desperately tried to hide has come back to haunt her.

Finally Home

The son of a wealthy banker, Hank Paulson poses as a lumberjack to carve out his own identity. But in a stagecoach robbery gone wrong, he meets Amelia Martin, a a soon-to-be schoolteacher with a vivid imagination, a gift for making things grow, and an obsession with dime novels. As the town is threatened by a past enemy, Hank might just be the hero they all need. Can he help without revealing who he is? And will Amelia love him when she learns the truth?

Books by JL Crosswhite

Romantic Suspense

The Hometown Heroes Series

Promise Me

Cait can't catch a break. What she witnessed could cost her job and her beloved farmhouse. Will Greyson help her or only make things worse?

Protective Custody

She's a key witness in a crime shaking the roots of the town's power brokers. He's protecting a woman he'll risk everything for. Doing the right thing may cost her everything. Including her life.

Flash Point

She's a directionally-challenged architect who stumbled on a crime that could destroy her life's work. He's a firefighter protecting his hometown... and the woman he loves.

Special Assignment

A brain-injured Navy pilot must work with the woman in charge of the program he blames for his injury. As they both grasp to save their careers, will their growing attraction hinder them as they attempt solve the mystery of who's really at fault before someone else dies?

In the Shadow Series

Off the Map

For her, it's a road trip adventure. For him, it's his best shot to win her back. But for the stalker after her, it's revenge.

Out of Range

It's her chance to prove she's good enough. It's his chance to prove he's more than just a fun guy. Is it their time to find love, or is her secret admirer his deadly competition?

Over Her Head

On a church singles' camping trip that no one wants to be on, a weekend away to renew and refresh becomes anything but. A group of friends trying to find their footing do a good deed and get much more than they bargained for.